A DEVIL IN EVERY DARK CORNER
AMANDA BRAUN BOE

CONTENT WARNING

Even though Imogen, Carmen, and Lulu love nothing more than relaxing with donuts and lively banter, A Devil in Every Dark Corner is still a novel about the hunt for a supernatural murderer, and contains dark elements that may not be suitable for all readers. Such elements include:

-Explicit magical violence and torture
-Discussions of grief, loss, and death
-Murder
-Death of a child
-Parental death
-Explicit gore, blood, and dismemberment
-Monsters of all shapes and sizes, demons, and other supernatural entities
-Exorcism
-Guns, chainsaws, knives, and other weapons
-Detailed visions of murdered people
-Stalking
-A toxic relationship
-References to past trauma
-References to past alcohol use
-Kidnapping
-Hypnotism of adults and children
-Bogeyman-ish scene with a child
-Extreme burns
-Mind control
-Extended confinement in a dungeon

Please use discretion and care while reading.

Now let's join Otherworldly Investigations. Carmen has a slice of exorcism cake with your name on it.

FOR MY STARFISH

This is my problem with modern-day monsters, Scully. There's no chance for emotional investment.

—

Agent Mulder, *The X-Files*

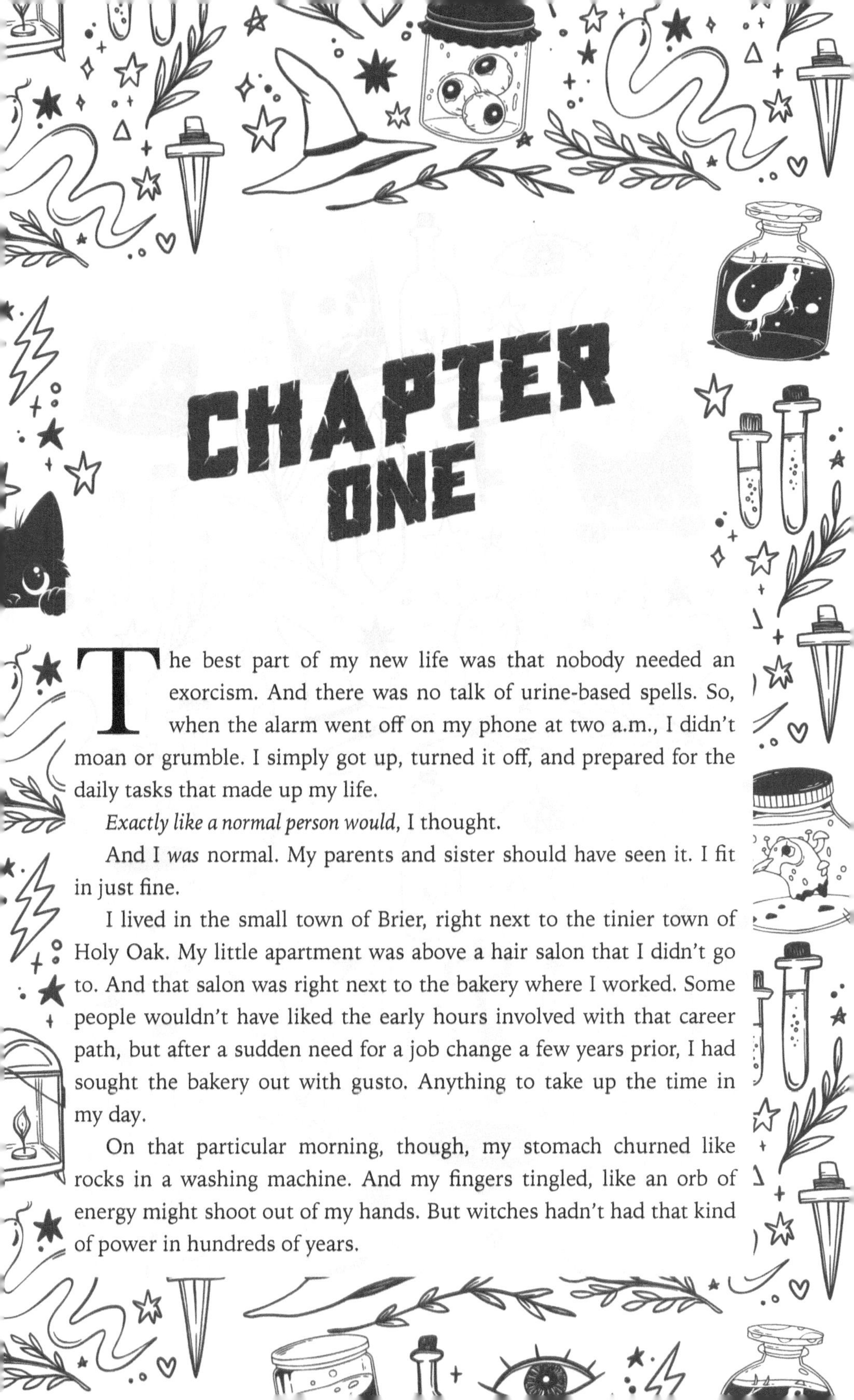

CHAPTER ONE

The best part of my new life was that nobody needed an exorcism. And there was no talk of urine-based spells. So, when the alarm went off on my phone at two a.m., I didn't moan or grumble. I simply got up, turned it off, and prepared for the daily tasks that made up my life.

Exactly like a normal person would, I thought.

And I *was* normal. My parents and sister should have seen it. I fit in just fine.

I lived in the small town of Brier, right next to the tinier town of Holy Oak. My little apartment was above a hair salon that I didn't go to. And that salon was right next to the bakery where I worked. Some people wouldn't have liked the early hours involved with that career path, but after a sudden need for a job change a few years prior, I had sought the bakery out with gusto. Anything to take up the time in my day.

On that particular morning, though, my stomach churned like rocks in a washing machine. And my fingers tingled, like an orb of energy might shoot out of my hands. But witches hadn't had that kind of power in hundreds of years.

I looked at myself in the full-length mirror. I was ordinary in every way. I had brown hair and brown eyes. I was average height. As usual, I dressed in gray to blend into the background.

"Listen, Imogen," I said. "You're perfectly fine. You don't have to be a witch. And you don't have to do anything you don't want to. Not one damn thing. You made your choice. A stomachache is not a portent of doom. Plenty of people get them. Normal people. They get up, do what they have to, and go to bed. Sometimes, if they're lucky, maybe they get takeout Indian food. Stop being a witch, bitch."

I nodded to reassure myself, even as my phone rang wildly on my bed. It was the fourth call in two days. They weren't afraid to call at 2:15 a.m. They knew I was up. My parents knew my schedule. Eventually, I would have to answer. And I didn't fucking want to.

If it's that bad, they'd show up, I thought. *So, Carmen must not have cut her leg off with that chainsaw or anything.*

I scratched Buster Keaton, my fluffy orange cat, beneath his chin. He purred like everything was OK, the fool.

"Cross your tail, Buster," I whispered. "Pray that I can just get up and make bear claws every day until I'm dead."

Listen, being a witch isn't great, so I didn't think I was missing out by turning my back on it. To put it mildly, witch powers are shit. People assume you can flash a sinister glance at your enemy's field, and presto, their crops are decimated. I've always thought that was a little over-the-top, myself. Apparently, those people never heard of group therapy. Sure, witches had mojo like that back in the day, but it all started going downhill in the 1700s. Instead, modern witch magic is like a horror movie where a teen wanders through a dark house, desperate for their flashlight to work. But instead, it flickers again and again, and then goes out right when you see the monster's sharp teeth. That's magic: a crappy flashlight. Powers that work just enough to get your hopes up. Then the letdown. Then afterward, you have to deal with indigestion. Indigestion if you're lucky.

But on the upside, I'm great at card tricks, gambling, and I can grow one hell of a weed-free garden.

The second annoying part of being a witch is that everyone who knows about my family inevitably asks if we are descended from someone in Salem. Yikes. Listen, those were all innocent people who were slaughtered. I mean, Rebecca Nurse was everyone's kind old grandma and was basically hanged because she took in a Quaker orphan.

I've always wanted to dramatically tell people that humans are the real monsters, but unfortunately, I've met enough monsters over the years to know that isn't the case.

Lulu's Bakery, where I worked, had been around for about fifty years. It was a cute little place with exposed brick and rows of glass cases just waiting to have hot rolls lined up in them. Smells of sugar, oil, and coffee had seeped into the walls. Any self-respecting ghost should have haunted that place, where they could have gotten damn fine crullers, instead of haunting decaying farmhouses, hoping to scare someone cleaning out their grandpa's old shed.

Baking was a perfect choice for me because magic was a lot easier to control when you had something to work with: making a jinxed stew, reading enchanted poems or phrases aloud, stirring hexed cement, or growing a row of lucky zinnias. It was easier on the system than trying to create something out of nothing.

Trying to perform magic outside your abilities used to be a hot topic at the witch reunions. Some were convinced that practicing ancient, powerful spells was the only way to recharge old abilities. But nobody wanted to do much other than talk about it. After all, performing lesser spells made you sick enough. Nobody wanted to run the risk of swelling up and resembling an abstract painting. No witch was ever too interested in investigating that theory...except perhaps my sister, Carmen.

After avoiding my parents' call, I went to work and pretended everything was normal. I spread butter on dough, sprinkled cinnamon sugar that I may or may not have enchanted, and rolled it up into Minnesota's best caramel rolls. My boss's name was Lulu, too. She kind of looked like the picture of her grandma, the original Lulu, which hung out by the fresh hamburger buns. In the photo, Lulu stood with a snarky smile, rolling pin in hand, like she was going to whack the photographer. This Lulu was just as brassy. She had shoulder-length hair that was platinum blonde with orange ends. She was stuck in the early 2000s with her animal print tops, thick belts, and jean skirts. According to their family lore, grandmother and granddaughter also shared an ability to make you feel like the biggest idiot alive with one pointed stare.

The morning passed as we finished up the caramel rolls, filled donuts, and took breaks, so Lulu could sing along to a 1990s love ballad.

Back on the day of my job interview with Lulu's Bakery, I couldn't stop my leg from shaking. We sat across from each other at a folding card table. I was nervous because the interview had to go well. I couldn't go back.

Lulu glanced back and forth between my sparse one-page resume and my sweaty face.

"I've been in here a lot," I said, nervously.

Be normal, for the love of God.

Lulu ate a powdered donut, her smile warm and welcoming.

"I thought I knew you," she said. Lulu always sounded like a vivacious used-car salesman. "You've been in here with your fam."

"Yeah," I said, excited that a normal conversation was happening with a normal person.

"And that gal with the red hair and the 1950s cocktail dress."

"That's my sister, Carmen," I said.

"Sister?" she asked. "Wow. You two are opposites, huh?"

"Yep," I said. I sat there in head-to-toe gray, right down to my thrift store jacket. But blending in had been useful at my old job. If you had to kill a werewolf in front of someone, it could be a little traumatizing. Some people didn't like acknowledging that the other-worldly existed, and it was nice to just slip back into the shadows with your neutral clothes. Carmen never followed that rule. Instead, she tried to figure out a client's favorite dessert. Then she made and delivered it, usually with a pocket demon sticking out of her coat.

"She has fantastic style," said Lulu.

"She is uniquely herself," I said.

Lulu glanced down at my resume again.

"This resume is almost as short and bad as mine," she said, laughing.

I felt alarms go off in my head.

Lulu leaned in. "Listen," she said. "I had some rough years in my twenties. I never did anything for long, except for maybe partying. I was lucky my parents had this place. Everyone thought I'd run it into the ground. I lost a lot of people because of my drinking, but my mom and dad never lost faith in me. And more importantly, I never lost faith in myself. So, here we are. I haven't had a drink in ten years. And I might be what you'd call responsible."

The tension eased out of my body.

"This is how my resume looked," she said. "I'm not trying to get in your business or anything, but when I saw it earlier, I thought maybe we had something in common."

I stared at her, wondering how to get out of this.

"What was it with you?" she asked. "If you don't mind me asking."

"I was in business with my family," I said, slowly. "Not like this one, but… I hit a rough patch."

Lulu nodded, waiting for me to continue. I didn't want to continue, but what could I do?

"Otherworldly Investigations," I said. The nervous twang in my voice ramped up. "Looking into scary stuff. Terminating it if need be."

Lulu studied me like a nature documentary, then raised an eyebrow.

"Otherworldly," she said.

I nodded.

"So, you and your family dealt with demons and monsters?" she asked. There was no humor in her voice. It made me feel like passing out.

"Yep," I said, sweating. "And ghosts."

Lulu smiled and winked at me like we were both in on something. We weren't.

"I know what you mean," she said. "I have a few ghosts in my attic, too."

My face went cold. It was happening again. I had told the honest-to-God truth, but people weren't hardwired to believe, and it was hard to force them.

Once, we got a call from an older lady just north of Kirkwood. She had some rowdy little pocket demons squatting in the rafters of her garage. They growled and threw wood and rocks down whenever she went out there to tie flies for fishing. She knew she was calling Otherworldly Investigations. And she knew that I was a witch. But when I stood in her garage and looked up at the bat-sized demons scurrying around, she just couldn't make herself believe it.

"How long have the little demons been here?" I asked.

"The mice showed up about a week ago," she said, her eye twitching. I nodded. Even after I had them out and loaded in an animal carrier, she refused to believe. She stared through the metal bars at the little tan demons and shook her head.

"I've always hated mice," she said.

I snapped back into reality and stared at Lulu across the table. The last thing I wanted to do was start our relationship on a foundation of lies. I decided to do the stupid thing and try to convince her.

"Monsters really do exist," I said. "And demons. And ghosts. And my family investigates them. Like Sam Spade. But with spells. And exorcism projectile vomit."

Lulu picked up the rest of the resumes sitting on the table and threw them in the trash can beside her.

"I know it exists," she said. "A lot of bad things exist. And they're hard to talk about."

"But," I said, knowing that she still didn't think I was literal.

"Don't worry that I'll judge you," she said. "You're a character, that's for sure. But so is my brother, Louis. You'll fit in good. Just come to work on time and try hard, and things will be fabulous."

I can't say I didn't try, I thought.

She reached out her hand and I shook it.

It didn't take us long to be friends. We both liked trashing bad movies. And she was another cat person, although I was pretty sure hers wasn't a familiar. Sometimes, she'd joke about the cryptid and demon thing, but not too much because she thought it was a sensitive topic. It was, but not in the way she thought.

I met plenty of people who didn't believe, and sometimes it was annoying. But then, other times people believed right away. Depending on the situation, I wasn't sure which was worse. Believers were apt to get killed.

"Hey, gal," said Lulu. She definitely sounded like she wanted something. She slid up next to me as I gave Trisha the last powdered donut holes to bring to the front. "I have a great idea."

"I hope it doesn't involve me," I said. The last great idea she had was a girls' spa day. I ended up with more of a rash than when I used witchcraft to hurry a pizza up in the oven.

"You're so cantankerous," said Lulu, smiling. "Let's go to the casino tonight."

"Can't we just stare at nothing?" I asked, sighing. "Or watch a movie?"

"I like being lazy too," said Lulu. "But we're turning old. The other night, when I stopped by, we yelled to each other like deaf old people for five minutes about ketchup."

"Good," I said. "I want to be old. I never want to be out at night again if I can help it. For the first thirty years of my life, it seems like I was out all night, every night."

Lulu nodded, thinking she knew the kind of nights I meant. I actually referred to incidents like when Carmen slashed a giant demon bug in half with her chainsaw. The whole thing ended with me covered in goo.

"I know what you mean," said Lulu. "We'll just play the quarter slots."

"Go with Trisha or Sam," I said.

"I never win when I go with them," she said. "But I always win when I go with you, lucky Immy."

Witchcraft made you exceedingly good at playing the quarter slots.

"And I promised my niece the newest PlayStation for Christmas," said Lulu. She nudged me with her elbow a bunch and winked. "So, I could use some luck."

The tropical trees and birds went around and around on my machine. I breathed deeply and sneezed.

Three bright toucans clicked into place and the whole machine lit up red.

"Holy crap," I said, feigning surprise. "I won!"

"I tell you what," said Lulu. "These are our machines."

I sneezed again. I learned how to disguise my witchcraft when I was five. Coughing worked too. Anything that masked the quick words you chanted under your breath.

"Sorry, Imogen," said Lulu. "I always forget you sneeze so much when we come here. Think you're allergic to their carpet cleaner? It's strong."

"I think so," I said, sneezing again.

Her machine lit up.

"Holy shit!" said Lulu, laughing. She'd won twelve hundred bucks.

I waved goodbye to Lulu as she got into her car, then I walked through the rest of the dark parking lot to my vehicle. The place was quiet and cold and sat right next to a swampy marsh that was frosty from the wintry air.

Walking in the dark alone was never a good idea. I'd seen a lot of people get hurt that way. Not just hurt by perverts and jackasses, but also by werewolves and the occasional drunk demon. But after all of my years in Otherworldly Investigations, I still hadn't taken my own advice.

I unlocked my car door and then stopped. I felt his presence right away. I looked up and there he was, a thin guy with greasy hair.

"Hey lady," he said. He lifted a gun to my face. "You won pretty big in there. Eight hundred, right?"

I said nothing.

"Give it to me and everything will be fine."

I scanned him up and down, trying to figure out what he was. Maybe he was the reason my parents had called. Perhaps an angry leprechaun that needed quick cash?

"What are you?" I asked, unafraid. "Some hard-on-your-luck demon?"

He lowered his gun for a second. His face contorted like I was the weirdo. Just your average dick, then.

"What are you smoking?" he asked. "Just give me the damn money."

"Are you serious?" I asked. "You're robbing me? That's perfect. Thank you *very much*. Could this day get any shittier?"

"The world *is* shit, lady," he said. "Now fork it over, or I *will* shoot you."

"Come on," I said. "I didn't even want to come here."

Suddenly, the man fell over on his side. The gun clanked onto the pavement.

"What the?" he said, trying to sit up. Some brown, frosty weeds from the swamp had tied themselves around the jerk's feet. They pulled him slowly to the icy water.

"What the hell?" he said. "What's going on?"

"Maybe slight drowning will teach you not to be an asshole," I said. I walked with him as he was pulled toward the water.

He tugged and tried to break free, but the weeds were now wrapped all the way up his abdomen.

"Help me," he said. "Wait, are you doing this?"

I smiled and kept whispering the incantation.

"Lady, never mind. Keep your money. Just let me go."

His foot dipped into the water, and he started crying.

"Holding women at gunpoint isn't very nice," I said.

He nodded, still crying.

"It tends to stick with people," I said. "Makes them afraid."

"I'm sorry!"

I had slowed the pace down a bit. The water was barely over his calves. But he thought he was being murdered.

"I think you should treat women with a little more class and respect," I said. "When you were a little kid, back before you were a scumbag, what was life like? Did you play with your friends? Did you laugh and have fun?"

Big tears streamed down his face.

"My friend Eddie used to come over after school. We'd set up tracks for our Matchbox cars. I had a crush on his older sister. She was way out of my league."

"That's not saying much," I said.

He was submerged to his knees now.

"Just think how ten-year-old you would feel if he knew he'd become this," I said. "Intimidating women and pissing your life away. He'd be fucking disappointed."

I leaned toward him.

"Why are you doing this?" I asked.

"I'm sorry," he said. He was submerged up to his waist. "I owe my cousin money. He's a serious guy. I can't rip him off again."

"Listen, jackass," I said. He was shoulder-deep in water. "You are going to leave here. You are going to get a quiet job and live a quiet life somewhere else. And you're never going to bother another woman again. You hear me?"

He nodded.

"Because I'll know if you do."

"Yes," he said. "I won't. Please."

I muttered under my breath, and the weeds loosened themselves. The guy pulled them off, but then he just stayed in the water, staring at me like I was a monster.

"Remember," I said, turning around. I walked calmly to my car, got in, and gave him one final stare as I drove away, just to send home the feeling that he'd had an encounter with a devil.

"Moron," I said to myself.

CHAPTER TWO

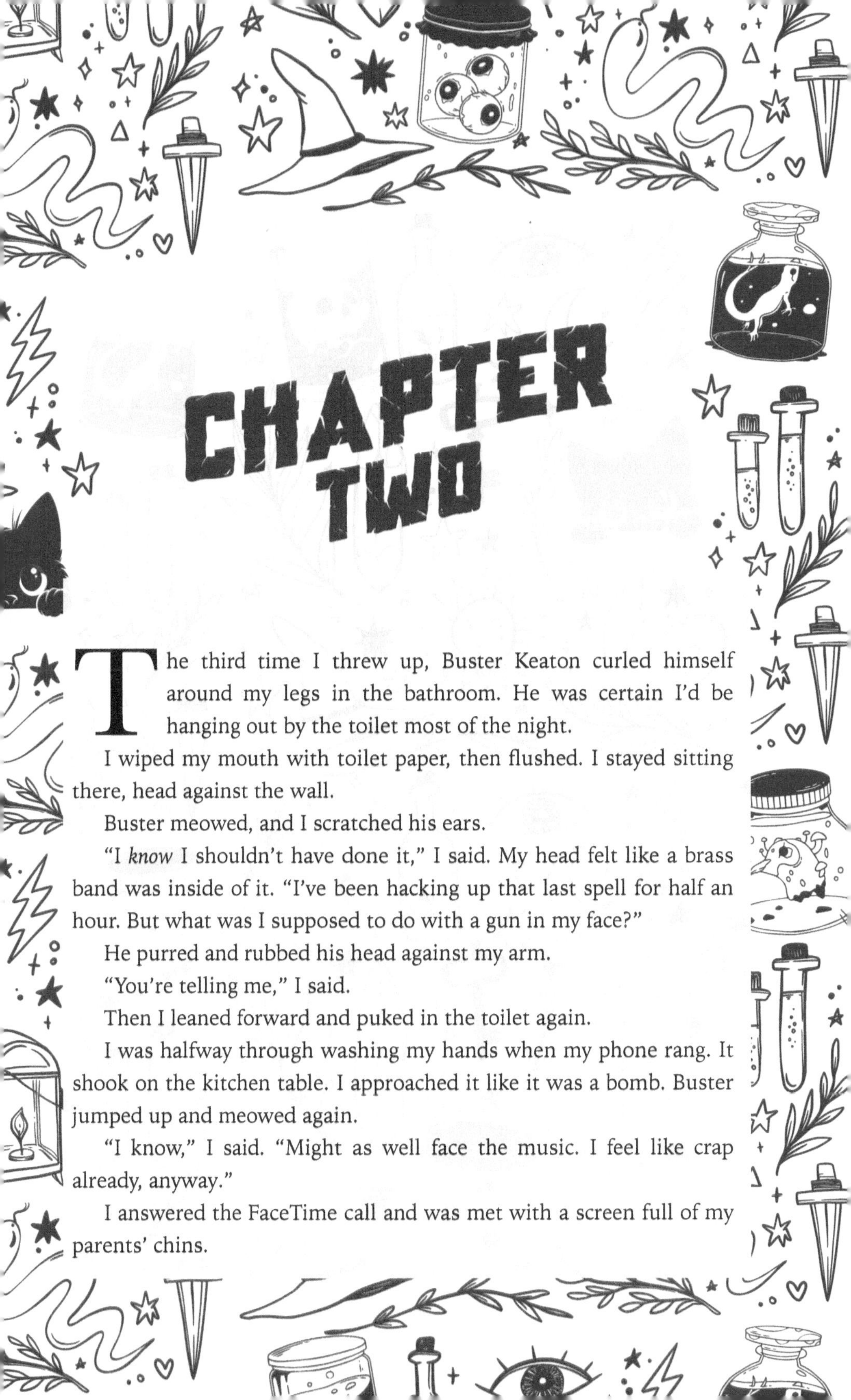

The third time I threw up, Buster Keaton curled himself around my legs in the bathroom. He was certain I'd be hanging out by the toilet most of the night.

I wiped my mouth with toilet paper, then flushed. I stayed sitting there, head against the wall.

Buster meowed, and I scratched his ears.

"I *know* I shouldn't have done it," I said. My head felt like a brass band was inside of it. "I've been hacking up that last spell for half an hour. But what was I supposed to do with a gun in my face?"

He purred and rubbed his head against my arm.

"You're telling me," I said.

Then I leaned forward and puked in the toilet again.

I was halfway through washing my hands when my phone rang. It shook on the kitchen table. I approached it like it was a bomb. Buster jumped up and meowed again.

"I know," I said. "Might as well face the music. I feel like crap already, anyway."

I answered the FaceTime call and was met with a screen full of my parents' chins.

"Imogen!" said my mom. "We finally got through!"

"You look so pale," said my dad. "Have you been taking those multivitamins we sent you?"

"Put your phone down a little, guys," I said. "I can't see anything but pores."

My parents sat at their dining room table. My mom was a tiny lady with big eyes, thick, speckled glasses, and short, dark hair. She never swore and had a golly, shucks kind of attitude. Once, when I was eight, she finished my costume for the school's production of *A Christmas Carol,* then joined my dad to cleanse a house of a particularly obnoxious poltergeist. She rounded out the day by showing up to my play early, so she could sit in the front row and record me for posterity. Actually, most of her days were spent like that.

Whereas my mom was petite and unassuming, my dad was large and loud. He was a big guy, measuring in at about six and a half feet tall. He had an unkempt tuft of thinning red hair. Dad hated the expense and hassle of shopping at big and tall stores, so instead, he had a bizarre fashion sense based on what he could easily find. That day, he wore a sweater featuring a lightning storm and some running horses. The angriest I had ever seen him was in 1997 when a rag-tag group of vampires had decided they wanted to bring about the end of the world by turning or killing as many humans as they could find. Their scheduled date for the apocalypse? Super Bowl Sunday. And my dad's team, the Green Bay Packers, just happened to be playing against New England. My dad had a hand-held radio tied to his belt all day, listening to the score as we hammered stakes through hearts, and threw salt around. I never heard so much swearing from one person in one day. Green Bay won, by the way.

"Look, Madge, she *is* pale," my dad said. "Flu. Definitely the flu."

"Oh, dear," said my mom. "You can't even eat a bowl of reduced-sodium chicken noodle soup under a full moon. It's just a waxing crescent now."

"And I don't have any soup," I said.

"Oh, my, that's even worse," said my mom.

"It's not the flu anyway," I said. "I just did too much magic today."

My mother's concern immediately turned to excitement. She did a happy little shuffle in her chair.

"How wonderful," she said.

"You didn't use magic to help you change a flat tire, did you?" asked my dad. "That's what I did last week when we had that snow. I got a rash like you wouldn't believe."

"It's true," said my mom. "I had to rub the fat of a chupacabra all over his neck and chest to finally make it go away. Very icky."

I stared at them for a moment.

"No," I said, slowly. "I used it to win some money at the casino, then scared a jerk who tried to take it from me."

"That's my girl," said my dad. "Stand up for yourself. Dirty bastards."

"You need to get a little magic toolbox to help you," said my mom. "We can put a few bones in there, maybe the tongue of a…"

"That's all right," I said. "That kind of thing doesn't happen very often."

"Tell her now," said my dad, nudging my mom.

"Petey, give me a minute," whispered my mom. "I was trying to ease into it. Have a pleasant conversation and then slip it in."

"Slip what in?" I asked.

"Well," said my mom, flustered. "We need you to come home tomorrow morning, sweetie."

"Why, what's wrong?" I asked. "Is Carmen all right?"

"Carmen's fine," my mom said.

"Tell that to her snout," my dad whispered.

"We just need to sit down and have a family meeting," said my mom.

"About what?" I asked. "Because if it's a family meeting about a certain family business, I already said I'm done."

"You can't be done," said my dad. "It's in your blood."

"It's just that me and your dad are taking a little vacation," said my mom.

"First time in fifteen years, Immy," my dad said, interrupting. *"Fifteen years."*

"And we need you to help your sister in case anything pops up," said my mom. She lowered her voice to almost a whisper as she added, "Like a case, or something."

"You know as well as I do that Carmen is perfectly able to investigate ghosts or battle pixies all by herself," I said. "She's probably looking forward to it."

"That's just the thing," said my mom. "Carmen can't do much of anything right now, in her condition."

"She can dig," said my dad. "She can dig really good. Herd cattle."

"That's right," my mom said, giggling. "She can, can't she?"

"What the hell are you talking about?" I asked.

"Carmen turned herself into a Pembroke Welsh Corgi," said my mom.

"And she can't change back," said my dad.

"A corgi?" I asked.

"You know, sweetie," said my mom. "The dogs the Queen liked. They're the breed of the fairies. I always thought it would be nice to have one, but not this way, of course."

"It's awkward for all of us when she has to go to the bathroom," said my dad.

"I know what a corgi is," I said. "How did this happen? I didn't know it was even possible. When's the last time a witch has been able to turn into an animal?"

"You know how your sister is with magic," said my dad. "She's always trying to push her luck."

"This is all stuff that we can go over at the family meeting tomorrow morning," said my mom.

"Wait a minute," I said. "I haven't agreed to anything."

"You can't just let your sister lie around like a dog," said my dad. He couldn't help laughing.

"Petey," said my mom, scolding him. "It's not funny."

"This is just your way of trying to get me back in the business," I said. "I know it."

"Imogen Abernathy," said my mom. "Do you want proof that your sister is a dog? Do you want me to go up to her room and get her on the phone, so you can see her big, Yoda ears and her tiny stub tail?"

My dad was now crying from laughter.

"If you don't come home tomorrow morning, I will be forced to take drastic measures," she said.

"Excuse me?" I said. "I'm thirty-two. I'm not a little kid anymore."

"No, you're not a kid," said my mom. "And neither am I, which means that we can both do what we want. Which means if I want to, I can come sit at your bakery day in and day out, eating donut holes, commenting on the coffee's strength, getting out baby photos, and embarrassing you until you agree to come home."

"You'd never do that," I said, sweating.

"Wouldn't I?" she asked. "I once sat in a car for a week, staking out a house I knew a certain demon liked to frequent. I packed lunches in a cooler and had enough trail mix to feed a thousand campers. I only ever left that car to pee in a grove of trees fifty feet away. A bakery is a lot more comfortable, with a public bathroom, heat, and all the sweets I can handle. Being an adult doesn't just mean doing what you want, Immy. It's also about facing responsibility. And remembering that family is important, no matter what age you are. But I *will* play the mom card if I have to. I love a good caramel roll."

I sighed. I hadn't seen my mom this worked up since her run-in with the invisible gnome. That dude was a big pervert.

"I'll be there at eight," I said.

My mom clapped her hands.

"Perfect," she said. "I'll make your favorite for breakfast. And don't worry, we have real maple syrup in the fridge."

"Fantastic," I said, sarcastically. "Because that's what I was worried about."

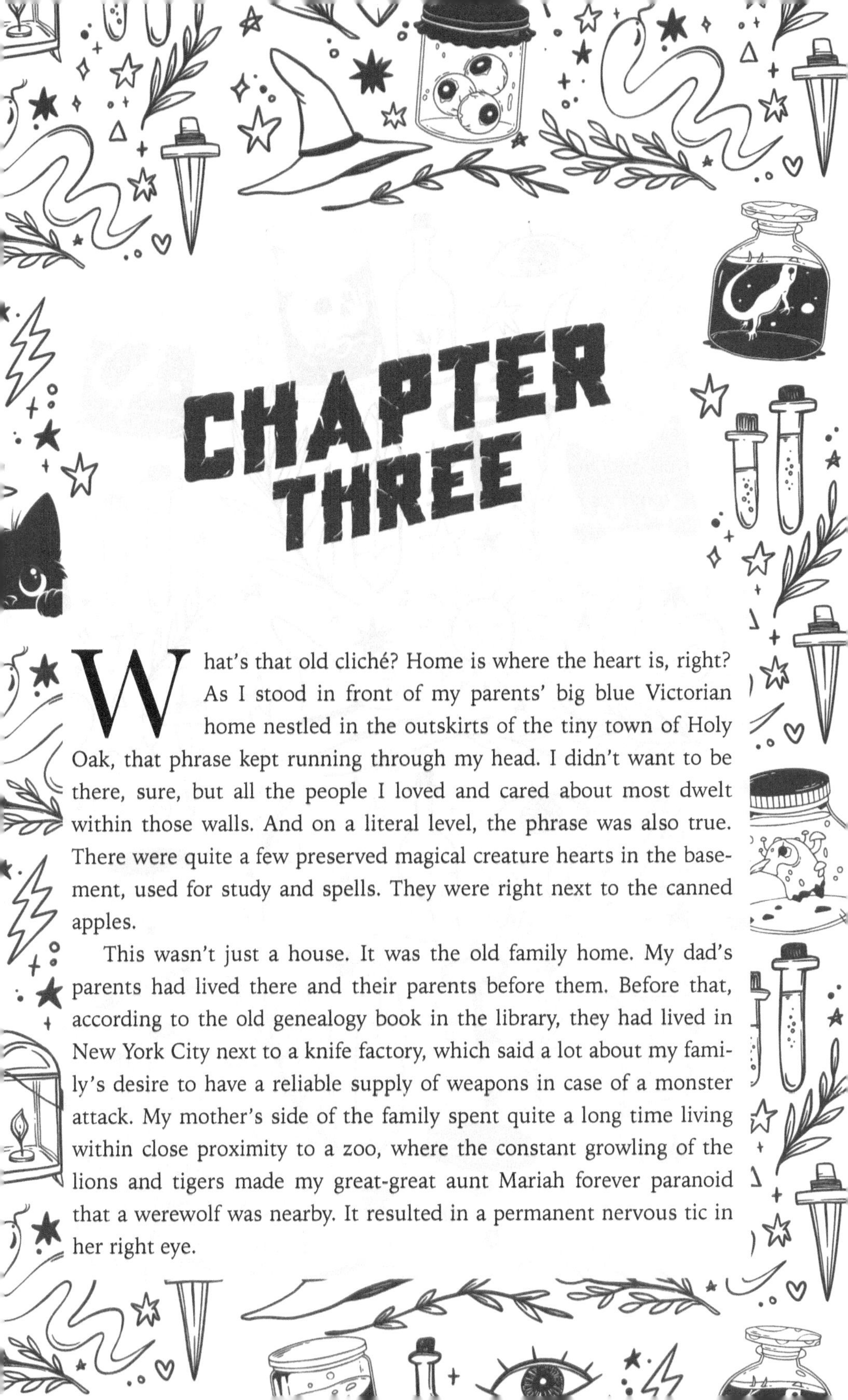

CHAPTER THREE

What's that old cliché? Home is where the heart is, right? As I stood in front of my parents' big blue Victorian home nestled in the outskirts of the tiny town of Holy Oak, that phrase kept running through my head. I didn't want to be there, sure, but all the people I loved and cared about most dwelt within those walls. And on a literal level, the phrase was also true. There were quite a few preserved magical creature hearts in the basement, used for study and spells. They were right next to the canned apples.

This wasn't just a house. It was the old family home. My dad's parents had lived there and their parents before them. Before that, according to the old genealogy book in the library, they had lived in New York City next to a knife factory, which said a lot about my family's desire to have a reliable supply of weapons in case of a monster attack. My mother's side of the family spent quite a long time living within close proximity to a zoo, where the constant growling of the lions and tigers made my great-great aunt Mariah forever paranoid that a werewolf was nearby. It resulted in a permanent nervous tic in her right eye.

My parents' home was situated on thirty acres right outside of town. To the west, it bordered vacant land owned by elderly Mr. Peterson, who left it as tall grass for pheasant hunting. Behind the house to the northeast were the woods where, as children, we liked to search for fairies. Unfortunately, we never found them, but we did find a troll who taught Carmen how to identify plants and flowers useful in making spells and charms. Finding me disinterested in all things witchy, the troll instead taught me how to swear.

Directly behind our home was the greenhouse that Carmen had built to grow the many plants and flowers that she used in the spells the troll had first taught her years before. She also saved space to grow tomatoes from heirloom seeds so, according to her, they actually tasted like something instead of the flavorless red blobs for sale at the grocery store.

Further back behind the greenhouse were several old, and let's be honest, shitty-looking white sheds. We didn't go in them very often. They contained Christmas decorations, lawn ornaments, random crap that Carmen's demons brought home, and items that I liked to pretend didn't exist.

Outlining the entire property was the closest thing to a fence that my witch family could muster. Every ten feet was a large rock, about the size of a chic, hefty throw pillow. They had been there since the house was built, and by the time I was born, they were all covered in a good deal of green, shaggy moss. Everyone around town just thought they were my ancestors' idea of decoration, or perhaps an answer to the question of what to do when you find a bunch of big rocks in your field. But if they had taken the time to roll one of those rocks over, they would have seen a lot of old Latin symbols written on them. It was our security system. ADT for witches who didn't want angry cryptids or demons walking up to the front door.

I put a foot on the creaking porch and stopped. Every inch of that house held a memory. That was where I had sat one morning as a young teen when Carmen glided out of the house to show me her very first sewing creation: a green and yellow striped 1940s asymmetrical button-down dress. That was when she was ten years old. Her long red hair flew in the air as she spun around.

"Do you like it?" she asked, beaming.

"Sure," I said. "It's nice. Is it for a costume party?"

Carmen laughed. "No, silly. I'm going to wear it when we hunt those water monsters tonight."

"But you'll get blood on it," I said.

"Don't worry," said Carmen, skipping around the deck. "I used stain-resistant fabric!"

"I don't know what to say to that," I said.

"Do you and mommy and dad use code words when you hunt monsters?" asked Carmen.

"What do you mean?" I asked.

"In movies, they always use code words," said Carmen. "That way they can let people know something bad is going down without giving it away to the bad guy."

"We've never done anything like that," I said.

"Can we, can we?" asked Carmen, jumping up and down.

"Sure, fine," I said. I pulled her down to sit next to me. She was so excited that she still bounced as she sat.

"Our code word will be 'fried eggs,'" said Carmen. "I can say, 'There are fried eggs at your three o'clock,' or, 'I think there are fried eggs in that building.'"

"OK," I said. "But why fried eggs?"

"Because we'd never say it normally," said Carmen. "We always have scrambled eggs."

I snapped out of my reverie and grabbed the doorknob. I barely opened it when a small corgi ran through the hall and jumped up into my arms. Its minuscule tale wiggled like mad.

"Immy!" said the dog. She smiled at me.

"God," I said, holding my dog sister out in front of me. "It *is* you. You're a dog."

Carmen laughed. "Isn't it marvelous? I'm almost embarrassed that I was going for a Cavalier King Charles Spaniel."

"I have to put you down," I said, lowering her to the ground. "This is too weird, even for us."

Carmen patted her paw on the ground. "Sit down on my level, Immy. It hurts my little doggie neck to stare up at people for so long."

I shook my head and slid down to the ground. Just then, my parents walked up.

"Immy!" said my dad. He gave me a firm pat on the back.

"You're right on time for breakfast," said my mom. "I'm so glad you girls have always been punctual."

"You wouldn't want to be late to an exorcism," said Carmen. "That's just bad manners."

"How long have you been this way?" I asked.

"Gee," said my mom. "I'd say about a week, wouldn't you, Petey?"

"Probably," said my dad. "You should see the crafts she's made with sticks."

"Really?" I asked.

"Yeah," he said. "She's chewed them down into some really beautiful stakes. They'll be handy for the next vampire raid."

"Mom," said Carmen. "Bring the mirror to show Immy."

My mom was like an excited kid as she scooted into the dining room. She was back a few seconds later with a full-length mirror. She leaned it against the opposite wall, in front of me and Carmen.

I sat with my sister, the corgi, next to me. But in the mirror, Carmen looked the way she usually did. She was my normal, red-haired, twenty-eight-year-old sister, staring at me with green eyes. She sat with her knees off to the side, wearing a 1940s sailor dress.

"That's interesting," I said, looking back and forth between the corgi next to me and her human reflection in the mirror. "What are you thinking? The dress must be a clue. Water, right?"

"We tried quite a few baths and salves," said my mom. "All they did was make her smell good."

"The mint was very relaxing," said Carmen.

"Then we stumbled on the reflection thing when your mom groomed Carmen," said my dad.

"I think what we have to do is grab that dress out of her closet," said my mom. "And take it to a south-flowing river to wash it. Then we'll wring it out and set it to dry on the bed right where she usually sleeps."

"Then just to seal the deal, we'll make an Abernathy stew," said my dad. "Maybe with a little more kick than usual."

"That's where you come in, dear," said my mom. "We all need to be here to stir."

"That's a lot of magic for one day," I said. "And I was already throwing up last night."

"That's why you should have answered your phone earlier," said my dad. "We'll all be rough tomorrow, but you'll look like thirteen miles of bad road."

"Thanks," I said. "I appreciate that."

"That's why we're having our big breakfast," said my mom. "We're going to carb up like it's a triathlon. No one leaves the table until the Belgian waffles are all gone."

Carmen put her paw on my hand.

"And I made you some crêpes with a Nutella filling," she said.

"You made crêpes?" I asked. "As a dog? How?"

Carmen winked. "I have my secrets."

I stared at her. "Secrets…to making crêpes as a *dog*?"

"This snout comes in handy," said Carmen. "I'll leave the rest to your imagination."

My parents ushered us both into the dining room, where the long table was filled to capacity with a starchy-carb lover's feast. My mom lifted Carmen into an old high chair and made a plate for her.

"Good thing we never got rid of this old girl," said my mom. "Of course, I always thought it would be used again for a baby."

"I thought you were only going to needle me about re-joining the business," I said. "Not about my womb, too. Let's stick to one argument."

"Oh no, sweetie," said my mom. "I've used needles on a lot of creatures. But definitely not you. That would be against my code."

"Remember the needles under that demon's pillow that one time?" asked my dad. He shoved waffles into his mouth. "Classic."

"If you have an evil vampire or monster as a hostage and want to get info out of him," said Carmen, her little corgi butt wiggled with excitement over this topic, "remember to have Gregorian chanting on in the background while you stick the needles under his fingernails. It drowns out the screaming."

My parents nodded in unison.

I cut up my crêpes and waffles into tiny bits and doused them in syrup.

"Can't we get through one meal without talking about torture?" I asked. This was almost as bad as Thanksgiving, the holiday where my dad always recounted the story of carving up a giant spider instead of a turkey. The green slime in that tale always ruined my appetite.

Carmen pawed at her highchair.

"I want to talk about Immy," she said. "I want to hear all about her adventures at the bakery. It must be delightful. So romantic and delicious. I love a good beignet."

Everyone looked at me, waiting for me to tell one hell of a bakery story, or any story. But, of course, I had no life, so…

"Buster Keaton is doing good," I said, slowly. "Still orange and fluffy."

"Aww," said Carmen. "Norma Shearer really misses him."

Just then Norma, a fluffy white and orange cat, slid by my legs, hissing. She was pissed that I'd taken her brother with me.

"I, uh, get up, go to work, and go to bed," I said.

Everyone stared at me. Carmen's dog smile beamed, waiting for me to get to the excitement. These people were too used to slasher stories. I opened my mouth, trying to think of something. Then I closed it again. My family looked around at each other, then at me again. I felt my face go red.

"Oh, shut up," I said. "Go back to talking about torture."

Generally speaking, adult relationships with siblings can be complicated. After all, you no longer have Legos to bond over. Some adult siblings are competitive, some have no real relationship with each other, and others begrudgingly put up with one another. That's not the way it was with Carmen and me. Ever since we were kids, Carmen had always looked up to me, waiting with Christmas-morning excitement for the day she'd be old enough to tag along and help with otherworldly jobs.

Even as an adult, she always seemed eager to know my opinion or get my advice. And I had *no idea why*. Because let's face it, Carmen was perfection. She seemed to know how to do everything, and was, at any given moment, mastering a new skill. I realized this early on when I once walked by her bedroom when she was twelve. She sat like Snow White on her bed in a homemade cream Welsh country dress. A black ribbon was tied in a bow on her head. But instead of little bluebirds dressing her, she played the bagpipes to her winged pocket demon, Horatio. He was the most human-looking of the pocket demons. He reminded me of a little gargoyle hooked onto the side of an old church. Except those statues might have looked a little prettier than him.

"Since when can you play the bagpipes?" I asked.

"Horatio taught me," she said, smiling. "Right after my last knife-sharpening lesson."

Years later, when she was well into her teens, we were about to head out to our latest job, when Carmen rushed downstairs with her hands full.

"Immy," she said. "Look at these baskets. What do you think?"

One was a white woven basket with an intricate green checker design. The other was a rustic basket woven with thin branches. It had a big red bow on the side.

"We have to go," I said. "Did you make those?"

"I weaved them last night," said Carmen. "Which one do you think goes better with an exorcism?"

I stared at her. "I don't think I can choose," I said, slowly. "Why are you bringing a basket to an exorcism?"

"Don't be so silly, Immy," she said. "You can't just carry the exorcism cake in your hands."

"Cake?" I asked.

"Of course," she said.

"Is it Devil's food?" I asked.

"It's not too on the nose, is it?" she asked.

Later at the exorcism, one Tobias Leech, the man who needed our particular service, sat bound with ropes in an old wooden chair. The walls heaved and rattled as he blurted Latin. Blood ran out of his mouth while he talked.

I flipped through one of our old books, looking for the right incantation, while Carmen took the cake from its basket. *You're Exorcised!* was piped neatly on top of the cake in chocolate icing.

"Would you like some, Mr. Leech?" she asked, displaying the cake before him. He immediately spat blood into Carmen's face, narrowly missing the cake.

Carmen calmly put her creation down and wiped the blood off her face with a homemade knitted hankie.

"We'll wait to eat until you're feeling better," she said, evenly. Then, with her cool demeanor intact, she reached out and grabbed Mr. Leech's neck in a death grip, and lifted him off the ground.

"Don't do that again, you naughty little demon," she said. Then she threw him onto the ground.

I stood, mouth agape.

"How the hell are you that strong?" I asked.

Carmen smiled and smoothed the crease out of her dress. "You should see what I bench press," she said.

Later, when the demon had vacated his body, Mr. Leech got a kick out of that cake. He became one of Carmen's many friends made on the job, whether they were people haunted by unruly ghosts or individuals tortured by angry garden gnomes. They liked having someone to talk to about their otherworldly experiences, given that their own friends and family didn't believe them. Getting a homemade quilt didn't hurt, either.

But Carmen's seminal moment probably came one blustery October day when we tracked a mothman-type cryptid to an abandoned barn. It had been on a week-long binge of attacking people and terrorizing small pets. But we were woefully unprepared when we entered that barn. The creature flew down at us from the rafters with its talons bared and quickly relieved us of every weapon we had. We were crouched behind some hay, wondering what the hell to do, when Carmen spotted something on the dusty shelf in front of us.

There, between the old Cool Whip containers full of nuts and bolts, was something orange and white. Carmen crawled over and reached onto the shelf.

"Be careful," I whispered.

"Immy," she said, quietly. "It's a chainsaw!"

It was a STIHL 038 Magnum, to be exact. Its chain was rusty from sitting so long.

"Isn't it darling?" asked Carmen, whispering.

"Sure," I said. "But I don't know how to run a chainsaw. Do you?"

It was a little heavy, so Carmen set it on the ground. She wedged her high heel into the handle to hold the saw down, then pulled the cord to start it. It only took two pulls for it to sputter to life.

Carmen smiled at me with more than a little satisfaction.

"I can try," she said.

She tore out into the middle of the barn. I chased after her, screaming her name. But I didn't need to worry about her safety. The fight only lasted about three minutes. In the end, Carmen's face and neck were covered in creature goo and blood.

She revved the saw and smiled.

"It runs pretty good," she said. "But I think it needs new gas."

According to Carmen, that's the day she found out that true love existed.

CHAPTER FOUR

Carter wrapped a faded superhero blanket around himself.

"Daddy," he said. "Can you check again?"

Sam grabbed his young son's hand and walked with him back into the boy's bedroom.

"Sure thing, sport," said Sam. "But I know there isn't a monster in your room. See that nightlight? That's a special one me and your mom got. It's made to keep monsters away, so you don't have to worry."

Sam sat his son back down in bed. The boy didn't look so sure about the nightlight.

"How do you know that it'll work?" the boy asked.

"We looked at the reviews online," said Sam. "This was definitely the best nightlight for keeping monsters away."

Sam looked in the closet and under the bed. He even pulled his son's bookshelf away from the wall to make it look like he was being thorough.

"You're 100% monster free," said Sam. "Let me tuck you in."

Carter pulled the covers under his chin like he thought something might bite him.

Sam kissed his son's head. "Your mom will be right next door," said Sam. "And I'll be down in the garage finishing up that birdhouse. Tomorrow, I'll be ready for you to paint it. Won't that be fun?"

Carter nodded slowly, but still didn't smile.

Sam kissed his son again, then walked to the door.

"I'll even leave the bedroom door open," said Sam.

Carter nodded again.

"Goodnight, sport," said Sam. "Love you."

"Night, daddy," said Carter. "Love you too."

Sam turned off the main bedroom light and walked away. His wife, Eliza, was reading in their bedroom down the hall. She looked up when he walked in.

"Is he feeling better tonight?" she asked.

"I don't know," said Sam. "I'm not sure if he bought the monster-eliminating nightlight thing."

"I've been reading about it," said Eliza. "And I don't know. Kids being afraid of monsters is normal, but like this? Maybe we should have him talk to someone. He was absolutely terrified to go to bed the other night, Sam. I've never seen anything like that."

"I kind of remember being scared of something in my closet when I was a kid," said Sam. "But that's just because I watched *Child's Play* too young."

"If this nightlight doesn't help, we'll have to think of something else," she said.

"For sure," said Sam. He kissed his wife. "I'm going to finish that birdhouse. Maybe messing around with it tomorrow will take his mind off things. Don't wait up."

"All right," she said. "Love you."

At three in the morning, Carter's eyes flew open. He had been sleeping fitfully, and the moment he woke up, he was already covered in sweat. He felt *it* watching him again. Even with the nightlight, it was still there. He could almost see it standing there in the doorway out of the corner of his left eye.

Carter couldn't breathe. He dug his fingernails into his palms under the blanket. The woman stood there, breathing with that rough stopping and starting. She didn't say anything, like always. But he knew she was there. He knew if he looked over at her like he had *that first time,* she'd be staring at him with her strange face. She wore a long brown dress that reminded him of a dirty rag. Her face was the face of an old woman with nothing but wrinkles. But the eyes and mouth were dark slits, and the face curled up at the edges. It wasn't really her face at all, but a dirty, leathery old mask. Carter had committed this all to memory from only catching a glimpse of her once. Once had been enough.

It almost seemed like she was a mirage standing there, or a cardboard cutout. She was completely still. But then every so often her long, jagged fingers would flick, and Carter knew that it wasn't all in his head.

She had been bothering him for a week and a half now. Why him?

In a moment of courage, Carter flipped over on his right side, pointed away from the woman in the doorway.

You're not really there, he thought. *Monsters aren't real.*

For a minute, it seemed like nothing would happen. Maybe the old woman was gone. Or maybe she *hadn't* been there at all. But then there was a squeak at the end of his bed. The sound of springs as someone sat down near Carter's feet.

Carter pulled the blankets tighter around himself and shut his eyes. But he still heard that awful woman's breathing. Then something changed. He swore he heard something. Was it a voice? Was she speaking? He had never heard her speak before. He felt like something cold and angry had wedged itself against his chest. Silent tears ran down his cheeks. He felt something sharp reach around his foot. The raspy voice got a little stronger.

"Too much," she said. "Far too much."

What would she do? The grip on his foot got tighter.

Years later, Carter wondered what made him do it. It's almost as if something took possession of his body. It was a moment of bravery that he should have been proud of, had it not been for the repercussion that followed.

Carter threw the blanket off himself, grabbed the signed baseball from his nightstand that he'd just gotten the summer before, and threw it at the woman. It went through her like it was nothing. Like *she* was nothing.

Then suddenly she was gone. Or was she? There was angry barking by the foot of his bed, but it was too dark for Carter to make out what it was. He could just see the outline of something bristly sliding out of his room. Its angry nails scratched against the hardwood floor.

Carter waited a moment, then flew out of his room like he was on fire. He sped into his parents' room and jumped on the bed. His mother, Eliza, immediately sprang up and grabbed him.

"Baby, what's wrong?" she asked, holding him tight.

"She's there," Carter screamed, crying. "She's there again. She's always there. She wants to kill me."

Carter felt relief seep into him. Now his parents would understand the danger. Now they'd know how serious this all was. He had never been able to put it into words before.

"Oh, baby," said Eliza, rocking Carter back and forth. What should she do? What should she say?

"It's going to be all right, honey," she said, kissing him.

But then the house filled up with screaming. It was like nothing Eliza had ever heard before, full of anguish, fear, and hate. It was coming from the garage, where Sam must have fallen asleep while finishing the birdhouse.

Eliza sprang out of bed. Carter held her tight. But the sound of screaming, barking, and chewing paralyzed her with cold. It was the sound of torn flesh battering the night—of darkness filling up with blood.

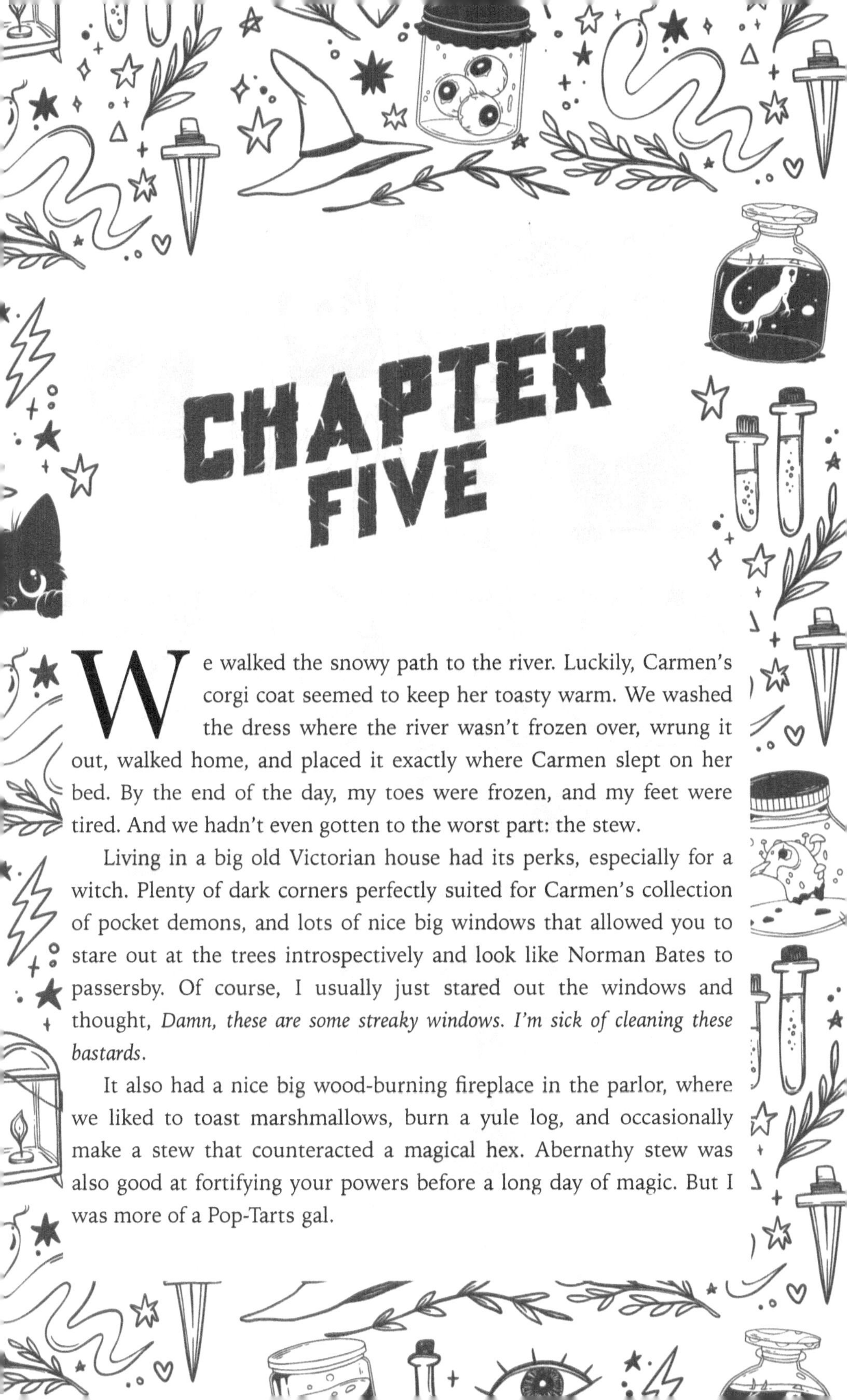

CHAPTER FIVE

We walked the snowy path to the river. Luckily, Carmen's corgi coat seemed to keep her toasty warm. We washed the dress where the river wasn't frozen over, wrung it out, walked home, and placed it exactly where Carmen slept on her bed. By the end of the day, my toes were frozen, and my feet were tired. And we hadn't even gotten to the worst part: the stew.

Living in a big old Victorian house had its perks, especially for a witch. Plenty of dark corners perfectly suited for Carmen's collection of pocket demons, and lots of nice big windows that allowed you to stare out at the trees introspectively and look like Norman Bates to passersby. Of course, I usually just stared out the windows and thought, *Damn, these are some streaky windows. I'm sick of cleaning these bastards.*

It also had a nice big wood-burning fireplace in the parlor, where we liked to toast marshmallows, burn a yule log, and occasionally make a stew that counteracted a magical hex. Abernathy stew was also good at fortifying your powers before a long day of magic. But I was more of a Pop-Tarts gal.

My mom had a cast iron pot bubbling over the fire. She tossed a few herbs in and stirred.

"What is that smell?" I asked, walking up.

"It's your supper," said my mom, stirring again.

"We're multitasking," said my dad. "Cuts down on the dishes."

"I think it smells good," said Carmen, wagging her stump tail.

"I'm not eating Abernathy stew," I said. "That stuff is nasty."

"We've really gotten the knack of masking the flavor in different foods," said my mom. "You'll like it."

"It's chicken and wild rice soup," said my dad. "Your favorite."

My mom sprinkled something black into the stew and handed the wooden spoon to Carmen, who took it in her mouth. Then she lifted Carmen over the pot, so my sister could stir it. A large bone moved beneath the surface of the soup.

"What kind of bone is that, mother?" I asked. "Tell me that's a regular soup bone."

"Lots of soups have bones, dear," said my mom. "It gives the broth flavor. Be more of an adventurous eater."

"Adventurous eater," I muttered under my breath. "I've inadvertently eaten giant slug goo."

"Again, with the slugs," said my dad.

Each of us stirred in a different ingredient. I was lucky when they got around to me. I was only dealt a bunch of oregano.

Then my mom got out the kosher salt, and with a gloved hand, she tossed in a goodly amount.

"Whoa," I said, grabbing her arm to stop her from adding more. "Take it easy."

"Maybe you should all have the leftover spaghetti," said Carmen.

"It'll be fine," said my dad. "We're taking one for the team."

"Say that to your blistered mouth," I said.

"A few blisters are worth Carmen turning into herself again," said my mom.

"I don't know," I said, staring at my sister's wagging hind end. "She makes a pretty good dog. She hasn't chewed up shoes or anything."

"Thanks," said Carmen, smiling. "But it would be hard to run a chainsaw."

Mom ladled the soup into big bowls, and we all sat there by the fire, choking it down. Carmen tried to lap it up as fast as she could with her long tongue. The rest of us took the slow and steady route.

"Oh, dear," said my mom, putting down her spoon. "It really is gosh-awful, isn't it?"

"Yep," we all said in unison.

That night, Carmen curled up on the damp dress that was spread out on her bed.

"Cross your fingers that this works," I said, turning her light off.

"I will when I have fingers to cross again," she said.

I smiled and closed her bedroom door. Now all we could do was wait until morning.

"It's taking too long," said my dad. We all sat at the dining room table the next morning with bowls of uneaten cereal in front of us. Our faces were splotchy from too much magic. I felt like I had thrown myself out of a moving vehicle and landed face-first on a gravel road.

"It must not have worked," he said.

"Give it time, Petey," said my mom. "Maybe she's stuck half-and-half, and needs a moment to compose herself."

"I hope not," I said. I had visions of my sister turning into a demented dog centaur. "Like a human head coming out of a corgi body?"

"Or a corgi head coming out of a Carmen body," said my mom.

"I love this game," said my dad. He pointed at me. "If someone put a gun to your head, which would you rather be: a corgi with the head of a human, or a human with the head of a corgi?"

"Which version gets you out of eating dog food?" asked my mom.

I shook my head. "Can't we just gossip about the neighbors like normal families?"

Just then, I heard high heels on the stairs. Carmen bounded into the room in a 1940s mustard shirtwaist dress. Her head wasn't a corgi head. Just her normally sleek, coiffed hair and beaming expression. She seemed 100% dog-free.

"Thank God," I said, slapping the table. I stood up. "Well, it's been real."

My mom grabbed my arm and guided me back down into the chair.

"What took you so long?" asked my dad. "We thought you'd become a brand-new mythological creature."

Carmen slammed a big old book down onto the table and smiled. We all jumped at the noise.

"I feel marvelous," said Carmen. "Great work, everyone. And good thing you took a picture of me before I changed back, mom."

Mom nodded and patted her iPhone.

"I've just been distracted by research," said Carmen, opening one of the witch books from our library. It was Morgan's *Monster Miscellany*. It had old-timey monster pictures in it.

"I kept dreaming about a dog last night," said Carmen. "And I'm trying to find it in here."

"I wonder why you could have had dogs on the brain," I said, sarcastically.

Carmen shook her head. "No, Immy, this wasn't a nice dog like me. I barely saw it, like it hid just beyond the foot of my bed. But in the moonlight, I could make out its coarse fur sticking up. Like it was growling at me. I think I was afraid… Isn't that wonderful?"

"This calls for some tropical smoothies," said my dad, standing up. My mom clapped her hands excitedly and followed him into the kitchen.

"You think this is a new case?" I asked, distracted.

"Could be," said Carmen. "And great timing, too, because I just finished making our new business cards."

She reached into her pocket and slid one across the table. It was solid black. The silver lettering read *Otherworldly Investigations*. Underneath that, it said, *Imogen and Carmen Abernathy*. The back listed our parents' home address and both of our cell phone numbers.

"Wait a minute," I said. My body filled with tension. "You can't have my number on here. I don't want a bunch of people calling me."

"How can we solve people's otherworldly problems if they can't call us?" asked Carmen.

"*We?*" I asked. "Who's this *we* you're talking about? You have a demon in your pocket?"

Carmen gently patted the pocket of her dress. "As a matter of fact, I do," she said. "But you know I was referring to you, silly. You know you love investigating the otherworldly. Taking care of monsters. Helping people."

I stared at her, perplexed.

"How the *hell* do you figure that?" I asked. "I'm the only one of us four that does nothing but complain about it. I bitch, I moan, and I lose my temper. I gripe about it so much that even I get sick of my own voice. The last thing in the world I do is *like it.*"

Carmen waved away my comment and smiled.

"That's just your shtick," said Carmen. "Everyone knows that. Like a temperamental artist. Do you think painters are happy painting all the time? Do bakers jump for joy with how every roll turns out?"

I crossed my arms. It had just been a matter of time until I was forced to deal with this.

"This is in your blood, Immy," said Carmen. "Some people can look at walls and tear them down, build them back up, and wire everything perfectly. They were meant to renovate houses. Some people get their first kitten when they're young and know from that moment on that they're going to be a vet. And some people are born right there in the kitchen, with their hands deep in bread dough. They're meant to craft beautiful sourdough loaves and enticing desserts. But that's not you, Immy. You were born in the light of a full moon, with fickle witch blood running through your body. You played with ghosts before you played with other children. You knew what a werewolf howl was before you were six. You know the otherworldly is real. And if a monster is hurting someone, you know how to stop it.

And when something is that deep in you, you can't just walk away from it."

I sighed deeply. I didn't want to make eye contact, afraid that I'd agree to something.

"Plus, it took me a whole week to make those cards by hand," said Carmen. "So out of the kindness of your heart, you should at least help me while mom and dad are on vacation."

She smiled like this was a political debate, and she had stacked up some serious points. I leaned back in my chair while Carmen turned to her book. She shook her head at the image of a certain dog and turned the page. I knew it wasn't the right dog either, of course. And I knew it because I had been having those dog dreams too. I had been having them since my parents had first tried to call me. It was one of the reasons why I had a dull pain in my gut. The other reason was that Carmen's words had been like a surge traveling up and down my spine. I wasn't going to admit it to her, but I was seriously worried that my little sister knew what the hell she was talking about.

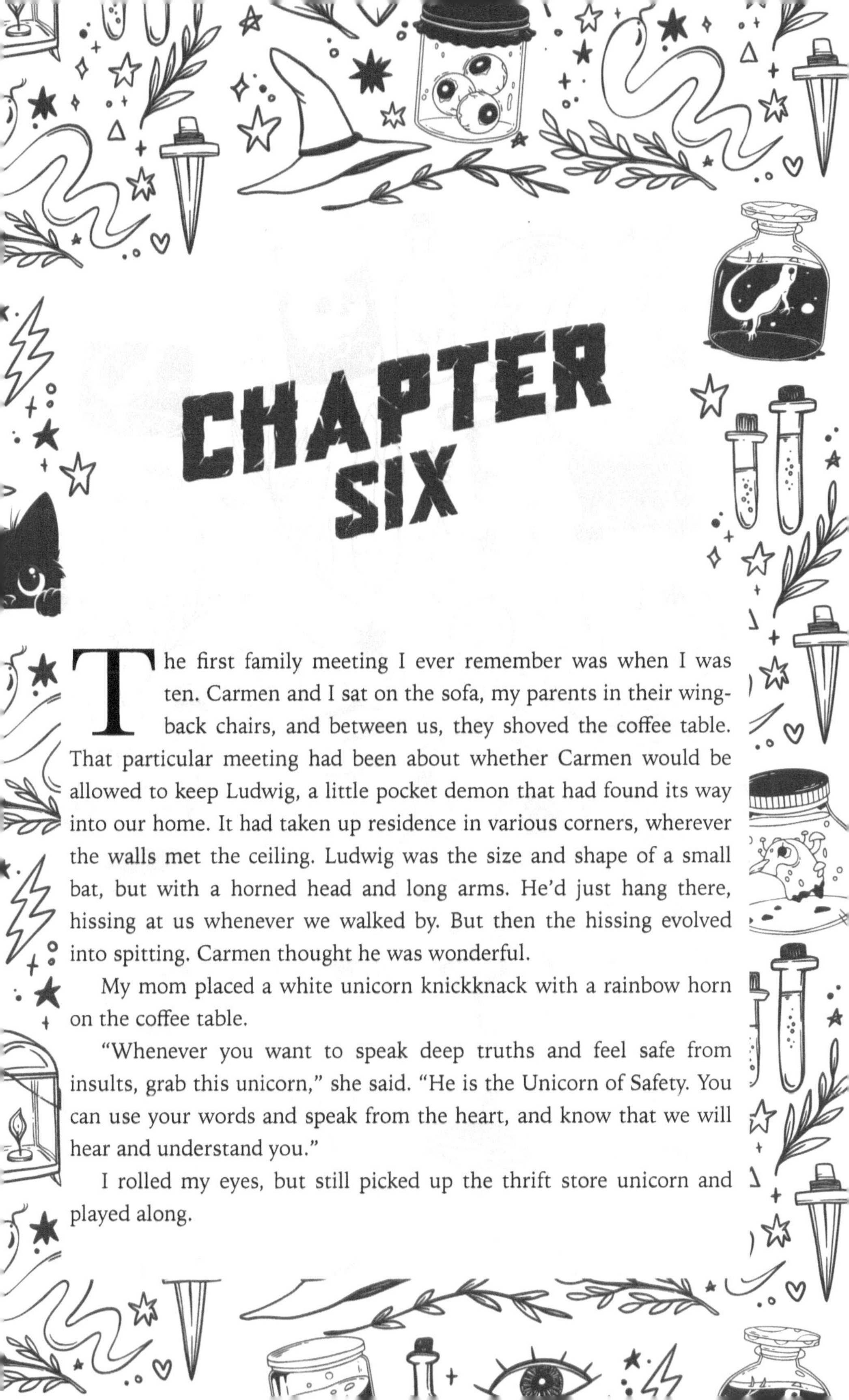

CHAPTER SIX

The first family meeting I ever remember was when I was ten. Carmen and I sat on the sofa, my parents in their wing-back chairs, and between us, they shoved the coffee table. That particular meeting had been about whether Carmen would be allowed to keep Ludwig, a little pocket demon that had found its way into our home. It had taken up residence in various corners, wherever the walls met the ceiling. Ludwig was the size and shape of a small bat, but with a horned head and long arms. He'd just hang there, hissing at us whenever we walked by. But then the hissing evolved into spitting. Carmen thought he was wonderful.

My mom placed a white unicorn knickknack with a rainbow horn on the coffee table.

"Whenever you want to speak deep truths and feel safe from insults, grab this unicorn," she said. "He is the Unicorn of Safety. You can use your words and speak from the heart, and know that we will hear and understand you."

I rolled my eyes, but still picked up the thrift store unicorn and played along.

"Ludwig hisses at me every time I go by him to the bathroom," I said. "Yesterday, he threw poop at me while I was brushing my teeth."

"We hear you and understand you," my family said in unison.

I handed the unicorn to Carmen. She took it with her tiny fingers.

"But it's a devil, and it's fun," Carmen said. She had learned early on that quoting lines from *Mystery Science Theater 3000* was a good way to convince my parents of anything.

"That's another valid point," my parents said.

It was eventually decided that Ludwig could stay, with some verbal and written warnings. But he must have thought the whole thing was hokey too because, by the time the meeting was over, he had flown out of the house and into the big maple tree outside the bathroom, where he resides to this day. If you're ever in our bathroom freshening up, don't freak out if you suddenly have poop that looks like rabbit pellets thrown at the closed window. That's just Ludwig's particular style of greeting.

Even though I was now thirty-two and Carmen was twenty-eight, the family meetings were still the same, right down to the unicorn.

I sat at my place on the sofa, drinking my tropical smoothie. But there seemed to be more of a palpable excitement to this meeting, not like the last one where we debated reupholstering the wingback chairs.

"Petey, would you like to begin?" my mom asked.

My dad nodded. "Now, Immy," said my dad, taking the unicorn. "You know that on Monday, me and your mom are going on our first vacation in fifteen years. But what we haven't told you is…that's just part one."

"Part one?" I asked. "Of what?"

"Of seeing the world," my dad said. "We're checking the whole thing out. Gonna see what the rest of the world has for chips. I hear they have a lot of neat, different chip flavors."

I looked around at my family. They watched me like I was something that might explode, and therefore needed careful monitoring.

"So…" I said, slowly. I was perplexed. "You're going to investigate the otherworldly all over the world now?"

Mom and dad laughed. "The only thing we're investigating is a pitcher of margaritas on the deck of a Princess Cruise," said my dad.

"I don't usually indulge," said my mom. "But the strawberry ones are so refreshing."

Carmen clapped, excited for them. "Remember to send me old-timey postcards, mom," she said. "I'll make a collage."

"I don't get it," I said, putting the smoothie down. "How are you going to be a part of Otherworldly Investigations?"

"We aren't," said my dad. "We're retiring, kid."

"We'll still help you girls out from time to time," said my mom. "But we really want to scale back."

I felt some kind of popping go off in my head. My whole face turned red. I looked down at my hands and found that they trembled. My family still stared at me, nervous.

Carmen grabbed the unicorn and held it out to me.

"Do you need the Unicorn of Safety, Immy?" she asked, cautious.

"She really looks like she needs that unicorn," said my dad.

"Oh, dear," said my mom. "Remember your language in this house before you lose your muffins, young lady."

I nodded. It felt like I swallowed lava. "What the flip," I said, slowly, "are you flipping talking about? Give me that unicorn."

I grabbed it from Carmen. "I said I didn't want to flipping investigate monsters anymore. I was sick of getting flipping tackled by creatures and puked on by people afraid of ghosts. You flipping lost your shiitake when I quit. And now you're doing the same flipping thing. You can leave, but I *can't*? You flipping flippers are flipping kidding me!"

"We hear you and understand you," they all said.

My dad reached over and grabbed the unicorn. He looked like he needed a drink. "We put in our time," said my dad. "You know how many apocalypses we averted before you were even born? We've worked hard. Now it's time to enjoy the money we ground our knuckles to the bone for."

"Most of the money you ever made came from your sham psychic readings and ripping off gas station casinos," I said.

"But we had to gather a lot of herbs and roots for the incantations to rip off those casinos," said my dad. "Sometimes, we had to drive clear to Wyoming for the right shrubbery. Way out of the way."

"Plus, those psychic readings weren't all shams," said Carmen. "Remember the lady from Bismarck, Mom?"

"That's right," said my mom. "She did end up meeting a tall, dark stranger. How was I to know he had two wives already?"

"Did you think we were going to keep investigating monsters and ghosts until we keeled over?" my dad asked.

"Yes," I said, exasperated. I still trembled. "That's exactly what I thought."

My mom smiled kindly. "That's silly, honey," she said. "We couldn't do that. I have a touch of arthritis in my knees already."

I leaned forward and put my hands on my knees. An old familiar wave of jittery numbness ran up my body. It had been a while since this had happened. I gulped in breaths like one of my old goldfish. Carmen rubbed my shoulder. My mom was suddenly there with a glass of water, while my dad shoved some kind of homemade lavender candy my way. After a moment, the feeling subsided, and I leaned back on the sofa. I sighed and placed my shaky hands on my lap.

"Here's the Unicorn of Safety, dear," said mom.

I took it. "That happens whenever I think about *that* day," I said. My voice wavered like a pre-teen. The words came out of me faster than I meant them to. "You know what the last case was like for me. It was...a bunch of bullshit. Do you remember all the broken stuff? Do you remember me in bed? You guys acted like I was nuts for not getting over it right away, for wanting out. You wanted to sweep it under the rug...or under the *shed*, and move on. I guess I was supposed to forget it all right away like a robot."

My parents stared at the ground. Carmen slid up next to me and put her head on my shoulder.

"We hear you and understand you," she said, quietly.

I felt tears on my cheeks. When I looked up, my parents were tearing up too. My dad took the unicorn.

"We handled all that like idiots," said my dad. He stared at his feet. "You know it, and we know it. Wasn't the first time, either. We've been sorry about that since the day you quit. You were so excited about the future, about what you thought your life was going to be like. Well, you know we were excited too. But sometimes life is cruddy, and people are even cruddier. We're sorry, Imogen."

"We are," said my mom, her voice wavering. "We're very sorry."

I nodded. Carmen wrapped her arms around me.

"I understand if you don't want to investigate with me, Immy," she said.

I shrugged. "I don't know," I said. "I don't know what I want. It's like that old saying, something about every time I think I'm out, they keep pulling me back in. *They* being magic and monsters. It's like the otherworldly won't leave me alone. Even if I was in a cave in the desert all by myself, I'd probably still dream about it, or wake up with Ludwig in a corner flinging poop at me."

We all laughed a little, but quietly.

"We probably won't be able to retire without turning a corner in France and running into a vampire," said my dad. "It's just in our blood. It's drawn to us, or we're drawn to it. One of the two. But... you know your mom has always wanted to see the world."

"I know," I said, reaching over and grabbing her hand. "Sorry, mom. I do want you to go."

"And I don't want to ruin your life, Imogen," she said, almost crying again.

"You ruin my life?" I asked. "Not a chance. Go on your trip. I'll stay here and help Carmen if anything comes up. If I want to stay and keep going with Otherworldly Investigations after that, I will."

"And if not, we'll think of something else," said Carmen.

"Yeah," I said, starting to feel the pain in my body subside a little. "We'll think of something."

We all sat there silent for a second.

"That was probably the most emotional family meeting since the pocket demons stole the Christmas roast," said my dad, exhaling loudly. "Dirty rotten bastards."

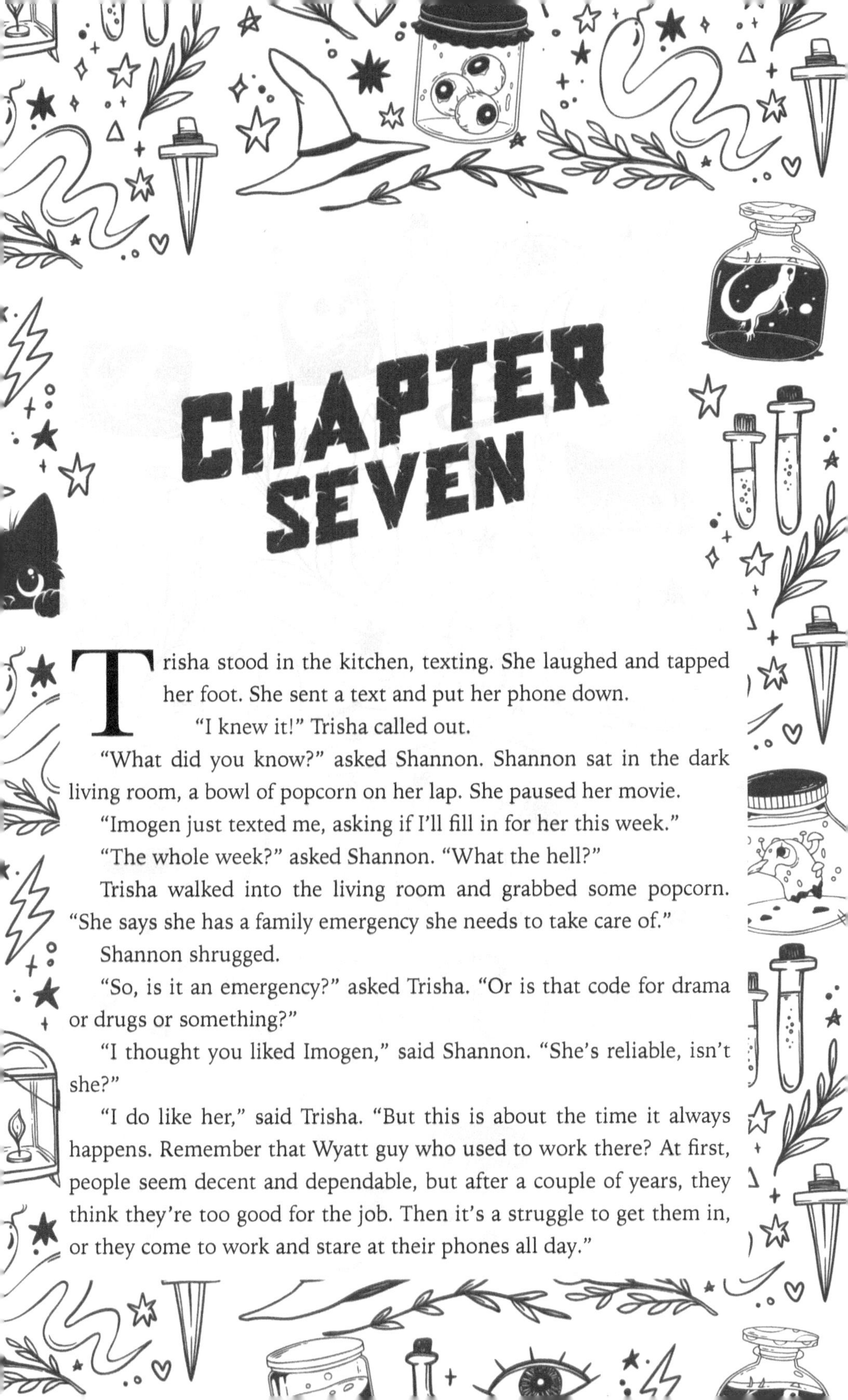

CHAPTER SEVEN

Trisha stood in the kitchen, texting. She laughed and tapped her foot. She sent a text and put her phone down.

"I knew it!" Trisha called out.

"What did you know?" asked Shannon. Shannon sat in the dark living room, a bowl of popcorn on her lap. She paused her movie.

"Imogen just texted me, asking if I'll fill in for her this week."

"The whole week?" asked Shannon. "What the hell?"

Trisha walked into the living room and grabbed some popcorn. "She says she has a family emergency she needs to take care of."

Shannon shrugged.

"So, is it an emergency?" asked Trisha. "Or is that code for drama or drugs or something?"

"I thought you liked Imogen," said Shannon. "She's reliable, isn't she?"

"I do like her," said Trisha. "But this is about the time it always happens. Remember that Wyatt guy who used to work there? At first, people seem decent and dependable, but after a couple of years, they think they're too good for the job. Then it's a struggle to get them in, or they come to work and stare at their phones all day."

"You're going to feel so bad if her dad died or fell off the roof putting up Christmas decorations."

"I would," said Trisha. "But I've never been wrong yet."

Trisha took another handful of popcorn, then looked at the bowl.

"Whose popcorn is this?" she asked.

Shannon frowned a little, then scrunched down in the sofa, like she was trying to disappear.

"Damn it, Shannon," said Trisha. "And my milk is half gone. I label everything."

"Come on," said Shannon. "We shop at the same store. All our crap looks identical. I just grab."

"Hence the labels!" said Trisha. "And what are you watching? How can you stand this crap? People are always getting their entrails ripped out. What is that? The blood doesn't even look like blood. Looks like melted pink lollipops."

"It relaxes me," said Shannon.

"How the hell can that guy getting his eyes ripped out relax you?"

"You explain your convoluted love stories, and I'll explain my convoluted horror," said Shannon.

Trisha shook her head and ate another handful of popcorn.

Shannon dreamt about her allergies. She was seven years old again, over at her dad's house. Her father had just gotten a puppy from the animal shelter. Shannon crawled on the floor up to the dog, laughing as they touched noses. Then the scratchy eyes and sneezing fit started.

Shannon woke up to Trisha standing over her, nudging her to get up.

"What are you doing?" asked Shannon, rubbing her face. Her eyes and nose really *were* itchy.

"You'll never fricking believe this," said Trisha. "That dog is back."

Shannon got up and looked out the window.

"No," said Trisha. "It's downstairs."

Shannon almost laughed. It was ridiculous. "How did it get in the house?"

"I don't know," said Trisha. "But I heard something. I went halfway down the stairs, and it was standing in the kitchen. So, I slammed the door and came up here."

"Someone is being a scary creep," said Shannon. "Everyone knows I'm allergic to dogs. Someone must have let it in here to be an ass. I told you to lock the door!"

"I thought I did," said Trisha. "Bet it was that Ted prick across the street. But to be sure, tomorrow morning we're going around town to ask. If your dog's a mean old bastard, why do you let it run?"

"How are we going to get it out?" asked Shannon.

"We'll have to wrangle it," said Trisha. "I'll get the broom from the closet, so I can shove it toward the door without getting too close."

"What am I supposed to do?" asked Shannon. "My eyes are on fire already."

"Just wait up here," said Trisha, walking toward the door. "Unless I scream that I'm being bitten."

"That's reassuring," said Shannon. Shannon walked with Trisha to the hallway. She turned the hallway light on as Trisha grabbed the broom from the closet. Then she watched Trisha walk down the stairs.

"I'm telling you," whispered Shannon, tiptoeing. "Someone let that dog in here to rob us or murder us."

Trisha shook her head. "You should watch my romantic comedies instead."

Trisha reached the bottom of the stairs, then opened the door. When she disappeared on the other side, the growling began. Shannon leaned forward to hear better. She scratched her nose.

There was a rough bark and another few snapping barks.

"Come on," Trisha's muffled voice said. "Get out of here, you mean bastard."

There was another bark, and then a lower growl. The dog sounded mad, sure, but maybe not as mad as when they had first seen it in the front yard two weeks before. That first time, it acted like it wanted to pounce on them. Its gray and black hair had stood up on end. It had growled and barked for a long time before Trisha shooed it away. Maybe it was getting used to them. Trisha had always been an animal person.

Shannon stood there in the quiet.

The dog must be out of the house by now.

She touched her nose and eyes. They hardly even felt sore anymore.

That's weird.

Then the lights in the hallway flickered once, twice, and went out completely.

Shannon's eyes widened. She let out an anxious whisper and saw her own breath.

"Shit," she said. "Someone did let that dog in here."

Shannon took each step down the stairs with quiet precision, trying not to make a sound. The kitchen door was still closed, and she kept an eye on it as she carefully opened the drawer to the end table at the bottom of the stairs. She quietly grabbed the Mace that was always kept there. Shannon held it with a grip so tight it made her hand clammy. Then she cringed as she tried to turn the knob on the kitchen door without making it squeak.

At first, she didn't see anything. The kitchen island was in the way. But as she made her way around it, the streetlight shined in on something heaped on the floor. It was Trisha.

Shannon's mind couldn't make sense of the scene in front of her. There was something spread all over Trisha and the linoleum. Part of her knew that it was blood, but the other part couldn't figure out how that could be. They had just talked upstairs. And there had hardly been any noise, and no screaming. Plus, it wasn't even that big of a dog. Mean, sure, but still a little smaller than her cousin's yellow lab. Trisha looked like she had been attacked by something bigger. The heap of her on the floor was…consumed. There were bloody bits of fabric and pieces… This had to be some gag.

Something deep and frightened within her warned her to run, but instead, she found herself leaning forward to look at the heap.

It must be a mannequin. It must be a joke.

Then there was something else. Something immediate. A cold feeling on her back. Shannon touched herself and looked at her fingers. Blood.

How was she bleeding?

Shannon turned around just in time to see a kitchen knife run across the top of her leg. That felt wet too.

Is this shock?

Shannon was still trying to make sense of things when a figure stepped closer. She had on a dirty brown dress and wore an old, wrinkled mask that curled up around the edges.

Shannon opened her mouth, but no noise came out.

"I think I should spare you the pain," the figure said. Her voice was quiet and crisp, like a cold wind coming to life. The woman pointed down at Trisha. "I think I should spare you the pain."

The woman lifted the knife back and then brought it down toward Shannon. Shannon grabbed at the woman's arm. The woman struggled as Shannon kept hold. Then Shannon reached forward and clamped down on the woman's arm with her teeth. She bit down hard for Trisha, like the angry dog that they were both so wary of.

The woman hardly made a sound. Shannon broke free and spat blood. Then suddenly the knife was there, cutting into Shannon's upper arm. She was somehow on her back on the hard linoleum floor.

How did I get here?

The woman loomed over her. Shannon reached for the Mace and sprayed like she intended to use the whole thing. She did. The woman backed away long enough for Shannon to shoot up.

How is she not screaming? How is she not hurt?

Then the woman was at her again. Shannon struggled to get to the door. She knew she had been cut again, somewhere. The door was only a few feet away.

Shannon felt woozy as she leaned onto the cupboard. She looked down at herself and saw blood dripping from her ripped pajama pants. She needed to hit this woman. She needed to make sure this didn't happen to anyone else.

She felt the woman behind her, so Shannon grabbed the only thing within reach. Shannon clamped her sweaty, bloody hand onto the popcorn bowl and hurled it at the woman's face. As soon as it made contact, the woman stopped. Uneaten popcorn, unpopped kernels, and salt covered the woman's dress. The figure stood there, looking at herself like she'd been covered in acid.

Shannon didn't look back as she ran through the door. She didn't stop to think how silly it was that an old metal bowl of popcorn had done anything. After all, it was hardly the only part of the night that didn't make sense.

Shannon didn't think about the ice and snow against her bare feet, or the footprints of blood that trailed behind her in the moonlight. She wasn't sure if she was shaking from cold or shock as she ran out onto the street. All she knew was that she wasn't going to look down at her body again. She wasn't going to see how bad it was.

Soft snowflakes hit her face. They were so bright in the light of the approaching vehicle that they reminded Shannon of the sparkles that had covered her bedroom ceiling as a child. She wasn't going to look down at her body. Because she was going to be fine. She *had* to be fine. She had to tell people what had happened.

The man from the car had such sad eyes when he approached her. Did he run toward her? Shannon wanted to tell him everything. And somehow, she wanted to tell him that it was terrible because it had been such a pretty night, too. She grabbed him with bloody fingers to tell him. But as they leaned down in the snow, and her tired eyes blinked rapidly against the snowflakes, Shannon opened and closed her mouth, somehow unable to find the right words.

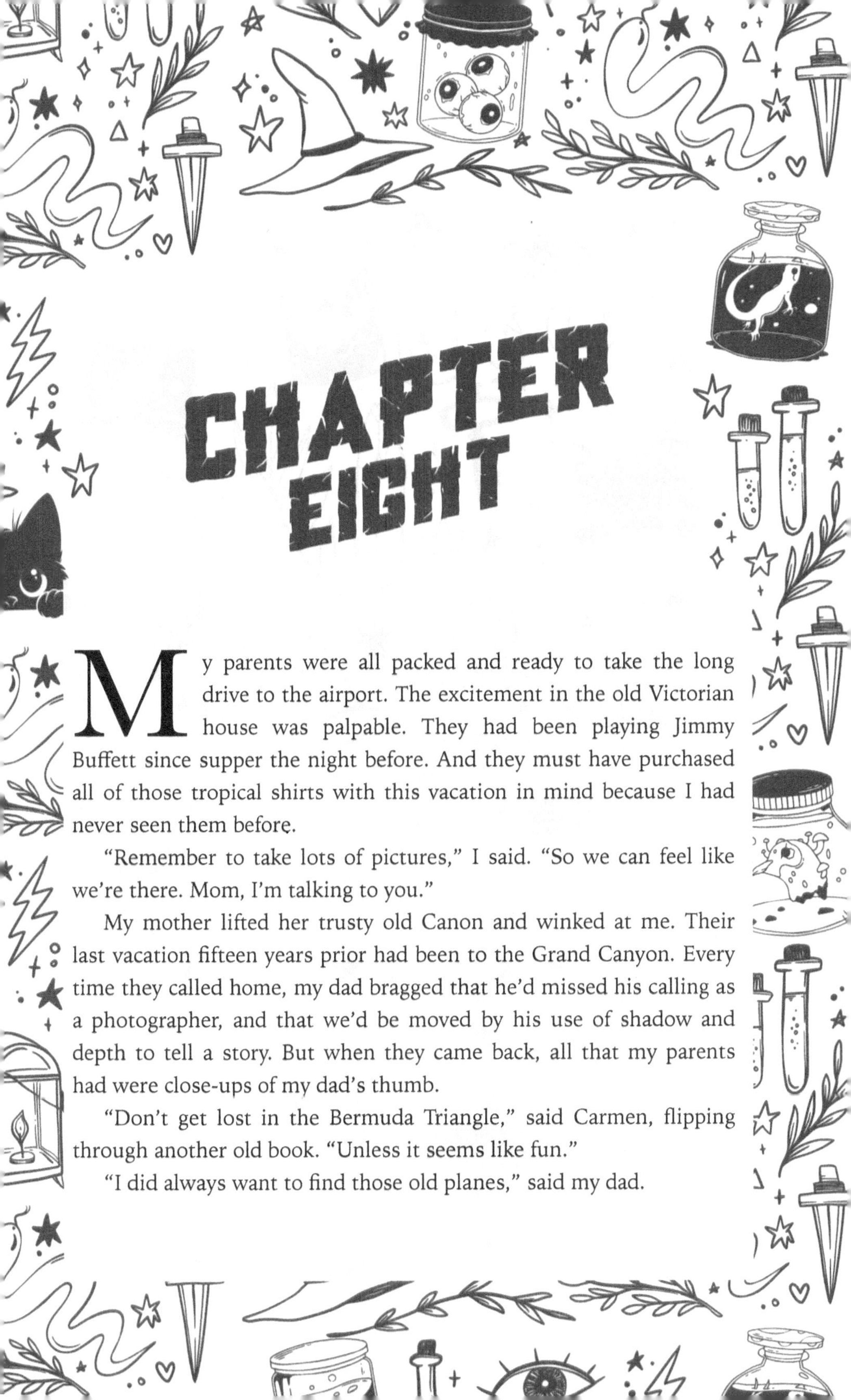

CHAPTER EIGHT

My parents were all packed and ready to take the long drive to the airport. The excitement in the old Victorian house was palpable. They had been playing Jimmy Buffett since supper the night before. And they must have purchased all of those tropical shirts with this vacation in mind because I had never seen them before.

"Remember to take lots of pictures," I said. "So we can feel like we're there. Mom, I'm talking to you."

My mother lifted her trusty old Canon and winked at me. Their last vacation fifteen years prior had been to the Grand Canyon. Every time they called home, my dad bragged that he'd missed his calling as a photographer, and that we'd be moved by his use of shadow and depth to tell a story. But when they came back, all that my parents had were close-ups of my dad's thumb.

"Don't get lost in the Bermuda Triangle," said Carmen, flipping through another old book. "Unless it seems like fun."

"I did always want to find those old planes," said my dad.

I helped my parents haul their luggage out to the car. While I shoved my mom's huge suitcase into the trunk, Ludwig hissed and growled at us from the nearby ice-covered tree.

"I'll be homesick for the little things like this," said my mom, staring at the angry demon.

"It's just like a Norman Rockwell painting," I said.

We moved a little further away from the tree when the spitting began. Our feet crunched in the snow. The cold was like a living thing, circling around us.

"He seems madder since I got back," I said.

"Maybe he missed you," said my mom.

"Where's Carmen?" I asked. "It's freezing. And we'll be lucky if we can get all your luggage in the car free of demon scratches."

"It's just that time," said my dad. "She's in the shed."

I immediately went stiff. Of course, Carmen was in the shed. Someone had to go to the shed every day. Pretty soon, only Carmen would be around to go into the shed. I knew they had to do it, but somehow it was still a jolt.

"Do you want to go help her?" my mom asked, quietly.

"No," I said, rigid. "I don't."

"It's all right, kiddo," said my dad. "Let's not get all wound up again. This is supposed to be a fun day."

"I'm sorry," I said. I tried to will the tension to leave my body. "I'm not wound up. I just don't know why you bother."

"We can't let it starve, sweetie," said my mom.

"Why not?" I asked, shrugging.

"That's my girl," said my dad. "Tough. Fight the assholes."

"I wouldn't let it die," I said, contemplating. "But I think I'd let it starve, just a little bit."

My mom patted my shoulder. "You don't mean that."

"I think I might," I said.

When Carmen got back, she said nothing about feeding *that thing,* but instead surprised my parents with a homemade tropical quilt that they could enjoy on cooler nights on deck. It even had a few little devils poking around the corners of some squares.

"To remind you of home," she said.

We all hugged and said various mushy things to each other. And in keeping with our family's idiosyncrasies, there were explanations of where they kept the emergency holy water that only they knew about, and numbers to call if the apocalypse came before they were scheduled to return.

When their car had disappeared down the road and the snow had settled, Carmen straightened her coat dress and said, "I hope I get caught in the Bermuda Triangle, just once."

"Was it this dog, Immy?" asked Carmen. She held an old book up to me. It had a faded yellow painting of an Irish Wolfhound.

"You know as well as I do that it wasn't that dog," I said. I took a big drink of coffee and sighed for the tenth time that day.

"Don't lose heart," said Carmen. "We'll find it."

"We've been at this for hours," I said. "Let's scoop snow until our backs hurt. That would be more fun than this."

"I don't know why you didn't say anything when you first got here," said Carmen. "We both dreamt about dogs. It has to mean something."

"Maybe it means that we need a new pet," I said.

Buster Keaton and Norma Shearer hissed at us from their plush bed nearby. I thought they'd be in jolly moods when I brought Buster back from my apartment. After all, it had been a while since they'd seen each other. But after the initial joyful reactions, their moods toward us had soured.

"All your demons are sure acting like…demons today," I said.

Norma hissed again.

"Same to you, pal," I said.

"Immy, stop arguing with the cat and help me find this demon dog."

"How do you know it's a demon?" I asked. "How do you know it's a case at all?"

"Why else would we both dream about it?"

"Maybe we're just weirdly in sync," I said. "Witch intuition. Must mean that a dog show is airing somewhere in the world tonight."

"You know certain visions of angry dogs are portents of doom," said Carmen. "You have to be more careful, Immy. We don't want to be caught off guard while it's just the two of us."

"I think you're becoming paranoid *because* it's only the two of us," I said. "You act like because the other two investigators are off gallivanting on a cruise ship, something bad is bound to happen. What are the chances of a big case coming our way, just when mom and dad leave? We'll probably have to cleanse a house and that's about it."

Carmen shook her head. "You say that now," she said. "But you'll be eating your words when a demon hound is eating *us*."

I laughed. "Maybe you should calm down and stop looking for a devil in every dark corner."

Carmen raised an eyebrow. "But the devils are there, Immy, whether I look for them or not. You know that."

Carmen bent down and made cooing noises. A little pocket demon named Benedict scurried out from under the corner hutch, aiming straight for Carmen's outstretched hand. He looked just like a little guinea pig, except instead of fur, he was covered all over in what felt like a thousand cockleburs. Carmen held him up, and he nudged his prickled head lovingly against her neck.

"See?" she said.

"No fair," I said. "I didn't mean little guys like him."

"But the others are there, aren't they?" asked Carmen. "Everywhere. Sure as sugar."

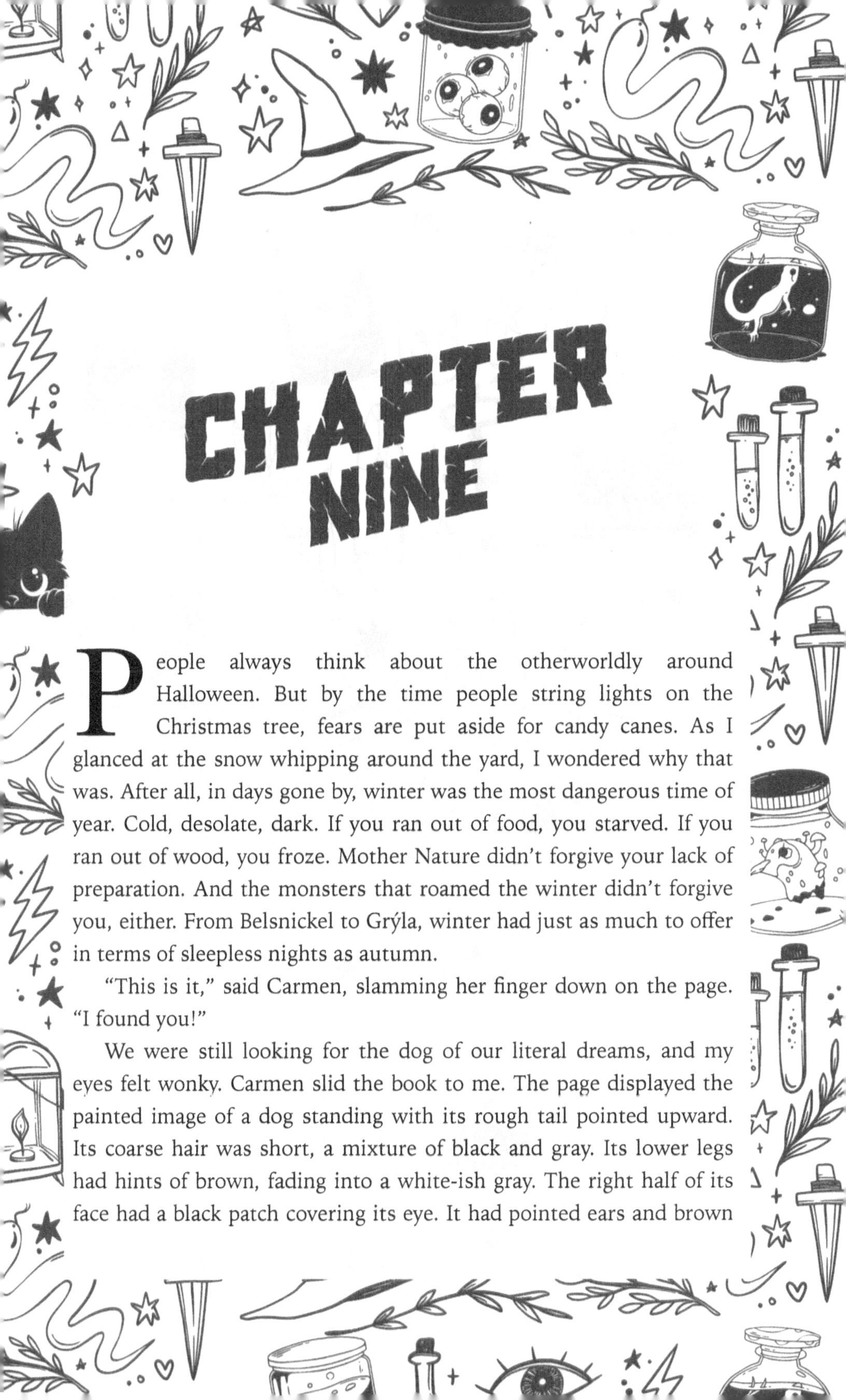

CHAPTER NINE

People always think about the otherworldly around Halloween. But by the time people string lights on the Christmas tree, fears are put aside for candy canes. As I glanced at the snow whipping around the yard, I wondered why that was. After all, in days gone by, winter was the most dangerous time of year. Cold, desolate, dark. If you ran out of food, you starved. If you ran out of wood, you froze. Mother Nature didn't forgive your lack of preparation. And the monsters that roamed the winter didn't forgive you, either. From Belsnickel to Grýla, winter had just as much to offer in terms of sleepless nights as autumn.

"This is it," said Carmen, slamming her finger down on the page. "I found you!"

We were still looking for the dog of our literal dreams, and my eyes felt wonky. Carmen slid the book to me. The page displayed the painted image of a dog standing with its rough tail pointed upward. Its coarse hair was short, a mixture of black and gray. Its lower legs had hints of brown, fading into a white-ish gray. The right half of its face had a black patch covering its eye. It had pointed ears and brown eyes. In thick, straight lettering, the script above it read *Australian Cattle Dog or Blue Heeler*.

"Blue heeler," I whispered. And for a second, I saw my breath. The picture darkened, a phenomenon most people would have blamed on the gloomy sky and storm outside. But I knew it was because of something altogether different.

I closed my eyes and saw the dog again at the foot of my bed. But it wasn't my bed at all. And not my room. There were baseball players taped to the walls. A model plane hung from the ceiling. There was a signed baseball on the nightstand.

Who am I?

Then suddenly I was down in the kitchen. But this wasn't my kitchen. Even in the dark, I saw the wall color was blue, with white cupboards and a faded butcher block island. I looked down. There was something there, huddled in the corner. It was a person. She wore a yellow sweatshirt with the letters UMD near the cuff of one sleeve. But she was on her stomach. I couldn't see her face.

Have I seen that sweater before?

I blinked a couple of times and was back in the dining room with Carmen. She leaned in, studying me. She poured more coffee and handed it my way.

"Are you with me, Immy?" she asked.

"I am now," I said.

The lights flickered. We didn't look at the antique fixtures, but instead at each other. We never broke eye contact, even when the book before me seemed to whisper something too quiet to hear.

Then the lights brightened again. Everything was normal and warm. Like the moment before had never even happened. And still, we stared at each other. Then, slowly, the expression on Carmen's face changed from blankness to a shit-eating grin.

"It's a case!" she whispered.

"Son of a bitch," I said.

The effect was immediate. As soon as the otherworldly moment happened, the pocket demons came out of their corners, looking around like the sky might fall. They ran for the front door and sat there, like cats waiting to get out. The cats were there too, actually.

"Babies, what's wrong?" asked Carmen, leaning down to them.

There was a chorus of spitting and meowing, popping and babbling.

"They must think there's some bad mojo going on with that blue heeler," I said.

"But you can't just run away, my darlings," said Carmen. "We won't let anything hurt you. And it's much too cold out there, especially for little demons like you."

"Bribe them, Carmen," I said. "They could get hurt out there."

"That's right," said Carmen. "Come with mommy. We'll always protect you, the way you protect us. Now, how about I turn the heat way up and make you all some apple cider with Red Hots?"

That seemed to do the trick. All the demons followed Carmen to the kitchen. In about ten minutes, they each had dainty cups of apple cider. They downed it with fervor. The house was about ninety degrees.

A pocket demon named Barnaby whizzed by my head. He laughed and clapped his paws together with delight. He was like a tiny polar bear, but with a horn in the center of his head. To make some of the non-flight demons a little more cheerful, Carmen had gotten out one of the old spell books and decided to risk the rash. After a moment, half a dozen usually flightless demons were lazily drifting around the room. Norma Shearer and Buster Keaton floated by me, and I scratched their ears. They purred at me for the first time in days.

"I love you, you know," I said to them. Then I broke eye contact with Buster. My gaze drifted to the entryway where Lulu stood, drenched from the heavy snow outside. Her eyes were red and swollen like she'd cried the whole way to our house. But the sight of a bunch of pocket demons and two cats hovering in the air, and the sight of Carmen at the center of it all with a spell book, had understandably morphed that sadness into shock.

"Carmen!" I whispered, waving at her to cut it out.

"Oh!" said Carmen. Slowly, the demons and cats wafted gently to the ground. But that didn't seem to help matters. Lulu just stood there, pointing and stuttering. For a moment nobody said anything, then Carmen smiled.

"You're right on time!" said Carmen. "We just made cider. And I have a charcuterie board in the fridge that's simply divine."

CHAPTER TEN

Carmen draped one of her homemade quilts over Lulu's shoulders. We all sat at the dining room table while Lulu drank cider from an old chipped tea cup. Her hand shook every time she set the cup back down on the saucer.

"Could you go over that one more time?" asked Lulu.

For the third time, I explained that our witchcraft abilities were real…just like I had said all along. And so was our family business, Otherworldly Investigations. And I also had to inform her that monsters and ghosts, were, in fact, not just weird metaphors. It was a lot for anyone to take in. Lulu stared at her drink.

Finally, she took a deep breath and asked, "Really? Even Bigfoot?"

"Yes," I said.

"The Loch Ness Monster?" she asked.

"Yes," I said.

"Pretty much any cryptid you can think of is real," said Carmen, smiling.

"Cryptid?" asked Lulu.

"That's the technical sort of term for all of those monsters that people wonder about," I said. "Like the Jersey Devil, krakens, etc."

"And demons are real too, obviously," said Lulu.

Carmen lifted Barnaby. "Of course," she said.

Lulu's hand shook again. "So… God, the Devil, angels?"

"If we're going to talk about God and the Devil, I think I better bring out that soothing chamomile tea," said Carmen.

I patted Lulu's hand. "The verdict is still out, but nothing much surprises me anymore."

Carmen put the tea down in front of Lulu.

"I really thought you meant symbolic demons and monsters," said Lulu, holding her teacup for dear life.

"It's normal for people to not want to believe," said Carmen. "That's usually when I empty my pockets."

"You need to stop doing that," I said, eyeing Carmen. "I don't like our ratio of hyperventilating to non-hyperventilating clients."

"Oh, Immy," said Carmen, dismissing me. "They don't all take it that bad. Look at Lulu. She's fine."

Lulu did not, in fact, look fine. She looked like something stunned and rigid that had been forcibly molded into a chair.

"I'm having a hard time with the demon thing," said Lulu.

Barnaby must have understood her because he reached out and licked her hand.

"Good baby," said Carmen, smiling.

"So then, you guys aren't evil, right?" asked Lulu. "You're not like the witches gathering to kiss Satan's butt in *Haxan: Witchcraft through the Ages*?"

Carmen and I shot each other surprised looks, then burst out laughing.

"That's a good one," I said, wiping the tears away. "We've never been asked that. I don't remember any clandestine pacts. Do you, Carmen?"

"I have monthly subscription boxes that I can't seem to get out of," said Carmen. "But other than that, no."

"The key thing to remember is that witches, demons, ghosts, and cryptids are just like humans in that some are lovely, like Carmen here, and some are complete assholes. It just depends upon the creature," I said.

Lulu took this in. "You said your powers are cruddy compared to witches of the past?"

I nodded.

"But Carmen was levitating those demons," said Lulu. "That seems pretty powerful."

"And I was recently a very cute little corgi," said Carmen. "I'm going to do a watercolor self-portrait of my time as a dog when I have a free moment. I'll send you a copy."

"Carmen is always trying to push the limits of her abilities," I said, shooting my sister a parental glance. "Luckily, she has a diet rich in Omega-3s and oatmeal."

"That's true," said Carmen. "And I have all my babies."

"Babies?" asked Lulu.

"All the pocket demons scurrying around are Carmen's friends/babies/pets," I said. "They fortify her power a little bit, like bran flakes. But they don't have enough oomph to make her powers what they would have been, had she been born four hundred years ago."

"I see," said Lulu. She was starting to brighten up a little bit. Honora, a pocket demon that always reminded me of a platypus, had taken up residence on Lulu's lap. She petted her tentatively. "Why do you call them pocket demons?"

"Because they're a demon you can fit in your pocket, silly," said Carmen. "Just think of them as demonic Beanie Babies. Sometimes, I forget they're there until Benedict rolls out of my hair."

"And what made you want to start Otherworldly Investigations?" asked Lulu. "Is that just a witch thing, or?"

"There aren't too many things you can do with limited powers nowadays," I said. "And usually, demons and cryptids are drawn to witches, so it just became a logical career path. Our family has been doing this kind of thing for generations."

"You can also be a forty percent reliable fortune-teller," said Carmen. "Or count cards in Vegas."

Lulu nodded. "So, why is that, with your powers? Why are they cruddy? Can you strengthen them?"

People always fell into two categories: the talkers and those that seized up. Sometimes when people found out that witches, monsters, and ghosts existed, they wanted you to cleanse their house, so they could go back in and forget the whole thing had ever happened. I imagined them later in their homes rocking back and forth in a chair while watching sitcom TV, desperate to make their lives feel normal again. The other group always asked questions, so they could better come to terms with the way the world worked. They needed to make sense of it. That way it didn't seem so frightening. Lulu was definitely part of the second group. I knew it was only a matter of time until she asked about the Salem Witch Trials.

"For a while, that was a hot topic for witches," I said. "But nobody at the witch reunion even brings it up anymore."

"Witch reunion?" asked Lulu.

"I always make the bars," said Carmen, excited. "Immy's in charge of the punch. It's quite good. The secret ingredient is…sherbet."

Lulu looked at Carmen like she was nuts. "Neat," she said.

"Some say that the only real way to get our powers back is to get in league with one of the big guys," I said.

"Fairies," whispered Carmen.

"But others say that's a lot of garbage too," I said. "It's hard to separate fiction from the truth in our world."

"But I thought you said that these little demons helped you with your powers," said Lulu. "But fairies... Does that mean fairies are demons?"

"I certainly hope so," said Carmen. "At the very least, they're definitely not angels, from the stories I've heard."

Carmen and I gave each other a high five.

"If you look back at old records, there are lots of stories of witches coming into contact with fairies," I said. "And then somehow getting powers. You even see accounts of that in the Salem Witch Trials. But fairies have been dwindling for a long time. Some say that dwindling fairies means dwindling witchcraft abilities."

"I see," said Lulu, thinking. "Were those women really witches at Salem?"

"No!" Carmen and I said it in unison, trying to hold back our disgust.

"Those poor people," I said. "Slaughtered for absolutely no reason…"

Lulu bent her head down over her chamomile tea. After a moment, silent tears streamed down her face. I shrugged at Carmen. I never knew how to deal with big shows of emotion.

"Immy," said Carmen. "You broke her!"

"Sorry," I said. "I thought I was the only one who had strong feelings about Salem."

Carmen stood over Lulu and put her hands on her shoulders.

"There, there," said Carmen. "It's all right."

"It's not that," said Lulu. She said each word between gulps of tears. "It's just—I can't believe I forgot. I knocked on the door and nobody answered, but I heard talking, so I thought it would be OK to come in…"

"It was," said Carmen.

"And I was going to tell you right away, but all this happened," said Lulu. "I'm a terrible person. I can't believe I forgot. For a little while, I forgot!"

"Forgot what?" I asked.

Lulu took her hand away. Her brown eyes sparkled with tears. "Sam and Trisha are dead," she said.

"Holy shit," I said, standing.

"Those are the people you work with, Immy?" asked Carmen.

I nodded. "Were they delivering meals?" I asked. "Was it a car accident?"

"No," said Lulu. She talked slowly, staring off into space. "That's the weird part. Sam's wife, Eliza, called me Saturday morning…and then Trisha's brother called me Monday. It happened on different nights. They were both attacked."

"Attacked by what?" asked Carmen, leaning in.

Lulu took a long sip of tea. "By a dog."

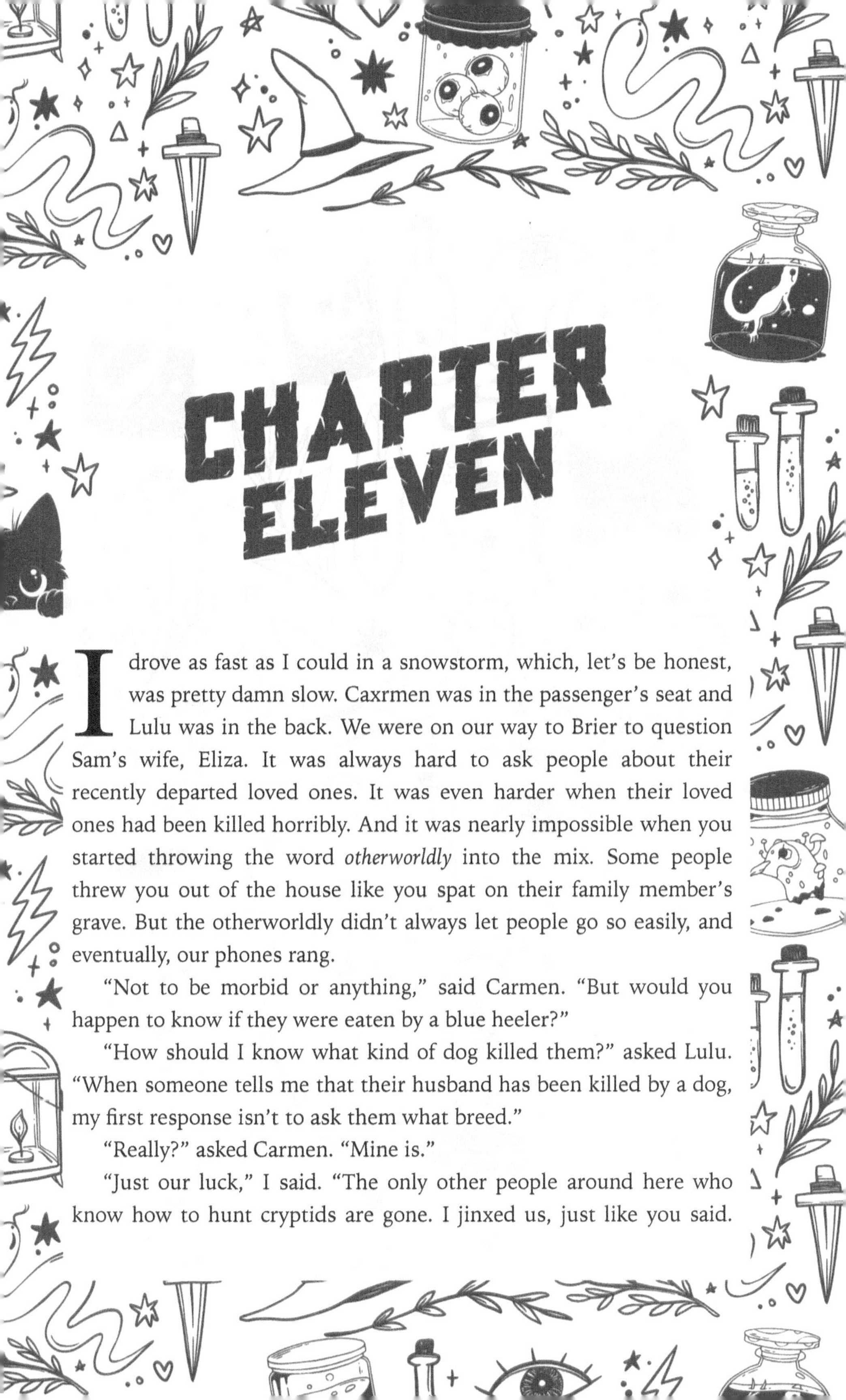

CHAPTER ELEVEN

I drove as fast as I could in a snowstorm, which, let's be honest, was pretty damn slow. Caxrmen was in the passenger's seat and Lulu was in the back. We were on our way to Brier to question Sam's wife, Eliza. It was always hard to ask people about their recently departed loved ones. It was even harder when their loved ones had been killed horribly. And it was nearly impossible when you started throwing the word *otherworldly* into the mix. Some people threw you out of the house like you spat on their family member's grave. But the otherworldly didn't always let people go so easily, and eventually, our phones rang.

"Not to be morbid or anything," said Carmen. "But would you happen to know if they were eaten by a blue heeler?"

"How should I know what kind of dog killed them?" asked Lulu. "When someone tells me that their husband has been killed by a dog, my first response isn't to ask them what breed."

"Really?" asked Carmen. "Mine is."

"Just our luck," I said. "The only other people around here who know how to hunt cryptids are gone. I jinxed us, just like you said.

We could have had a ghost infestation or a little exorcism to deal with, but no, we get an old-fashioned monster hunt."

"Do you think it's a blue heeler werewolf?" asked Carmen. "We haven't had a werewolf in a long time. I didn't care for the last one. I picked hair from my shawl for weeks."

"Is it because of me?" Lulu asked. "Did I make some monster mad? And now it's killing all of my employees?"

"Have you refused service to any hairy men recently?" asked Carmen.

"It might be because of us," I said. "Some monsters have a bone to pick with witches."

"Do you live alone?" asked Carmen.

"Yes," said Lulu.

"She'll have to stay with us, Immy," said Carmen. "She might be next on the list."

"Are you serious?" asked Lulu. She had continued her look of stiff immobility in the back seat. She was like petrified wood. "There goes sleeping ever again! Not that I was planning to do much, anyway."

"We'll keep you safe," I said. "You already have an advantage over most people. You know that the otherworldly exists, and you're with people who can help."

"And the pocket demons and I make a lovely crème anglaise," said Carmen. "It has a little kick."

We turned the corner onto Sam and Eliza's street.

"Do you feel that, Immy?" asked Carmen.

"I certainly fricking do," I said.

"What? Feel what?" asked Lulu, leaning forward.

I pulled into the driveway and parked.

"You know that feeling when you just get done puking?" I asked. "That complete emptiness? It's like that."

"That doesn't sound good!" said Lulu. She fiddled with her gloves like she might rip them up. "What does that mean?"

"It means that we aren't going to find the cryptid here," I said. "It's long gone."

"How are you going to find anything out?" asked Lulu. "Eliza will think you're nuts."

"We have our ways," said Carmen, winking.

I opened my door. "No, we don't," I said. "We're not doing anything like that until we have no other choice."

We got out of the car and looked around. The gray sky matched the snowy gray ground. Everything was still and quiet, like the hands of a clock had come slowly to a stop. Winters could be like that. But the hollow feeling in my gut told me that more than the serene emptiness of a winter's day was at work.

"See that," I said. "No birds. Not a one."

"It *is* winter," said Lulu.

"But birds are usually attracted to me for some reason," said Carmen.

"I see that," said Lulu, glancing at Carmen's deep green wool coat dress, tied at the middle with a crimson sash. "You look like they dress you in the morning."

"A reanimated bird once did," said Carmen. "It's a funny story, actually, unless you're squeamish."

Carmen grabbed a huge casserole dish out of the trunk. Then we walked up, and I knocked lightly on Eliza's front door. Little Barnaby hunkered down deeper into Carmen's pocket.

"The demons are skittish," I whispered. "I think all ghosts and cryptids have left the area."

"How many are usually around here?" asked Lulu. "The town only has two thousand people."

"Way more if you count the ones in the cemetery," whispered Carmen.

Just then, the door flew open. We all looked down. A small, fair-haired boy in a baseball cap stood in front of us. To say that he was crestfallen would be an understatement. He looked around us like he hoped someone else might come up the sidewalk.

"Carter!" said Eliza, hurrying up. "I told you not to answer the door!"

"I thought it was daddy," he said, staring down at the ground.

Eliza was struck dumb for a second. We all stood there awkwardly as she put a shaky hand on her son's shoulder.

"How about you finish coloring that picture for me," said Eliza. "You know I love fairies."

Carter trudged back over to his plastic kid's table and picked up a green crayon. Lulu hugged Eliza, who looked like she was doing her best to stop from crying. Then we were ushered over to the sofa. We sat down and Carmen put the casserole on the coffee table.

"I told him, but he doesn't understand," whispered Eliza.

"It's like that with little kids," said Lulu.

We all nodded.

"Thanks so much for bringing this over," Eliza said, pointing at the food.

"Of course," said Carmen. "You just put it in the oven at 400 degrees for about forty-five minutes. And there's a loaf of garlic bread, too."

"Thanks," said Eliza.

Nobody seemed to know what to say. I always hated when a case started like this. Old-timey ghosts were so much easier, or cryptids on a spree of scaring people. But this was the worst. What could we ever say to Eliza to make things better? To ease her pain? Nothing.

"We were so sorry to hear about your husband," said Carmen. She had always been so much better at connecting with people.

"Thank you," said Eliza. She stared off into space. "It doesn't make any sense. The cops don't get it either. He was in the garage. The door was closed. Was the door open earlier because he was cutting wood and there was dust? Did Sam let the dog in because it was cold out? He always liked dogs."

We all looked at each other.

"Did you ever see the dog before?" I asked. "We live outside Holy Oak, and the people in the farm near us let their black lab run wherever it wants."

"No," said Eliza. "I've never seen a dog running around, except Mrs. Murphy's Pomeranian once."

The scratching noise of a crayon against a coloring book stopped. I glanced across the room. Carter sat there, staring at us. Then, slowly, he looked back down at his book and began again.

The ears of a fox, I thought.

"It's just so scary," whispered Eliza. "That there's a dog out there attacking people. And poor Trisha. It must seem friendly at first, for people to keep letting it in."

Later, Lulu asked if she could see a mural Eliza was working on. Carmen and I decided this was a good time to approach Carter with one of Carmen's most reliable secret weapons.

"The name of the game is double chocolate chunk cookies," said Carmen. She set the plate down in front of the coloring book. "Would you like one?"

Carter brightened when he took one of the massive cookies. He ate it like he fully intended to have three more.

"They're my favorite too," said Carmen, taking a bite.

We sat down next to Carter. The crayons were scattered all over the place. His coloring book of choice was strangely topical.

"Is that a fairy?" asked Carmen.

Carter nodded. "I colored Bigfoot too, see."

He turned a few pages back. He had colored Bigfoot with a mixture of brown, tan, and green crayons.

"I like it," I said. "But my favorite are probably the mysterious big black cats of England. Have you heard of them?"

Carter shook his head but looked intrigued.

"I always liked the Loch Ness Monster," said Carmen. "But fairies are fun too. I haven't met one yet, but I hope to."

Carter smiled the way little kids do when they find out an adult shares their interest.

"That's the bad part about grownups," said Carmen. "Most of them don't believe in fairies and Bigfoot. But we do, don't we, Immy?"

"I've had coffee with Bigfoot," I said. "Nice guy."

"Really?" Carter asked. He looked like we just told him that Santa was real.

"Yes," said Carmen. She lowered her voice. "So, if you ever see something that you don't think other adults will believe, just tell us because we definitely will."

Carter's face turned serious. He grabbed a crayon and went back to coloring. But after a second, he stopped.

There were a few other coloring books on the table. A couple of pages had been ripped out and thrown on the floor in a crumpled heap. One was a picture of a dog.

"You don't want to color the dog?" I asked, picking it up.

Carter shook his head.

"Did you see the dog?" Carmen asked, slowly. "The other night?"

Carter picked up another cookie and nodded.

"Where was it?" asked Carmen.

"My bedroom," said Carter.

My mind snapped back to the vision of me in the bedroom, of the baseball players on the walls.

"Tell me about it," said Carmen.

Carter shrugged. "I was in my bed, and it was there, growling."

"Then what happened?" I asked.

"It left," he said. "So, I got my mom."

Carmen and I looked at each other.

"Anything else?" asked Carmen.

The little boy was quiet for a long time.

"Remember," said Carmen. "We believe things other adults might not."

Carter grabbed the whole plate of cookies and shook his head.

We pulled out of Eliza's driveway and headed for the hospital.

"What did you learn?" asked Lulu.

"Carter knows more than he's saying," I said. "I hate when we play the magic card and kids don't bite. Makes it more complicated."

"We could always use stronger tactics," said Carmen, in a sing-song voice.

"No," I said. "We'll see what Shannon knows, and if we still have questions, then we'll do it your way."

"What way are you guys talking about?" asked Lulu.

"Just sprinkling a little dust on their faces," said Carmen. "It always gets people talking."

"She wants to drug them," I said. "Hypnotism dust. It works pretty well, but it's kind of a hassle. Some people get goofy. You kind of have to babysit them. And it's always made me feel a little icky afterward."

"I'm not going to lie," said Lulu. "That's pretty messed up."

I shrugged.

"You try holding a hundred people's hands when they can't come to terms with the fact that their neighbor's a werewolf," said Carmen. "After a while, you'd drug them right away too, to get to the fact-finding."

"Touché," said Lulu.

"I glanced at Carter's bedroom," I said. "It's definitely where I was in my vision."

"Some serious magic happened in that garage," said Carmen. "And I felt it upstairs too. Did you?"

"Yep," I said.

"We need to know more, Immy," said Carmen.

"The newspaper says that Shannon was attacked too," I said. "So, she should be able to give us some more info about this dog."

Shannon was flipping through channels when we entered her hospital room. She settled on some game show from the 1980s.

"Hi," she said, surprised.

Carmen could hardly get her bouquet of peonies and amaranth through the door.

"Wow," said Shannon. She cringed as she propped herself up in bed. She had a blanket pulled up to her chest, but I still saw the bandages all over her arms. "Those are beautiful flowers!"

"Thanks so much," said Carmen. "I made the arrangement myself. About a year ago, I built a greenhouse in the backyard to grow herbs and flowers. You know, to help me become a more powerful witch."

Shannon snorted as she laughed. Lulu and I looked at each other and let out an awkward chortle.

"Ha," I said, making eyes at my sister. "That's a funny *joke*."

"Are you feeling better?" asked Lulu.

"I guess," said Shannon. "It all seems like a terrible dream. Trisha and I have lived together for years. And I've known her since I was thirteen. Sometimes she drove me crazy. I mean, the woman labeled her Corn Nuts, so I wouldn't eat them. Like I'd eat that crap. But I can't imagine never laughing together over another crappy movie. I can't believe it. We liked most of the same things and hated all the same people..."

"That's what really counts," I said.

"I know," said Shannon. She wiped away a tear. "She was a gem— an absolute gem."

Lulu put her hand on Shannon's scratched fingers.

"Listen," said Lulu. "We just saw Eliza, and she's pretty shaken up."

"I heard about that," said Shannon. Her eyes filled with tears as she shook her head. "Poor Sam."

"She's really worried about that dog," said Lulu. "We told her we'd try to figure out where it came from. We thought you might be able to help."

Shannon played with her blanket.

"We saw it in the yard a couple of times," said Shannon. "It always came around sunset, or after dark. It stood in the backyard, barking or growling. That drove Trisha crazy. Getting barked at in your own yard."

"Was it this dog?" asked Carmen. She held up her iPhone with a picture of a blue heeler.

Shannon nodded. "But I didn't see it the other night," she said. "I only heard it downstairs, growling. Trisha woke me up, saying it was downstairs. I don't know how it got in. Trisha went down to get it out. I didn't want to get too close. I have bad allergies."

We all looked at each other. If I had raised my eyebrow any higher, it would have been in my hairline.

"Sorry," said Carmen. "I thought you were attacked by the dog."

"No," said Shannon. "It got quiet downstairs. The lights went out, so I was worried that someone let the dog in. I went downstairs and Trisha was already dead."

"But you're hurt," said Lulu.

Shannon looked down at herself. "I went downstairs and the dog was gone. I was attacked by the lady in the mask."

Carmen dropped her iPhone. Barnaby poked his head out of her pocket, and Carmen gently shoved him back down.

I grabbed a folded newspaper that sat on Shannon's bedside table. "What lady?" I asked. "We never heard anything about that. There's an article in the Brier Herald that says you were attacked by a dog, just like Sam."

"I know," said Shannon, annoyed. "I'm so pissed. I told the cops what happened. I don't know if they're trying to keep it quiet or what. But you know that newspaper is trash. They can hardly spell. They mix up people's obituaries. And now this. I don't get it."

"Eliza *did* say that she didn't understand how the dog got into the closed garage unless Sam let it in," said Carmen.

"I bet that lady let it in," said Shannon. "That's what I kept saying to Trisha too. You wouldn't let that mean thing in on your own."

"I'm so sorry, Shannon," said Lulu. "I had no idea."

"I just want everyone to know," said Shannon. "That's all I care about. People need to be able to protect themselves from that whack job."

"What did she look like?" I asked.

"It was dark," said Shannon. "But I could tell she was wearing a long brown dress. Like something you'd wear to the Renaissance Festival. And she had some old mask strapped to her face. A weird, leathery thing. It reminded me of masks in creepy old pictures of Halloween from the 1930s. It was wrinkly, like an old woman with a pointy nose. The mouth and eyes were just jagged holes. And it was all curled up around the edges. She took one of the kitchen knives and…you know…"

"How did you get away?" asked Carmen.

Shannon smiled, but it was a smile without any humor in it. She was angry and scared.

"It was so stupid," she said. "I felt like I was going to pass out, but I wanted to hit her once, so maybe I could crawl away. The only thing in reach to hit her with was the bowl of popcorn that we were eating earlier."

"Really?" asked Lulu.

"She just stood there like she couldn't believe it," said Shannon. "I remember thinking the metal clanking on the floor was so loud."

A silver bowl, I thought. *Salty popcorn.*

It felt like sound had been sucked out of the room. None of us knew what to say.

"I hope the police find that lady," said Shannon. "But I don't think you gals should go looking for that dog."

A cold trickle of air seeped in through the windows.

"I think it would be a bad idea," said Shannon.

CHAPTER TWELVE

"You could have stayed at our house if this makes you uncomfortable. I know it makes me uncomfortable," I said.

"Don't be so dramatic, Immy," said Carmen. "This is just a little hypnotism dust to help the investigation along. It's harmless."

"Are you kidding me?" asked Lulu. "Sure, this is all creepy as hell, but kind of fascinating too. Plus, I can handle myself. I box at home for exercise."

I pointed at Carmen. "She's going to be your protégé, not mine," I said.

We were on our way back to Eliza's house to find out if they had ever seen this mysterious woman.

"So, it's always been just you guys and your parents, investigating mysteries?" Lulu asked.

I stared blankly at the snowy road in front of me. Carmen glanced my way, nervous.

"Actually," said Carmen. "A couple of years ago, there was another guy who helped us every once in a while."

Lulu nodded, staring out her window. "So, if things ever get too tense," she said, "maybe he could come help."

"Not bloody likely," I whispered.

"This is incredible!" said Eliza, staring at the layered hummingbird cake on the table. We brought along apple cider, too. The plan was to get Eliza and Carter full of enough rich treats that they'd be as sedate as you get after eating Thanksgiving dinner. Then Carmen would walk behind them and sprinkle the dust on their heads. It was a lot easier than trying to put it in food. You wouldn't believe how many times people ended up with the wrong slice of cake. It got awkward.

We sat down at the table, and Carmen began carving up slices.

"Yum!" said Carter, taking a plate of cake.

Eliza stared at Carmen. "You can bake, do woodworking, fix things, and make your own clothes. Is there anything you can't do?"

"I can't fly!" said Carmen. "Yet, anyway."

Eliza got a big kick out of that. Lulu and I rolled our eyes.

"If anyone at this table finds a way," said Eliza. "It'll be you."

"Thanks," said Carmen. "Have some cider."

"I've never had it with Red Hots before," said Eliza.

Carmen filled all of our mugs with a generous amount.

"It's good!" said Carter, wiping his mouth.

"Drink it all," said Carmen. "I swear it's not poisoned!"

Eliza laughed. Lulu shook her head like witches were hopeless. I tried to use my eyes to tell Carmen to stop being suspicious as hell. But she just smiled and winked back.

"This is fun," said Eliza. "You should come over more often. I've been trying to get a game night go—"

But Eliza never got out the rest of her sentence. Instead, both she and Carter slouched down in their chairs, resting their heads on the table. Cider spilled everywhere.

"Holy shit," said Lulu, standing up.

"What the…" I said. Then I looked at Carmen, who wore a satisfied smile. "Carmen! You weren't supposed to put the dust in the cider!"

I pushed it away. "How did you know which glass we would end up with? You could have drugged us!"

"Oh, Immy," said Carmen. She wiped up the spilled cider. "You know I'm nothing if not careful."

By the time we had Eliza and Carter resting on the couch, I had dissolved into a fit of nervous laughter.

"Look what you did," said Lulu. "Your sister's gone full hyena."

"Do you want to hold Horatio for comfort, Immy?" asked Carmen.

I wasn't supposed to be a witch anymore. I wasn't supposed to hunt monsters. I wasn't supposed to investigate murders where people were mauled. Thanks, but no. And I sure as hell wasn't supposed to drug people to uncover the secrets they were too scared to talk about.

"All I can say is I hope the Devil *is* Tom Ellis," I said. "Because I'm pretty sure we're all going to hell now."

"Don't be so dramatic, Immy," said Carmen. "Hypnotism dust has been used by witches at parties forever, and by witch parents to find out which kid took all the cookies from the jar. It's better this way. He was obviously too scared to tell us what happened."

"We're still making him go over the whole thing," I said.

"But he won't even remember," said Carmen. "They'll both wake up hours from now feeling fresh as a daisy."

"It might save lives," said Lulu.

"That might be true," I said. "But it still won't help me sleep at night."

Just then, Carter sat up straight, put his arms at his sides like they were wings, and began hooting.

"What the hell is going on?" asked Lulu.

"He thinks he's an owl," said Carmen. "It is hypnotism, after all. This is a common side effect."

"Are there other side effects?" asked Lulu.

"Scurvy," I said, rubbing my temples.

"Are you serious?" asked Lulu. "Doesn't that make your gums bleed?"

For the first time in a long time, Carmen seemed a little peeved at me.

"We're just going to have to hope that doesn't happen," said Carmen, frowning.

"I'll second that," said Lulu.

Carmen sat down next to Eliza and whispered in her ear.

"Eliza," said Carmen, slow and melodic. "Listen to my voice. Are you there?"

Eliza's eyes flew open, and she began to speak in rapid, fevered tones.

"What language is that?" asked Lulu.

"Latin," we both said.

"What is she saying?" asked Lulu.

I leaned in as Eliza repeated some of the same words, now in more of a sing-song voice.

"It's strange," said Carmen. "I don't understand. Something about a sheik and a prophet. Do you understand it, Immy?"

I squinted as Eliza said the same words over and over. Then I nodded.

"I know what this is," I said, crossing my arms.

"What?" they both asked.

"Eliza is reciting, in Latin, the lyrics to the 1982 hit 'Rock the Casbah.' By The Clash, I believe."

Carmen nodded.

"I have to hand it to you, ladies," said Lulu, putting her hands on her hips. "You're breaking this case wide open."

"Let's get down to business," said Carmen. "Enough, Eliza."

Eliza stopped mid-sentence, closing her eyes again.

"Hear my voice," said Carmen. "You are guided by my voice. You are perfectly safe. Now, go back to the day when the dog attacked Sam. Where are you?"

The whole room seemed to get darker. It wasn't just me. Lulu looked around too. It was as if the snowy clouds outside had completely blocked out the sun.

"I'm in bed," whispered Eliza. Her face turned to a frown. "I'm scared."

"Why are you scared?" asked Carmen.

"I'm reading a parenting book," said Eliza. "Carter is terrified that there are monsters in his room. And I don't know what to do."

"I wasn't expecting that," whispered Lulu.

"What does the monster look like?" asked Carmen, leaning in.

"I'm not sure," said Eliza. "Carter won't say. But...when he comes to bed, he says that *she* wants to kill him."

Carmen looked at me, and I nodded.

"Sleep now," said Carmen. "When you wake up, you will think this was all a dream. You will feel light and hopeful."

Eliza rested her head back on the sofa. Then Carmen scooted over next to Carter.

"Carter," said Carmen. "Everything is all right. I need you to tell me about the night the dog was in your room. You will be perfectly safe. Nothing can harm you. But we need your help. Will you tell us?"

Carter nodded. Carmen took Barnaby out of her pocket and put him on Carter's lap.

"This is my friend," said Carmen. "You can pet him if you feel nervous."

With gentle fingers, Carter rested his hands on Barnaby, who cuddled into his new pal's sweater.

"Tell me about the dog," said Carmen.

"I only saw it for a minute," said Carter, quietly. "It was kind of hidden in the dark. It went out into the hallway."

"That's the only time you saw it?" asked Carmen.

Carter frowned. He seemed unsure of how to answer.

"What about the monster Eliza was talking about?" I asked.

Carmen nodded. "Carter," she said. "Is the monster in your room the dog?"

Carter shrugged. "Kind of," he said. "The dog is the lady, and the lady is the monster."

We all gaped at each other.

"Ask him that again," I said, nervous.

"Carter," said Carmen. "Are you saying that the woman and the dog are one?"

Carter nodded, holding Barnaby closer for comfort.

"Shit," I said.

"Is that bad?" asked Lulu.

"It's more complicated," said Carmen. "Carter, tell me about the lady."

"She showed up one night," said Carter. "I woke up and felt her there, standing in the corner. She stood and watched. I pretended she wasn't there. I pretended I was sleeping. But she stayed until the sun came up."

"How many times did you see her?" asked Carmen.

"Every night for a week and a half," said Carter.

"Holy shit," said Lulu. "No wonder Eliza was freaked out."

"Poor kid," I said.

"Does she do the same thing every night?" asked Carmen.

Carter nodded as Barnaby burrowed further into his sweater. It was as if the pocket demon was just as nervous about the story.

"Sometimes, she stands in the closet and watches me through the crack," he said. "And sometimes, she sits in the rocking chair. But she always stares."

"What does she look like?" asked Carmen.

"I don't know," said Carter. "I thought she was old, but it's just her mask. She's got a long, brown dress on. Her fingers are the only things that move."

"Now remember," said Carmen. "My friend Barnaby is with you to keep you safe. He won't let the lady hurt you. Tell me about that night with your dad."

"They got me a night light to stop monsters," said Carter, his voice rising. "But it must have been broken because she was still there. Standing by the hallway, so I couldn't get out."

Lulu shivered. The temperature in the whole room seemed to drop twenty degrees. I looked up toward the ceiling. It felt as if the house itself was creaking to life.

"I turned over," said Carter. "But she sat on my bed. She talked to me. She never did that before."

"What did she say?" asked Carmen.

"Something about *too much*," said Carter, cradling Barnaby.

I wrapped my arms around myself, trying to keep the cold out.

"Then what happened?"

"I reached up and threw my baseball at her," said Carter. "Then it's like she turned into the dog and left. I ran to tell my mom. That's when we heard it in the garage."

We all stood there in the quiet living room, not knowing what to do next. The very air felt like it was listening to us. As if a thousand ears were waiting to hear, waiting to report back to their master.

Light tears slid down Carter's face. Carmen leaned over and grabbed Barnaby. As she lifted him up, the pocket demon brushed the tears away from the boy's face with his thick paw.

"Sleep and feel light, Carter," whispered Carmen. "When you wake up, you will be happy, knowing you have friends that love you."

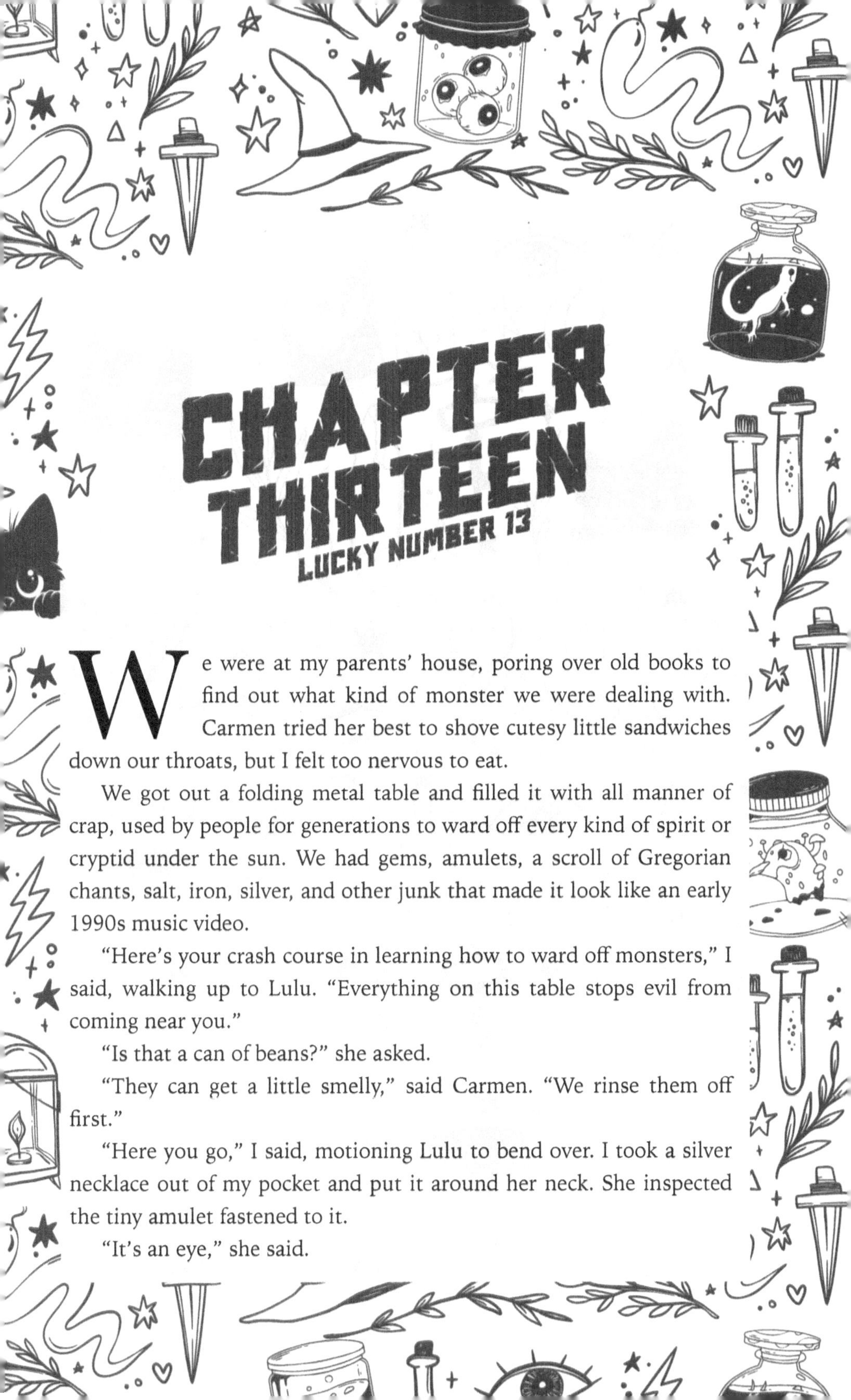

CHAPTER THIRTEEN
LUCKY NUMBER 13

We were at my parents' house, poring over old books to find out what kind of monster we were dealing with. Carmen tried her best to shove cutesy little sandwiches down our throats, but I felt too nervous to eat.

We got out a folding metal table and filled it with all manner of crap, used by people for generations to ward off every kind of spirit or cryptid under the sun. We had gems, amulets, a scroll of Gregorian chants, salt, iron, silver, and other junk that made it look like an early 1990s music video.

"Here's your crash course in learning how to ward off monsters," I said, walking up to Lulu. "Everything on this table stops evil from coming near you."

"Is that a can of beans?" she asked.

"They can get a little smelly," said Carmen. "We rinse them off first."

"Here you go," I said, motioning Lulu to bend over. I took a silver necklace out of my pocket and put it around her neck. She inspected the tiny amulet fastened to it.

"It's an eye," she said.

"Eyes have been used to protect against evil for a long time," said Carmen. "Got to keep that evil eye away. People used to paint them on buildings, ships, cups…"

"Cups?" asked Lulu.

"You don't want a monster to go down your throat when you're drinking ale," said Carmen.

"I'll keep that in mind," said Lulu. "I'm also going to take this iron rod, just in case."

Carmen revved up her trusty 038 Magnum. We both scowled at her for the gassy smell, and she quickly turned it off.

"You should see how upset monsters get when I start this," said Carmen. "I sprinkle the chain with holy water."

"Although, to be fair, they're usually miffed about the chainsaw either way," I said.

"That's so true," said Carmen.

"Is this thing a werewolf or what?" asked Lulu.

"I don't think so," I said. "Werewolves are big. And they don't switch back and forth so fast. If you turn into a werewolf, it's going to be an all-nighter."

"What kind of creature can change back and forth from a person to a dog?" asked Lulu.

I shrugged. "There are several possibilities," I said. "Could be the Aswang. It's a kind of ticked-off vampire that changes into a dog. Or it could be some kind of angry fairy, but like I said, fairies are rare."

Lulu pointed at Carmen. "Didn't you say you were just a corgi?"

Carmen's eyes sparkled.

"I *did* change into a dog. Witches can change into dogs, Immy. Witches can change into a couple of different kinds of animals if they have the power."

I tapped my foot, nervous.

"You think this could be a rogue witch?" I asked.

Carmen smiled, and my mood instantly soured.

"Well, then I guess it's going to be an awkward reunion this year," I said.

"That changes things, Immy," said Carmen. "We better gather a few more things to ward off witches."

"You have stuff in your house to ward off *you*?" asked Lulu. "Do you put it by the remote, so only you can watch Netflix?"

"You've been reading my diary," said Carmen. "Salt's a good one. We can't stand it. That's why whenever we cook, we use the thirty percent less sodium blend. And we have to wear rubber gloves when we sprinkle it."

"You people have complicated lives," said Lulu.

I tried to take a couple of deep breaths, but my body didn't want to.

"Who the hell could it be?" I asked. "Transforming like that is tricky shit. And nobody at the witch reunion has even been an asshole the last couple of years."

"You can't be an asshole or people would be suspicious of you," said Carmen. "Just look at Ted Bundy."

Lulu opened her mouth to talk, but was interrupted by a loud banging at the front door. We all jumped. It had been so calm, with the snow drifting slowly to the ground. The thing about living on the outskirts of town was that we got used to the quiet, and the only people who came over were looking specifically for us.

The banging continued as we got up from our chairs and peeked around the corner, into the entryway. Who the hell would come to our house banging like that?

Carmen took a few tentative steps toward the entryway when the painful moaning started, then the banging came again.

"Is that the dog?" asked Lulu. "Or the lady? Or whatever? Should I grab the salt and rod or what?"

"Yes!" I said.

We got closer. The banging continued.

"Wenches!" someone said. It was a male voice, deep and loud. "I know you are at your dwelling. I can smell your flesh!"

"Are we dead?" Lulu asked, lifting the rod. "Is someone here to kill us?"

"Who the hell is that?" I asked.

"What do we do, Immy?" asked Carmen. "He doesn't seem like a very polite guest. Should I get the saw and gems?"

The banging stopped, and the voice rang out again.

"Do not be afraid," he said. "I have not consumed human flesh for many a moon. Since long before your grandparents and their grandparents before them were runny-nosed little human babies. I seek refuge! Do you not aid the pathetic, weak, and frightened? For I am one such soul today! Open the door, lest my large, beautiful form be ripped into food for scavengers."

"He sounds like he escaped from Shakespeare in the Park," said Lulu.

"I'm not sure about that," I said, putting my hand on the doorknob. "It's winter."

Against my better judgment, and with all three of us holding various gems and charms, I slowly opened the heavy wooden door. The pocket demons, along with Buster Keaton and Norma Shearer, had vacated to the safety of closed cupboards, loose floorboards, and the crawl space below the hutch.

I was just peeking an eye out to see who the visitor was when a massive force shoved the door open. Two giant hooves stepped into the entryway. We all retreated a few steps, stunned by the image before us. He was a minotaur, that was obvious. I had never seen a full-grown one. I'd only ever seen a picture of a baby one, sent by my uncle during his trip to Crete. But this guy was something else. He was ten feet tall, so our high ceilings came in handy. His chest, legs, and arms were built like an actor signed on to star as a comic book hero. His bull head was massive, with horns sticking out as thick as my arm. And, in typical minotaur fashion, the only thing covering his nether regions was a belt and loin-cloth, *Beastmaster*-style.

"Oh, God!" said Lulu, screaming. "It's the Devil! It's the Devil!"

"Ha, ha!" said the beast. "I have still got it. I can smell that this one is new to monsters. Look at how afraid she is! Cower, puny one!"

"Screw you, asshole!" said Lulu.

Before we could say anything or stop her, Lulu lunged at the minotaur with the iron rod, whacking him hard in the thigh. He yelled out, hopping up and down on our antique floors.

"Mean, puny one!" said the minotaur. "Did I not say that I was needy and sought refuge? Refuge me!"

I put my hand on Lulu's rod, nodding for her to lower it.

"He's a minotaur," I said. "And I think he's a nice one. He couldn't get on the property otherwise."

It was a fact that I had forgotten myself for a moment. Monsters banging on your front door will do that.

"Oh!" said Lulu, looking a little embarrassed. She dropped the rod and shrugged at the hulking figure, who sat on the floor. He cradled his leg like a baby. "Sorry about that. I didn't realize you were a nice monster."

"Nice monster," said the minotaur, moaning. "And to think, in my prime, I feasted upon the heads of many a human with delight. Human heads are sweeter than… You…what is your favorite food?"

"Me?" I asked. "I guess I'm partial to French silk pie."

"Yes!" said the minotaur. "Think of the freshest, sweetest slice of French silk pie, and know that it pales to the sweetness of your delicious head."

"I…don't think we know each other well enough for you to say things like that," I said.

"What a lovely day this has turned out to be," said Carmen, smiling at the minotaur.

"But do not fear," said the minotaur. "For many moons ago, your long-expired ancestor saved me from the clutches of death, so in return, I eat no human flesh, just animal flesh…and occasionally soup."

"Which ancestor was that?" asked Carmen, excited.

"Ignatius Abernathy," he bellowed.

We looked at each other.

"I have no idea who the hell that is," I said, shrugging.

"I'll have to look that one up in our genealogy book later," said Carmen, beaming.

"What was he like?" I asked.

"He was an insufferable cad," said the minotaur. "But take no offense, for most people are. Yes, he was a lying, thieving, whoring scumbag. But helpful in a pinch."

"Sounds like most of my relatives," said Lulu.

"Well, Mr. Minotaur, come in," said Carmen. "Come into the parlor."

The minotaur followed Carmen into the living room. He sat on the ground with his legs crossed. Carmen disappeared for a moment, then reappeared with a large mixing bowl filled with coffee, and our Thanksgiving serving tray covered in cookies.

"At least there are some who still treat guests as kings," said the minotaur.

Lulu kept nudging me. She pointed at the minotaur and whispered, "A devil! I bagged my first devil!"

I gave her the thumbs up, then interrupted the conversation Carmen was having with the minotaur about whether it was weird for him to eat beef. It wasn't.

"You seem to know who we are," I said.

"Your puny family is known to me," he said. "I have watched your dealings since my encounter with your ancestor."

"My sister is known for her hospitality," I said. "And for being cordial and having friends. But not me. I'm virtually friendless, thought of by most as a bitch, and more than a little rattled by a current matter we're dealing with. So, excuse me for cutting out the pleasant chit-chat, but who the hell are you and what the hell do you want?"

The minotaur slapped his hand against the floor in amusement. It made us all bounce a little bit. It was something he liked to do quite a bit. Norma Shearer, who had just emerged from under the hutch, turned around and hid again.

"Yes," said the minotaur. "We shall cut the crap! You are Imogen, you are Carmen, and you are..."

"Lulu Marin," said Lulu.

"And as for me," he said, puffing up his chest, "I'm Hector the minotaur!"

I tried to hide a laugh.

"You find my name amusing, little human?" he asked.

"Do you try to make *Hector* rhyme with *minotaur*?" I asked.

He shot hot air out of his nose, then put a hand to his chin, considering.

"I enjoy when it rhymes, yes," he said. "We all have our little things."

Carmen grabbed at the gray arm of my sweater.

"Can we keep him, Immy?" she asked. I shook my head.

"And you're here because?" I asked.

"As I said, I seek refuge from the one who would do me harm. And you are known for protecting the pitiful."

Carmen sat down next to Hector.

"Who wants to harm you?" Carmen asked.

"I was in Iowa when I first smelled her," said Hector. "I haven't been to these shores in many suns, so I came here last year to wander the prairies, climb the mountains, and reminisce about times gone by."

"Sounds fun," I said, trying to hurry this up.

"Indeed," he said. "But then one day, while bathing in a river, I caught a scent in the air. A scent that I have not smelled in so long that one would think the memory dead. But I will never forget *that day*."

"What smell was it?" asked Carmen, resting her hand on Hector's arm.

"It was the smell of rotten eggs, of burned dreams, and sharp thistles."

Air caught in my throat.

"She tried to do me harm that day long ago," said Hector. "The day your ancestor saved me. There is no grudge too petty for her. So, I know she will come for me."

Slowly, the pocket demons and cats wandered into the living room, circling Hector. It was easy to see now—they were all so frightened. We could soothe them like children, but they were tuned into some other frequency. They felt the shadow coming in around them. I had felt it for days, too, like a cold draft creeping up my toes, then taking over my whole body. All you could hear was the tick of the grandfather clock as we all stood there, nervous.

"She has been here for a while," said Hector, "hiding in the dark corners. She is waiting for the right time to get her hands on us all. Monsters and demons have all fled this place, seeking refuge on distant shores or calming waters. But I knew the best place was with those who could protect the world from her."

"And who is she, exactly?" asked Lulu.

Hector nodded. "This place is protected from dark magic and dark creatures?"

"Of course," said Carmen.

"Then I will dare to utter her name," he said. "I would not do so otherwise."

We leaned in. We sat on the edge of a knife, waiting to hear the name of the danger that surrounded us.

"She is..." said Hector. "The Thistle Witch."

Silence wrapped around the room, but when Carmen and I made eye contact, we couldn't help laughing. The pocket demons and cats joined in, rolling around the floor in amusement.

"Do not laugh at me," said Hector, banging his hand again. "No one laughs at Hector!"

"I don't get it," said Lulu. "What's so funny?"

"There's no such thing as the Thistle Witch," said Carmen. "It's like the boogeyman. It's a story witches used to tell to frighten their kids. Kind of morbid, really. I love it."

"Someone from the reunion probably just lost it," I said. "Like Donna, maybe. She always has a snide remark. And she takes it as a personal offense if you don't eat her congealed potato salad. She'd kill for that stuff. I know it."

"But I saw the Thistle Witch with my own eyes!" said Hector.

"I believe you saw someone who *told you* they were the Thistle Witch," I said. "People pretend to be other people all the time in this line of work. Carmen once pretended to be Morgan Le Fay."

"And Baba Yaga," said Carmen, looking proud.

"That woman could have been anyone," I said. "It's not like you could check her ID."

"So, you believe in every monster except this one?" asked Lulu.

"I don't believe in Santa Claus either," I said.

"Don't say that, Immy," said Carmen. "Christmas is just around the corner, and if you don't believe, you don't get presents."

"If you saw her as I did," said Hector. "You would have no doubt. She first appeared to me as an angry spotted dog, then her form changed into that of a masked woman."

The laughing stopped. The pocket demons went quiet too, looking up with surprise. There couldn't have been a more spot-on description of the creature we were dealing with. But it seemed like a big pill to swallow. Could it just be that this creature had appeared first to Hector, and now again to us, pretending to be the Thistle Witch to create an aura of fear and mystery? Or was the Thistle Witch real after all, like the giant squid getting taken off the cryptid list? The Thistle Witch was just a story people with magic told their children, and an old-fashioned one at that. It was something our grandparents heard when they went to bed. Not for the first time this week, I was left feeling unsure.

"I don't even know where to start with all this," I said. "What do you think, Carmen?"

Carmen patted Hector's arm like he was a child.

"I guess you better tell us how you met up with the Thistle Witch," she said.

Hector gulped coffee from his mixing bowl. Logs crackled in the fireplace as everyone in the room—witch, demon, and human—sat listening to Hector's tale.

"Many moons ago," Hector began. "I wandered around the rough mountains of my homeland."

He ate a cookie in a single bite, sending crumbs everywhere.

"First, I should say," said Hector. "You may or may not have heard a rumor that minotaurs like a good treasure. I am here to say the stories are true. Nothing fills my large heart with joy like a chest full of rare jewels…except maybe human flesh to dine upon."

I rubbed my temples and sighed.

"A friend of mine disclosed to me the whereabouts of a certain hidden treasure," said Hector. "At least, I thought he was a friend, paying me back for killing a giant serpent that attempted to throttle him. But it turns out he was enamored of my mate, Jade. So, he sent me into the mountains to find the gold and rubies with the secret intention of sending me to my death."

Carmen drank a mug of hot cocoa, enraptured with the story Hector told. I didn't feel the same kind of joy hearing about cryptids and legends. I just wondered how it would end up biting me in the ass.

"I found the place that was marked upon the ancient map," said Hector. "It was night, a beautiful, long night. And the moon was huge and delicious, like the head of a pale human, waiting to be plucked and eaten."

"Lovely bedtime story," whispered Lulu.

"I began to dig," said Hector. "With my giant, strong hands I lifted mounds of dirt and threw them aside, hungry for the beautiful treasure below. I did not heed the sudden change of light, the darkening of the world that took place around me. And I did not heed the growling that began ringing in my ear. After all, minotaurs deal with wild animals all the time. Why would this day be any different?"

I opened up my hands and saw how sweaty my palms were.

Why can't I be left alone to make donuts until I die? I thought.

"The dog appeared before me like a monster stumbling out of a dream," said Hector. "One moment I was alone, then the next moment it was there, growling and biting at me. I grabbed my trusty spear to throw at the creature, but it vanished as quickly as it had appeared. That was when I knew that there was dark magic afoot. But I cared not, for I am Hector, known for my bravery. There are few monsters roaming this Earth that stir fear within this hardened heart.

I wanted to see the smile on Jade's face when I returned with the beautiful gold. Many treasures are guarded by fearsome creatures."

"Like minotaurs," I said.

Hector pounded the floor.

"Yes!" he said, laughing. "Quite true."

He ate five more cookies. The pocket demons shielded their heads as the crumbs fell on them like raindrops.

"The treasure was buried deep," said Hector. "But soon I hit wood. I rubbed away the last bits of Earth. You can imagine my disappointment when I realized that I had uncovered not a chest of fine jewels, but instead a pauper's grave. Nothing more than a shoddy, cheap box."

Carmen had a notebook on her lap. A whole page was nearly filled with her perfect penmanship. That was the Carmen way. She was thorough with note-taking on cases like this. You never knew what details might be important. They might come in handy ten minutes or ten years from now on a different case.

Carmen had a quilt around her shoulders, and as she wrote, she pulled it tighter around herself. Despite the crackling fire, wisps of cold air trickled in around us.

"I wanted to know what wretched soul was buried so far from the rest of humanity," said Hector. "So, I pulled apart the box. Perhaps you think me cruel for doing so, but back then I thought little of humans, and even less of their final resting places. Humans were just weak, frightened babies, bent on pushing out magic and monsters and labeling us evil."

The wind picked up. Heavy flakes smacked against the windows.

"That was when the dog appeared again," said Hector. "It stood where a tombstone ought to be, snarling and kicking. I saw it better now. It was gray and black, with a black patch over one of its eyes. It was clear the thing was quite mad or evil. I still thought it was merely a guardian, so I demanded that the specter who claimed ownership of this place show itself. And that was when the dog transformed."

"It became the woman in the mask," said Carmen.

"Indeed," said Hector.

"Was it a leathery mask, curled in at the edges?" I asked.

"Quite," said Hector. "And she wore a corseted brown dress."

My stomach felt like a hard, heavy mass.

"I asked if the place I disturbed was her grave," said Hector. "She shook her head, then said, 'It is my home.' I asked if she was a vampire. She shook her head again, and said, 'Vampires are my dolls. I play with them until I break their bones. I am the Thistle Witch.'"

"This isn't sounding good at all," whispered Lulu.

"It was clear that I spoke to a rather powerful entity," said Hector. "Minotaurs are not afraid, but nor are we stupid. This seemed like a good time to take my leave."

Hector took another gulp of coffee. He seemed to be getting more nervous as the story went on, as though the Thistle Witch might appear just by saying her name.

"I told her that I meant no disrespect," said Hector. "That I thought this was only the grave of a pointless human. But she would have none of it. 'Disrespect is all you meant,' she said. 'I have a reason for being, and that reason is torture. That reason is pain.'"

Hector stared out the window. He put his hand up to his face, contemplating.

"To this day, I'm not sure how it happened," said Hector. "It seemed that suddenly it was much later. The moon was in a different place in the sky, and I was waking up. I was tied to large stakes buried deep in the Earth. I felt a strange, painful numbness in my right leg. With groggy confusion, I lifted my head to see the Thistle Witch bent down over my leg, cutting it from ankle to knee. She stared into my eyes the whole time she did her grizzly deed. She used an iron knife, one that made her own hand crackle and burn in pain. The smell of her putrid flesh and my flowing blood was enough to sicken the bravest of creatures. I am not afraid to say I cried out in pain many a time. But she stayed steadfast in her work, watching me and cooking her own flesh."

This isn't any witch from the reunion, I thought.

"What kind of witch would do that, Immy?" asked Carmen. "She seemed to enjoy her own suffering."

"A very twisted one," I said.

"With her deep cut complete," said Hector, "she disappeared from view, then reappeared with a pot full of something. I cried in agony again when she lifted the lid, burning herself again. It was filled with red-hot coals."

"Oh, God," said Lulu, shaking her head.

"I have met many creatures that enjoy torture," said Hector. "Especially torturing humans. But I have never seen anything like the kind of fevered pleasure she got from both hurting me and hurting herself to cause me pain. Bare-handed, she reached in and grabbed the coals. Her flesh sizzled as she rammed them into my open wound. She filled the whole length of the cut. I am sure that all monsters and animals were cleared from the mountains, scared off by my tortured screams cracking the night. The cut filled, she sat upon my injured leg, to smash the hot coals and wound together. She watched me as I screamed, but said nothing. Finally, when I was silent again, she lifted her hands to show them to me. Then she crawled over and rubbed her dead, charred palms against my face."

"Good grief," I said. "How much more of this is there?"

"Be merry, tiny Imogen," said Hector. "I was just about to say that the Thistle Witch was reaching into my mouth to rip my tongue out when your ancestor arrived."

"Thank goodness," said Lulu.

"He told me later that he had been tracking me for days," said Hector. "It was clear, by looking at his dress and his swagger, that he was nothing more than a rake. 'Please do not harm my new friend, there,' he told the witch. 'For I will be needing him presently.' She turned on Ignatius with the only emotion I had seen her emit thus far. She swore at him, stating her displeasure for warlocks and witches everywhere, and told him that she would torture him when she was done with me. He made a snide remark about the state of her hands already, and how they wouldn't be up to the task. That's when she lifted her hands to reveal that they were as smooth and unblemished as a baby human's."

"How could she do that?" asked Lulu.

"That's a very powerful witch," said Carmen.

"She advanced slowly upon Ignatius," said Hector. "The slow, methodical way she walked toward him was like a big cat stalking its prey. She took her time because she knew she could easily smite us."

Hector leaned over and rubbed his right leg. There didn't seem to be a scar.

"That is when Ignatius told her that he wanted to make a deal," said Hector. "The witch brightened at this, but seemed dubious about what bargain they might strike that she would be interested in. It seemed to me that Ignatius was somehow familiar with her story because he said that the Devil had forgotten her there. That her purpose in life had been fulfilled, and she was now left wandering the world. So, he said that he would make her a grand promise in return for our freedom."

I sat up straight.

"What was the promise?" I asked.

"I am not sure," said Hector. "They went off together for some time, binding their pact together with dark magic. The weather turned foul, with blustery winds and hail. So, I knew whatever promise they had made to one another was dastardly. When they returned, she was pleased, indeed. Later, when I tried to get the answer out of him, Ignatius was unresponsive. He only changed the subject, and said it would be a burden for later generations."

Carmen and I made eye contact.

"He does sound like a scumbag," I said.

"You should have seen her then," said Hector. "Standing in her grave. It was more frightening somehow than when she tortured me. She never broke her gaze as she gathered the dirt and pulled it back down into the hole where she stood. When it was up to her neck, she stopped and said, 'When you return home, your mate will be dead. And someday, many moons from now, you, too, will die by my hand.' Then she sank beneath the surface, buried again."

The room was quiet for what seemed like endless moments. I felt my heart racing. Then Lulu slapped her leg.

"Anyone have a cheerful story to lighten the mood?" she asked. "Something about a deer and cat becoming best friends?"

"There isn't even a mark on your leg now," said Carmen.

"A witch's powers back then were something to behold," said Hector. "It would make you and your tingly fingers feel much shame."

"Lovely," said Carmen, smiling.

"Why exactly was our ancestor tracking you?" I asked. "Why did he want you so bad that he'd make some big, Earth-shattering deal?"

"He sought a mermaid," said Hector, frowning. "And he knew I could find her. I helped him. It was the least I could do after he saved me from the witch and healed my leg. Minotaurs have honor."

"What did he want the mermaid for?" I asked.

It almost seemed like Hector blushed.

"It is not relevant," said Hector. "It has nothing to do with the Thistle Witch. Suffice it to say, they had once had quite the steamy romance, and your ancestor wanted to rekindle it."

"That's enough, thank you," I said. "I don't need to know more about that."

"Was your mate dead?" asked Carmen. She had such empathy for everyone.

"Indeed," said Hector. "The sunlight and strength of my life was snuffed out that night. That is how I know she will keep her promise to kill me. Now that you have heard my tale, you must protect me. Whatever promise was made has obviously come to fruition, or she would not be here. So, as I said before, shelter me!"

"Of course," said Carmen. "You can stay here. We'll protect you."

My hands got sweatier. My heart thumped louder. I wasn't ready for this. Why couldn't it have been a little ghost? A lake monster? And then there was the problem of Hector. He was massive and cumbersome. There was only one place around here built for something like him, and my breath caught in my throat when I thought about it.

"He could barely squeeze into the parlor," said Lulu. "Where the hell will he stay?"

"I will stay in the dungeon, of course!" said Hector.

Carmen and the pocket demons shifted their eyes to me, waiting to see what I'd do, and how I'd react. I stood like a mannequin.

"What dungeon?" asked Lulu. "You don't have a dungeon, do you?"

"Of course," said Hector. "I shall stay in the dungeon you built below your shed, the one where you imprisoned the demon that was once Imogen's mate."

Lulu stood, hands lifted in shock.

"Wait, wait, wait," said Lulu. "What the hell is he talking about? Someone forgot to tell me something about something."

"Son of a bitch," I said, leaning back and crossing my arms. Waves of anxiety crashed through me like water against rock. "I have to go into that damn shed."

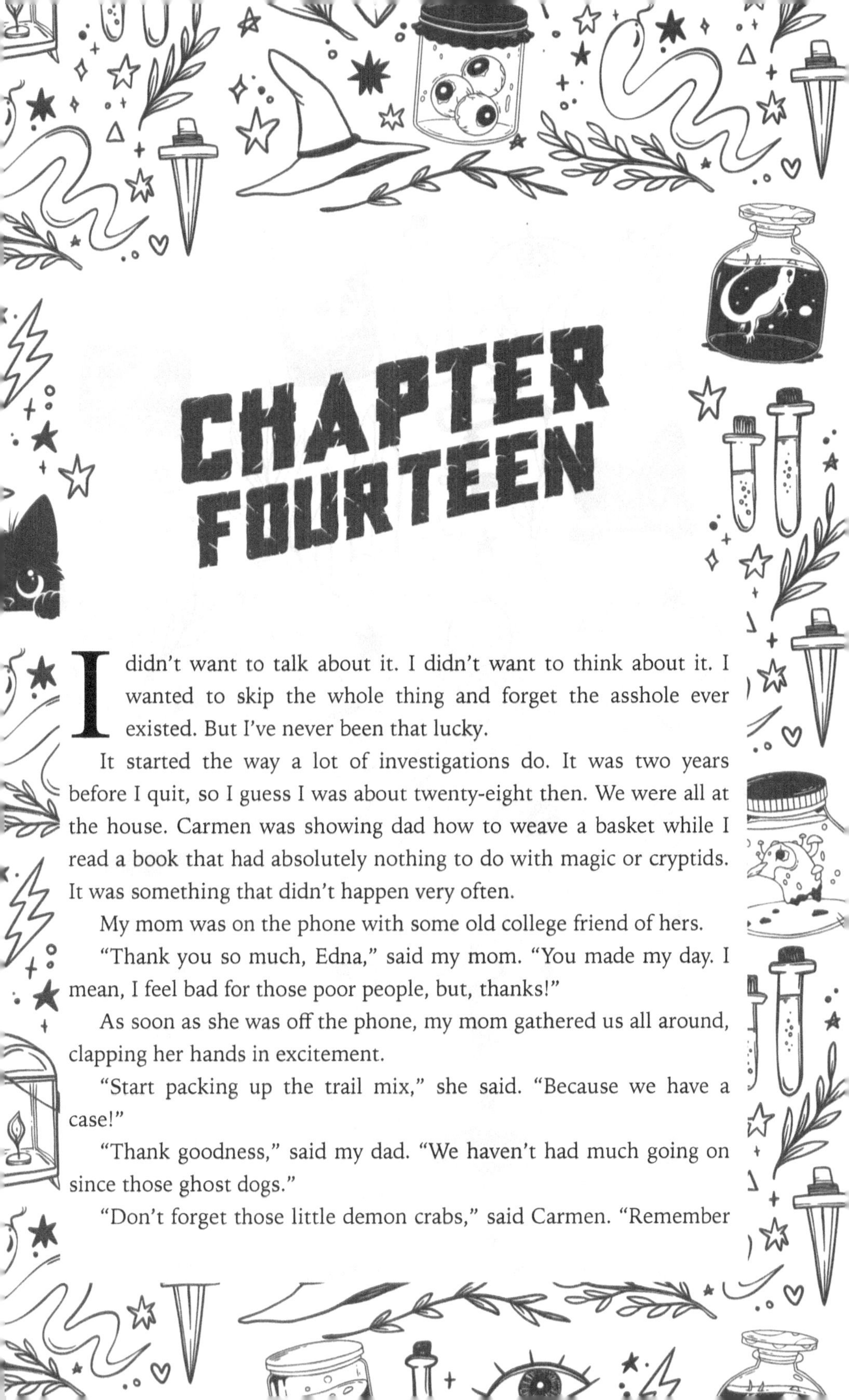

CHAPTER FOURTEEN

I didn't want to talk about it. I didn't want to think about it. I wanted to skip the whole thing and forget the asshole ever existed. But I've never been that lucky.

It started the way a lot of investigations do. It was two years before I quit, so I guess I was about twenty-eight then. We were all at the house. Carmen was showing dad how to weave a basket while I read a book that had absolutely nothing to do with magic or cryptids. It was something that didn't happen very often.

My mom was on the phone with some old college friend of hers.

"Thank you so much, Edna," said my mom. "You made my day. I mean, I feel bad for those poor people, but, thanks!"

As soon as she was off the phone, my mom gathered us all around, clapping her hands in excitement.

"Start packing up the trail mix," she said. "Because we have a case!"

"Thank goodness," said my dad. "We haven't had much going on since those ghost dogs."

"Don't forget those little demon crabs," said Carmen. "Remember how angry they were, trying to snap your fingers in half when you picked them up? So cute!"

"That was Edna," said my mom. "You remember her, Petey. I was the one who always woke her up when she fell asleep in astronomy class. She couldn't help it, poor dear. Dr. Taylor would turn the lights off, so we could see the projected sky on the ceiling, and the sweetheart was snoring in two minutes."

"She was the one with the crazy big hair," said my dad. "Of course, they all had crazy big hair back then. Mostly because of hairspray, but Madge here found a spell that worked even better."

I shook my head, smiling.

"Edna says that there have been reports of some weird deaths by Superior, Wisconsin," said my mom. "Right next to the lake. It looks like the people were mauled."

"How wonderful!" said Carmen. "For us, not them, of course."

"That's what I said," said my mom. "And other people have reported seeing some weird creature by the water. They're describing it as half otter, half dog."

Carmen hopped up, her dress flowing around her like a ballet dancer.

"I'll be ready in ten minutes!" said Carmen. "Just let me pack some clothes and demons."

"Your college friend knows that you're a witch?" I asked. "And that you investigate the otherworldly?"

"Of course, dear," said my mom. "She's known since we were both freshmen. I got a ghost out of her dorm room during our second semester there."

"You were in the right place at the right time," I said.

"She paid me back in haircuts," said my mom, smiling. "She was taking business classes to open her own salon."

Kathleen Mackenzie of Superior, Wisconsin, was one of the good clients—the kind that didn't need any convincing that the other-worldly existed. My mom and I chatted with her while dad and Carmen drove around the places where the creature had been sighted.

"I know monsters are real," said Kathleen. We sat on her wet wooden porch. It was a cold day, especially with the breeze from the lake. But we sat outside anyway, so Kathleen could smoke. Everything was green from the recent rainfall. I used to notice things like that. I used to think simple things were beautiful.

"You sure it's OK if I smoke?" asked Kathleen. Her eyes were red, and her whole face looked raw.

"That's fine," said my mom. My mom detested smoking. She sat away from the table, so she wouldn't be caught in the smoke trail. She held the mug of coffee Kathleen had given her for warmth. I sat on the railing, looking out at the deep blue of Lake Superior.

"It's funny," said Kathleen. "I was just worrying about Chace a little while ago because he's been acting so different since his dad and sister died. But look at me. I haven't smoked in twenty years."

She brushed something off her shirt and stared out at the water.

"Then the other day, I went out to get gas," said Kathleen. "Just to get out of the house for a few minutes. I went in the station to grab a bag of chips, and there they were. So, I thought, *What the hell?*"

I nodded and took a sip of coffee.

"Who cares?" asked Kathleen. "Nothing matters now. Sure, I still have Chace. I love him, but he's always been independent. He's out of school. Has a good-paying job. He doesn't need me."

"Children always need their mom," said my mom. "No matter what age they are. Right, Immy?"

"That's right," I said, nodding. "Nothing like having a mom to talk to."

"I guess," said Kathleen. "But with girls, it's different. Alice still needed me. She was only thirteen. She was my miracle baby. And Burt...we were high school sweethearts. I've known that man since the first day of kindergarten. And now they're both gone."

"We're so sorry," said my mom. "I know this is painful, but did you ever see the monster?"

Kathleen nodded.

"Burt and Alice liked to go fishing," she said. "There's a rocky place just a little further down the beach here. It's only a three-minute walk. I was in the house one day when Burt called me. He said, 'You have to come down here and see this weird animal we found.' Of course, I thought they were just kidding around, but I went down anyway, and there it was."

"What did it look like?" I asked.

"The body was like an otter," said Kathleen. "But its legs and head reminded me of a dog. The tail was really long. That creature looked so weird. It was kind of a dark, sleek brown. It was hissing and spitting. Alice was obsessed with trying to take a picture or video of it. Kids and their phones, you know? But she couldn't get a good one, and it swam off."

My mom nodded. Kathleen put out her cigarette and crossed her arms.

"Their fishing trips turned into monster-hunting trips," said Kathleen. "It didn't take long for the stories to spread. Then one day, they took some burger with them."

"Was that the last time?" my mom asked, quietly.

"Yep," said Kathleen, messing with her shirt again. "They were trying to bait it, bring it in. Not to hurt it or capture it. Alice never would have gone along with that. She's an animal lover. They just wanted a picture that wasn't a blur."

Kathleen Mackenzie was all out of tears. She lowered her head like she might cry after all. But she had already done that for two weeks straight. Her eyes had run dry.

"Jacob showed up at my door," said Kathleen. "He's the cop. He lives a mile down the road. I used to babysit him back in the day. Anyway, Burt and Alice hadn't even been gone that long. They weren't even gone long enough for me to worry. That monster must have come up on them almost as soon as they were by the water. They were found by a couple of teenagers."

"I'm so sorry," said my mom. "They were…mauled?"

Kathleen's nod was almost undetectable. "I had them cremated."

"We were right again, by God," said my dad, when we reconvened at a park. "It's a dobhar-chú."

"Every eyewitness describes our toothy friend the same way," said Carmen. "Half dog, half otter. And look, this child's drawing of it made it into the town newspaper. The fiery eyes are a nice touch, don't you think?"

"Now that we know what we're looking for," I said. "We just have to draw it out into the open."

"The raw burger Alice and Burt used obviously worked," said my mom. "Actually, it worked a little too well. The mean bugger just went from appetizer to the first course."

"We'll be more prepared than they were when this thing comes out of the water," I said.

The dobhar-chú was a cryptid native to Ireland. It was also sometimes called the king otter or the water hound. It liked to crawl out of the water and scare people and, occasionally, rip them limb from limb. Some might wonder why an Irish cryptid was in Wisconsin. Firstly, sometimes monsters just liked to wander. They got bored and wanted to see something new or take a vacation. Secondly, when people started moving to new countries, they didn't just bring their names, languages, and favorite recipes. They also brought their monster stories. And monsters are bound to their tales, no matter where their tales might go. And that's how you can end up with a banshee terrorizing an elderly woman at a nursing home in Sioux Falls, South Dakota.

We placed raw meat at several locations where the king otter had been seen, but he never showed.

"There are too many people milling around, Immy," said Carmen, looking through her French antique field binoculars at a beach we were monitoring. "The dobhar-chú might have a taste for humans now, but he sure as sugar isn't going to come back here when there are twenty people with cameras waiting for him."

"I know," I said. "This beach is like a mall. The other two places the dobhar-chú was spotted are crowded too."

"You know what that means," she said, lowering her binoculars. Barnaby playfully tugged at the straps from the safety of Carmen's silk pocket.

"He's going to find a new place to kill," I said.

The call came two days later. We were in our hotel room. We had a map of the town and local beaches spread over the table. Mom and dad circled places they thought the king otter might go next.

"Here's a tranquil spot," said my mom.

"I think it's like a lover's lane of the lake," said my dad. "A great place to kill people."

I took the phone out of my pocket when it started ringing. I stared at it, questioning whether to answer.

"Who is it, Immy?" asked Carmen.

"No idea," I said.

"Better answer it, kiddo," said my dad. "Could be something about the case."

"You always say that," I said, putting the phone up to my ear. "And it's always somebody telling me that I may have already won fabulous prizes."

"Hello?" asked a hurried voice on the other end.

"This is Imogen Abernathy," I said. "Who is this?"

"Thank God," said the voice. "This is Chace Mackenzie. I got your number from my mom."

"Good," I said. "We've been meaning to talk to you about the case, if that's all right."

"Listen," he said. "You have to come now. I just stopped at home to see my mom. She left a note here on the cupboard."

"What does it say?" I asked, nervous. I motioned for my family to get up.

"It says that she's going to find the dobhar-chú," he said. "And that she doesn't want it to get away with killing dad and Alice."

"Shit," I said, grabbing my stuff.

"I feel like something bad is going down," said Chace. "That's not like my mom. I'm worried she's going to get hurt."

"We're going now!" I said, as we ran out of the hotel. "We'll find her."

We found Kathleen Mackenzie, but not the way we wanted to. First, we went to all the places where the dobhar-chú had already been. But there were too many people around, and it didn't take long to realize that Kathleen had been thinking just like us. She knew the monster would go where it could stalk one solitary person.

We found her on a tiny beach where trees obscured it from the road. It was mostly rocks, with just a little sand. It looked like a fisherman's secret spot.

At first, we thought she was sitting with her legs in the water. But people don't usually stick their jeans into a lake. And then the sunlight reflected off something metal. I put my hand in front of my eye to block the glow. It was a large can of tuna that she had poured all over the beach. Just the kind of smelly food that would lure a hungry cryptid in.

I walked around the cattails, and that's when I saw the blood. It dyed the tiny beach pebbles a dark copper brown. A tear ran down Carmen's face as she bent down and rested her fingers on Kathleen's hand.

"Poor dear," said my mom. My dad came up behind my mom and

put his hand on her shoulder. There was nothing else that could be said. Nothing else that could be done.

Carmen and I sat with Chace Mackenzie on the wooden steps of his parents' porch. His face was blotchy. He had a beer in his hand and a few days of stubble on his face. His hair was sticking this way and that from restless nights.

"I don't have anything," he said, running a hand through his hair. "I don't have anyone."

"I'm so sorry," I said, feeling helpless.

"Is there anyone you can stay with?" asked Carmen, softly.

Chace's only answer was silence.

"I wish she thought I was worth more," he said, taking a sip of beer. "You know what I mean? We lost a lot. A lot. Our hearts were broken. But she didn't think about what she still had. We still had each other."

"People don't think right when it comes to monsters," I said, trying to sound supportive. "But believe me, she loved you. She just had her mind on revenge."

Chace nodded and put down his beer.

"I guess you guys probably see people pissed off at monsters all the time," said Chace.

"You should have seen the family that went after a vampire by themselves," said Carmen. "There were a lot of puncture wounds that day. And in weird places."

Chace laughed in the sad way that makes you know that nothing will ever make a person laugh or smile their fullest again.

"So, are aliens real?" he asked, after a long silence.

"Who knows?" I said.

"OK, here's one," he said. "Are you related to anyone from Salem?"

"No!" we both shouted.

We never found the dobhar-chú. Sometimes cases ended like that. The monster sightings dwindled to nothing, and you were left with a lot of dead ends. Sometimes the cryptid knew you were on his trail. And sometimes somebody else caught him, and you never found out.

But sometimes something else happened entirely. It was a possibility I never considered until the dobhar-chú case. But afterward, I never forgot it. Sometimes a case isn't just about the cryptid, or the ghost, or the *whatever* at all. There's something else going on beneath the surface. And you don't know it's there, even though your job is to watch and wait and follow and find. In the process of investigating, sometimes something insidious attaches itself to you. And you don't suspect a thing until the *thing* is just about ready to choke you.

CHAPTER FIFTEEN

Chace pulled up to my parents' house in his green minivan.

"Come on, babies," said Carmen, leading the demons outside to welcome our friend. They wore new sweaters that Carmen had knitted. "Chace is back!"

"What is it this time, ladies?" asked Chace, shutting his van door behind him. "Are you on the trail of a sinister chupacabra? Or is it a demented werewolf?"

Buster Keaton rubbed against Chace's leg, leaving long orange hairs on his jeans.

"That's why I love you, Buster, my man," said Chace.

"It's angry old Aunt Mae," I said, walking down the steps.

"What's wrong with Mae?" asked Chace.

"Mae had a heart attack when she found out that her kids were going to rip down the old homestead when she passed away," I said. "And wouldn't you know it? When she had said heart attack, she just happened to be by her ridiculously large staircase."

"This isn't going to end well for Mae, is it?" asked Chace.

"It's the perfect recipe for an angry spirit," said Carmen, looking too excited about gnarly poltergeists. She was like a Bond villain as she petted Ludwig. "Now, she's haunting the new house where her home used to be."

"You're kidding me!" said Chace. "That poor old lady died because they were going to tear down her house…and when her kids saw that it *literally* killed her, it didn't cause a change of heart? Damn. Nice family."

"And it was such a pretty house," said Carmen. "Lots of old dark woodwork and creepy corners. A good place to die."

Chace and I laughed.

"That's the thing about people," I said, crossing my arms. "They're assholes."

"Maybe," said Chace. "But not you two ladies."

Carmen put Ludwig in his tree and motioned Chace to come in.

"I know she's not," I said, pointing at Carmen. "But the verdict is still out on me."

"I don't think so," said Chace, smiling at me. "Not at all."

I shook my head. "Come inside, you nerd," I said, rolling my eyes.

The case of old Aunt Mae was the first investigation that Chace assisted with. It wasn't like he volunteered or anything. Actually, he was a little hesitant about it.

"It *would* be awesome to see a ghost," he said, eating scrambled eggs. We all sat at the table, eating a huge breakfast in preparation for the ghost hunt. "I just don't know what I can do. It's not like I have witch powers or anything. I'm a janitor. If the ghost has a fuse that needs changing, I can probably do that."

"Our powers aren't exactly wondrous to behold," I said. "I made a bar of chocolate appear once at a birthday party. That's probably the coolest thing I've ever done."

"Don't sell us short, Immy," said Carmen. "Maybe if we keep practicing, we'll be like Great-Great Aunt Hortense. She burned her house down once with a spell. It was an accident, of course. She was trying to make it rain to clean the bird poop off the siding, but still…"

"Magic isn't everything," I said. "It didn't help old Fred Astaire and Ginger Rogers, here."

The dancers I referred to were my parents, who ate their breakfast with ice machines strapped to their backs. They had recently decided to take up a new hobby together. At first, they considered downhill skiing, but my dad didn't like the hill aspect. They finally settled on salsa dancing. They figured that with their witch/warlock abilities, they'd be able to bust a move in no time. Instead, all they busted were their classic bodies. They looked like they had just gotten out of boot camp with their raw feet, sore legs, and pulled backs.

"What was wrong with paint by numbers?" asked my dad. "Or a bulldog puzzle? Those are low-impact couple activities. Is that so wrong?"

"I wanted something active, Petey," said my mom, cringing as she leaned over to drink coffee. "I wanted to keep our bodies young."

"We sure as hell succeeded," my dad said, readjusting his ice machine.

"Maybe yoga next time," said my mom.

"Why didn't you use witchcraft to ease your backs?" asked Carmen, drinking her tea like a refined Titanic passenger.

"We did," said my dad, annoyed. "This is all the better we got."

Chace, Carmen, and I exchanged glances, trying not to laugh.

"We won't be good to anyone today," said my mom. "And the owners wanted the ghost out as soon as possible. Would you consider going with the girls, Chace? Just so there's a third person there?"

"Yeah," said my dad. "That Mae is a mean old bag."

"All right," said Chace. "But if this ends up being like *The Shining*, I'm going to piss myself."

It ended up taking a large amount of sage, Carmen reciting multiple incantations, a thorough scattering of salt, some roses, and me insisting the ghost leave, for Mae to finally take a hike. We learned that Chace had a good set of lungs when the walls started weeping. And when the ghost accosted him on the stairs, crawling slowly up them to attack him, I was fairly certain he would never go on another investigation.

"Look at that," said Carmen, watching Mae stalk Chace. "She wants to terrorize him. Isn't that cute? Must be because he's a newbie, huh?"

"Probably," I said, hiding a laugh.

"What do I do?" asked Chace, desperate. "Throw the salt in her face?"

"Sure," I said. "Can't hurt."

Getting doused in salt bought us enough time for Carmen to finish her incantation. All in all, it was a normal day at the office. When the ghost was gone, and we were paid, there was nothing left to do but pack up and go home.

"How was your first investigation?" I asked Chace.

"I think I need a beer when we get back to your place," he said.

"That's nothing," said Carmen. "Wait until you see your first demon. The human haters are particularly memorable. Feisty. You better have a good detergent."

"I might have to work up to that," said Chace.

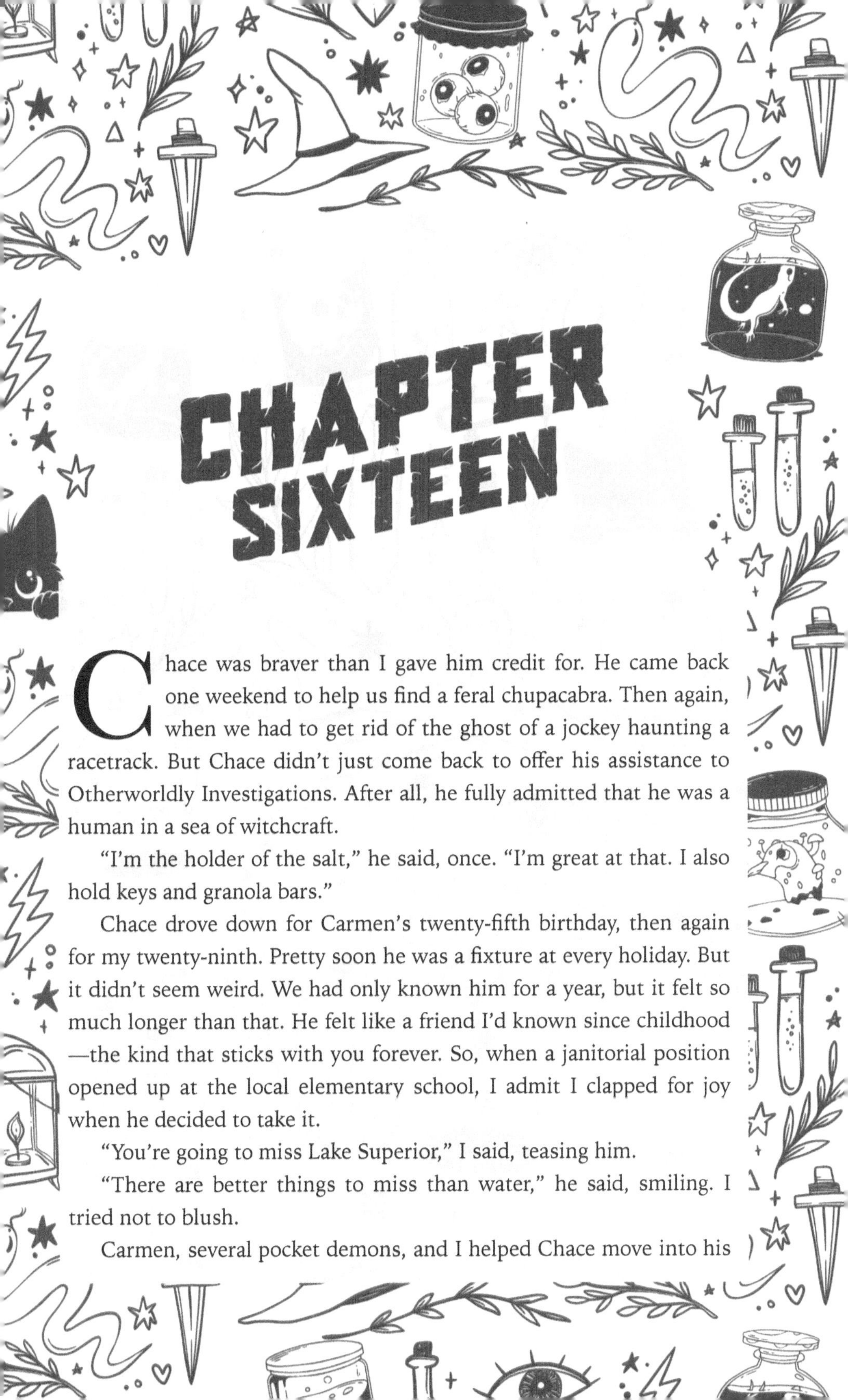

CHAPTER SIXTEEN

Chace was braver than I gave him credit for. He came back one weekend to help us find a feral chupacabra. Then again, when we had to get rid of the ghost of a jockey haunting a racetrack. But Chace didn't just come back to offer his assistance to Otherworldly Investigations. After all, he fully admitted that he was a human in a sea of witchcraft.

"I'm the holder of the salt," he said, once. "I'm great at that. I also hold keys and granola bars."

Chace drove down for Carmen's twenty-fifth birthday, then again for my twenty-ninth. Pretty soon he was a fixture at every holiday. But it didn't seem weird. We had only known him for a year, but it felt so much longer than that. He felt like a friend I'd known since childhood —the kind that sticks with you forever. So, when a janitorial position opened up at the local elementary school, I admit I clapped for joy when he decided to take it.

"You're going to miss Lake Superior," I said, teasing him.

"There are better things to miss than water," he said, smiling. I tried not to blush.

Carmen, several pocket demons, and I helped Chace move into his house in Holy Oak. It was on the other end of town, but that isn't saying much when your town had about eight streets. We were bringing in the last few boxes when Chace came into the house singing. The pocket demons shoved their hands and paws over their ears.

"We're finally done!" he said, throwing the box down. "Where did I get all this crap?"

Carmen and I laughed as the demons pulled out his clothes to sleep in a box.

"And you didn't even pack weapons," said Carmen. "They take the longest to bring in."

"I'm here, and the boxes are all in the house. You know what that means?" asked Chace.

"That it'll take you two more weeks to put it all away?" I asked.

"Maybe," he said. "But it also means I can finally say: Imogen Abernathy, will you go out on a date with me?"

Carmen explained the concept of dates to her cat, while I stood there, smiling. It was a question I had been meaning to ask him, too.

We sat at Dave's pizza. It was everyone's favorite restaurant in Holy Oak because it was the only restaurant. It had fake chipped wood paneling on the walls and brown, shaggy carpet on the floor. Everyone knew not to touch the underside of the tables because they were covered with gum that people had stuck there in the 1980s.

"Here's a question," said Chace. We were drinking milkshakes, waiting for our pizza to come. "Probably the most important question you'll ever be asked. Ready?"

"I'm ready," I said, pretending to be serious.

"What's the worst first date you've ever been on?"

"So many to choose from," I said, laughing. "OK...when I was seventeen, I went out with Toby Boots."

"You should have stayed with him," said Chace. "Just for the name. That's a great name. Toby Boots."

"Toby was very artistic," I said, playing with my straw. "He was kind of Goth, just a little. It took him a long time to get his hair right. It was black and longer, and he had to get it spiky with gel and flipped to the left."

"This is wonderful so far," he said. "Were you also Goth?"

"I may have owned black lipstick for a short period of time. But when you're a witch, the whole Goth thing seems superfluous."

"And where was your first date?" asked Chace.

"It was here," I said, laughing. "Because it's the only place in town."

"Does it make you miss him?"

"Totally," I said. "I think I'll call him later. No, but on our date, he came with a handwritten document for both of us to sign, stating that neither of us would be dishonest to our true, authentic selves."

"I hope you took a picture of it!" said Chace. "I can't believe you didn't go out on a second date."

"I did. We went out for eight months."

We both laughed so loud that the cook came out of the kitchen to look at us.

"He had this thing where he didn't want to watch movies," I said. "He said they were too mainstream. He only wanted to watch films that he made himself."

"What were his movies about?" asked Chace, excited.

"There was a long one about dandelions. I'm not joking. But then he broke up with me, so he could go out with Britney Mitchell. They both worked at the fabric store."

"I wonder where old Toby is now," said Chace.

"I stalked him online about a year ago. Now, he lives in Windom. His hair is short and blond, he has a wife and three kids, and he watches movies. His favorite movie is *Bedknobs and Broomsticks*."

We both laughed again.

"He's making up for lost time," said Chace. "Just think how psyched he's going to be when he gets to the Pixar movies."

"I know," I said. "So, what's your worst first date?"

"I guess that would be… Don't laugh. Her name was Mackenzie Anderson."

I swatted Chace's arm.

"You jerk," I said, laughing. "You teased me about Toby Boots. If you two had gotten married, and she decided to change her name, it would have been Mackenzie Mackenzie."

The waitress brought out our pizza. She rolled her eyes at us as she returned to the kitchen.

"I was sixteen, I think," said Chace. "I thought we'd go bowling. But she had this super close family, and a couple of nights before the date, she called and said her older brothers wanted me to go out on a family date first, so they could get to know me."

"Abort mission!" I said.

"I was all sweaty and freaked out," said Chace, remembering. "I just wanted to bowl and eat tots. But I thought, *OK, we'll probably just go to Hardee's or something*. But no, they picked me up, and we all went to a wild game feed at some American Legion her parents always went to."

"Oh, no!" I said, cringing. "Did you enjoy your snake burger?"

"No," said Chace, disgusted. "And I thought it would be fine because my grandma always said that they have normal things at wild game feeds, too. But they didn't. Not a damn thing! There were elk sloppy joes. That was the closest to normal. I ate one of those. And then about fifteen dinner rolls."

I laughed as I took a bite of pizza.

"Then her brothers started giving me a hard time. And they had me eat ostrich. Don't do that. Don't *ever* do that."

"Don't worry," I said.

"And every time I ate something, I'd sit there for a couple of seconds, wondering if I'd puke. Then her oldest brother tricked me into eating rocky mountain oysters. I didn't know what they were!"

I had my head bowed in laughter. It was a good thing we were the only two customers at that dive.

"Then I was in the bathroom for fifteen minutes," said Chace, laughing. "And Mackenzie got annoyed because she thought I was making a big deal about nothing. But it wasn't *nothing*. It was alligator and wild boar. And it was not good."

"So, there wasn't a second date?"

"No," he said, taking a sip of his Coke. "I just spent the rest of high school hiding in the janitor's closet whenever she walked by."

"I hope you think this date is better than that one," I said, smiling.

"It definitely is."

When we said goodnight later, I decided to kiss him, just to see what it was like. It seemed like something that could develop into a habit.

On Christmas day that year, Chace brought over his mom's famous cheese ball. We sat around the tree opening presents like a family. Because we were. So, I didn't think it was corny at all when I opened a little box, thinking it was the earrings I wanted, only to find an engagement ring with a shiny, dark ruby.

"I helped pick it out," said Carmen, with a coy smile. "It reminded me of something you'd find if you had to dig up the corpse of a flapper."

"I love you, Imogen," said Chace, getting down on one knee. "I thought my family was gone. I never realized when I met you that you were my family, too. I can't imagine my life without you. Will you marry me?"

We decided that we didn't want a long engagement, and we didn't want anything big. We'd get married in a couple of months with just my parents, Carmen, and a few little demons.

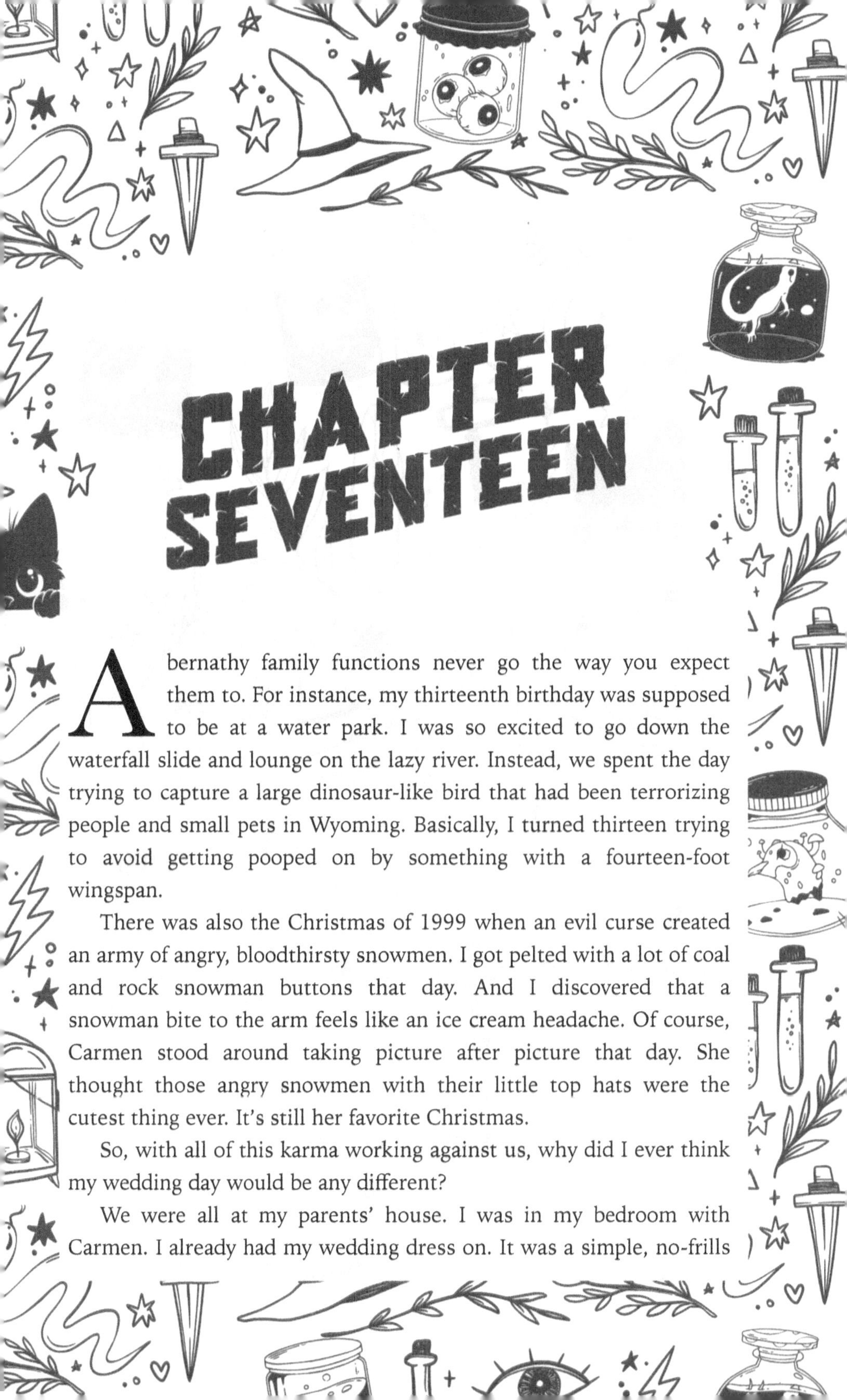

CHAPTER SEVENTEEN

Abernathy family functions never go the way you expect them to. For instance, my thirteenth birthday was supposed to be at a water park. I was so excited to go down the waterfall slide and lounge on the lazy river. Instead, we spent the day trying to capture a large dinosaur-like bird that had been terrorizing people and small pets in Wyoming. Basically, I turned thirteen trying to avoid getting pooped on by something with a fourteen-foot wingspan.

There was also the Christmas of 1999 when an evil curse created an army of angry, bloodthirsty snowmen. I got pelted with a lot of coal and rock snowman buttons that day. And I discovered that a snowman bite to the arm feels like an ice cream headache. Of course, Carmen stood around taking picture after picture that day. She thought those angry snowmen with their little top hats were the cutest thing ever. It's still her favorite Christmas.

So, with all of this karma working against us, why did I ever think my wedding day would be any different?

We were all at my parents' house. I was in my bedroom with Carmen. I already had my wedding dress on. It was a simple, no-frills gown. Just the kind I wanted. It had a little beading, and thin cap sleeves because I didn't feel like pulling up a strapless dress all day. And for my feet, I decided on comfortable, simple flats. Carmen was my maid of honor, but I told her to wear whatever she wanted. Being given free rein like that meant that on my special day, she decided to get out the big guns and dress herself up like a Victorian cover model, in a pale purple corseted dress with delicate ivy embroidery across the chest and some kind of crazy hat with a big white feather hanging out of the side.

"You look amazing," I said, making her twirl around. "That's your finest work yet."

"Thanks so much, Immy," she said. She looked me up and down and clapped her hands. "I love your dress, too. It's so absolutely Immy. But I thought maybe this might go with it."

She grabbed a flat box from on top of my dresser and opened it up. Inside were two delicate, long white gloves, with shiny buttons stitched up the outer sides.

"I love them," I said, tearing up. "They're perfect."

Carmen hugged me tightly. Barnaby poked his head out of her dress and squealed at getting slightly smashed.

"Happy wedding day, Immy."

"Thanks, Carmen," I said, holding her.

That's when my wedding day stopped being fun. There was noise on the stairs and my parents stormed through my bedroom door. They were already dressed for the ceremony, but the fact that they were also brandishing a hatchet and club told me nothing good was about to happen.

"No way," I said, raising my hand to them. "Don't you dare. I don't want to know anything about it."

"It won't take long, dear," said my mom. "It's just a little demon slug infestation at a farm an hour north of here. You won't even get your dress dirty. And you look so pretty."

"A real vision," said my dad. "Couldn't feel happier. But should we kill some demons quick?"

"Absolutely not!" I said. "Killing monsters always takes longer than you think it will. If you think it'll take an hour, it'll take three."

"I'll bring my 038 Magnum," said Carmen, delighted. "That'll make quick work of them. Then cake!"

"I don't see how you think we'll stay clean," I said, my face turning red. "This is so ridiculous. Can't we just be normal once?"

"The longer we stand here and argue, the more of this precious, beautiful day we lose," said my dad.

He lifted an old instant camera and took a picture of me.

"Let's hit the trail," he said.

Chace ran up the stairs and into my room, so winded that he could hardly talk.

"I got all the weapons in the two cars," he said, panting. He was already dressed in his dark blue suit.

"You're in on this?" I asked, hands on my hips.

"I'd feel bad if we didn't go," said Chace, shrugging. "All I'd be able to think about while cutting the cake is people getting eaten by slugs."

I threw my arms, fed up.

"Fine," I said. "Let's go."

As we left the house, Chace put his arm around me and said, "By the way, you're a vision of loveliness."

"Yeah, yeah," I said.

I didn't, in fact, stay clean. None of us did. All the slugs ended up being in the farmer's barn. He'd been able to lure them inside and trap them before his family suffered from anything grislier than getting slightly gooey.

We went in through the barn windows and immediately got down to business. They yelped and hissed, jump-crawling at us instantly. They had three rows of teeth circling the inside of their wide mouths.

It *did* only take us an hour to kill them, but nobody had informed me that when you strike a hatchet into an angry, dog-sized slug, it explodes like a child popping a birthday balloon. The slug goo went everywhere—on my dress, in my hair, and all over my face.

I stood there, staring at myself. I was covered head to foot in what looked exactly like snot. I emitted a noise that sounded a lot like growling. I was stricken immobile with anger.

"I want a do-over," I said, exasperated.

Carmen took care of most of the slugs with her chainsaw. Unlike me, she didn't seem to mind getting goo all over.

"It doesn't smell bad at all," she yelled over chainsaw noise. "A lot better than werewolf sweat."

When we were about done, Chace was cornered by a feistier slug on the opposite side of the barn from me. It whipped Chace's hatchet out of his hand with its thick, wormy rear end, then knocked him down. I yelled to Carmen, and she was on them in a second. The slug was just biting down on Chace's leg when Carmen's chainsaw made contact. It exploded, sending candy red goo and yellow pus everywhere. After all that slime, Carmen's dress color was indecipherable.

When it was all over, Carmen wiped her face and bent over to help Chace up. She patted him on the back, but then something weird happened. I'm not even sure why I noticed. Carmen's face went blank and pale as Chace let go of her.

"I'm good," said Chace. "Just a little bite. Let's get married!"

My parents and Chace stood in a corner, discussing the slugs. They were pumped about the exciting events, and the large quantity of pus. My dad started to tell the tale of other slugs he had encountered. But I don't remember what he said. I was too focused on Carmen staring at Chace's back. I had never seen my sister's face so devoid of emotion. Anyone else might have written it off as Carmen being annoyed that the wedding day was a mess, or upset that her nice Victorian ensemble was ruined. But for some reason, when I saw Carmen's foreign facial reaction, it stirred a feeling in me that I had never known before—a kind of wispy, nervous agitation in the chest. The feeling that everything inside me was draining away. Standing there, I never could have imagined that the feeling wasn't just some one-time sense of dread, something that eventually evaporates like dew in the morning. I never could have imagined that the feeling was just making its first of many house calls, like a guest you can't get rid of.

My dad was speeding again. He and my mom had headed back in one car, and they were now so far ahead that we couldn't see them. My mom was paranoid about having the appetizers ready for the wedding, even though it was just us.

Carmen, Chace, and I were in the other car. We had to get back and see if we could get the slug juice cleaned off us before meeting the justice of the peace at the park.

I was in the back seat, wiping goo off my arms with paper towels. Then I passed the roll forward. Chace was in the passenger's seat. He eagerly grabbed them and wiped off his face.

"We won't be able to say our wedding day wasn't memorable," said Chace, grinning.

"Just the kind of memory I was hoping for," I said.

Carmen drove with one hand on the wheel. She stared at the road like a zombie. She didn't take any paper towels. She let the goo harden on her. And she didn't say anything. She was in a whole different place. She bit the nails of her right hand, nails that she had just carefully applied polish to three hours earlier. I wanted to lean forward and ask what was up, but whenever I opened my mouth, nothing seemed to come out. Instead, I stared out the window, thinking of everything except the wedding that was about to happen.

"Immy," said Carmen, finally. Her voice startled me. In Carmen time, it had been centuries since she had talked. Chace didn't seem to notice. He looked out his window and hummed.

"Yeah," I said. I tried to hide my nervousness, not knowing why.

"Remember when I went on my first investigation with you and mom and dad?" she asked. "Remember how I made my first dress for it?"

"Of course," I said, picturing her twirling in delight.

"Remember how I told you that story about *fried eggs*?"

A tight cold took hold of my chest. My forehead was instantly sweaty as I remembered the code word for danger that Carmen and I had decided on when she was only ten.

"I remember," I said, my voice even.

"I love when you two tell stories," said Chace, smiling and looking off.

"There are fried eggs in the front seat," said Carmen. There was no urgency in her voice. She knew better than that.

"Fried eggs," she said. "So, get ready."

"What?" asked Chace, looking around to figure out what Carmen meant.

Chace was a little confused, but still unconcerned. It took him quite a few seconds to realize that Carmen had veered off the road. I grabbed my seat and recited a protection incantation just as we dipped into the ditch. Chace gasped and yelled out as Carmen aimed the car to ram his side right into the approaching power pole.

I was still crawling out of the back seat and onto the brown grass of the ditch when I heard Carmen's door slam. She zipped around the front of the vehicle, her stained Victorian dress clinging to her like a dirty dish rag. I remember thinking how strong she was as she opened Chace's door. She was steady and calculated as she ripped him out and shoved him onto the ground. She was like a bird building a nest, taking charge of a job that needed doing.

"What's going on?" I asked. I stood up, dizzy and confused, but unhurt. It was clear that Carmen had successfully performed a protection spell, too. She didn't have a scratch on her.

Chace wasn't faring as well. He was on the ground, curled up in a ball so tight that I couldn't see if anything was broken.

My heart pounded as I tried to bend down to help him. But before I could, Carmen pulled a knife out of the layers of her clothing and, without a moment of hesitation, ran the blade through Chace's shoe, clear down into the ground.

Chace and I both yelled out at the same time, him in pain and me in complete confusion.

"What are you doing?" I asked, shoving her away. "Are you insane?"

"That's barely a scratch, Immy," she said. "It would take more than that or a car accident to hurt a demon."

"What?" I asked. My head filled with buzzing, and I saw black spots in front of my eyes.

Chace sat on the ground, his foot still skewered into the Earth. He didn't look surprised by the accusation. It made me dizzy all over again.

"I saw it at the barn with the slugs," said Carmen. "That slug bit him and tore his skin, but when I got a look at it, I realized it wasn't a normal bite. It looked like the slug just tore his rubbery jacket. I saw his real skin underneath. Those purple-blue scales that some demons have."

Chace shook his head, staring off into space. The knife in his foot didn't seem to bother him.

"You've known since the barn?" I asked. "Why the hell didn't you tell me?"

"There are lots of demons, Immy," said Carmen. "Like little Barnaby here. Such a sweetie. And they're perfectly wonderful. I thought maybe he was afraid to tell us he was a demon, thinking we wouldn't accept him. I was trying to think of what kind of demon he could be, then I realized that if Chace Mackenzie was a real man, that meant that this demon is…"

"One of the human haters," said Chace, looking up at us. "The kind you warned me about on my very first ghost hunt. I thought that was pretty funny."

He pulled the knife out of his foot and threw it aside. He was about to stand up when Carmen pulled her chainsaw out of the trunk and held it down toward him.

"Stay on the damn ground," said Carmen. She took a breath, trying to calm herself. "Please."

I had never heard Carmen so angry. Her jaw was rigid, and her nostrils flared like a bull. But this was Chace. He was goofy Chace, who liked to dance with my mom in the kitchen—who liked to have debates with my dad over what quarterback was absolutely pathetic. How could this be real? The spots in my eyes got worse. I bent down and inspected his torn leg. His skin hung loose, like a floppy cloth over shimmery, scaly flesh.

"Don't worry," said Chace. "All the best songs are about heartbreak."

"It's true, isn't it?" I asked, feeling cold and prickly all over. "You killed Chace Mackenzie, and now you're wearing his skin?"

"Sure am," he said, matter-of-fact.

"How long have you been in there?" I asked. My face felt so taut.

"Sorry, but your taste in men really *is* this bad," said Chace. "It's been me in here ever since that first phone call."

I stared into his eyes, the only thing he hadn't stolen from that poor guy that I had never known. There were so many things I could have said, so many things I wanted to say. And there were so many tears I wanted to shed. But maybe I didn't want to shed them. Because I didn't want to give that cowardly bastard the satisfaction.

I felt my leg lift out from under me. I kicked the man who wasn't Chace right in the chin, sending him careening backward. I had never knocked anyone out before. He looked so silly crumpled on the ground, like the waste of space he was.

"At least we both got to throttle him a little bit, huh, Immy?" said Carmen, resting an arm around my shoulder. But somehow, I couldn't speak just then.

The pocket demons wiggled out of Carmen's clothes and inspected the man who wasn't Chace, walking around him and sniffing.

"You might as well call mom and dad to come back and pick us up," I said. The mid-September day had grown cloudy, and the cold breeze seemed to saw me in half. I grabbed a spare sweater from the trunk and threw it on over my forgotten wedding dress.

"Dad will be thrilled," I said. "He can finally test out that new dungeon."

CHAPTER EIGHTEEN

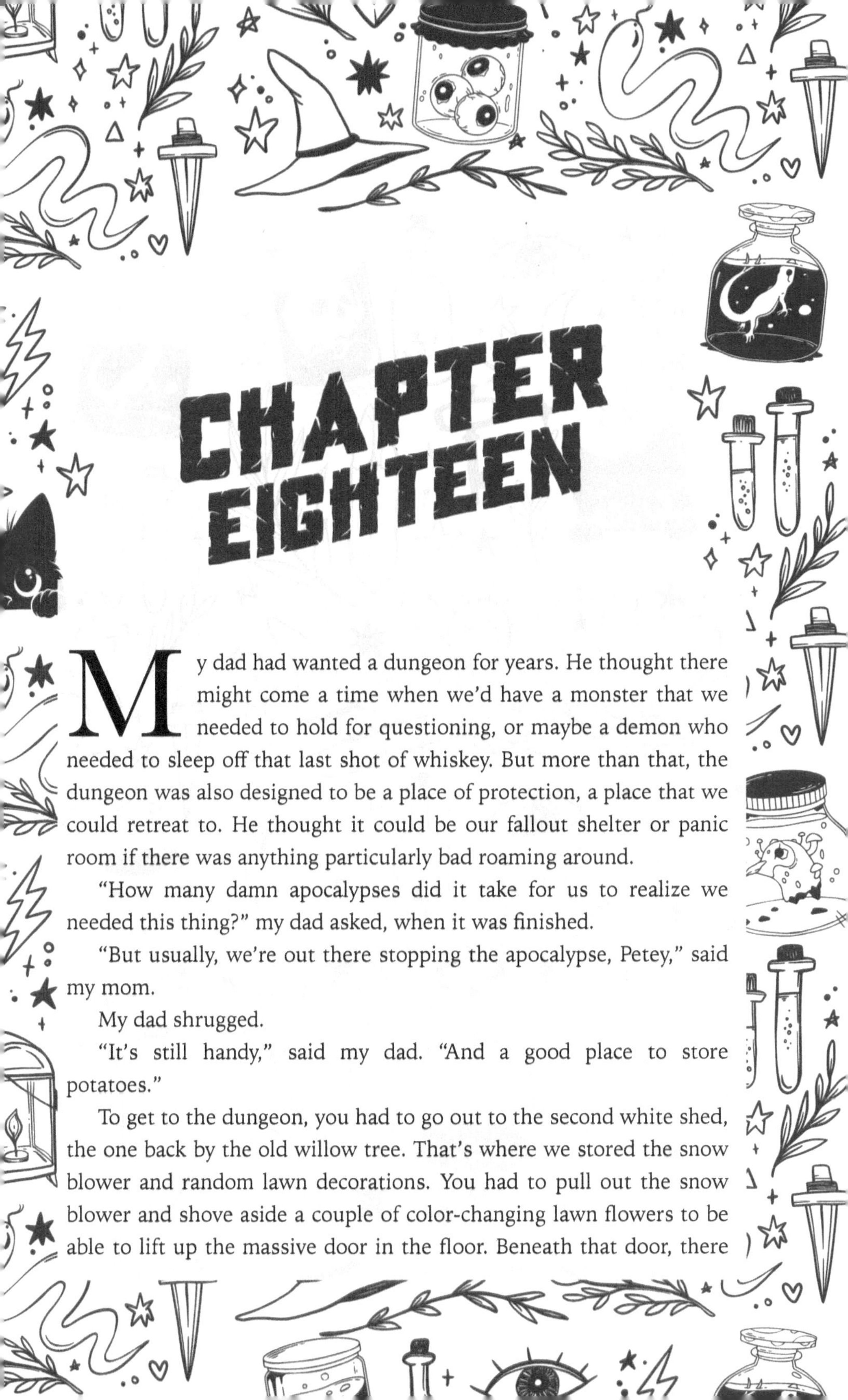

My dad had wanted a dungeon for years. He thought there might come a time when we'd have a monster that we needed to hold for questioning, or maybe a demon who needed to sleep off that last shot of whiskey. But more than that, the dungeon was also designed to be a place of protection, a place that we could retreat to. He thought it could be our fallout shelter or panic room if there was anything particularly bad roaming around.

"How many damn apocalypses did it take for us to realize we needed this thing?" my dad asked, when it was finished.

"But usually, we're out there stopping the apocalypse, Petey," said my mom.

My dad shrugged.

"It's still handy," said my dad. "And a good place to store potatoes."

To get to the dungeon, you had to go out to the second white shed, the one back by the old willow tree. That's where we stored the snow blower and random lawn decorations. You had to pull out the snow blower and shove aside a couple of color-changing lawn flowers to be able to lift up the massive door in the floor. Beneath that door, there was a wide staircase leading down into the ground. When you hit the bottom, you were about twenty feet below the surface. Then a big hallway led to a right turn that opened to a large room. The room was about thirty by thirty feet. In the far-left corner was a jail cell. There were little lights all over the ceiling that we were able to power through our combined magic and a little help from the pocket demons.

It was a place designed as a safe haven for creatures that needed to hide, or as a jail for creatures that we didn't want to get out. The iron bars on the jail cell ensured that whoever was put in there, couldn't get out unless someone helped them out. But that wasn't the only protective magic at work down there. Lining the whole outer edge of the room and hallway were witch bottles cemented down to the floor. Inside were hairs, nails, and other items of protection against malevolent forces. Finally, the walls were covered with Gregorian chants that both kept evil at bay, and stopped anything harmful from being able to leave.

"None of us better turn into an asshole," I said, when we painted the chants on the wall. "We'd never be able to get out of here."

"But we're still witches," Carmen said. "I don't think I'd want to stay in here a whole day. You'd have a rash from hell. Or maybe heaven."

As a last bit of protection, we painted eyes on each of the steps coming down into the dungeon. Even if something bad was able to get by one of the steps, it would never be able to get by thirteen.

In the history of Otherworldly Investigations, the only creatures to inhabit our dungeon for a lengthy period have been Chace Mackenzie, eight sacks of potatoes when my dad had a hankering to make a large batch of soup, and the pocket demon Horatio when he got into the RumChata and, let's be honest, turned into a little bit of a bitch.

Of course, all that protective magic ended up working against us. It made it really hard to bring evil demons down to the jail cell. We wrapped the still unconscious Chace in a bunch of blankets, so he couldn't see where he was being taken if he woke up. Then my dad and I carried him downstairs. After two steps, he woke up and began thrashing around. My dad barked at him to shut up, and we continued descending the staircase. Chace writhed in pain and screamed words I didn't understand. With each step, the blankets turned bloodier and bloodier. Finally, on the dungeon floor, we hauled Chace to the cell and unrolled him. Both he and the blankets were drenched with blood. My dad put on some gloves and closed the cell door, then locked it. Chace didn't move or react to being locked in. Having your evil insides liquefied will do that.

Mom and Carmen had to feed him Abernathy stew for six days after that, or he would have died. Even with that, though, he wasn't fit to talk for two weeks. And all those witch bottles and chants on the walls had their effect too. From then on, he always looked like the sickest man on Earth, about to expire from an unknown illness. It was proof of the darkness that existed beneath his stolen skin.

"Imogen Abernathy," said Chace. "You *do* care."

He sat on the floor of his cell, legs crossed. When Chace had recovered from his blood-spewing, we decided it was time to question him and see what the hell this was all about. I was totally prepared to receive zero closure, which was a good thing, because I didn't.

"Do I?" I asked, crossing my arms. "Could have fooled me."

"Your mom and sister nursed me back to health," said Chace. "And now here I am, ready to hang out with you forever. You can't let me go, can you?"

"I was in favor of letting you die," I said, monotone.

"It's true," said Carmen. "She had so many wicked intentions that I'm surprised she can get in and out of this dungeon."

"I do have a bad cough, though," I said. "And personally, I think that when we're done with you, we should drag you right back up those stairs and throw you out with the garbage."

If possible, my comment made Chace look even sicker.

"You can cut the sarcasm and stop acting like you're the one with the power here," I said. "Because you know how uncomfortable we can make it for you. So, I suggest answering our questions."

"This whole thing is just so sad," said my mom, frowning. "I can't do it. Petey, stay with the girls. I'm going to go perform that exorcism in Kirkwood to cheer myself up."

My dad nodded as my mom ascended the stairs.

"Are you going to play ball?" I asked.

Chace crossed his arms and nodded.

"Damn right," said my dad. "Why the hell did you do all this? How'd you get involved with the dobhar-chú case?"

Chace picked his nails and sighed.

"You people are so stupid," he said. "I took that dobhar-chú from his home by Niagara Falls and drove him all the way to Superior. It's a good thing I bought the reinforced animal trap because he was pissed. I dropped him at the outskirts of Superior, thinking if he killed anyone, it would be close enough for you to hear about it. I figured the dobhar-chú would be so angry about being displaced he'd be sure to maul some passerby. And he did."

I exchanged glances with my dad and Carmen. This was the guy we'd trusted for two years. The guy I had almost married. I felt sick.

"As soon as I saw what he did to Burt and Alice Mackenzie, I went to find any other member of the family. Chace was sitting in a park, playing his guitar for little kids. He was giving them lessons. He was a soft, mellow, easy-to-kill guy," said Chace.

"You're an asshole," I said.

"And I fooled you," he said, smiling. "I fooled a bunch of witches and tiny demons for two whole years. That's *pretty* bad. Your magical abilities really are shitty, aren't they?"

Carmen bit her lip. There was nothing she hated more than being confronted by how much witch powers had deteriorated in the last four hundred years.

"I dug out all of Chace's insides. Then I rubbed myself in a camou-flaging ointment. It's my family's specialty. Every week or so I had to take off the skin, spray it out, then reapply the ointment to myself. But overall, I was impressed. The skin has held up nice."

"We don't need so many details about you skinning that poor kid," said my dad.

"As soon as I assumed Chace's identity, I ran into a problem. You had just gotten into town and the dobhar-chú was nowhere to be found. He had killed those two people because he was scared, but then he decided to do something about it instead of sitting in Superior in a huff."

"He went back home," said Carmen.

"Yep," said Chace. "There I was. I hadn't even met you yet. So, I came up with a different plan."

I felt that nervous emptiness in my chest again.

"You killed Kathleen," I said. I could still picture her sitting on her deck, heartbroken. "That's right," said Chace. "It was easy to lure her there. She wanted to spend time with her son so badly. All I had to do was make it look like a mauling, and plant some tuna. Then I wrote the note and called you. I had to meet you, you see. It was all part of the plan."

"But how in the world did you know that we'd come up to Superior to investigate the dobhar-chú?" asked Carmen.

"Sounds like quite a leap," said my dad. "There are hundreds of otherworldly cases all over the country. It seems like a lucky break that we chose that one."

"I didn't know that you'd come to Superior," said Chace. "You see, I've been playing the long game. I'd been roaming the country killing people and setting up cryptids for over a year before you bit. You're some of the only witches who investigate the otherworldly anymore. Most of them are just palm readers and gamblers. A much safer profession. But none of them would do. It just had to be you, the monster-hunting witches descended from monster-hunting witches."

"You have some beef with us?" I asked. My whole body felt tired.

"I certainly do," said Chace, standing up. "I needed you, Imogen. I needed your heart, specifically. I needed you to love me, and then I needed to break your heart. I was planning on breaking it on our honeymoon. Would have been nice and quiet. No witnesses. Just us alone in Saint Croix."

"Why the hell did you want to break *my* heart specifically?" I asked, fed up.

"You're so special," said Chace, almost putting his hands on the bars. "Don't you realize how many dark, sweet spells require the broken heart of a witch? Like resurrection spells, for instance. Resurrection spells for demons. One that could bring back my family. Like I said, the long game."

"And I suppose you wanted one of our hearts because my ancestors killed yours, right?" I asked, shaking my head.

"That's it," said Chace, smiling. "You don't still want to give it to me, do you? Your sister always has a knife on her somewhere."

"Talk like that to my daughter again, and I'll ram an iron rod up your ass," said my dad. "I don't care how much it burns my hands."

"Why did our ancestors kill yours?" asked Carmen.

"I guess probably because killing humans is kind of our thing," said Chace. "Better hobby than gin rummy. And your skin. Yum. Like a Fruit Roll-Up."

"That's what I thought," I said, sighing.

"People are like cattle," said Chace. "You'll never make me feel bad about killing them. And they're getting more like cattle each day. Dumb. Gullible. Most of them can't even do math in their heads anymore."

"I don't like the way he's insulting cattle," said Carmen. "And math."

"You were right to worry," said Chace, staring at me. "Remember that night in bed? You told me you were so scared that you'd spend the rest of your life in Otherworldly Investigations…"

Carmen and dad stared at me. I felt my face go hot and cold at the same time.

"You were *so* right," said Chace. "We had all those plans, but they were make-believe. And now you know, don't you? That you're never getting out."

"I don't need a man to get me out of anything, dickwad," I said.

"I know," said Chace. "But now you know that anywhere you go, a monster will be there. Any house you live in will have a vengeful ghost in the basement. Magic will always find you. You'll never escape. And any lover you have will just be a demon in disguise."

He smiled, happy with himself.

"At least I was able to torture you," said Chace. "I guess I got a little revenge, then. I was actually thinking of making the moves on Carmen first. But she was too weird even for me."

Carmen walked quickly over to the cell, reached through, and grabbed Chace by the neck. He was gagging by the time my dad and I pulled her away. She shrugged us off and inspected her burnt arm, which had touched the iron bar of the cell. Then she calmly readjusted her black and white checkered 1930s housedress.

Chace sat on the floor, sputtering.

"I lost myself for a moment," said Carmen. Then she kneeled down, looked in at Chace, and said, "You evil, misogynistic, egomaniac, rat bastard. Don't ever make the mistake again of thinking any woman is waiting to fall at your feet."

Chace rubbed his neck and nodded.

"I love my daughters," said my dad. He gave us both firm pats on the back. I put my arm around my sister and flashed Chace an angry smile.

"I'm sorry my family stopped your family from slaughtering a bunch of innocent people," I said, mocking him. "Sob, sob. Now, me and my family are going to leave you here. With just your own annoying voice and the chants on the wall, giving you those beautiful blisters. And you can contemplate how, if you ever get out of here, you'll only be getting out to die. Because I don't think you can take those stairs again."

Chace stared at me, then looked away, sullen.

"And don't you even think of eyeing any of my potatoes," said my dad.

Chace sat there, watching nothing, as we turned around and left him to rot.

When I reached the top stair, we turned around and lowered the door back down on the dungeon. Then we put the snow blower and lawn decorations back over it. I didn't say anything as we locked the shed door and walked back up to the house. I looked calm and placid, and I felt no emotion as I walked through the kitchen, up the stairs, and into my bedroom.

I looked around at all the items in my room: the striped curtains on the windows, the pictures on the walls, the knick-knacks, and the books on the shelves. I felt nothing. Then I saw the little box on my dresser. I picked it up and opened it a crack. The little ruby glimmered at me. I felt no emotion as I opened my mouth and screamed. I felt no emotion as I hurled the ring at the window and witnessed tiny chips of ruby break away and catch the light before falling on the floor. And I felt no emotion as I tore apart my room, heaving the bookshelf onto the floor, breaking the mirror on the dresser, throwing my clothes everywhere, and tearing at my wedding dress until segments of delicate fabric separated with a soft breaking rip.

I threw my lamp against the wall, watching the violet ceramic base crack into hard chunks. Then I felt it—a soft hand on my shoulder. Carmen stood there, frowning. She quietly sat down on the bed. Without words, she pulled Barnaby and Horatio out of her pockets and set them aside. Then she reached out and patted the bed next to her, motioning for me to sit down. I didn't even realize that I was crying until I flung myself down into her, drenching her dress in my tears. I held my arms tight around her as I cried. It felt like we stayed that way forever, holding on to each other. Over the sound of my crying and heartbreak, I heard Carmen. She patted my back, and in a gentle, calming voice, said four simple words, over and over again.

"I love you, Immy."

But of course, you can't just hold someone and make a situation all better again. Over the next couple of weeks, I hardly left my room. Whenever my parents asked me if I wanted to help with an investigation, I said no. After doing that about ten times, they finally got fed up.

"You can't just sit here like this," said my dad. "You can't just let that bastard win."

"Don't you get it?" I asked. "I don't want to do this anymore. I don't want to be this anymore."

"A demon hurts you and your reaction is to up and leave and go work at a bakery?" asked my dad.

"The powdered donut holes are good, sweetie," said my mom. "But we don't get it."

"It doesn't have anything to do with Chace," I said. "He was just the final straw."

"Straw of what?" asked Carmen. She looked so worried. Ever since we were children, the plan for our future had always been Otherworldly Investigations.

"I haven't wanted to live this way for a long time," I said. "I want to be normal."

"You can't ever be completely normal," said my mom. "Your excellent poker skills tell you that."

"And I don't want to be thirty, still living at home," I said.

"Nobody's telling you to stay at home, Immy," said Carmen. "It's just convenient to have the weapons centrally located."

"I don't want to be part of the business either," I said. "I want out."

"You make us sound like the mafia," said my dad. "Which is cool. But we're not. You sound like you don't even like us."

I put my hands up, exasperated. Then I marched back up to my room. Being an old house, I clearly heard my dad downstairs.

"All her life, she's never slammed that bedroom door," he said. "At sixteen, she wasn't slamming that door. Now she's thirty, and she's slamming that door."

"Oh, Petey," said my mom.

"She's gonna fix that door if she wrecks it," said my dad.

Later that night, I sat on a wood stump in the backyard. I stoked a campfire until I had tall flames rising out of the pit. I stared into the burning logs until my eyes hurt and felt hazy when I looked away into the blankness of the night.

I felt someone sit down next to me. I didn't have to look to know who it was. I heard the familiar bird-like chatter of Minerva, a pocket demon that looked like a small, bright yellow dragon with a thin tail and shimmering wings. She loved the chance to get outside and was excited to be next to a roaring fire.

"Good baby," whispered Carmen, petting Minerva on her lap. "Stay."

I didn't say anything. I poked the fire with a long stick.

"Is that your wedding dress in there, Immy?" asked Carmen.

"Sure is," I said.

Carmen shook her head. "The people at David's Bridal wouldn't want to hear that," she said.

"Want a marshmallow?" I asked.

Carmen looked at me with a raised eyebrow.

"I think I'll wait until the dress fumes and fibers burn away," she said.

I reached my hands closer to the fire to warm them.

"You can't see why I want to leave?" I asked, quietly. I didn't want to fight with my sister, not after she had shown me so much sympathy.

"Of course, Immy," said Carmen. Her voice was so soft I could hardly hear her. "People do lots of different things in life before they find their way. Before they find what they want to do."

I nodded, feeling like there was a big *but* coming up.

"A lot of people leave home long before they're thirty," said Carmen, still stroking Minerva. "Some people go off to college on the other side of the country or the other side of the world, and from then on, only go back home on holidays."

"What's the big problem, then?" I asked. "I'm only going a couple of miles away."

Carmen held Minerva like she was grasping the demon for comfort as she struggled to find the right words.

"You're going about this in such a strange way, Immy," said Carmen. "It gives me a cold feeling in my stomach. It makes me nervous somehow. You're acting like some desperate teenager who wants to be emancipated from his family."

"I just want to live my own life," I said. I placed a marshmallow on the end of a stick and put it into the fire.

"You can have whatever life you want," said Carmen. "You can go wherever you want. Mom and dad and I have never tried to force you to stay here. It's just…"

"What?" I asked. I couldn't look at her. I only stared into the fire.

"The way you want to cut and run like this," said Carmen. "It makes me wonder what place we'll have in your new life. You want to get away from magic and witchcraft, but your family *is* magic and witchcraft, Immy. If you want to separate yourself from it, where does that leave us? If I call or text you in a week, will you answer? How about the week after that? Will you respond to me? Or will you let more and more calls go to voicemail? Will you phase us out a little more each day, ashamed of us? Will you invite me to your apartment? Will you introduce me to your friends?"

I couldn't answer her. I let my stick and marshmallow fall to the ground. A large ball of guilt formed in my stomach, taking up too much room to ever think of eating. And the way Carmen's voice sounded… I didn't need to look at her to know that she had begun to cry. I had never made my sister cry before. Not even when we were kids, and it was my fault that she had skinned her knee coming down from our tree fort.

"I just can't get rid of this awful feeling," said Carmen, letting the tears fall down her face. "The feeling that what's really going on is that I'm sitting next to my best friend, and she's telling me she doesn't want me anymore."

Before I could say anything, Carmen got up, silent as a specter, and disappeared back into the darkness. I only caught a glimpse of her head, bent down in sorrow as she clutched Minerva tight to her. Her red dress whipped in the wind as she was swallowed up by the night.

Carmen was right, of course. She was right about everything, the way I guess she always was. That's the way it is sometimes with sisters and best friends. They see things and understand things about us that we don't understand ourselves. It took me a while to realize that I really *was* running from my family, and maybe Chace didn't have as much to do with it as I thought. But of course, that didn't stop my fists from clenching when I thought about him or stop my heart from aching.

And despite what Carmen said, I did find myself standing and staring at my phone when she called, letting it ring sometimes, and then feeling terrible about it afterward. But of course, she forgave me. That was the Carmen way, too. And how I knew I didn't deserve her. She was far, far too good for me. And that was how I knew that when I started working on the case of the Thistle Witch with her, I'd have a hard time not staying in Otherworldly Investigations for good. After all, how could I break Carmen's heart again? How could I threaten our bond when she had only ever shown me compassion?

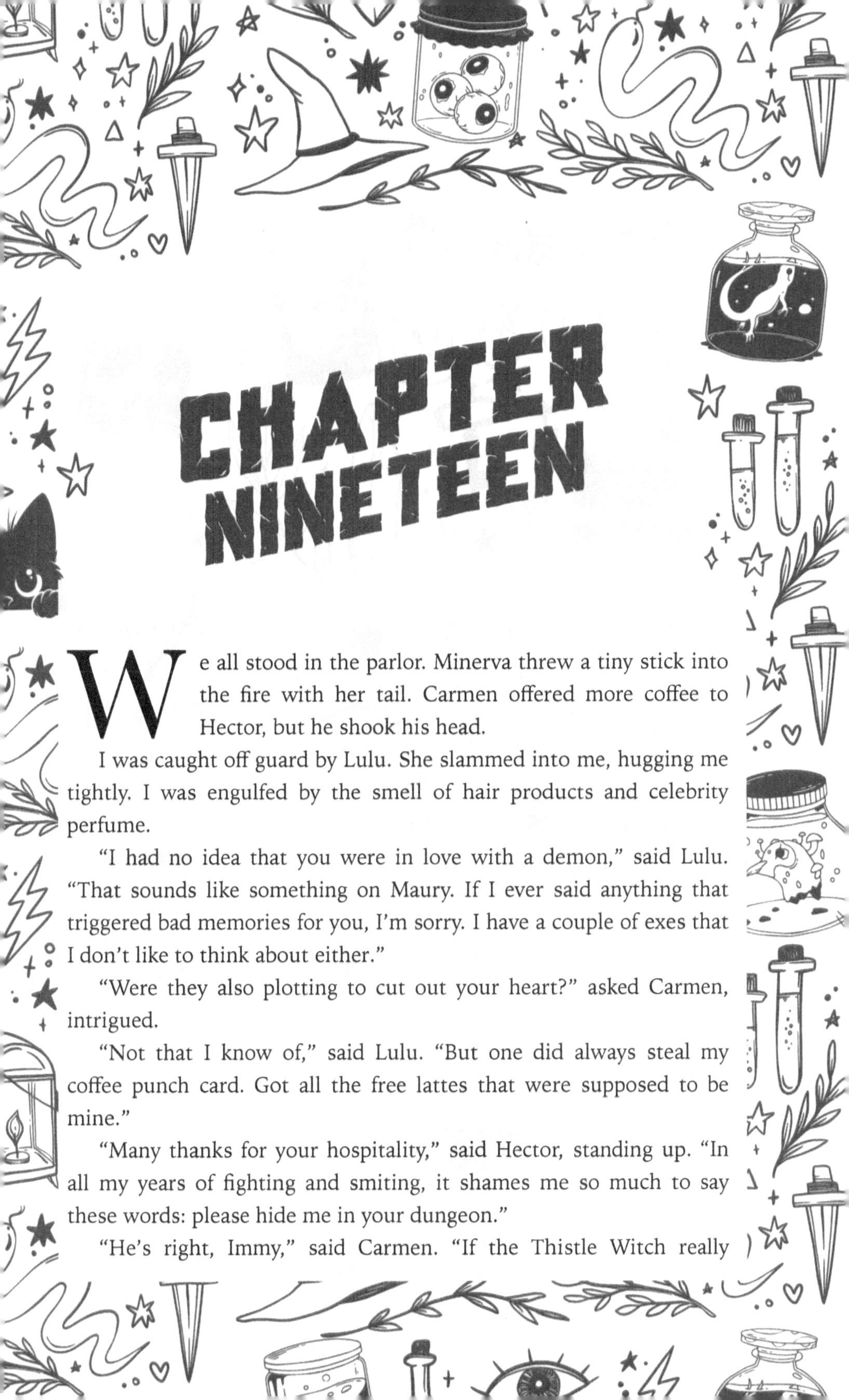

CHAPTER NINETEEN

We all stood in the parlor. Minerva threw a tiny stick into the fire with her tail. Carmen offered more coffee to Hector, but he shook his head.

I was caught off guard by Lulu. She slammed into me, hugging me tightly. I was engulfed by the smell of hair products and celebrity perfume.

"I had no idea that you were in love with a demon," said Lulu. "That sounds like something on Maury. If I ever said anything that triggered bad memories for you, I'm sorry. I have a couple of exes that I don't like to think about either."

"Were they also plotting to cut out your heart?" asked Carmen, intrigued.

"Not that I know of," said Lulu. "But one did always steal my coffee punch card. Got all the free lattes that were supposed to be mine."

"Many thanks for your hospitality," said Hector, standing up. "In all my years of fighting and smiting, it shames me so much to say these words: please hide me in your dungeon."

"He's right, Immy," said Carmen. "If the Thistle Witch really wants to harm Hector, we should get him down there fast, so she can't track him."

"I know," I said. We turned to leave the parlor, but then I stopped and looked at Hector. "How did you know that I was in a relationship with a demon?"

"Come, come," said Hector. "As I said, I have been keeping track of your family for years, and even if I had not been, I would still know the story. Your entanglement is all the witch community talks about. You are a cautionary tale of what not to do, and why playing the slots is a better career than monster hunting."

"I'm an after-school special," I said.

"You don't mind that I'm coming down here, do you?" asked Lulu. We walked slowly down the dim stairs of the dungeon, except for Carmen, who seemed to float down them like a 1930s dancer. I was impressed that Hector got down into the dungeon at all. The fact that he could pass by each step was proof that he'd turned over a new leaf, and left his human-eating days long behind him.

"Why would that bother me?" I asked.

Lulu shrugged. "This seems like some serious family drama," said Lulu. "I know how that is, and how you don't really want to advertise it."

"It's fine," I said. "You just better not be another monster in disguise."

"No worries there," said Lulu. "It must take a different kind of monster to spend two years washing out skin and putting it back on."

Carmen gave me a mom-like pat on the arm as we rounded the turn. I always wondered what it would be like to see Chace again. I felt a rush of adrenaline in my face, just like I expected I would. But then when it faded, I was left with an odd sensation, a feeling that I wanted this thing out of our dungeon, the way you want an old, broken TV out of your basement.

Time hadn't done much for Chace's appearance. His face was even blotchier than the last time I'd seen him. And his whole visage looked sunken and wrinkly. Any normal person might have written off his appearance as the ravages of age, or possibly an advertisement for why you shouldn't do drugs. But I knew the real reason was because his skin was wearing out. Soon his whole face would melt away, like when Carmen first tried making a homemade pie crust, and the thing sank to the bottom of the oven.

Besides looking ill, his time in the dungeon had also taken a lot of the wind out of Chace's sails. He looked like a plant that had been battered in a rainstorm, droopy and more than a little pathetic. Against my better judgment, I felt bad for him. But I squashed those feelings deep down inside myself, deciding that if I was going to feel anything, it was damn well going to be apathy.

"Imogen," he said. His voice was crackly and rough. He cleared the gunk out of his throat. He looked at me like he had never expected to see me again. And that had most definitely been the plan. "Why are you here?"

That's when I noticed he had some books on the floor of this cell, a wooden chair, and a few bags of chips. Carmen was the kindest person on Earth, even to those who deserved it the very least.

"Who the hell is that?" asked Chace, pointing at Hector.

"I am Hector the minotaur. And you are obviously overstaying your welcome in that fleshy abode you have made for yourself. Have a little decency, man, and let that poor soul have some rest."

"I would," said Chace. "But I think the skin acts as a barrier against the protective charms. Stops them from doing so much damage."

"By the looks of you, that's saying something," said Lulu.

"Who are you?" asked Chace, squinting at her.

"Lulu," she said. "I've heard a lot about you."

"Oh," said Chace, surprised.

"Don't get excited," said Lulu. "She left out the good stuff, if there is any."

"Hector is going to stay with you for a while," said Carmen. "He needs a safe place to lie low."

"I've never had a roomie before," said Chace. He took a sip of water like a man in the desert. "It'll be a hoot."

"Indeed," said Hector. "We can swap stories of bending and breaking humans to our will. And dining upon them in delight."

If Hector had forgotten about his decision to refrain from consuming human flesh, he was reminded by the judgmental looks we gave him.

"But of course, I am now a reformed minotaur," said Hector, embarrassed. "So don't tempt me, demon."

"You're in charge, Bessie," said Chace.

"I am neither a cow nor a woman cow," said Hector. "But I understand the slight."

"Where the hell did you pick this guy up?" asked Chace.

I ignored him and instead glanced into his cell. Curiosity had gotten the better of me, and I wondered how he had passed the time for the last couple of years.

"Reading anything good?" I asked, raising an eyebrow.

"The classics," said Chace. "Dickens, The Brontë sisters..."

"Is that *The Monk?*" I asked. "Tisk, tisk, Chace. Doesn't the demon carry him away and throw his body onto the sharp rocks at the end?"

Chace's face was even and tired, but amused nonetheless.

"You've gone and ruined it for me," said Chace. "And I love a good demon beat down. Now what do I have to live for?"

A thought suddenly crossed my mind. But the idea of involving Chace in anything we did made me more than a little nervous.

Always ready to fulfill her duty as the protective sister, Carmen pulled me away.

"What are you doing, Immy?" whispered Carmen. "I didn't think you'd want to talk to him."

"I don't," I whispered back. "I just thought he might know something about the Thistle Witch."

"Do you think it's safe to ask him questions like that?" asked Carmen.

"Probably not," I said. "But what the hell is he going to do? It's not like he can go anywhere."

We decided we should be fair and consult Lulu on the matter, given that she was likely also in danger from the Thistle Witch.

"Should we ask Chace about the Thistle Witch?" Carmen whispered to her.

"Why the heck are you asking me?" asked Lulu. "Does it involve jelly-filled donuts in some way?"

That apparently settled, we approached the cell again.

"I need to ask you a question," I said. "Will you give me a straight answer?"

Chace blinked a couple of times, considering.

"I think this is the part where I make a request," he said. "You'll have to give me something if I answer your questions."

I sighed. Nothing was ever easy, was it?

"What do you want?" I asked, impatient.

"In exchange for answering questions, I want...one of Carmen's chocolate meringue pies," said Chace.

His answer didn't compute with me for a moment. Truth be told, I'd seen people do a lot of things for Carmen's baked goods. There was once a fistfight at the local county fair over the man who had won her apple turnovers, and the poor bastard who had come up short. But Chace had been one of the few who never seemed particularly interested one way or another by Carmen's mastery of sugar.

"What the hell?" I asked. "I thought you'd ask for your freedom or...*literally* anything."

"What good is my freedom?" asked Chace. "You told me once that I wouldn't make it past those stairs again. If it wasn't true then, it's definitely true now."

"Fool," said Hector, approaching the cell. "I would have asked for a mighty club or perhaps some soup."

"What do you know about the Thistle Witch?" I asked. I blurted it out before I had a chance to second-guess myself.

Chace had such a funny look on his face. He stared at us like we were nuts, which said a lot, coming from a guy living in borrowed skin.

"You bored or something?" asked Chace. "You aren't around for two years, then when you show up you ask about the boogeyman?"

"You don't believe in the Thistle Witch?" asked Carmen, leaning in.

"No," said Chace, slowly.

"But you're a demon," said Lulu.

"So?" asked Chace. He talked to us like we were dumb kids. "Those are just stories witches used to tell to scare their kids. Nothing like warping youth, huh?"

"They are not tall tales," said Hector. "I saw the Thistle Witch for myself years ago, and now she is coming after me to satisfy her bloodlust. I am sure of it."

Chace shook his head. "Someone is trying to look scary," said Chace. "I once told a guy I was the Devil...the real, actual Devil... before I ate him. Demons and monsters say crap all the time."

"We think she's telling the truth," I said. "That she really is the Thistle Witch. She transforms from a blue heeler into a woman. She has a mask. She's just like the stories witches used to tell."

Chace still didn't look convinced. He sat down in his chair like he was ready for this conversation to be over.

"What do you want with me?" asked Chace.

"Hardly any of our books about demons or cryptids say anything about the Thistle Witch," said Carmen. "Just that she sneaks into a young witch's room to frighten them. Or sometimes she's a dog that you can hear growling during the witching hour. Occasionally, she abducts witches or warlocks and eats them. That's about it."

Chace sighed like someone above discussing such silly things.

"All the monsters and demons are fleeing," said Hector. His voice was urgent and clear.

That got Chace's attention. He stared off into space. At first, he looked like he wasn't thinking about anything, but then he began to tap his foot nervously. Sweat formed at his hairline.

"You can't feel it down here because this place is protected," said

Hector. "But if you were above ground, you would feel that there is an emptiness in the air."

"Didn't you guys feel that when we went to Eliza's?" asked Lulu.

Carmen nodded. "Even my babies tried to scatter at first," said Carmen, petting her pocket. "Until we convinced them to stay."

"This whole area feels drained of magic and monsters," I said. "Why would that be?"

Chace swallowed. He looked like he was starting to believe in Santa.

"Because she hates all magic," said Chace. He inhaled deeply. "And would just as soon kill a monster or witch as look at them. If this crazy witch is actually real, you're all screwed."

"Why?" I asked.

"Your version of her story is pretty tame," said Chace. "Demons tell a different version. In it, she's pretty powerful and pretty pissed off."

"That's great," said Lulu. "Pissed about what?"

"She doesn't need a reason," said Chace. "First, the Thistle Witch doesn't just come to a witch's house to freak out kids or occasionally eat people. That's not very scary, and a lot of creatures eat people."

"Like you," I said.

"I'm forced to abstain, remember?" asked Chace. "Anyway, in the legend, the Thistle Witch was the thirteenth child of a thirteenth child…"

"That's a fabulous start," said Lulu.

"This was in England somewhere," said Chace. "The legend isn't specific on that. A woman named Mary Smith, who was a witch, was hurrying down a lane during a rainstorm. She was nearly trampled by a carriage carrying Harold Martin and his wife, Bonnie. Any feelings of remorse for almost running her down disappeared when Harold realized that Mary was a witch. He hated witches and happened to be incredibly drunk at the time, so he didn't mind cussing her out and telling her what he thought of her and witches in general."

"I've definitely never heard this before," said Carmen. She glowed at old tales of witchcraft. "I always remember jerks."

"In the accident, Mary twisted her ankle," said Chace. "But she was also pissed about the verbal lashing Harold gave her. Witches were still pretty powerful back then. This was the early 1700s. Mary could tell Bonnie was pregnant, so she silently cursed the couple. She decided that since they hated witches so much, she would curse their thirteenth child to be one, and not only a witch, but one that would bring them nothing but suffering."

Barnaby stuck his head out of Carmen's pocket, then ducked back down again. He didn't seem to like where this story was going.

"But the story goes that Mary's spell worked better than she meant it to," said Chace. "When the baby was born, it didn't cry. It didn't make a sound at all. It just stared at the doctor and his assistant. When he held her up, all the candles in the room went out. And the clocks stopped at the moment she was born, which just so happened to be three in the morning."

"The witching hour," I said. "That's just perfect."

"It's also called the Devil's hour," said Chace. "Which might be more fitting for the story."

I felt that same sensation again, that unnerving feeling that always came on whenever anyone talked about the Thistle Witch. It felt like there was something under my skin, squirming around to get to the surface. And a paranoid fear that if I turned around, she just might be there.

"The child was never named," said Chace. "I'm not sure how she became known as the Thistle Witch. It could be because she wasn't exactly a cuddly baby. People were frightened of her from birth. Her father only lasted three days. It's as if he went insane. He couldn't stand to look at his own child. So, he took a red-hot poker and fused his eyes and mouth shut. They found his body deep down in a well, quite a while later. But the only thing left of him was his torso. His head, legs, and arms had mysteriously vanished."

"This sounds like the woman I encountered," said Hector. "The same evil surrounds her."

"Bonnie lasted a while longer," said Chace. "After all, the baby needed nourishment from her. But as soon as the Thistle Witch was able to walk and speak and function like any small child, she didn't need anyone. Bonnie was found hanging from a tree, her hands and feet cut off. The doctor and assistant supposedly died in a similar fashion."

"I should have stuck to making dinner rolls," said Lulu.

"Who *is* watching the bakery?" asked Carmen. She was like a kid who remembers piano practice a month after the fact.

"I have more siblings and cousins than you can shake a stick at," said Lulu. "And they all owe me big for watching their kids all the time."

"Can we return to the problem at hand?" said Hector. "We need to know how she will slaughter us."

"You need to work on your optimism," said Carmen, patting Hector's arm.

"It went on like that," said Chace. "She took care of her twelve brothers and sisters. That's when she learned she could turn into different animals. Her favorite was a blue heeler. She loved to disguise herself as a dog, and then maul people who tried to shoo her away."

"Nice, clean fun," I said.

"But she didn't stop there," said Chace. "Like I said, Mary Smith's spell worked too well. She really *did* create a monster. She created a self-hating witch. And that's a bomb waiting to go off. The Thistle Witch didn't care how far a spell went because she didn't care if she hurt herself. Because she hated herself, you see? She hated *all* witches. And she didn't exclude herself from them."

"She would be terrible at the reunion," said Carmen.

"Soon, her ultimate goal became destroying Mary Smith and her family," said Chace. "The very woman who made her. But she enjoyed revenge and didn't want to do it fast with a knife or club or poison. That wouldn't have been any fun for her."

"What did she do?" I asked, swallowing. "I'm almost afraid to ask."

"Remember what I told you about her parents?" asked Chace. "How they were missing body parts? Well, nothing went to waste for the Thistle Witch. She was tinkering with a new spell. Something no other witch has ever tried. Sure, some witches have reanimated their favorite cat or tried to bring back good ol' Uncle Bob. But no witch has ever seriously tried to create a monster out of the dead. Except for her."

I looked down and realized that my hand was on my stomach. I was holding myself for comfort. But nothing was going to comfort me now that I knew what we were up against.

"She took all of those body parts," said Chace. "And bound them together with dirty thread and spells and dark words. She wove them together into whatever creature she wanted. A mindless, thoughtless killer, one that answered to her alone. A body part murder machine."

"Nope," said Lulu, throwing up her hands. "It's like that movie. I don't do horror movies. Especially with people sewn together. No, thank you."

"What kind of monster did she make?" I asked.

"Legend says she made three different ones," said Chace. "To rip apart whoever *really* pissed her off. The first was a giant spider. The story goes that it was twelve feet high. Its body was made from a bunch of different witch and human heads bound together in a big blob. The legs of the spider were made from witch and human arms and legs that were woven together. People heard it coming, too. The heads screamed the whole time. But nobody got away. How can you escape something that's made for destruction?"

You could have heard the tiniest bug scurry around the floor of that dungeon. None of us knew what to say. Carmen's eyes were huge. I couldn't tell if she was trying to process what we had heard, or trying to think of ways we might defeat her. My mind was completely blank. I was too afraid to be anything but blank.

"The kicker of the story," said Chace. "Is that, according to legend, the Devil himself was so impressed by the Thistle Witch's coldheartedness and sadism, that he rewarded her by making her a demon. So, witches and the Devil can't be too chummy if he rewarded her for slaughtering a bunch of them."

We stood in silence, digesting everything. Finally, I exhaled. It felt like I had been holding my breath since we had first come down to the dungeon.

"Do you see?" asked Hector. "She has her mind fixed only on revenge. She will stop at nothing until her task is complete. At least I can feel at ease now, knowing that I am safe here until she has been defeated."

"You are," said Carmen. "We built this place ourselves. There are lots of protective amulets you can't even see. They're buried in the walls."

"Wait a minute," said Chace, his voice rising. "He can't stay down here if she's after him. I don't want that bloodthirsty monster after me. I never did anything to her, but she'll kill me just for standing next to him."

"What are you so worried about?" I asked. "I thought she was like the Easter Bunny."

"I think you've tortured me enough," said Chace, scared. "Having me down here with him when she comes calling is a little extreme. You really think she's coming for him?"

"She isn't coming," I said. "She's *here*. She's already killed people. And she hates Hector for disturbing her grave once."

"And she's after me and Imogen for some reason," said Carmen. "But we can't figure out why. It's something about a pact our ancestor made with her a long time ago."

"You know anything about that?" I asked.

"No," said Chace. He was circling his cell like a trapped animal, desperate to get out. "I don't know anything about a pact. Now get that minotaur out of here. I don't want to be an accessory after the fact."

"This is one of the safest places you could be when we go up against her," I said. "Probably even safer than the house."

"Don't say that," said Lulu. "That's where you have me staying."

"You don't get it," said Chace. "Look at Hector. Look at how scared he is."

"How dare you," said Hector. "I could smite you with my little finger. Do not try to dirty my mind with your demon tricks when I am just starting to feel better."

"He knows how powerful witches used to be," said Chace. "You are nothing in comparison. You're like two little kids with card tricks, going up against Houdini. You are so far out of your element that it's impossible to fathom. You are going to fail. And you're going to get us all killed."

I stood a half inch from his cell bars. My body was rigid and tense.

"You underestimated us once," I said. "And that ended up being pretty stupid on your part. Maybe you shouldn't underestimate us again. We're stronger than you realize, asshat."

Chace shook his head, annoyed.

"This isn't about me hurting you and lying to you, Imogen," said Chace, frantic. "Put away your pride for a second. You can't just make yourself more powerful. So, there's no way you can go up against her and win. You have to make a deal with her like your ancestor did, or run."

"I don't think making deals with evil entities is wise," said Carmen. "It always backfires in movies."

We turned to leave.

"You all right here, Hector?" I asked.

"Splendid," said Hector. "I can feel the strength and safety in this place. I feel calmer than I have in ages."

"No," said Chace. He did everything short of rattling the bars. "Get him out of here. Or let *me* out!"

"Let you out?" I asked. "You have me perplexed. Didn't you just say a few minutes ago that your freedom was pointless because you'd never make it up the stairs?"

"I'd rather die going up the stairs than die from being mutilated by her," said Chace.

I stared at him for a moment, then turned away. He had told us about the Thistle Witch, but that didn't mean I trusted him. If we let him go, and he lived, who knew what he'd do? He might even make a pact with the witch. It wasn't a leap to imagine him doing such a thing.

"Don't worry," I said, walking down the hallway. "This is the safest place you can be. And I'll have Carmen bring you that pie."

As we walked up the stairs, Chace kept yelling and begging to be set free. Hector sat there, telling him to be calm.

"Imogen!" he yelled. "Imogen! You and Carmen are just as bad as she is if you let her kill me!"

As we lowered the door back down to conceal the dungeon, Chace's words were cut in half. But the echo of his panic still reverberated on the floor. We stared at the door, watching his terror bounce the pebbles and dirt. I wondered if he was right. I wondered if we were fighting a losing battle. And I wondered if there was a line somewhere that I had crossed. I didn't want Chace in that dungeon. I didn't want him in my life at all. But I didn't want to let him out, either, in case he ran to her. What did that say about me, making him stay down there in eternal discomfort? I tried to push the unease out of my mind. After all, Chace was a demon who had made his name by lying and tricking. So, why couldn't I banish the feeling that I was doing something, or everything, wrong?

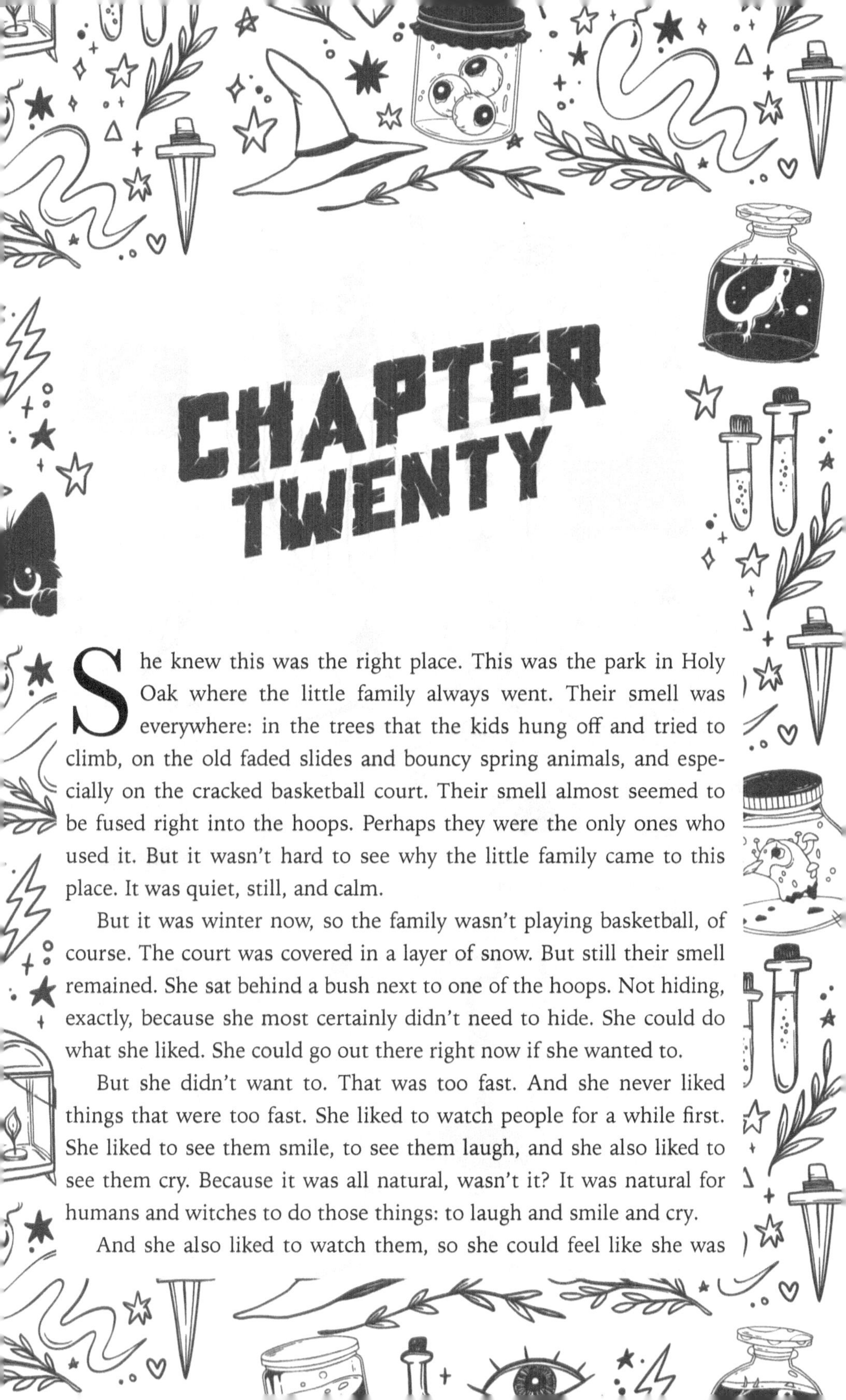

CHAPTER TWENTY

She knew this was the right place. This was the park in Holy Oak where the little family always went. Their smell was everywhere: in the trees that the kids hung off and tried to climb, on the old faded slides and bouncy spring animals, and especially on the cracked basketball court. Their smell almost seemed to be fused right into the hoops. Perhaps they were the only ones who used it. But it wasn't hard to see why the little family came to this place. It was quiet, still, and calm.

But it was winter now, so the family wasn't playing basketball, of course. The court was covered in a layer of snow. But still their smell remained. She sat behind a bush next to one of the hoops. Not hiding, exactly, because she most certainly didn't need to hide. She could do what she liked. She could go out there right now if she wanted to.

But she didn't want to. That was too fast. And she never liked things that were too fast. She liked to watch people for a while first. She liked to see them smile, to see them laugh, and she also liked to see them cry. Because it was all natural, wasn't it? It was natural for humans and witches to do those things: to laugh and smile and cry.

And she also liked to watch them, so she could feel like she was with them. She could feel like she was a part of them. Because she *was* a part of them. Of course, she was, and a very important part, too. She was the period at the end of the sentence.

On this particular day, the family had come to the park to sled down the nearby hill. The dog could easily see them from where she sat. Little wispy snowflakes began to fall, and the kids caught them in their mouths. Then they put down their tiny plastic sleds, scooted forward with their feet, and slid down the hill. It sounded a lot like sliding down Styrofoam, the air was so cold and tight. They hooted and whooped when they reached the bottom, then turned around and went back up again. They never slid down particularly fast, and the hill was barely even a hill, really. But the kids laughed and smiled, so the dog decided that this must be what the family considered fun.

The parents slid down a couple of times too, but they mostly stood off to the side, taking pictures. It wasn't hard to see why. These little kids wouldn't be little kids for very long. Someday, they would come back home all grown up. And the parents that took pictures now would have gray hair and lines all over their faces. Then they would all sit down at the table together with coffee in front of them and look at the big book of pictures and remember this day. This day would be the thing they talked about, looked back on, reminisced over.

The dog wagged her tail when she thought of this. What a happy day that would be. Reminiscing over days gone by. Wasn't that a favorite pastime of humans?

And for a moment, the dog wondered what would happen if she walked out from behind that bush and trotted up to the little family. The boy and girl would surely run up to her and pet her. Every child wants a dog, so they would beg until their parents were nearly fed up. Then they'd make signs and no one would claim her, so the family would keep her.

I've never done that before, thought the dog.

And perhaps she'd have a fenced-in backyard and a big fancy dog house, and she'd never have to be anything other than a dog again. She'd never even consider changing back to herself. After all, she had stayed a dog for longer before. For a lifetime once, really. Just for a change.

And they'd feed her dog biscuits and dog food, and she'd eat them and nothing else, except for maybe a few table scraps. And she'd be such a good dog. Such a very good dog. Sitting beneath the table on mornings when they had waffles for breakfast. She could almost imagine the little boy sneaking her a bite. She could almost taste the syrup.

But there isn't time, thought the dog. The realization deflated her. There were *other* things to do, after all. And she realized that if the family put up signs about a lost dog, those sisters would just come looking for her. They knew who she was, after all. That was more than clear. And it wasn't the right time yet. Her creation wasn't built yet.

Wouldn't those sisters be mad when they realized what their ancestor had done? It was just like a witch or a warlock to do something like that. He threw all of his descendants to the wolves, and for what? She had been waiting for this day for such a long time. Those sisters and their parents had been slipping up for a while, but that last stunt had really put them over the edge. And the audacity to slip up by copying *her*? She couldn't just let that go. She had to do something. So, she couldn't be a good dog. Not right now, at least.

She sat there in the snow as the wind picked up and blew flakes against her. She almost felt like she could cry. She was wistful, watching the little family, because of course, she wouldn't be their good dog. And of course, these little kids would never be adults. And their parents would never be old. They'd never get a chance to flip through that big book of pictures and smile about times long ago in the park they loved.

It wasn't fair, not really fair at all. She could have been their good dog. It would have been so nice to be their good dog, sitting on the porch, wagging her tail. But somehow or another, she never was good, was she? Whether she was human or dog, she never ended up being good. And she *knew* she could be good if she wanted. She would be so *good* at being *good* if she really put in an effort and tried. But she never really tried, did she? She wondered why that was.

She decided next time she'd be good. Next time, she'd be good for sure. She'd be somebody's good dog, just as soon as this was all over. And if not next time, surely the time after that.

The dog walked out from behind the bush and approached the little family on the hill. It took a moment for them to spot her. The kids were tackling each other in the snow as their parents watched and laughed.

The little boy noticed her first and squealed in absolute delight, just like she knew he would. They all smiled at her, even the parents. They were ready for her to be their good dog. Their smiles were so warm and welcoming as she trotted up to them. They smiled and smiled and smiled. And then somehow their smiles stopped.

She knew it was because they had seen her teeth.

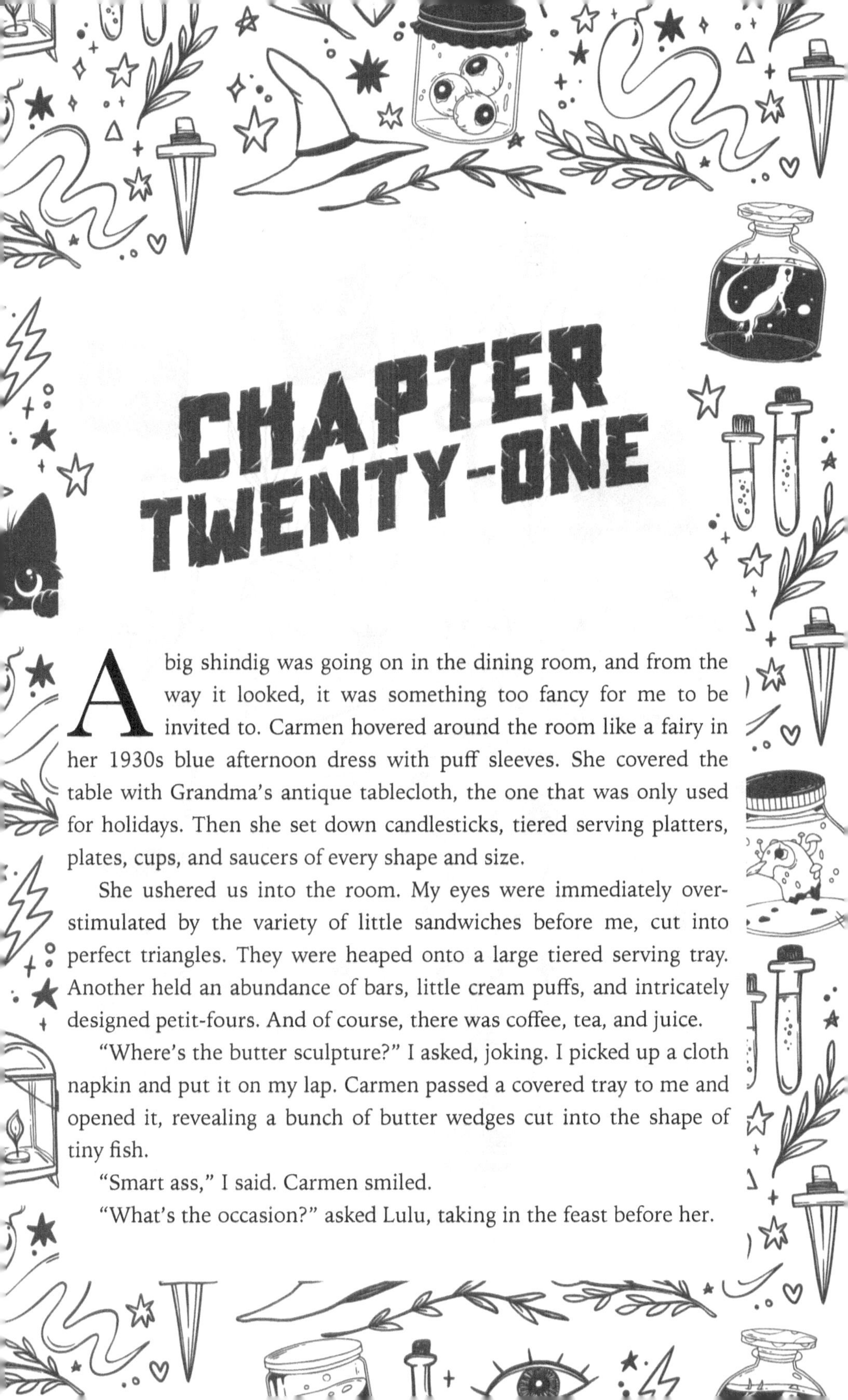

CHAPTER TWENTY-ONE

A big shindig was going on in the dining room, and from the way it looked, it was something too fancy for me to be invited to. Carmen hovered around the room like a fairy in her 1930s blue afternoon dress with puff sleeves. She covered the table with Grandma's antique tablecloth, the one that was only used for holidays. Then she set down candlesticks, tiered serving platters, plates, cups, and saucers of every shape and size.

She ushered us into the room. My eyes were immediately over-stimulated by the variety of little sandwiches before me, cut into perfect triangles. They were heaped onto a large tiered serving tray. Another held an abundance of bars, little cream puffs, and intricately designed petit-fours. And of course, there was coffee, tea, and juice.

"Where's the butter sculpture?" I asked, joking. I picked up a cloth napkin and put it on my lap. Carmen passed a covered tray to me and opened it, revealing a bunch of butter wedges cut into the shape of tiny fish.

"Smart ass," I said. Carmen smiled.

"What's the occasion?" asked Lulu, taking in the feast before her.

"She always does this during intense cases," I said. "One nice meal in case we die."

Lulu pulled her hand away from a petit-four. I guess she had been hoping for a less morbid answer.

"I also bake to help me think about a case," said Carmen. "Or whenever I'm stressed about a case."

"Which is it this time?" I asked, taking a bite of my chicken salad triangle.

"I talked it out with Horatio and Barnaby all night," said Carmen, motioning to her pocket demons, who sat at their kiddy table, enjoying snacks. "And we're not sure."

"That spoils my appetite," said Lulu. "I was hoping it was some pre-Christmas thing you did."

"Either way, you've outdone yourself," I said, taking a sip of coffee. "Did you roast your own beans?"

"Of course," said Carmen. "Nothing but the best in case we end up as dog food."

"When did you have time to do all of this?" asked Lulu.

"Don't be silly," said Carmen, waving the air. "If you had the traumatic dreams I have, you'd hardly sleep either."

Lulu leaned toward me and asked, "Is this what holidays are like?"

"At Christmas, she makes a traditional British pudding," I said. "Then gives everyone a homemade gift and a brand-new weapon. Last year, I got a flail."

"Maybe I should drop hints about a gift card," said Lulu.

As we ate our assortment of sandwiches and treats, Carmen looked through a series of papers in a plain beige folder.

"Look at this, Immy," she said. "We never even thought to ask Eliza and Shannon about Sam and Trisha's corpses."

"That's not easy to bring up in a conversation," said Lulu, grabbing a cookie.

"What is that?" I asked.

"It's the coroner's report for both Sam and Trisha," said Carmen. "It looks like Sam was left sans arms and legs, like Harold Martin from the legend."

"I don't know why I bother trying to eat around you people," said Lulu.

"And poor Trisha was left with even less," said Carmen. "But I won't go into that. I want to enjoy my cupcake."

"Where did you get the coroner's report?" asked Lulu.

"I have my inside people," said Carmen, smiling.

"Poor Keith," I said. "When you two were kids, he had allergies all year round. His nose was so raw I thought it would fall off. He didn't exactly seem like police material."

"He's much better now," said Carmen. "I gave him a charm to ward off the hay fever and cat allergies. Now he'll be good for life as long as he never finds out the charm contains urine."

I shuddered. Why did spells always contain pee and bones and nasty, gooey substances? Why couldn't they call for queso and a nice smattering of Auntie Anne's pretzels?

"What's the next step?" asked Lulu. "What do we do now to stop the Thistle Witch? Get some weapons ready? Make some potions? Confront her?"

Carmen held on to her cupcake with the grip of a tiger.

"Where were you a few minutes ago when we discussed stress baking versus contemplation baking?" asked Carmen. "I haven't figured out the next step. But I will."

"Take it easy," I said. "Your poor cupcake doesn't deserve that. She's an evil monster, but she's still a witch like us—so at least we know what we're facing. Not like that time with the invisible gnome."

"She's far more powerful than us, Immy," said Carmen. "She's not like every other witch. Hence, the petit-fours. If only we were stronger. Turning myself into that beautiful corgi was a good first step. Now we just need to keep going."

"It could take us our entire lives to be more powerful," I said. "You've been trying to turn into an animal for six years. And you'd still be one if we hadn't exhausted ourselves changing you back. I still have a little bit of a rash from that in a place I'd rather not talk about."

"What else can we do?" asked Lulu. "Fight her? A chainsaw and some guns should be able to take care of just about any monster, right?"

"Yes," I said, thinking. "But we have to be smart about this, since she's been around for a long time. She has more experience than us. Since she's a witch, at least we know what would irritate us. We just have to take those things and magnify them to really annoy her. Holy water is a good bet. We also have plenty of salt and witch bottles. Maybe we should whip up a few potions. We'll need to gather some of our hair…"

"And we need to be fast, Immy," said Carmen. "We should confront her within a couple of days. We don't want her monster to be ready."

"How do you know it's not ready now?" asked Lulu.

"Because she's not out on the road right now, taunting us," I said. "She's only killed two people that we know of so far."

"She probably needs quite a few bodies to make a monster as big as the one Chace described," said Carmen.

"What do you think she'll make?" asked Lulu. "It better not be some big bug again."

Carmen clapped her hands. "I hope it's something festive since it's the holiday season. Maybe a big gingerbread man or elf. If I'm going to get mauled, she can at least have the decency to maul me with something Christmassy."

Our gloomy tea time/murder investigation was suddenly interrupted by the ringing of the 1930s black Bakelite telephone in the parlor. I swore and grumbled as I walked over to it, complaining, not for the first time, that in our line of work we should have something with caller ID like every other sucker that still had a landline, instead of something that just *looked cool*.

"Otherworldly Investigations," I said. I always held my breath whenever I had to answer the phone that way. Sometimes, it ended up being the propane guy or some neighbor. Then, when you saw them at the grocery store, they didn't want to look you in the eye. It was, however, a great way to get rid of telemarketers.

"Imogen?" asked my mom on the other end.

"Hey, mom," I said, relieved. "I'm glad it's you. Things are getting weird here."

I heard my dad mumble in the background.

"What was that?" I asked.

"Just wait, Petey," said my mom. She changed to speakerphone, so I could hear them both.

"I said it's also going weird here," said my dad. "At least everyone's nice. Very hospitable."

"You wouldn't happen to be working on a case, would you, dear?" asked my mom.

"Carmen!" I said. Carmen floated up next to me. Lulu followed. "I thought you said that you sent mom and dad texts to let them know what was going on."

"Oh," said Carmen. Her face was blank, then turned sheepish. "I lied, Immy."

I felt like throwing that old phone right in the garbage can.

"What a time for you to start being inconsistent," I said.

"I'm so sorry," said Carmen. "I just wanted them to enjoy their trip."

"I think our situation trumps shuffleboard night," I said.

"You wouldn't have a shuffleboard night," said Lulu. "You'd want to play that during the day, so you could see."

By this time, mom and dad were distracted by someone with a gravelly voice asking if they wanted to go in the hot tub.

"Sorry about that," I said, putting the phone back up to my ear. "I'm just facing certain doom with Abbot and Costello here. What's happening on your end?"

"Our trip has ended up a little different than we thought," said my mom.

"How's that?" I asked.

"We've been hijacked by a band of demons and monsters," said my dad. "This chupacabra keeps going on about how the jets in the hot tub are wonderful on his back. I should try it out."

I pulled the phone away, then put it back again.

"Excuse me?" I asked.

"The ship has been taken over by a ragtag group of monsters and demons," said my dad.

"Does that happen often?" asked Lulu, whispering. "Or is it weird?"

I shrugged. "It's definitely a new one."

"I guess we know where all the monsters went," said Carmen.

I felt my stomach toss and turn. How could we protect the people around here and somehow help my parents? They had faced a lot of apocalypses in their day, but they'd never been at sea with a ship full of monsters.

"Are they treating you all right?" I asked. "Are you OK?"

"We're the only people left," said my mom. "We got to our room, then I guess we must have been drugged. When we woke up, we had already left port. Then all the humans besides us were kicked off when we stopped at Grand Cayman."

"You mean they didn't hurt anyone?" asked Carmen, leaning into the phone.

"They're great," said my dad. "Kinda weird to see some of them in swimsuits, but they sing some damn fine Tom Jones karaoke."

Hooting and hollering echoed in the background. My dad didn't seem to be exaggerating at all. A Princess Cruise full of demons and cryptids seemed to be the recipe for a great time.

"So, you're having fun?" asked Carmen.

"I think this is the best vacation we've ever been on," said my mom. "Even though I guess it is technically a kidnapping. I'm trying not to think about that too deeply. I just want to enjoy my fancy balcony dinner."

"Sure beats that ghost town bus tour," said my dad. "Those bus bathrooms were horrendous."

"Take pictures!" said Carmen.

There was a strange glassy noise on the other end.

"What was that?" I asked.

"That was Phillipe refilling your dad's iced tea," said my mom.

"I thought you said there weren't any people on board," I said.

"Phillipe is a pocket demon," said my mom. "He's from Fort Lauderdale."

Carmen shoved her face into the phone. "Bring him home with you," she said.

Why on Earth would a band of demons and monsters steal a cruise ship to party down with my parents? It sounded like the silliest thing I'd ever heard of. And somehow, it also sounded like Carmen's idea of a dream vacation.

"I'm not exactly sure what to say," I said. "We're having slightly less fun here. What the hell is going on?"

"Sorry, dear," said my mom. "I'm just so distracted. Some of these monsters are really throwing their inhibitions to the wind. I think I'll just stare at the ground."

"And there's a centaur steering the boat," said my dad. "Can you believe that?"

"We've got a minotaur in the dungeon," I said, flatly. "So yes, I probably can."

"A yeti named Devon told us that almost all cryptids and demons have fled the Midwest," said my mom. "They're afraid of some witch. That's when we got worried and thought we should call."

"They're afraid of the Thistle Witch," I said. "She hates witches and made some pact with an ancestor of ours. Now, I guess she's decided it's time to kick our asses. Know anything about that?"

"So, she's actually real," said my mom. She sounded full of concern and worry, the way only a mom can.

"What ancestor?" asked my dad.

"Ignatius Abernathy," said Carmen. "The genealogy book doesn't say much about him. There's a big black smear next to his name."

"That's because he was a jackass," said my dad.

"Petey," said my mom. "Watch your language. But yes, he was. He left his wife and eight kids high and dry, and went off with some mermaid he was infatuated with."

"I kind of hate that guy," said Lulu.

"Do you know anything about Ignatius and his pact with the Thistle Witch?" asked Carmen.

"Sorry, sweetie," said mom. "We thought she was a legend, too."

There was silence as all of us thought. What could we do? If the demons and cryptids wanted them there, what could my parents say? It's not as if they could jump off the ship and start swimming.

"I wish we were there with you girls," said mom.

"I don't," said my dad. "We've got mini golf later."

"Thanks," I said, sarcastically.

"I'm just joking, kiddo," said my dad. "We can't get out of here, anyway. And it's not like we haven't tried. We were going to try a relocation spell when we got close to land, but a demon took our supplies. It would have been a long shot. We don't have that kind of oomph."

"Why are they keeping you with them?" asked Carmen. "Why didn't they kick you off with the rest of the humans?"

"They think we can protect them," said my mom. "In case that witch comes after them when she's done with you."

"That's comforting," I said, sighing.

"Aww," said Carmen. "They like you."

I had always been equal parts impressed and annoyed at how my sister could take moments of high stress, and instead of focusing on the aspect of us being screwed, she instead focused on how cute devils and cryptids were.

"We're basically calling to tell you to be careful," said my mom. "And remember, over the years we've practiced a lot of potions for times like this. You know what to do."

"And remember those emergency numbers hidden behind that picture," said my dad. "If worse comes to worst, they might help."

"Yes," said my mom. "Don't hesitate to call *that* number."

My dad grumbled something about the cost of calls at sea.

"We'll text you to keep you updated about our situation," said Carmen. I glared at her. "For real, this time."

"And we'll text back if we think of anything useful, sweetheart," said my mom.

"You're the strongest people I know," said my dad. "Don't be afraid of that bastard. And never let her see you sweat. Love you guys. Now I'm going to see a demon about some bourbon."

"Love you, sweeties," said my mom.

We tried to answer them, but they had already hung up. We stood there a long time, listening to the dial tone. I felt like we were all glued to that spot by the gravity of the situation. Nobody was coming to help. We had to figure this out on our own.

The clang of fancy teacups and plates snapped me back into reality. Norma Shearer and Buster Keaton were helping themselves to a couple of chicken salad sandwiches, while the pocket demons Honora and Benedict had left their kiddy table to steal cookies off a serving tray.

"What should we do now, Immy?" asked Carmen.

"Just what mom and dad said. Did they sound like they were very worried about us?"

Carmen and Lulu hesitated, then shrugged.

"Your dad sounded more worried about mini golf than anything else," said Lulu.

"That's because they know we're capable," I said. "We've been training our whole lives for this."

"Except me," said Lulu. "I trained to be a hairstylist, but dropped out to bake. It's more fun anyway."

"But that means you're still good with scissors," said Carmen. "That might come in handy if you need to stab something."

"Damn right," I said. I felt a little like a general rallying the troops. All I needed was the tapping of a drum in the background. "Are we adults or what? Or are we going to sit here sucking our thumbs? We act like we've just been sent off to college, and we're fumbling at our first adult party."

"This is a good speech," said Lulu. "I feel like you're drawing from your own past experiences."

"I'm sick of this," I said, stamping my foot. Carmen nodded excitedly, ready to embrace my pep talk. "I'm thirty-two years old, damn it. I'm not even close to being a scared kid anymore. And I'm not going to act like one. And Carmen, you're twenty-eight. You are ready for this. Think of all the monsters we've faced together. Just the two of us, without anyone's help. Countless exorcisms. Cleansing houses of angry spirit after angry spirit. One even scratched the hell out of my back."

"And don't forget that evil invisible gnome," said Carmen. "He was a little bitch."

"And we've sent a lot of other monsters packing," I said. "Without anyone else's help. And you, Lulu, you're… Actually, I don't know how old you are."

"I'm thirty-six," said Lulu, eating a petit-four. "But I'd like to think I have the emotional intelligence of someone in their golden years."

"Sure," I said, not wanting to lose my momentum. "You're not scared, are you?"

"Of course, I'm scared," said Lulu. "I just realized all of this existed, but like that guy says in that movie, 'I'm as mad as hell, and I'm not going to take this anymore!'"

I nodded. "So, we don't have to be intimidated by this witch just because she's our first really big solo case. We've killed monsters and sent cryptids crying to their momma. And we can handle this, too. We're going to make some potions, get some weapons ready, and go kick her thistly ass."

We hooted, hollered, and patted each other's backs.

"I feel good," said Lulu.

"I feel like we're going to kick her butt without batting an eye," I said.

"And I kind of feel like we could also kick the hell out of another team in football," said Carmen.

CHAPTER TWENTY-TWO

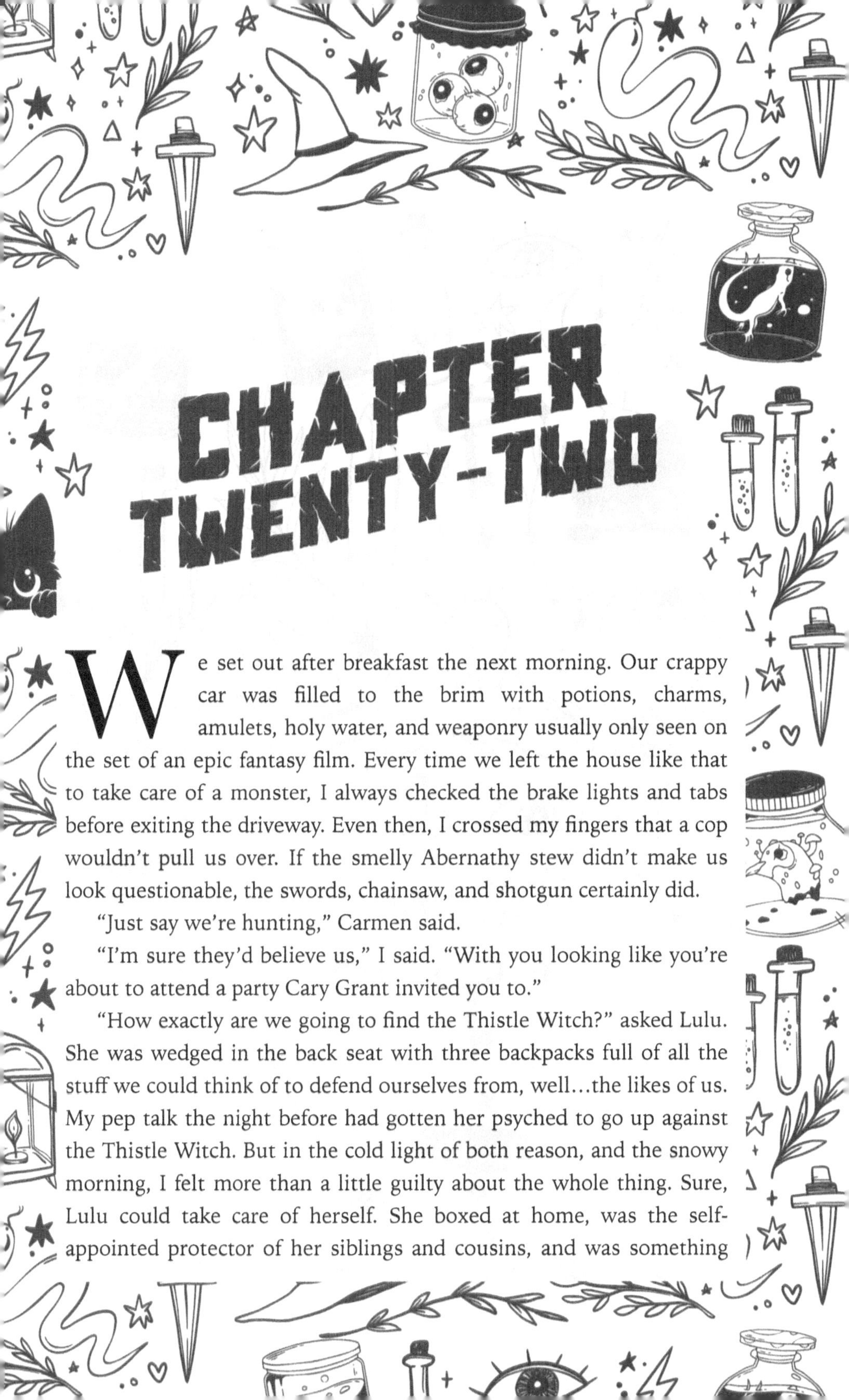

We set out after breakfast the next morning. Our crappy car was filled to the brim with potions, charms, amulets, holy water, and weaponry usually only seen on the set of an epic fantasy film. Every time we left the house like that to take care of a monster, I always checked the brake lights and tabs before exiting the driveway. Even then, I crossed my fingers that a cop wouldn't pull us over. If the smelly Abernathy stew didn't make us look questionable, the swords, chainsaw, and shotgun certainly did.

"Just say we're hunting," Carmen said.

"I'm sure they'd believe us," I said. "With you looking like you're about to attend a party Cary Grant invited you to."

"How exactly are we going to find the Thistle Witch?" asked Lulu. She was wedged in the back seat with three backpacks full of all the stuff we could think of to defend ourselves from, well…the likes of us. My pep talk the night before had gotten her psyched to go up against the Thistle Witch. But in the cold light of both reason, and the snowy morning, I felt more than a little guilty about the whole thing. Sure, Lulu could take care of herself. She boxed at home, was the self-appointed protector of her siblings and cousins, and was something else when she was in a parking lot with people who didn't know how to drive in the winter. But magic was still magic, and the Thistle Witch definitely had more magic than we did. People were already dead because they were associated with us. Thinking of the same thing happening to Lulu filled me with a sick chill.

"We'll find her," I said. "We have our ways."

Our way was not only effective, but thankfully, not even gross. It was also nice because it didn't involve standing over a hot cauldron. Actually, I had spent very little of my life standing over hot cauldrons. Instead, I had spent far too much time pulling hairs out of my head and shoving them into bottles, peeing in cups, and bending nails.

Carmen pulled a wooden flute out of her burgundy coat dress.

"Any requests?" she asked, lifting the flute to her mouth.

"'Free Bird,'" I said, cupping my mouth like I was shouting to a performer on stage.

"How about 'Greensleeves?'" asked Carmen.

"That was my second choice," I said, smiling.

"Is this going to find her?" asked Lulu. "Or is this what you do for fun when the internet is down?"

"Flutes are great for warding off evil," I said. Delicate snowflakes had begun to fall. The sky was matte gray. It was the kind of day that made you feel like a blue sky didn't exist behind it. "If a demon, monster, or ghost hears it, they usually retreat pretty quickly. But if the creature is powerful enough, it'll counteract the sound of the flute."

"Basically, we know we're close to the Thistle Witch if Carmen starts playing bad?" asked Lulu.

"That's about it," said Carmen, pulling the flute away from her mouth for a second. "I'm usually very good. I had eight years of lessons from the troll in the woods behind the house."

We drove down every street in Holy Oak while Carmen played her flute. This didn't take long, though, because we lived in a one-horse town. Literally, too. Mrs. Gorman on the other end of Holy Oak had one horse and only one horse. His name was Custard.

When we were finished with Holy Oak, Carmen's tune hadn't

suffered any. We got on the county road and headed over to Brier. "Greensleeves" was obviously Carmen's favorite song because she played it relentlessly. Halfway through the drive, I was not only bummed because of the evil we faced, but also bummed thinking about Henry VIII's wives. I was thankful when she mixed it up for a little while, switching to "Sheep May Safely Graze."

"We sound like a demented ice cream truck," said Lulu.

We did the same thing in Brier. We drove down every street, expecting the song to change. I felt like I was waiting for the bottom to fall out of my stomach. My hands were clenched on the wheel, wondering how much of a panic I'd be in when Carmen's flute faltered. I wanted to hear the music stop, but I guess I didn't want to hear it stop at the same time. Part of me wished the Thistle Witch had up and left, choosing someone else at the other end of the world to pick a fight with. But I knew if that happened, we'd just spend all of our time trying to find out where that place was and then book a ticket there.

I didn't know whether to grip the wheel tighter or let my hands loosen when we were finished with town. Carmen's tune hadn't changed.

"A tricky witch like you wouldn't live in town," I whispered. "You want seclusion."

I turned off on a gravel road and followed it until I hit another. We bounced up and down as we hit slushy spots and holes in the road.

"Are we going to drive down every road in the county?" asked Lulu.

"Yep," I said. "Good thing Carmen made sandwiches."

It was a nice day for a drive, I guess. It would have been relaxing if we hadn't been looking for a woman who wanted us dead. Lulu finished her sandwich, and for a moment, almost seemed like she was about to doze. But then we hit a spot where snow met loose gravel, and the jittery vibration woke her up again.

I turned down a tiny gravel road where the faded green sign said something like 6,503rd Street. The road curved and then went through some trees. Carmen's tune had become little more than white noise in the background. The snowy ground rose to our left, and I glanced to see a little boy and his cocker spaniel looking down at us from his yard as we passed. By his expression, we must have been the first people to go by in about three years.

The road sloped down. Then we passed a little creek surrounded by icy trees. I cranked my head to see if the water was completely iced over. As we drove by the last big tree by the creek, Carmen's flute faltered into a sputtering, hollow nothing.

I didn't realize that my foot was on the brake until my big toe started to hurt from pressing down on it. I didn't breathe as we sat on that thin little road. Lulu leaned up to us. We all looked about as rigid as the ice dams on the houses we had passed. There we were, in the middle of nowhere, the cold edging in around us. Carmen blew into her flute, but the only sound that came out was air.

"Is she there?" asked Lulu, pointing. The creek and trees curved back behind an old farm place. What had once been fields were now nothing but brambly weeds that barely poked up through the icy snow. A thin driveway about a quarter mile long led back to an old abandoned farmhouse. The driveway was covered with an untouched foot of snow.

The house looked like nothing but gloom. It was set way back on the property, nearly in the trees. From the deteriorating siding and broken windows, it was clear nobody had lived there for a long time. No person, anyway.

"Go closer to the driveway, Immy," whispered Carmen. It felt like the time to whisper, somehow. The punched-out windows of that house were like eyes looking at us. There wasn't a hint of wind, and the snow fell like a secret. It was a place that felt utterly empty, and somehow, at the same time, alive and watching.

I edged the car closer to the driveway.

"What are we doing?" asked Lulu. "If she's in there, she's going to see us and wonder why someone is going by so slow."

I picked up the pace and drove by the driveway. Carmen blew into her flute, but nothing came out. I guess I could have stopped right there, turned around, and headed up to the house. But somehow, I found myself still driving down the gravel road, going until Carmen's song flowed through her flute again.

I could keep driving, I thought. *All morning, all afternoon, and all night. How far away would we get by then? Far enough to be hard to track.*

But my foot stepped on the brake again. I had driven until some trees blocked our view of the house behind us, or perhaps blocked the house's view of *us*.

"What's the plan?" asked Lulu. "Should we leave the car here and sneak onto the property?"

Carmen was calm as she put her flute back in its case and set it by her feet.

"What do you think, Immy?" asked Carmen, trying to meet my eye. I hesitated for a moment, then looked at her.

"It doesn't matter," I said. "She already knows we're here. Can't you feel it?"

Carmen's expression faded into a little frown as she nodded.

"How do you know that?" asked Lulu, clenching the seat.

"It's like it was when we were at Eliza's," I said. "Only worse. I feel like I just threw up and *need* to throw up."

Lulu leaned back in her seat. "Shit," she said. "Good thing I brought that iron rod."

"I feel like a tool walking down the driveway like we're here to sell insurance," I said.

"We'll sneak in," said Carmen. "Like Lulu said. After all, maybe our feeling is wrong. Remember when you guys were on the hunt for that dinosaur bird in Wyoming when I was still too little to help? You had the feeling that the crazy lady from the diner was following you."

I stared blankly at Carmen. "She *was* following us," I said.

"But you all had the feeling that she was following you because she wanted to murder you and chop you into a million pieces," said

Carmen, smiling. "But really, she was following you because she was crazy and wanted to find a monster as some bizarre proof that evolution isn't real. Crazy, but not homicidal. So, your feeling was wrong. Get it?"

"No." Lulu and I said it in unison.

"Are we sneaking in?" Lulu asked.

"Sure," I said.

CHAPTER TWENTY-THREE

Each of us put a backpack on. Lulu held her trusty rod, I had my shotgun, and Carmen, of course, had her chainsaw.

We tucked ourselves behind some scraggly evergreen bushes, peeking through them to see the house in the distance.

"Isn't that heavy to lug around?" asked Lulu, motioning to Carmen's saw.

"It beats the alternative of being killed," said Carmen, smiling.

"That's true," said Lulu, swallowing.

"Focus, ladies," I said, keeping my voice down. I was afraid that, with her powers, the Thistle Witch might hear us. I was also afraid she had spies hanging around. "I think we can follow these bushes until they meet up with that grove back there. Then we'll stay low to the snow and weave through the trees until we reach the house's backyard. Going in through the back is best, I think."

"Let's do it, Immy," said Carmen.

I felt like one of the giant bats we captured once in Texas was flying around in my chest. With each step, it was harder to pretend that my gait wasn't shaky and unsure. When we hit the grove of trees and began edging closer to the house, it hit me how out of practice I was for all of this. Sure, I had intimidated that jerk in the casino parking lot and had used my magic to play the slots. But the last real time I had fought cryptids or demons with Otherworldly Investigations was when we had killed those slugs. I never could have fathomed as I sat in the car that day, fiddling with the beads on my wedding dress, how long it would be until I was on another case.

As I trudged through hard snow with shaky feet, I couldn't believe how different I was. I had burst into that barn in my wedding dress, completely sure of myself, thinking only about how the monster hunt was on an inconvenient day. There hadn't been fear about the battle to come. There hadn't been uncertainty in my mind or my step. Why couldn't I be that way now? Why couldn't I be sure of myself? Why did I have to change so much?

I picked snow-hearty cockleburs off my boot. Carmen and Lulu waited for me. I nodded, and we went forward again, creeping nearer to the house. I was just able to see the crumbling white siding through the trees when…

I opened my eyes and nearly stumbled. I looked down, expecting to trip over some stump. But there was only light, untouched snow around my feet. I steadied myself, dizzy from what had just happened. We should have been in the grove of trees to the west of the house, but instead, we were all on the long driveway. The broken mailbox creaked in the wind.

"Whoa," said Lulu, taking it in. "What the hell?"

"That's never happened to us before!" said Carmen, excited. "Amazing!"

"What's going on?" asked Lulu, pointing up toward where we had just been a moment before. "How the hell did we get out here?"

"Shit," I whispered, kicking the snow with my foot. "Nothing's easy, is it?"

"She must have a safeguard spell around the house," said Carmen, with more excitement than I thought was warranted for the woman who hoped to smite us. "Witches used to use these spells to protect their lonely cabins or fortresses. It made the place almost impenetrable to people that wanted in. Sometimes, they'd even camouflage a house completely to make it look like a tree, rock, whatever."

"Does that mean we're never going to get into this damn place?" asked Lulu.

"I sure hope not," I said. "A lot of the time, witches that performed those safeguard spells were protecting their houses from villagers with torches. Unlike them, we have magic. At least a little magic, anyway. Don't start betting against us yet. Come on."

We walked down the snowy path that made up the driveway. There was no point in retreating to the trees to try to be sneaky again. Getting beamed to your enemy's driveway kind of takes away the element of surprise.

I stepped in a tire dip and ended up with a boot full of snow. Then we walked, and we walked, and to change things up a bit, we walked a little more. I stepped in a tire dip and ended up with a boot full of snow. Then we walked, and we walked, and to change things up a bit, we walked a little more. I stepped in a tire dip and ended up with a boot full of snow. Then we walked, and we walked…

"Damn it!" I said, stopping. "If I walk in this same fricking tire dip one more time…"

"Fantastic!" said Carmen, looking back toward the mailbox, then turning forward to look at the house. We were still only a few feet from the mailbox. But we'd done enough walking to be up and down that driveway about three times.

"I need to stand still for a second," said Lulu, grabbing Carmen's coat for stability. "How are we not any closer to the house?"

We looked at the house and I took a few steps. Then I took a few steps again. Then I ran a little way. Then I took a few steps again. Then I ran a little way. Then I took a few steps again. Then I ran a little way.

Finally, I stopped and looked back at Carmen and Lulu. They were about two feet behind me. Carmen smirked.

"How was that for you, Immy?" she asked, smiling.

The driveway seemed to stretch out like a piece of gum that a child chews and then pulls to see how long they can get it. We could have walked up it forever, but we never would have gotten closer.

"Son of a bitch," I said, panting from the run/walk that I may or may not have just had. "Confronting this witch isn't going the way I thought it would."

"You thought it would go better?" asked Lulu.

"I thought there would be more weapons and blood," I said. "And fewer mind games."

"Just imagine having power like this, Immy," said Carmen. "Wouldn't it be lovely? For altruistic purposes only, of course."

"You'd never have to worry about people selling crap door to door again," I said.

"What now?" asked Lulu.

"Time to go to work," I said.

We threw our backpacks down into the snow, unzipped them, and pulled out whatever we thought was useful. Lulu threw some salt into the blanket of snow in front of us, while Carmen recited some Gregorian chants. I stirred a little pre-made stew and took a bite.

"Mmm," I said, cringing. "It tastes horrendous. We're starting to feel unwanted out here. My sister is a fantastic host, and it always makes her tear up when people don't return the favor."

Carmen continued chanting, but looked at me with a raised eyebrow.

Lulu elbowed me in the ribs. "What are you doing?" she asked. "She might hear you."

"She's her own security system," I said, loudly. "You know we're here, don't you? I have a lot of things that might interest you, if you just come out. Some pins, maybe? I've got this refreshing holy water. And look, Greenies dog treats. How can you say no to that?"

I gave Lulu and Carmen a bite of Abernathy stew, then we trudged a few steps. That wonky feeling of being stretched out didn't set in. I smiled at Carmen, then we all nodded to each other and ran like hell toward the house.

I'm not sure why, but as we approached the house, my eyes were glued to the bottom left window closest to the door. The closer we got, the less glare there was on the window. I could just make out a figure standing there, behind the shattered glass. A glimpse of a brown dress and a faded mask. Then we reached the front yard and…

We stopped short when the scenery changed once again. There was no longer a white house in front of us. There were no snowy trees. There wasn't snow at all, actually. Instead, we stood on dark green grass with thick, deep hedges reaching up far beyond our heads. We turned around in circles, taking it in. I ran my hand through the thick, piney-like texture of the yew hedges. They were so dense you couldn't even try to see through them. They must have been twenty feet tall.

"A hedge maze," I said, looking up toward the grim sky. I felt my heart in my throat. "That's nice."

For once, Lulu was at a loss for words. Instead, she stood with her hand gripped around that rod. Little dots of perspiration around her ears were the only sign that she was rattled.

Carmen took Horatio out of her pocket and held him tight. Then she closed her eyes and raised her head. She stayed that way for a moment, then opened her eyes again.

"I don't think we're still in that yard, Immy," she said. "Actually, I don't think we're really anywhere."

"What does that mean?" asked Lulu. She looked ready to smack anything that came around the corner.

"We're in a world created entirely by her magic," I said, stomping my jittery feet. "So, what does this mean? Let's see… well…we could be frigging anywhere, couldn't we? We could be in a closet that she hexed, or sitting in a mason jar on her dresser. This is an old-timey witch ass-kicking. It's almost awe-inspiring how doomed we are."

The longer we made fools of ourselves by fumbling to get to the Thistle Witch's front door, the more I realized that we were not ready for this. She was more powerful than the trinkets, stew, and salt we threw at her. We needed something stronger to get the job done. Or perhaps needed to *be* stronger. How to accomplish that, though, was a difficult question to answer.

"Getting turned into a demon by the Devil must have been like eating her Wheaties," said Carmen.

There was nothing to do but navigate the maze and find our way out, if that was even possible. We weaved around, turning here and there. Carmen held Horatio as she walked, closing her eyes when we got to a new turn or dead end. Then she petted him and whispered. He leaned in and whispered something back in his chirpy voice.

"This way," said Carmen, opening her eyes and heading to the left.

It went on that way for a long time—Carmen got Horatio's advice about which way to go, then we followed it, hoping for the best.

"Are we going toward the center of the maze or the exit, Carmen?" I asked, following as best as I could. I now carried both the chainsaw and the shotgun. It made it hard to keep up with a woman following the directions of an eager little devil.

"I'm not sure, Immy," said Carmen, picking up the pace. We looked a little demented, zooming around that dark hedge maze. But, looking back, we were more hexed than demented. "I'm going where Horatio thinks we need to be."

"He better think we need to be at home with a stiff drink," I said.

"What happens if we go to the center of the maze?" asked Lulu, huffing.

"Usually, there's a minotaur waiting to kill you," I said. "Hector would love the hell out of this."

"That's all right," said Lulu, smiling at her weapon. "I have experience with minotaurs."

I was caught off guard when Carmen stopped in front of us. It was all I could do to keep from plowing into her. I nearly dropped the chainsaw and gun.

"What the hell?" I asked, steadying myself.

"Look," said Carmen, pointing ahead.

A little girl in a drab, dirty dress poked her head around the corner, then disappeared again.

"Oh, no," said Lulu, whispering. "Not a little kid!"

"At least it's not an evil goblin," I said.

"Are you kidding?" asked Lulu, backing up. "In horror movies, kids are bad. They're always poking out from behind corners and fitting in places they shouldn't be able to fit. And then they reach out and grab you right before the scene changes."

"We need to keep it together," I said. That was pretty funny, coming from me. "This isn't a horror movie. We can handle this, remember?"

"Screw your pep talk," Lulu said, sweating. "I'm not going near that freaky kid."

But Carmen had already decided for us. She walked slowly toward the corner where the girl had disappeared. We reached out to pull her back to us, but she was already out of reach. She turned the corner, and that was it. We had no choice but to follow.

"Just great," whispered Lulu.

Who marches around the corner in a hexed hedge maze? That *had* to be some Otherworldly Investigations rule. And I knew another rule was never to split up when monstrous, magical things were out to get you.

Lulu and I took shaky steps as we approached the turn. Why wasn't Carmen saying anything? What was going on?

I felt a surge of adrenaline as we turned the corner and almost rammed right into both Carmen and the child.

"Son of a bitch!" said Lulu. She jumped at the sight of the girl just standing there, calmly staring. She looked like she could have played one of the poorer Jane Austen characters with her long, dirty muslin dress, tied just below the chest with a frayed blue ribbon. Her messy hair was covered with a faded white cap.

"This is Nancy," said Carmen, resting her hand on the girl's shoulder.

"Hello, Nancy," I said, looking into her deep blue eyes.

"Hello, miss," said the girl, in her thick British accent.

"Sweetie, what are you doing here?" asked Lulu. Lulu must have decided this girl wasn't a threat because she didn't amble toward us like that chick from *The Ring*.

"My sister put me here," said Nancy. "She put us all here."

Nancy pointed behind us. I held my breath when children walked out from behind corners. Some waved at us, while others didn't even bother to look over. They wandered through the maze and then disappeared behind various hedges.

"Your sister?" I asked.

Nancy nodded. "The Thistle Witch. She put us in here one by one when we made her mad. Those of us she didn't kill, anyway."

The three of us looked at each other. I could tell Lulu and Carmen felt the same combination of foreboding and sadness that surged through me. It felt like a cold trickle shooting through the body.

"How did you make her mad?" asked Carmen, bending down to Nancy.

The little girl scrunched her face as she tried to think. "It's hard to remember," she said. "It was such an awfully long time ago. But I think she got cross when I cried."

"Cried?" asked Lulu.

"Yes," said Nancy, looking off into the distance like she was remembering another life. "I cried when she killed mummy. She didn't like that. She didn't like that I was upset with her. That made her very cross."

On any normal day, hearing a tiny girl stuck in a hedge maze recount a tale of matricide would have been more than enough to make me sink into a chair, kick up my feet, and begin a diatribe about how the world was a festering alley dumpster of smoking garbage. But not that day. Something about facing my first monster in a long time had me off my game. I was just scared. Scared, damn it. And there was no other way to put it.

That old feeling that had been in me since Carmen's song first faltered came to a crescendo. We were not ready to face the Thistle Witch. Or at least, I was now thoroughly convinced that *I* wasn't ready.

I leaned back against the maze, oblivious to what was going on around me. All I knew was the ringing in my ears and the feeling of my heart pumping in my face. I was cold. I was hot. I was tired. I was wired. And then when the ringing in my ears subsided, I opened my eyes and realized that both Lulu and Carmen were there, steadying me. By the expressions on their faces, I had definitely startled them.

Nancy stared up at me.

"You had better retreat with your friend there," said Nancy, pointing at me. "She is like a few of my brothers and sisters. Magic makes her afraid."

"No, it doesn't," said Lulu, glancing at me. "She *is* magic."

"That may be," said Nancy. "But she is afraid, nonetheless. And she cannot face my sister in a state of such disarray."

Carmen put her arm around me. There was fear and concern in her eyes.

"She's right," I said, trying to catch my breath. "We're not ready. Or I guess *I'm* not ready. Can't you feel it? We're not strong enough yet. We're not prepared. She'll eat us alive."

"I know," said Carmen, frowning. "I knew it the moment I felt that emptiness at Eliza's. I hoped it was me being paranoid."

"Then let's get the hell out of here until we figure out another plan," said Lulu.

We turned to leave, but then Carmen stopped. She reached out for Nancy's hand.

"Come with us, Nancy," said Carmen. "We can get you and your siblings out."

Nancy stepped back with a sad look on her face.

"Get out to where?" asked Nancy. "I've been in here for so long now, where would I go? Everyone I ever knew or loved has been dead for so long that even their grandchildren are forgotten."

Her words slid through me like a somber tune that you can't shake.

"But I hope you find a way out," said Nancy, walking away. Then she stopped and looked back at us. "Oh, and mind the monster at the center of the maze. He's out of sorts most of the time."

Then as quickly as she had appeared, Nancy was gone.

"Good grief," said Lulu. "Is this one hell of a long day, or is it just me?"

"It's not just you," I said, glancing around. My feet were firm on the ground again, and I was able to take deep breaths without feeling cold. I felt fairly confident that I was ready for the next thing to kick us in the ass.

"Are we closer to the center or exit of the maze?" asked Lulu.

"Fabulous question," I said. "Carmen, any ideas?"

Carmen lifted Horatio and whispered to him.

"This way!" said Carmen.

We turned a couple of dark corners and then stopped dead. Sitting in the shadows, staring right up at us, was the angriest goblin I had ever seen. He had black eyes and rough, sunken skin the color of green mucus. When he saw us, he began grinding his teeth and laughing.

"I was kidding about the whole goblin in the maze thing," I said.

The goblin slowly got up. We hesitated to do anything. He looked pissed off, but most goblins usually did, so we wanted to wait for him to show his true colors before starting up the chainsaw. He ambled toward us.

"Maybe he's not so bad," said Carmen. "Are you, sweetie?"

The goblin smiled at Carmen, then whipped a switchblade out of his pocket and flicked it open.

"Holy shit," said Lulu, backing up. "Freaky bastard."

"Fried eggs in front of us," said Carmen, shouting. "Give me my chainsaw!"

I simultaneously gave Carmen the 038 Magnum and fired my gun. But he plowed into me as I shot it, so I only shot at the sky. The goblin aimed right for Lulu, knocking her down. Carmen yelled as she tried to pull the chainsaw over to start it.

The goblin was on Lulu, nothing but claws and teeth. He tried to grab hold and bite her. But she knocked him in the throat with her rod. She gave a good beating for a first-time monster hunter. You usually didn't see that kind of pummeling in a novice.

I walked over with a horseshoe and pressed it against the back of the goblin's head. He howled as the shoe burnt his rawhide skin.

Then he flew off Lulu and latched onto me, digging his teeth into my ankle. I was about to pelt him across the head again when Carmen swooped in with her chainsaw. There was a coarse buzzing sound of chain hitting bone, and then…well…that was the end of that.

Of course, using a chainsaw meant that blood splattered everywhere. It was all over the grass, hedges, and us.

"That's got to be about the grossest choice of weapon," said Lulu, looking at herself.

"Isn't it great?" asked Carmen.

"Where was the warning, Horatio?" I asked. I shook my finger at the blood-spattered pocket demon on Carmen's shoulder. "Thanks a lot."

"He must have thought we should do some monster hunting while we're here," said Carmen.

"How practical of him," I said, shoving the horseshoe back in my bag.

"You're bringing another demon next time," said Lulu, wiping the blood off her face. "You hear that, little guy? Don't make that cute face at me. You're on my list."

"There has to be a next time first," I said. Feeling as decisive as I could with a cloud of panic swirling around in me, I grabbed for the salt. Carmen held her saw steady as I coated the chain with it.

"What are you doing?" asked Lulu.

Carmen revved the saw and nodded at me with an approving grin.

"Trust me," I said. "I saw this on an episode of *The Simpsons* once."

It only took a moment for the yew branches to start flying. Carmen smiled as she cut a hole big enough for us to walk through. We followed her as she cut bush after bush, heading toward what we could only imagine was the outer edge of the maze.

"Isn't this going to piss her off?" Lulu shouted over the chainsaw noise.

"I hope so," I said. "If she doesn't want her maze destroyed, I guess she'll just have to beam us out."

Almost as an answer to my statement, thunder cracked above us. But Carmen didn't falter in her task. Ignoring the storm over our heads, she continued to cut through the hedges. And she didn't stop when the rain began to fall.

Carmen nudged a fussy yew branch free, and we walked through the hole…

The dizziness of being transported from place to place via magic was starting to feel a little too familiar. There we were, at the end of the driveway once again. Carmen's chainsaw was still running, and its harsh echo against the snowy mounds and naked trees left me feeling exposed. Carmen turned her chainsaw off and set it on the ground. The familiar creaking of the mailbox greeted us yet again.

But we didn't comment on how we had escaped or lament those poor children still trapped in the maze. We didn't stand in awe of the magic that allowed our adversary to protect herself and make us look like fools. Instead, we stood there, completely silent. Down the long driveway, sitting right near the house, was a blue heeler, watching us. It almost seemed fake, the way it sat so still in the snow.

Then I found myself taking a step forward. Carmen grabbed my arm. I blinked a couple of times and focused on the dog.

The evergreen bushes near the house sprouted thick, tangled shoots. They wound through the snow and up toward the dog. The dog remained where it was, unconcerned by the development.

I mumbled under my breath, and the weeds tightened around the dog's feet. Then they wound around its legs. Finally, the dog stood up. She fixed her gaze on me and growled. The second the noise left her throat, the weeds I had bound her with curled up and fell away.

Now free of my spell, the dog stood there, growling and baring her teeth at me. Sure, I knew the Thistle Witch wasn't like that jerk at the casino. I knew she'd be able to shrug off my vines with little effort. And I knew, for all my trouble, I'd be sick later. But for some reason, when I saw her standing there, I was filled with the need to show her that I was not afraid, even though fear was a light term for the terror that pulsed through me.

"We better go, Immy," whispered Carmen. "We need to think of something else."

There were a lot of things I wanted to say to that dog. She wasn't growling anymore. She just stood there, waiting and watching. I felt compelled to speak to her. I didn't want her to think she'd fazed us.

"It's been fun," I shouted to her, as Carmen ushered me away. I looked at Carmen's worried face. I could almost see her brain trying to plan our next move.

When I looked back to the yard, the dog was gone.

We walked down the snow-packed gravel road, headed toward the car. We all felt too tired and spellbound to talk. I stared at my feet, wondering what the answer to all of this was. We had fought a lot of magical creatures, but their magic was usually as pathetic as ours. I didn't want to admit that Chace was right, but I also didn't know what we were going to do. What could you say about a witch who could wallop you without even lifting a finger?

As my mind drifted, my eyes focused on something dotting the cold, white road. As we walked, the copper drops gave way to a thin stream stained on the hardened snow. Then we ran. As we came up to the car, Carmen pointed into the trees. But I had already seen them. It was hard not to. When Lulu spotted them, she looked away. It was a family, hanging in the tall oaks. To put it mildly, they were not whole.

Carmen held Lulu around the shoulders, comforting her in that way that only Carmen could. They didn't look at the trees. In fact, they both tried hard *not* to look at the trees, like any normal person would. But not me. I stared, thinking of what the Thistle Witch had done to her own parents, to the doctor and assistant, to the relatives of Mary Smith, to her own siblings, and to my friends. I stared until the bodies seemed to flicker, and then suddenly they were gone, along with the blood on the road.

"What does it mean?" asked Lulu.

"The Thistle Witch has killed again," said Carmen, quietly.

She took Horatio out of her pocket and nestled him. Lulu and

Carmen stood there, staring at me. They stared at me while I stared at the empty trees that swayed in the wind, shaking their branches in the cold air, like they were still trying to free themselves from the remnants of a dirty spell.

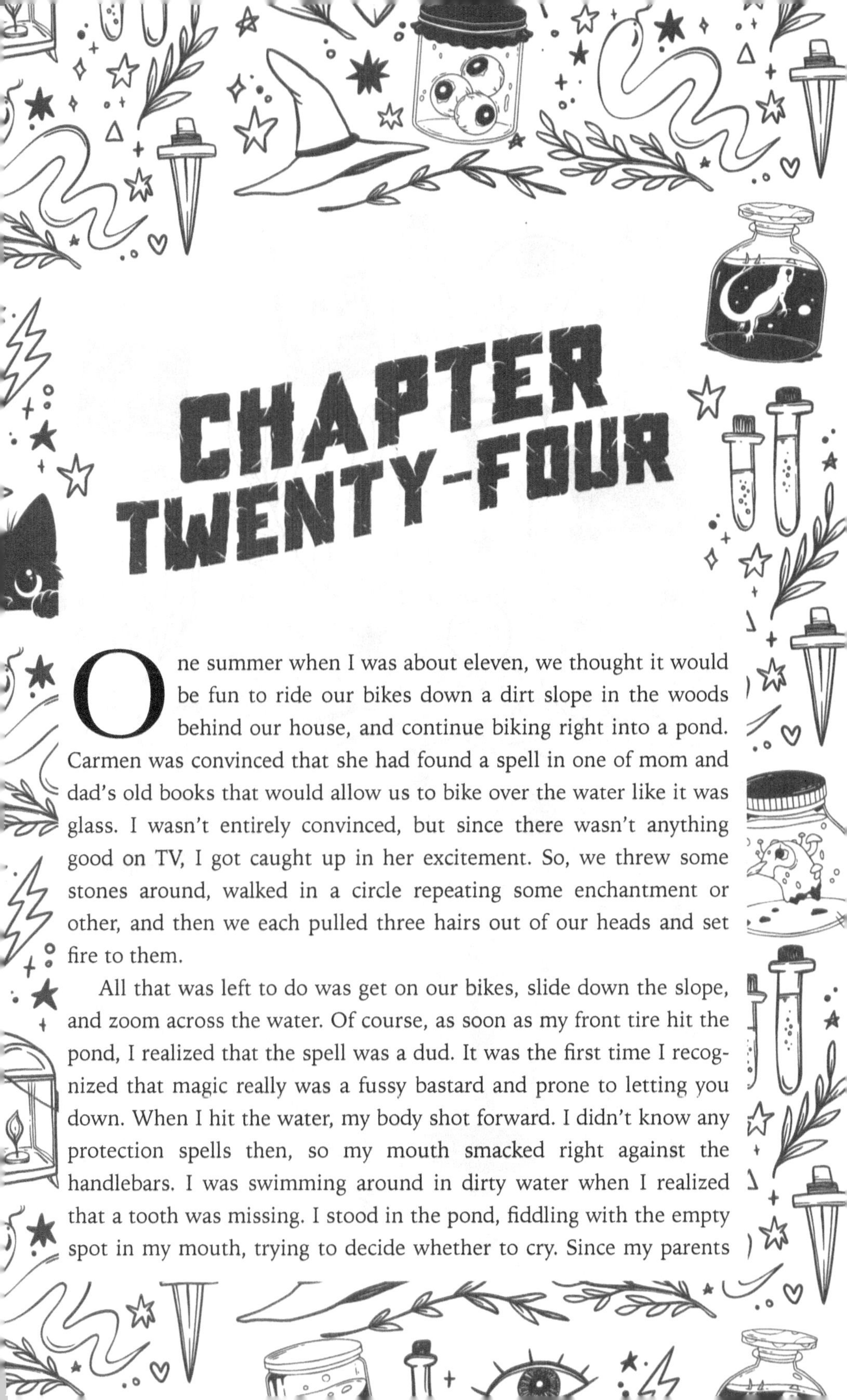

CHAPTER TWENTY-FOUR

One summer when I was about eleven, we thought it would be fun to ride our bikes down a dirt slope in the woods behind our house, and continue biking right into a pond. Carmen was convinced that she had found a spell in one of mom and dad's old books that would allow us to bike over the water like it was glass. I wasn't entirely convinced, but since there wasn't anything good on TV, I got caught up in her excitement. So, we threw some stones around, walked in a circle repeating some enchantment or other, and then we each pulled three hairs out of our heads and set fire to them.

All that was left to do was get on our bikes, slide down the slope, and zoom across the water. Of course, as soon as my front tire hit the pond, I realized that the spell was a dud. It was the first time I recognized that magic really was a fussy bastard and prone to letting you down. When I hit the water, my body shot forward. I didn't know any protection spells then, so my mouth smacked right against the handlebars. I was swimming around in dirty water when I realized that a tooth was missing. I stood in the pond, fiddling with the empty spot in my mouth, trying to decide whether to cry. Since my parents were up at the house, and since it was only a baby tooth, there didn't seem to be much point. But I did curse under my breath at my swollen, split lip.

Carmen had been behind me on her bike, and seeing me face plant into the water, she instead glided smoothly off toward the bank of the pond. She looked like a little cherub sitting on her bike with Barnaby on her shoulder. Her eyes were wide, both afraid that I was hurt, and afraid that she'd get blamed if I was.

Of course, I had willingly gone along with the scheme, so nobody really blamed Carmen. Plus, I was older and should have known better. My parents didn't say much, except my dad, who was impressed by my bruised lip.

"That's a beauty of a shiner," he said, giving me a thumbs up.

That reaction was fine with me. I was never big on feelings. Like a good homegrown Minnesotan, I had learned that feelings and emotions were things that you squished down inside yourself. You weren't supposed to let them come to the surface because then you might *make a scene*. And nobody ever wanted to *make a scene*.

Unfortunately, this did not hold true when Carmen was born. Maybe she was outside taming Horatio when the memo was sent, but Carmen seemed completely unaware that feelings were things you just weren't supposed to have. From her very first meltdown over nap time, it was clear that Carmen not only *had* feelings, but she also wanted to *discuss* those feelings. And horror of horrors, as Carmen grew up, my family realized that Carmen wanted to discuss *our* feelings too.

I hoped that it was a passing fad, but when the Unicorn of Safety was introduced, I knew we were in uncharted territory. I didn't want to tell everyone how I felt when Carmen accidentally liquefied all of my Barney toys into a big plush mess when an early spell of hers backfired. And I didn't think it was important to discuss how I felt when my face smashed into those handlebars. But it became clear that warm June morning that Carmen had no plans to let it go.

I was in my room with a cold pack on my mouth when she first came in on tiptoes. She held a big plate in her little hands. Horatio sat on the plate, and when they had my attention, the little pocket demon pulled a napkin away to reveal two pieces of cinnamon sugar toast. Granted, the toast looked good, but my mouth was too sore to eat. I declined.

That made things even worse. Carmen not only had the guilt of being indirectly involved in my accident, but she also had the weight of having her peace offering declined. She ran from the room and came back moments later with a large pickle. I liked pickles, everyone knew that. But it was another thing I had to eat, so I shook my head.

I should have taken the damn pickle. Carmen's suffering was really at a fever pitch. I heard her run into her room. A half-hour later, she returned with a homemade card. Her face was squished up with worried anticipation over how I would react. I didn't think I could stand another second of childhood tension and sticky, marker-stained fingers. I took the card.

"Do you like it?" she asked in her little kid's voice.

"I love it!" I said, as enthusiastically as I could.

"Really?" she asked.

"Really!" I said. I smiled my biggest, fakest smile. My lip was on fire. But I mustered up my best acting skills because I didn't want Carmen to keep coming back.

"Do you like the colors?" she asked.

"I love them!" I said. And then to really sell it, I added, "The purple is great!"

I only ever got purple birthday cards after that.

Carmen grinned. She thought that accepting her gift meant that I was now open to a conversation about feelings. I was *not* open to a conversation about feelings. But somehow or another the Unicorn of Safety was suddenly in her hands. Before I could escape to the bathroom to take a three-hour shower, Carmen gently placed the unicorn on my lap. Her tiny fingers could barely hold it.

"Now," she said, smiling. "How did today make you feel?"

On a side note, that spell we performed to bike across water had the side effect of making our hair grow at three times the normal speed. Every week that summer, we had to sit and let my mom cut our hair in the kitchen. I didn't like to show those pictures to anyone. Mullets. Female mullets.

Growing up, I learned from books in our library that Carmen's emotional understanding had once been a common skill among certain witches.

Being an excellent cobbler was also a common skill among witches back in the day, I used to think, as I flipped through pages in those old books. *Why couldn't she have that skill instead? I'd love homemade shoes.*

For all my complaining, I knew Carmen's transformation of our family was a good thing. We went from people who never talked about anything, to a hugging clan that had family meeting nights. We also had family game nights, which usually led to another family meeting about whether someone used magic to make an ace appear.

It was hard to stay in a bad mood when Carmen came at you with her soothing voice and thoughtful homemade gifts. Actually, about the only one Carmen never changed was Ludwig. Instead, he always clawed at her hands while she cradled him and sang lullabies.

When we got home after sparring with the Thistle Witch, it was obvious by my prolonged silence that I was troubled by our encounter. I threw myself onto the couch and hoped that the answer to the problem of the Thistle Witch was located somewhere in the cobwebs on the parlor chandelier.

The house was a rush of activity around me. Carmen and Lulu texted my parents about our situation, then scurried to our library for spell books that my parents thought might help. There was also an impromptu self-defense lesson, and somehow in all the chaos, a calming face mask was placed on me. It didn't fit right, and the eye slits were on my cheeks. Still, I didn't move.

Carmen and Lulu didn't seem too rattled after meeting the Thistle Witch. Actually, they appeared optimistic. They sat in the dining room, planning how to take her on again.

"I think that weakening spell is the way to go," said Lulu, after Carmen explained it.

"Agreed," said Carmen. "It'll really give her a taste of our medicine."

Taking action to solve a problem was the thing *I* was supposed to be good at. Everyone knew that Carmen was the more magical sibling. I didn't have a problem with that. She knew the recipes for spells, hexes, curses, etc. And she also knew about famous magical figures and monsters. She was the studious one. The nerd. That's what she enjoyed, and that was another aspect of her character that everyone liked. I, on the other hand, was the take-action type. The one who made the plan. The one who clubbed things that needed clubbing. I would have been great in a 1950s action movie. After all, I already had the fake leather jacket.

After getting an epic beat down by a powerful witch, I should have *done something*. But I couldn't, somehow. Instead, I lounged on the couch, examining the inside of that pungent face mask, wondering what the hell was wrong with me. If I wasn't the take-action kind anymore, then what was I? Did I really want to be that, anyway? After all, I didn't want to be in Otherworldly Investigations, and I didn't want to be a witch. Or did I?

Of course, I knew that it didn't really matter what I wanted to be just then. Because a witch was after us, damn it. So, I had no choice but to be a witch. But still, I thought everything would have been easier if I could have been the woman I was at twenty-six, twenty-seven, or twenty-eight. How could I find my way back to that person, when I didn't even know what road had led me away from her?

Somehow or another, I ended up in the dining room with Carmen and Lulu. The face mask had been removed and my face had been washed. My cheeks felt hot. Suddenly, there was a sour cream and raisin pie in front of me, a treat usually reserved for my birthday.

Very fishy.

"Your favorite," said Carmen, in her chiming voice. "Have a big slice."

Lulu didn't need to be asked twice.

"It's good," she said. "My grandma used to make this all the time. Nobody does anymore."

I knew what Carmen was up to. Just like when we were kids, this was her way of opening me up. Her way of getting me to explain what was wrong and how I felt about my moment of panic earlier.

No way, sister, I thought. *Not happening.*

I scanned the room. I knew the Unicorn of Safety was lurking nearby.

"It's Immy's favorite pie," Carmen repeated. She looked at me, smiling. She was so kind. So understanding. A person you could really talk to.

Nope.

I took a bite. It *was* my favorite pie, but the Thistle Witch felt like a problem that even the magical combination of custard, raisins, and meringue couldn't solve.

"You don't like it," said Carmen, flatly.

"I like it," I said, with equal flatness.

"You don't seem like you like it," said Carmen.

"I promise I like it," I said.

Carmen's nose twitched.

"I used too many raisins," she said.

"You can't have too many raisins," I said.

"Are you hitting stems?" asked Carmen. "I know I checked for stems."

"There aren't any stems," I said.

"Then why don't you like it?" asked Carmen.

"I do like it," I said.

Lulu observed us the way scientists study animals to understand their social structures.

"You don't have to say you like it," said Carmen.

"I *do* freaking like it," I said, eating a huge bite to show her I liked it.

Seeing that I was not going to ease into this conversation, Carmen decided to do what no good Midwesterner *ever* did. She decided to look me straight in the eye and bring up the subject directly.

"Do you want to talk about it?" she asked.

"No," I said, talking with my mouth full.

"Are you sure?" she asked, with a shaky voice.

"No," I said.

"No…as in, you're not sure?" asked Carmen, confused.

"This is like tennis," said Lulu, amused.

"Why won't you tell me what's wrong?" asked Carmen.

"Why?" I asked. "You *know* what's wrong."

"Do you need the Unicorn of Safety?" asked Carmen.

"No," I said, a little louder than I intended.

"I'm afraid if we don't talk about it, you'll up and leave again," said Carmen, tears forming in her large eyes. She slid away from the table, pulled the unicorn from where it had been hiding on her lap, and put it down next to my pie.

Shit, I thought. *Now we have to talk about it.*

"I was fairly pathetic today, wasn't I?" I asked. I pulled the unicorn toward me in a defeated huff.

Lulu and Carmen raised their voices in protest, but I cut them off.

"I acted like a total newbie," I said. I slid my pie away. I just couldn't enjoy it. "Nancy said I was afraid of magic, and boy was she right. I used to be confident. What happened? I've never been shaky and unsure like that before. I never really wanted to be a witch, but magic never made me nervous. Ever since Chace, something inside me changed. Now, magic is something that I don't trust. I've been out of this thing so long that now it scares me. That's just the cherry on top of this whole vomit-filled milkshake, isn't it?"

"Nice visual," said Lulu, pushing her pie away.

"A witch who's afraid of witchcraft," I said, shaking my head in bitterness. "And not only that, but a witch who's afraid of witchcraft when we need to be more powerful to face a powerful witch. What a shitshow."

"You're being too hard on yourself," said Lulu, rapping her nails on the table.

"Am I?" I asked. "I look in the mirror, and I don't know who I am now."

"But people are constantly changing, Immy," said Carmen. "You can't expect to be the same person you were four years ago."

"I know that," I said. "But I kind of thought I would, you know, get better with age. Like a fine wine. But that sure was juvenile thinking. I'm more like that weird old juice at the back of the fridge with the slimy aftertaste."

They were both quiet for a moment.

"Balsamic vinegar gets better with age," said Lulu.

"And Gouda cheese," said Carmen.

"You guys are in better places than you were four years ago, aren't you?" I asked.

Carmen nodded. "My spell for transporting myself down to the guest bathroom is much better than four years ago. I got to the linen closet last month."

"Four years ago, I still hung out with people who acted like I was a science experiment for not wanting to drink," said Lulu. "So, I'm doing good."

"Now you're hanging out with us," I said. "Poor bastard."

"And you think you're just going downhill?" asked Lulu. "That's garbage."

"Is it?" I asked. "I'm not brave like I was then. Not at all."

Carmen put her hand on mine. "But Immy, you're the one who convinced us to go face the Thistle Witch today. You took charge of making the stew. You led us down the grove. You tried to figure out a way to get up the driveway. And when we were in that maze, you thought of the way out."

"Plus, you tried to vine her up," said Lulu. "That seems brave to me."

I shrugged. "You guys would have done all that without me," I said. "I just did it because we had no choice."

"But Immy," said Carmen, coaxing. "If that isn't being brave, then what is?"

"I was scared the whole time," I said. "I never used to be scared."

Carmen patted my hand and smiled. "That's just because you were young and stupid then, and didn't think about your mortality."

"Comforting," I said, pulling my hand away slowly.

"People have setbacks all their lives," said Lulu. "You don't just gradually have fewer and fewer problems until you're elderly. I've had so many setbacks. The second time I told myself that I was done drinking, I knew in my heart that I was still playing games. And a couple of days later, I went to a party I knew I shouldn't go to. I woke up later crying on somebody's rocking chair on their front porch. It was December and freezing in there. I was at a totally different party than the one I started at. I didn't know anybody, and I just sat there in the cold, knowing that something had to change. But do you think knowing that made all my problems go away, or made them suddenly easy to solve? Take it from me, being brave doesn't mean— *poof*—your problems are gone. It means facing your problems despite the fear that's still there. And that's just what you did today."

"That was beautiful, Lulu," said Carmen, leaning over to refill Lulu's coffee.

Lulu smiled. "What did I say? I've got the emotional intelligence of someone far beyond my years."

I took a deep breath, sighed, and pulled the pie toward me. Carmen seemed thrilled about my decision to eat.

"What?" asked Lulu.

"We've made a breakthrough with Immy," said Carmen. "I've been studying her for years now, and she's not exactly the most forthright with her feelings. I've learned to spot little details in her actions that reflect how she's feeling."

"Jesus," I said, taking a bite.

"See that?" Carmen asked Lulu. "Right there. When Immy is too nervous and bound up in her feelings, she just can't eat. Even foods she really loves. That's why I made the pie. I wanted to see how upset she was after today's events. Now that she's eating again, it signals that she's in more of a peaceful place emotionally. She's trying to look on the brighter side."

I had never heard my actions explained in such an astute, succinct way.

"I'd tell you to get another hobby," I said. "But you already have two hundred."

"Is that true?" asked Lulu.

"Of course," said Carmen. "Ask her."

They both stared at me, waiting for an answer. I took another bite and shook my head.

"You weird bastards," I said. "Let me eat my pie."

"Told you," said Carmen, smiling.

"I'm not happy about the way I am now or anything," I said. "But I guess maybe I should cut myself some slack. I'm trying."

As I finished my dessert, Carmen opened a book and showed me a promising spell she thought we might use to try to weaken the Thistle Witch's powers.

"Wait," Lulu said. "There's just one thing that I need to know."

"What?" asked Carmen.

"What the hell is a Unicorn of Safety?"

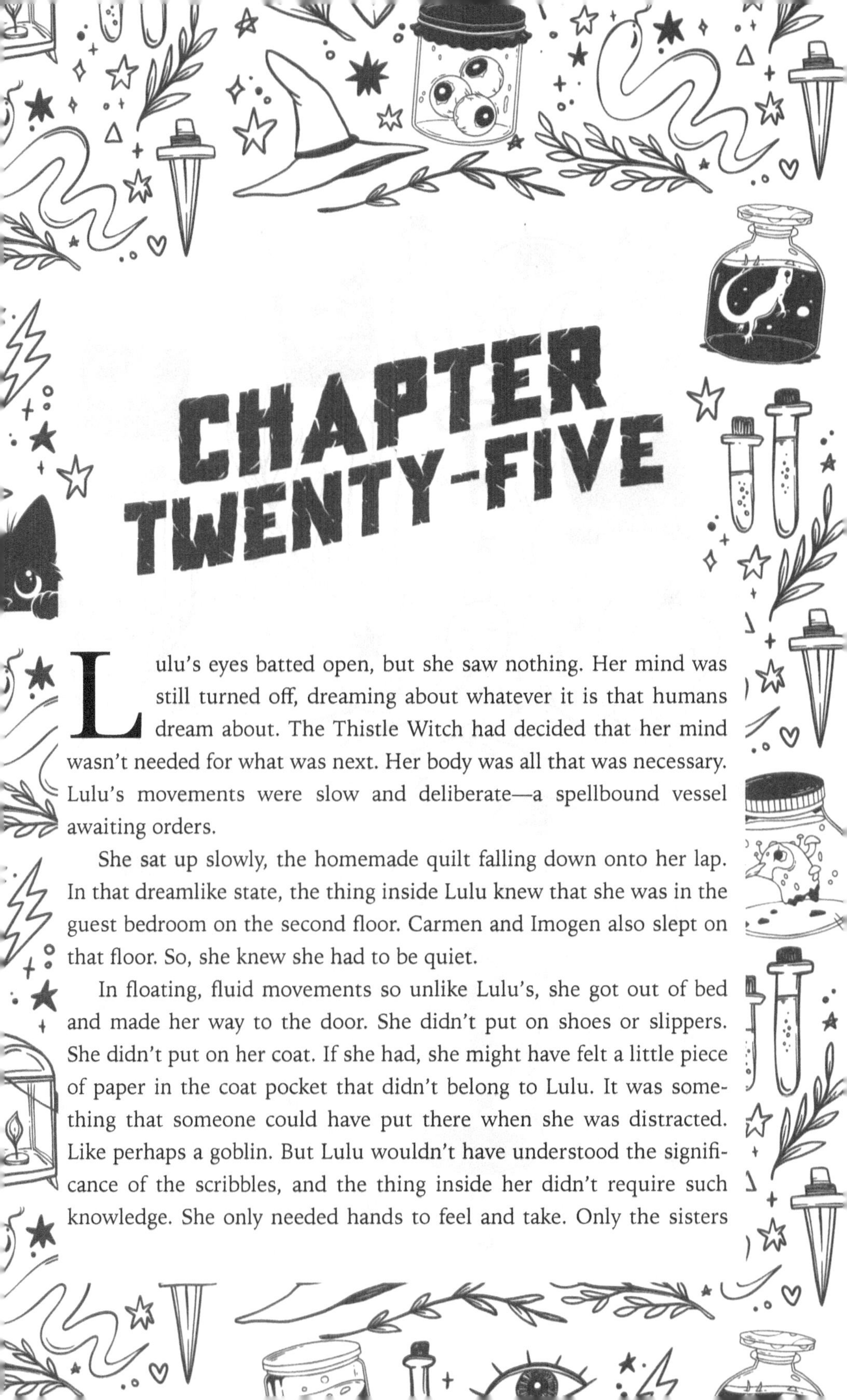

CHAPTER TWENTY-FIVE

Lulu's eyes batted open, but she saw nothing. Her mind was still turned off, dreaming about whatever it is that humans dream about. The Thistle Witch had decided that her mind wasn't needed for what was next. Her body was all that was necessary. Lulu's movements were slow and deliberate—a spellbound vessel awaiting orders.

She sat up slowly, the homemade quilt falling down onto her lap. In that dreamlike state, the thing inside Lulu knew that she was in the guest bedroom on the second floor. Carmen and Imogen also slept on that floor. So, she knew she had to be quiet.

In floating, fluid movements so unlike Lulu's, she got out of bed and made her way to the door. She didn't put on shoes or slippers. She didn't put on her coat. If she had, she might have felt a little piece of paper in the coat pocket that didn't belong to Lulu. It was some-thing that someone could have put there when she was distracted. Like perhaps a goblin. But Lulu wouldn't have understood the signifi-cance of the scribbles, and the thing inside her didn't require such knowledge. She only needed hands to feel and take. Only the sisters would have understood what that small piece of paper meant, and the Thistle Witch didn't want them to wake up quite yet.

Lulu crept down the hall. Her bare feet didn't make a sound on the old hardwood floors that were usually so prone to squeaking. From every dark corner, the little devils gaped, afraid to leave their sheltered places, afraid the infiltrating magic might somehow hurt them.

How did she get in? they thought, pulling the shadows tight around them like blankets. *This has never happened before. Evil magic should not be able to get in! It is protected.*

They squished themselves down smaller, knowing that even their combined magic was nothing against the masked woman's power.

As Lulu floated down the steps, Norma Shearer watched from above, hidden in the shadows atop the old grandfather clock. Braver than the rest, she hissed at the infiltration of dark magic, and the way it used her mother's friend. But the sounds from Carmen's familiar elicited no reaction from Lulu, who was already down at the bottom of the stairs. Feeling confident that the magic must not be able to harm them directly, Norma jumped as soundlessly as she could from her perch. Then she hung low to the ground as she scrambled down the hall to her mother's room. Buster Keaton was already there, mewing and pawing at Carmen's door.

Every drawer in the living room and kitchen was open. Lulu skulked from cabinet to cabinet, reaching in and feeling around. Her eyes stared straight ahead, as if the whole world was a white sheet that revealed nothing. She even opened a rusty candy tin, but all it held were old Canadian and British coins. Lulu backed away from the cabinets and stood listless in the center of the kitchen.

She blinked as the orders came in like an avalanche of white noise. Then she floated over to the sink and opened the flour tin, the sugar tin, and the pancake mix tin. She stuck her hand inside each, reaching around. Then in a shudder, she stopped, and made her way with floured hands over to a large jar sitting by a stack of take-out menus. It was filled to the brim with salt.

The white noise filled her head again as she plunged her hand into the jar and felt around. She did not spill a grain of salt as she pulled an old iron skeleton key out of the jar. She wrapped her long fingers around the key and held it tight. Her hands began to shake, and the reverberations spread throughout her whole body. She shook until her nose bled. Little drops ran down her lips. Then, at last, the shaking subsided. Lulu wavered back and forth. Then opened her hands again. Her palm was red and raw, and she held two identical keys. She stared off, waiting for a sign of what to do. Finally, she nodded and slipped one key into the pocket of her pajama pants. Then with a careful touch, she slipped the other key into the jar of salt, and set it back where she had found it.

There wasn't a squeak or a breath as Lulu slid out of the kitchen and into the hallway. The front door unlocked with a little click, and in a second, the cold nighttime swallowed Lulu up, along with the thing inside of her.

She doesn't hear us, Norma said to Buster Keaton. They were still outside Carmen's room, clawing with frantic paws at the old walnut door. *But she hears our mews outside, even when we're up in the darkest corner of the attic.*

And she heard me all the way from that little apartment, said Buster Keaton. *When I was meowing to come home. She is getting stronger. She would hear us outside her door.*

Norma and Buster hissed and growled in frustration.

This door is never locked, they said.

The little devils poked their heads out of their hiding places and blinked their beady eyes. One by one, each of them crawled carefully out to the familiars, whose shadows on the wall began to twist and turn and stretch into forms that were not very cat-like at all. The little devils gathered into a heap, and the familiars stepped on top of them, using them as a ladder. Up and up, they pushed the familiars, until the cats who were no longer cats reached the keyhole. They twisted and turned and pushed until they streamed through the tiny keyhole like black water, and fell like mist onto Carmen's floor.

As the mist settled on the warm bedroom floor, the two orange familiars once again sat there, peering up at Carmen's bed. Not missing a beat, they sprang up to her pillow.

She is still asleep, said Norma, pawing gently at her mother's nose. Carmen's face twitched at the feeling of the furry paw, but her eyes remained closed. Her breathing was soft and restful.

This is not sleep, said Buster. *It is that woman's spell.*

The familiars mewed and pawed, ruffling Carmen's hair. But still, she did not wake up.

We must wake her up, said Norma. *Before that woman uses Lulu for her wicked plans.*

But how can our magic counteract hers? asked Buster.

Just then, sparks shot through Carmen's door. The cats watched as the knob finally turned, and more than a dozen little devils streamed in, ready to help the mother who doted on them.

If we can't wake mother, asked Norma, *who can?*

Lulu's feet were red and shiny as she took careful steps in the snow. As she walked closer to the edge of the property, she became aware that the Thistle Witch stood there, just outside the line of protective stones that guarded the yard. The woman's dress blew in the chilly winter wind, but otherwise, she was immobile. The closer Lulu got to the witch, the louder the white noise in her mind became.

The Thistle Witch didn't make a sound, and neither did Lulu. The scent of cloves and dirt mingled when they came near each other. Then Lulu reached out her hand. The Thistle Witch took a thin yellow ribbon out of her dress pocket and placed it in Lulu's palm.

Then the Thistle Witch whispered something that was lost on the breeze. She motioned for Lulu to hold out her arm. Lulu did so, and suddenly the witch had a small lighter. The little flame flickered in the night. She held it under Lulu's arm, closer and closer to the skin. But Lulu didn't react, even when the flame rested against her, even when her skin burned. The witch nodded and pulled the lighter away.

Then the witch pointed back behind the Abernathy home, and Lulu nodded. As Lulu turned and made her way through the deep snow to the back of the Abernathy property, the Thistle Witch turned and paced up and down the road, waiting. When she passed under a streetlight, the blue heeler's tongue sprawled out of her mouth in satisfaction. If she wasn't going to be a good dog, then at least she could enjoy some suffering.

Lulu's body shivered in tight spasms as she ambled in a daze toward the blackness of the Abernathy backyard. She passed the first white shed and greenhouse without hesitating, then with careful steps made her way to the second shed.

The quiet darkness was deafening as she opened the shed door. With fast, steady motions, she removed the snow blower and decorations from the door in the floor. Then she lifted the creaking door and gazed down at the soft light of the dungeon.

The eyes on the stairs looked up at her in confusion.

The body can come down here, they seemed to say. *But the thing in the body is forbidden.*

Lulu smiled as she plucked the iron key from her hand and looped the yellow ribbon through the circle at the end. She double-knotted it on the key and took one final look. Then she threw it down the stairs. It landed with a quiet little plop on the dirt floor. She waited for a moment, listening. But no voice called out to her. And no one came to inspect what was thrown.

Good. Then they are asleep down there.

White noise swam in her head again, and she understood. It was up to the ribbon now.

As she made her way back up to the house, the wind battered her from every direction. She barely made it to the front porch without toppling over. The tracks she had made in the yard were already nearly gone.

Good.

Her feet didn't feel the wood as she put her foot on the step, and her hand didn't feel the metal when she put her fingers on the knob. But soon they'd be warm again.

As she walked back into the infiltrated home, a dog yipped out on the road.

Yes. Soon they'd be scalding.

CHAPTER TWENTY-SIX

I t wasn't a nice dream. In it, I was lying in bed. My head was filled with loud buzzing. It wasn't like bees exactly. It was like nervousness, getting stronger and stronger until a sound formed. And somehow, I knew it meant that *she* was in the room with me. It was like I was Carter again, in his room with the Thistle Witch at the end of his bed. But this was my room, in a protected home on protected property. But it still felt like she was there.

That's when I felt fingers run through my hair and brush up against my left ear.

I opened my eyes and launched out of bed. In my panic, all of my blankets flew off the bed and gathered into a big heap on the floor. I reached up and felt my head, expecting that nothing would be there. But there was a lump above my ear.

My heart banged in my throat as I peered in my dresser mirror. I leaned in and squinted. There was a little braid in my hair. The strands had only been woven around each other once or twice before the plait had been stopped. But it was there.

That's when I noticed the fuzziness of my reflection. I blinked a couple of times, thinking there was something in my eyes. But the dimness of the world remained. That's when I finally took a good long look in the mirror and saw something lying on my bed behind me. I held my breath as I turned around and made my way to the mattress.

"Son of a bitch," I whispered.

There I was, sleeping soundly in my bed. My mouth was open a little and my face was in a frown, suggesting that I really wasn't enjoying my dream.

"I'm still asleep," I said, staring at myself. Then I felt a surge of panic spread through me. "We're bewitched."

I bolted through the bedroom door and down the hallway, speeding into Carmen's room. I nearly ran into her as I came in. She sat on her dresser chair, watching the spectacle before her.

"What the hell?" I asked.

The real Carmen was lying in bed, dead to the world as Norma Shearer, Buster Keaton, and all the pocket demons attempted to shove her off the bed. Carmen was already on her stomach, and from years of my sister complaining that she could only sleep on her back, I deduced that her demon friends had already flipped her over once. They still had about two feet to go before she'd topple onto the hardwood floor.

"Isn't that sweet, Immy?" said the dream Carmen. "They love me. Look how hard they're trying. I think there are some monster cookies in their future."

"We're bewitched, aren't we?" I asked.

"I haven't bewitched myself this bad since I gave us both scaly legs when I tried to turn the bathroom into an aquarium. Remember?" asked Carmen.

I sighed, looking around. I still felt that hand in my hair. Usually, when we did too much magic and ended up bewitching ourselves as a side effect, I didn't feel watched like this or have the heebie-jeebies. It all felt a little too sinister.

Carmen didn't notice my unease. She was too busy watching the pocket demons try to wake her up.

"I got up about five minutes ago, and I've been pinching myself ever since," said Carmen. "Pinching both sleeping me and the *real* me,

I mean. But that didn't work. I was going to come find you, but my babies distracted me. I tried to help them shove me off the bed. But I guess I don't have any pushing power as dreaming me."

"Something seems off about this," I said. My words hung in the dark air of the room, making my neck crawl. "It feels creepy. And why do the demons want to wake you up so bad?"

Carmen shrugged. "They probably wonder why I'm sleeping so much. I usually get up around this time, and we do a craft like Christmas ornaments with construction paper or making your own shiv. And sometimes we have story time."

"Edgar Allan Poe poems?" I asked. Buster Keaton used his heft to try to get under Carmen's hip.

"It's usually either Winnie the Pooh or true crime," said Carmen.

I hid behind Carmen's curtains and gazed out her window. I don't know what I expected to find, but the yard was white, dark, and seemingly empty. I should have been prepared for just about anything, even something ridiculous. After all, we were in a dream, so clowns could have been doing backflips on the ice, and it wouldn't have meant much.

"What's wrong, Immy?" said Carmen. She joined me at the window, glancing at the nothingness outside.

"I can't shake the feeling that something's not right. I think we should check on Lulu."

Carmen led the way across the hall. I pushed the door open, expecting to either find Lulu sleeping, or to find an also bewitched Lulu standing there with her arms up, wondering what was going on. But there wasn't a dream Lulu, or a real one either. Her quilt was heaped up at the bottom of the bed, like she'd just gotten up and slipped away.

"Maybe she went to the bathroom," said Carmen, disappearing down the hall. But in a minute, she was back. Now it was Carmen's turn to look apprehensive. It made me feel less alone.

"I don't like this," I said, stepping onto Lulu's cold floor. "First my hair braids itself and now Lulu."

"Braids itself?" asked Carmen. She grabbed my hair and studied it.

"I wonder how that happened?" she asked. She sounded like she was nervous about the answer.

"I don't think it was us," I said. "I don't think we've bewitched ourselves. I think it was someone else. Want to guess who?"

"It can't be her, Immy," said Carmen. But she didn't sound sure. "You know the Thistle Witch can't get in here. There are protections buried in the walls of this house, scribbled under the paint, and attached under the siding. And then there are the stones around the property. Everything about this place stops cryptids and demons with wicked intent from strolling in."

"I know," I said, scanning Lulu's room. "But this witch is out of our league. Maybe her powers trump our protections. At least some of them, anyway. Maybe she can get around them."

"Maybe," said Carmen. I started poking around the closet. "What are you doing?"

"Help me look through Lulu's junk," I said. "Maybe the Thistle Witch passed something to her when we were out at that farmhouse. This place might be shielded from evil monsters coming in, but there's a chance a powerful witch might be able to slip a sinister object into a good person's back pocket before they walk across the property line."

Carmen was never afraid to get down to business. She looked through Lulu's books and flung herself into a pile of dirty clothes.

"But we never got close to the Thistle Witch," said Carmen, plunging her hand into a jean pocket.

"But Lulu was damn close to that goblin," I said. I opened the dresser drawers.

"Oh, dear," said Carmen. Her search for clues became more frantic after that.

I was on the floor, scanning under Lulu's bed, when I heard Carmen grab Lulu's coat. I barely even registered the crumpled noise. It sounded like a candy wrapper. Then a hush fell across the room.

"No," said Carmen. She hadn't sounded that crestfallen since the troll in the woods decided to escape cold Minnesota winters by moving out to California to live under a pier in Monterey Bay.

"What is it?" I said, shooting up.

"Just what you thought we'd find," said Carmen. She let the coat drop to the floor. She held a small sheet of crumbly paper, no bigger than a recipe card. Latin symbols written in the drippy ink of an old fountain pen crisscrossed it.

"They're not usually on parchment like this, are they, Immy?" asked Carmen. I took it from her with trembling, tingling fingers. There was no doubt about it.

"They're usually on papyrus," I said. "But it's a cursed tablet, all right. Son of a bitch."

"I've never seen one before," said Carmen, leaning over my shoulder.

"The last time we dealt with one was when you were a baby," I said. "Mom and dad left you with Aunt Joyce, but I screamed bloody murder to be taken along, so they did. I saw a lot of things I shouldn't have."

I had only seen the symbols on *that* tablet briefly, but I had passed by them in spell books a hundred times. Still, knowing what a cursed tablet looked like never prepared you for the moment you actually held one. It was a statement that someone in the world despised you, that they wished ill upon you, and that they were covering you with a fine mist of enchantment to use you however they wanted.

I wanted to set fire to the damn thing immediately, but I was fairly certain that wasn't possible. After all, I was just a dream.

"Last time a demon gave it to a man, didn't he?" asked Carmen.

"His name was Marv," I said. "He lived in Florida. The demon shoved the cursed tablet under his bed. It took us forever to find. Marv showed every sign of possession. We performed three exorcisms, and couldn't figure out what was going on. That's when mom whipped up a drink that let her detect unwanted magic. Marv was in such a bad way by the time we burned that thing. The demon had him climbing the walls, sliding across the ceiling, clawing himself up. They can get you to do just about anything."

Carmen pulled a lighter out of her pocket and lit it under the cursed tablet. The flame flickered around it, but didn't set the parchment on fire.

"We really need to wake up," I said. "That's the only way we can light this bastard up."

"And we need to find Lulu," said Carmen, putting the lighter away. "Who knows what the Thistle Witch has her doing?"

I set the tablet down on Lulu's bed, knowing we had to wait to face that. We left the room and passed by Carmen's door on our way downstairs. The pocket demons and cats still had about half a foot to go before Carmen would be propelled onto the floor. It was only a matter of time until they woke her up. I just hoped time was something we had.

We hurried down the stairs and into the kitchen, searching for Lulu behind every nook and cranny. I passed in front of the fridge and slid on something. I bent down and ran my finger through a dusting of flour on the floor.

"Why is this drawer open?" asked Carmen, peering into the large cabinet in the dining room.

I walked over and displayed my floury finger to her. She frowned.

"It's just a junk drawer," I said, reaching in and pulling out old phone chargers for phones nobody owned anymore.

"The Thistle Witch must have her looking for something," said Carmen.

"That's not encouraging," I said.

That loud, annoying buzzing blared in my ears again. It was like a teapot going off in my brain. This was all heading somewhere, leading to something. And it was something that I didn't want to face.

"I should have checked our coats and pockets when we left her house," I said, slamming the drawer shut.

"You couldn't have known," said Carmen. "Nobody could have. Like you just said, we haven't dealt with a cursed tablet in a long time."

"Of course, I should have known," I said, charging around the living room like someone who actually had a plan. "The Thistle Witch has had our number for a long time. It was stupid to think that we could go out and confront her on her own turf without some kind of retaliation. Stupid."

The buzzing in my ears waned to a dull hum. As I searched behind furniture for the missing Lulu, I became aware of another noise in the distance. It was quiet at first, like a displeased grumble. It was easy to drown out noises in a house that was usually filled up with pocket demon chatter. But the noise became a loud yip just as I opened a closet door. I stopped dead. My face turned cold as I stood listening to a dog bark in the distance. I looked at Carmen to see whether the sound was in my head or not. Carmen stared at the curtains with dismay. The Thistle Witch was out there.

I held my breath as we tried to look out the window without disturbing the curtain. The streetlight lit up the tiny paved road in front of the house. The asphalt was nearly covered with a thin layer of snow. The yellow light on the power pole made each flake look like a speck of gold, sparkling on its way to the ground. It would have been beautiful, had it not been for the blue heeler pacing back and forth. The dog didn't look at the house, but instead walked up and down the snowy street, happy with the bone that it carried in its mouth. Sometimes, the dog let the bone fall to the ground. Then it pounced on it, threw it up in the air, and caught it again.

"That looks like a human femur, Immy," whispered Carmen.

"I hope that cop friend of yours gets back to you tomorrow," I said. "We need to know who else the Thistle Witch killed."

The dog barked as the bone fell out of its mouth again. Snow flew everywhere as the blue heeler scrambled to retrieve its toy. The Thistle Witch was having a little too much fun, feeling like she had the upper hand so close to our house.

"This is a good time to confront her, isn't it?" asked Carmen, gently letting the curtain fall back into place. "She can't hurt us in a dream, right?"

I was quiet for a little too long to sound confident about my answer.

"Sure," I said, slowly. Carmen wanted more certainty than that.

"I've never heard of anyone being able to harm someone in a dream," said Carmen.

"Neither have I," I said. "But this is a witch from another time and place. We only know what we know. She has knowledge from a time when witchcraft was still serious shit. Who knows what she learned back there in the dark? She sounds like she's been hell-bent on revenge and destruction since she vacated the womb. When you want to hurt people that badly, who knows what you can do?"

Carmen considered this for a moment, biting her lip. Finally, she shook her head.

"I think she's psyching us out," said Carmen. "She's just trying to scare us."

"Obviously," I said, peering back outside. "And it's working, too."

"But if there's a chance that she can't hurt us because we're dreaming," said Carmen, "then this is the best time to talk to her. Soon the pocket demons will shove me off the bed, anyway, and I'll wake up. So, even if she does hurt us, we'll be out of dreamland soon."

I sighed. "If that was supposed to make me more confident, you fell short," I said. "But I don't think we have a choice. Lulu must be out there somewhere, freezing or torturing herself under the Thistle Witch's command. Or something equally unpleasant."

We didn't talk as we walked to the front door. I don't even remember getting there, actually. We were in a dream, but I still felt that numb sensation of walking toward something I wanted to run away from.

My hand was on the front door knob when Carmen stopped me.

"Now, remember," she said, her voice chiming. She looked me straight in the eye in the way that always made me feel uncomfortable, but also made me realize I was loved. "There's no shame in feeling afraid. I'm afraid, too. But one thing we're not going to do is *show* her that we're afraid. We're going to go out there and look at her like she makes us about as nervous as a giant bat hopped up on cold medicine. That giant bat wasn't scary, was he?"

"No," I said. "He was gross. There was a lot of cryptid cleanup that morning. Just how every sixteen-year-old wants to spend her Saturday."

Carmen nodded. "We'll look at her with confidence and act like she's that bat."

I grabbed an iron rod and then nodded at Carmen to take the other.

"She's that bat," I said.

Then we opened the door and walked out to see how much of a nightmare we were in.

CHAPTER TWENTY-SEVEN

Throughout my life, I have often resorted to spouting a lot of sarcasm when faced with an anxious situation. It must be a defense mechanism. A fourth-grade presentation that I did on manatees comes to mind as a prime example. Brad Martins was a bully in my class. His status as a popular kid, and the fact that his parents and my teacher were friends, gave him a free pass to say and do almost anything. He made faces at the poorer and scrawnier children, loved pushing his weight around, and enjoyed stealing anything anyone had.

I hated presentations and public speaking, and whenever I was forced to go up in front of the class, I always became as red as Carmen's hair. When I went up to explain how wonderful manatees were, Brad thought it was hilarious to scowl at me to psych me out, and then make a lot of chicken noises to let everyone know how nervous I was.

I guess something clicked inside me because that's when I lowered my poster and started heckling him right back, like an old stand-up comedian. I commented on his hair, ridiculously priced shirt, and how he was popular only because his parents had been born, raised, and would die in this dumb-shit nowhere town. If they lived in a big city, he'd be lost to obscurity like he deserved.

That was around the time I was led down to the principal's office to discuss my behavior. I got detention, but it was worth it. And Brad might have ended up with pocket demon poop in his desk a short time later.

When Carmen and I stepped out to confront the Thistle Witch in that dream, I was no less subtle.

"There's an ordinance on loose dogs in this town, you know," I said, trudging down the snowy sidewalk toward where the Thistle Witch stood on the road. "The people from the animal shelter in Kirkwood will be by in about fifteen minutes to bring you in."

Carmen walked next to me. Her gait was as nimble as a cat, ready to perform a spell if the need arose. The Thistle Witch dropped her bone and stared at us. She didn't growl or bare her teeth. Instead, she looked just like a dog interested in playing a game. Somehow that made me more unsettled.

"Luckily, they'll re-home you," I said. I stepped right up to one of the stones lining the yard, careful not to go beyond them, where she might be able to harm us. "But watch out for the spaying. That's an automatic service they provide to every animal they bring in."

Carmen and I stood on one side of the stones, the Thistle Witch on the other. We stared each other down for a second. Then I glanced at the iron rod in my hand.

"I don't suppose you want to tell us why you're doing all this?" I asked, whipping the rod in the air. "Or why you seem to hate us so much? I mean, I can see why you'd hate me. Everyone hates me. My face looks like this even when I'm not mad. But Carmen, everyone likes her. She brings her familiar to the nursing home every Saturday as a therapy cat. She was even homecoming queen back in school. I was the one heckling her from the bleachers."

Even in the confusing haze of the dream we were all in, I still felt magic at work. Something shifted slightly, like the screen on an old TV going wonky when the VCR is on the fritz. Then the feeling went away, and we weren't face to face with a dog anymore, but a petite woman in a mask.

"The dress I wore that night gave me a terrible rash," said Carmen. "The beading, you know? I had to make up a potion that involved quite a bit of spit to get rid of those bumps. But it was a nice honor."

From the moment we had walked up to her, the Thistle Witch had locked her gaze on Carmen. I saw her eyes deep within that mask, observing my sister, but revealing nothing.

Snowflakes that weren't really there landed on our shoulders. I had expected a little more action, or at least tough talk. After all, this witch had killed countless people with her human body part murder machines.

"Are you going to let us in on the secret?" I asked. "Tell us what the hell this is all about? Maybe tell us where you stashed our friend? And you know, if you're feeling extra charitable, you could give us a few hints on how best to smite you. Or…you could just leave. I'd take that. Wouldn't you, Carmen?"

"Absolutely," she said, nodding. "I have care packages up in my room. We could send you on your way."

"It's you," said the Thistle Witch. She pointed a thin finger at Carmen. The suddenness of her words startled me, but not her voice. With her Jersey Beast mask and dirty dress, I was expecting a cackling voice or perhaps something high-pitched, like an old cartoon witch that you'd watch on Saturday morning. Her voice was a whisper, sure, but it was a whisper that could have belonged to anyone.

"You are the reason," said the witch, her eyes still fixed on my sister.

Carmen stared back with troubled eyes and trembling lips. She reminded me of Judy Garland's sad expression after melting Margaret Hamilton.

"You broke the pact, and you will pay," continued the witch. She'd obviously never learned that pointing was rude because her finger was still aimed at my sister. "You will *all* pay, but you… I will know the color of your insides. I will tear your heart apart with my fingers."

That was more than enough to elicit a reaction from both of us. I yelled as I raised my rod. Carmen's face transformed from meek to resolutely pissed off.

"The hell you will," said Carmen. She raised her rod and lunged forward to meet the Thistle Witch on the other side of the stones. But before she could, a white-hot light blasted out of the Thistle Witch's hand. I had never seen anything like it before. No witch had been able to emit energy like that since the 1800s. The brightness filled up the world around us like a bomb going off. But I could tell as I fell back from the force, that it had been directed toward Carmen.

I was in the snow on my side when the world turned dark again. I scrambled up to look over at Carmen, but she wasn't there. Her rod was on the ground, red from heat. It melted a place around it in the snow. Nearby, where Carmen had stood, a puff of smoke rose up from the snow. Had she been hit?

I didn't realize that I was up until I was running at the Thistle Witch, cursing at her and swinging the rod. I lunged past the protective stones and out onto the street, raising the rod above my head. But when I swung it down through her, I was only swinging it through the air. I lost my balance on the ice, steadied myself, and then looked around. The Thistle Witch was gone, and so was my sister. It was lonely and quiet out on that nightmare street.

I raced back to the house, glancing at the smoke where Carmen had been.

"Shit, shit, shit," I said, as I slammed through the front door. I took the steps two at a time as I sped up them.

I pushed through Carmen's bedroom door just as the pocket demons and cats hurled my sleeping sister off her bed. It seemed to take hours for her to hit the floor. I held on to the walnut trim, still trembling from our encounter.

I wasn't sure what I thought would happen when Carmen hit the floor. But I wasn't prepared for her to slam onto the hardwood and disappear in a fine mist. Little droplets of smoke rose into the air before they faded away.

The demons stared at each other, chirping in alarmed, sputtering tones. I stood shaking and unsure. What had happened to Carmen? What the hell was I supposed to do? How was I going to wake up?

I slammed myself against the bed and yelled at Buster Keaton. I was just a dream, so I wasn't sure whether he'd hear me or not.

Good grief, I thought. *They're demons. They sure as hell better have some sixth sense about what's going on.*

"Buster," I yelled. "Can you hear momma? Can you hear me?"

At first, Buster stared off into space and put his ears back. But after yelling for a few more seconds, he pawed at his sister, then pointed to the air in my general direction.

"Good babies," I said. "Come on. Follow me! Follow me to my room."

The cats must have relayed what was going on to the others because as I ran down to my room, I had a dozen little devils behind me. They crawled, slithered, hopped, and flew at top speed toward my bed.

Buster and Norma hopped up on the mattress by my twitching feet. I whispered unintelligible words and frowned as I slept.

"I know that it's a shitty dream," I said to my sleeping self. "Hopefully, it'll be over in a minute."

I bent down next to Buster and whispered in his ear.

"You have to bite me," I said. "Bite me in the ankle to wake me up."

Buster put his ears down again. He didn't want to hurt his witch.

"You have to do it," I said, pleading. "You have to bite me. Carmen needs us. You know she's in danger. Bite me so I can help her!"

Buster meowed, long and loud. Norma nodded in agreement. He leaned his head down toward my foot and everything went dark.

I flew up out of bed, screaming. I reached down toward the pain. Buster definitely hadn't followed my directions halfway. He was still connected to my now flailing ankle. Finally, he released his teeth from my flesh and looked at me. I bent down and kissed him on the head.

"Thank you," I said. Then I threw myself out of bed and ran toward the door.

"Son of a bitch," I said, hopping on my sore, bleeding ankle. I sped down to Carmen's room. My stomach felt like it was filled with an agitated mass. I knew Carmen wouldn't be there when I stormed into her room, but the empty bed was still startling. I stared at it for a moment, eyes wide and heart thumping.

The pocket demons were all around, waiting for orders, waiting to see what could be done about Carmen.

"Outside," I said, turning out of her room. "Maybe she's still outside somewhere. That's where we were in the dream."

Barnaby and Horatio were outside before me. They bailed down the steps and ran around the snowy yard with their noses up, trying to smell for Carmen like a couple of bloodhounds. As they raced around the house, searching for their mother, I took slow, unsteady steps toward the place where Carmen and I had faced the Thistle Witch in our dream.

The sun was starting to rise as I put my foot down where Carmen had dropped her iron rod. The rod wasn't there, of course, because that had been a dream. The rod was next to the front door, by the shoes and umbrellas. But somehow there was still a melted spot in the snow, all the way down to the grass. How had the snow melted from something that hadn't really been there?

"That's not possible," I whispered, bending down to touch the spot. That's when I noticed something in my peripheral vision. A mound of snow moved a little. I stood up, expecting Barnaby or Benedict to pop out. After all, they were the snow lovers, and the pocket demons with the shortest attention spans. I bent down, ready to chastise them for giving up on looking for Carmen. But just as I opened my mouth, a little tan snout poked out of the snow.

"Immy!" said Carmen. She shook her small corgi head. Snow flew everywhere.

"You're all right!" I said. There I was, the one who hated PDA, picking Carmen out of the frozen mound and holding her tight.

"I have snow in my large ears, Immy," said Carmen, shaking her head.

"I thought you were hurt," I said, squeezing her. "I thought you were dead!"

"And I thought you didn't like hugs!" said Carmen, nuzzling my neck with her wet fur.

I set her down and crouched to her level.

"How is this possible?" I asked. "You should have woken up in bed. But I saw you hit the floor. You just disappeared. How can that be?"

"I'm not sure," said Carmen. She shook herself again to get the melted snow off her coat. "The Thistle Witch threw that ball of light at me. By the way, did you see that? Wasn't it amazing? No witch has been able to do that since Flora Delong back in 1872! Anyway, as that light came toward me, all I thought was, *If I were a dog again, I could scurry away to escape her blast.* And suddenly, I *was* a dog. She didn't see me get propelled back into the snow, I guess. I was stunned there for a long time. I couldn't move! Luckily, I'm one of the snow-loving breeds."

"But you still should have woken up," I said, confused. "That means that somehow you were able to manipulate your dream self and awake self in the same way the Thistle Witch was."

"I don't know," said Carmen. "It must be those spinach shakes that I've been eating for breakfast."

"That's powerful magic, Carmen," I said, slowly. I stared off, perplexed. "I don't know how you managed that."

"That's why I practice, Immy," said Carmen, smiling. Her tongue lolled out to the side of her mouth. We were quiet for a second, then we both looked at each other, knowing what the other was thinking.

"Do you think the Thistle Witch kidnapped Lulu?" asked Carmen, nervous.

"I don't know," I said. "But I'm getting the weird feeling that she was distracting us for some reason. We have to destroy that cursed tablet right now, and then figure out where the hell Lulu is. I promised we'd protect her, and so far, I'm doing a pretty crappy job."

We hurried up to the house. Carmen shuffled as fast as her little teddy bear legs could go. We were just through the front door when Minerva flew down the hallway, cackling in a high-pitched screech.

"What is it, baby?" Carmen asked.

Minerva gestured over to the basement door. It was never usually open. The pocket demons had a tendency to go down there whenever they were feeling a pagan inclination. We always gave them their privacy, so they could recite passages of the *Prose Edda* together in peace.

With the door open, it was easy to hear the persistent hum of something downstairs. If Minerva hadn't flown up to us, I would have brushed it off as Buster Keaton doing a load of laundry, but the sound was different from that. It almost sounded like…rain.

"Shit," I said. I pointed up the stairs. "Go get that cursed tablet right now!"

Carmen nodded and raced up the stairs. I followed Minerva down the basement steps and around the corner. The basement was unfinished, but the pocket demons liked it that way. It smelled more rustic, I guess. It was furnished with a 1980s tan sofa and chair with brown animal and tree accents. We had tried to replace them over the years, but Horatio wouldn't let us upgrade. A boxy old TV with a VCR sat in the corner, and the demons could often be found watching weird old 1940s cartoons. Lounging in the basement also meant they had easy access to the canned goods. They couldn't get enough pickled beets. And to top it off, the demons even had their own creepy bathroom.

It was a weird, dingy old bathroom that freaked us both out as kids. And that was saying something for Carmen because weird things were usually her bag. We used to dare each other to go into the basement with all the lights off, enter the bathroom, close the door, and sit on the floor for five minutes. I don't think we ever got to five minutes before running upstairs, certain that the ghost would get us.

The ghost in question was our great-grandmother, Euphemia. I once told a lie that her ghost was down there, waiting to chastise us even in death for being terrible, spoiled children. In life, she had been a bent-back shrew who never thought that children deserved much of anything—from clothes, to pizza, to love—based on the fact that, according to her, *she* had never received those things as a child, and she had turned out just fine, thank you very much.

"If you give a child love," she used to say. "They'll just expect more love."

Nothing was more vexing to Euphemia than children wanting more love. If anyone in our family could have haunted that bathroom, it was her. But after a while, I frightened myself into thinking that my own lie might be true, and I therefore hated that bathroom as much as my sister.

It wasn't hard to see why. Everything in there was partly to mostly crap. There was the toilet handle you had to keep pushing to make the water stop running, the shower head that was grimed over with calcium deposits, and the vanity mirror that had a broken hinge. Then there was the grubby old tile. Added to that was the melancholy yellow from the terrible lighting. The fact that the bathroom had never been updated was a testament to the fact that when you own a big Victorian house, you inevitably drown in the never-ending renovation projects. That's why I always fantasized about living in a small log cabin in the middle of the woods that could only be accessed via an ominous, winding path.

My feelings about that bathroom didn't change when I charged in and found Lulu standing in a huge cloud of heavy, hot steam. She stared like she was hypnotized, while boiling water pelted her face, chest, and stomach.

Minerva tried to turn off the tap while Honora tugged at Lulu's arm. But she batted them away and remained fixed in the scalding water.

I screamed for Carmen. I turned the water off and grabbed at Lulu's slippery skin. Bits of her arm flaked away as I pulled her out of the shower. She toppled over on me, and I held her tight on the bathroom floor, afraid that whatever spell she was under might compel her to lash out and hurt both me and herself. But she remained still as I gingerly wrapped her cherry-red skin in a towel. She was nothing but heat blisters. Her nose was red and raw. Her face was inflamed. But she didn't say anything. She was like a mannequin, glazed over on the floor.

I heard tapping on the wooden steps as Carmen's little paws ran down them. She had the cursed tablet in her mouth. She spat it onto the coffee table.

"Burn it!" said Carmen. Minerva flew over and blew a thin flame out of her mouth. The parchment crackled as the fire spread through it. Carmen's eyes were fixed on Lulu, who I ushered down to the sofa.

"She's burnt all over!" I yelled.

The cursed tablet burned quickly, turning to a black, curled fragment before disintegrating on the table. The change in Lulu was immediate. The haze in her eyes disappeared, and she looked around at us as if waking up from a dream. She almost smiled at Carmen, who sat there on the ground, wagging her little stump tail. Then a shadow passed over Lulu, and her face changed again. The pain had set in.

CHAPTER TWENTY-EIGHT

Lulu's screams had drawn all the pocket demons and familiars down to the basement. They held herbs and dark amber liquids in their clawed hands and paws. They offered them to Carmen as remedies for the puffy white and red blisters all over Lulu. Lulu reached up to her face, crying in pain.

"We have to get her to the hospital," I said. I sat next to her on the floor. "It's going to be fine. You're going to be all right."

"It hurts!" said Lulu. Her lips were swollen from the heat of the water.

"I know," I said. "We're going right now."

"We can do it, Immy. We can heal her."

"We can heal a blister or two," I said, "but not a whole body of them!"

"She might be in the hospital for a long time," said Carmen. "And who knows if the Thistle Witch will come back for her when she's in there."

"But we can't do it," I said, frazzled. "We're not strong enough. And you're a dog. You can't perform the spell like that."

"How silly of me," said Carmen. If a dog could have blushed, Carmen would have. "I almost forgot I was still a dog."

And then I felt that wonky, video-out-of-track feeling again. The same sensation that had washed over me when we were with the Thistle Witch. One moment I was looking at a dog, then the next moment, I was face to face with my normal sister again.

My mouth hung open as I stared at Carmen in her red housedress and fuzzy monster slippers.

"How the hell did you do that?" I asked, flustered.

"I don't know," said Carmen. She looked down at herself with amazement and pride.

"Last time, you were stuck as a dog for a week," I said. "And we could only change you back after performing a series of spells that took a whole day. And now you can just change back and forth at will? I don't get it."

"Neither do I," said Carmen. "I just thought, *you need hands to do this spell, so you better be human again.* And then I was."

"I know how you did it," said Lulu, lying there on the sofa. Even in pain, she still smiled at us. "Because when someone really needs you, you find a way to make your magic work. You're stronger than you realize. And that's how you're going to beat the Thistle Witch. Now, if you could please heal my lava skin, I'd appreciate it."

I wasn't sure this plan would work. The last time I had tried my own skin-soothing magic salve, I only swapped poison ivy for razor burn. But Carmen was sure of herself.

"We can do it, Immy," she said. "Trust me."

Barnaby had a big chunk of ginger in his mouth. He flung it into the mason jar with an enthusiastic grunt. If someone had been able to look in on us, they might have thought we were making our own vinaigrette. But when Carmen and I cleared our throats and hacked into the jar, all reasonable explanations would have disappeared. Plus, you know, we stood in a basement with a bunch of demons and a naked woman covered in blisters.

"Hope you don't mind spit," I said.

"I have a two-year-old nephew," said Lulu. She had her arms stretched out to cover her more delicate areas. "Most of what I deal with is spit."

Carmen sang a protective Gregorian chant as she mixed some crushed-up rowan tree leaves into the mixture.

"You'd be terrible in sales, Immy," said Carmen. "You're trying to get our customer to back out."

"Hospitals have drugs," I said. "Amazing drugs. And there's this thing called medical science that they use sometimes. It's out of this world. It's not just leeches and digging up corpses anymore."

"Knock it off, you two," said Lulu. "I'm freezing my butt off, and I feel weird being naked like this. And I'm sore. So quit whining and do your mojo."

"I'm not sure if this will work," I said.

Carmen dunked her finger in the mason jar, then drew a small spiral symbol on Lulu's cheek. I reached in and did the same, this time drawing the symbol on the back of Lulu's neck, right next to the chain of her eye necklace.

Lot of good that did against a witch with her power, I thought.

We repeated the symbol again and again, covering every square inch of Lulu's body. All the while, she stood there, cold and sore. She barely even cringed when we drew on her, though she had to be in intense pain.

She must really hate going to the doctor, I thought.

"This will be great practice for the Thistle Witch, Immy," said Carmen, drawing the symbol on Lulu's ankle.

"We're going to need more than this to beat her," I said, drawing the symbol on Lulu's arm. "We need magic like the magic she has. Old-timey ass-kicking magic. We can't stand around drawing symbols while her monster machine takes a bite out of us. And we can't get so drained when we do magic, either. We'll have to down cheap tacos and a couple of vats of nacho cheese like college kids to recuperate after this spell. I can feel it already."

"I'd rather have a bunch of scones," said Carmen.

"Could you do that?" asked Lulu. "Bring back the old witch magic?"

I shivered at the very thought of it. I was uncomfortable enough with shitty, card-counting Vegas witch magic. I didn't want to think about how out of control I'd feel with white light coming out of my hands.

"I have no idea," I said, sighing. "But we need to find out. And quick."

Carmen finished one last symbol on Lulu's foot, then stood up.

"There," she said. "Almost done. Ready, darlings?"

The pocket demons sat on the sofa, transfixed by our spell. Hopefully, their help had added a little something to our magic. Horatio dragged a dingy blue bucket from the bathroom. It was filled to the top with lukewarm water. He set it down at Carmen's feet and smiled. Carmen nodded and threw a little salt into it. She wasn't wearing gloves and her fingers turned red.

"All right," she said. "Hit the lights."

Minerva nodded and turned the old, faded light switch off. There weren't any windows in our ancient basement, so the room was instantly covered in blackness. The only beacon of light was Lulu, who shined like a science project in the darkness. The little symbols sparkled all over her like she had been covered head to toe in glow-in-the-dark paint. Carmen stood in front of Lulu with the bucket. She said a few words in Latin, and I repeated them. Then we both plucked a hair out of our heads and threw them in with the water. In the blue glow of Lulu's skin, I saw something run down Carmen's lip. She must have felt it because she twitched her nose, then reached up and wiped it away.

"You're bleeding," said Lulu, surprised.

"If that's the worst thing that happens today," said Carmen. "We'll consider ourselves lucky."

Then Carmen said something quick and guttural in Latin and threw the bucket of water straight at Lulu's face.

By the time Minerva had the lights back on, the pocket demons were at work sopping the water up with a bunch of old washcloths. They couldn't stand when their hangout was untidy. Lulu was hunched down, surprised at the suddenness of the water. Then she looked at her hands, her arms, and her stomach. The blisters were all gone. We had done it.

It was a moment that should have made me proud. But instead, I felt like I had been instantly stricken with food poisoning.

"I better sit down before I fall down," I said, grabbing the sofa. My legs felt like one of the gelatin molds some of the older witches used to bring to the reunion. Shaky and wiggly. Carmen collapsed down next to me.

Lulu made excited whooping noises. She alternated between cheering and asking where her clothes were. Carmen and I tried to look happy, but when you felt sick from magic overkill, you lost interest in everything. Everything except eating. Buster and Norma hopped up with cans of ginger ale. I forced myself to slam mine.

"Are you thinking what I'm thinking?" I asked, petting Buster.

"I was thinking we need to figure out how to strike back against the Thistle Witch," said Carmen. She grabbed some pastel taffy out of her housedress and popped a piece in her mouth. "And we also have to consider why the Thistle Witch bothered with Lulu. Why didn't she kill her to use for parts in her murder machine? Did she harm her in some way that we don't yet realize? Did she have Lulu perform some task while in a state of hypnotism? Hmm. There certainly is a lot for us to mull over. Is that what you were thinking, Immy?"

I was quiet for a moment, finishing my pop.

"Sure," I said.

"Really?" asked Carmen.

"No," I said. "That would have been sensible. Instead, I was thinking about tacos. The size of tacos, the quantity of tacos, and the fillings in tacos. And I was also thinking that now that Lulu's fingers aren't blistered, she could order us these tacos."

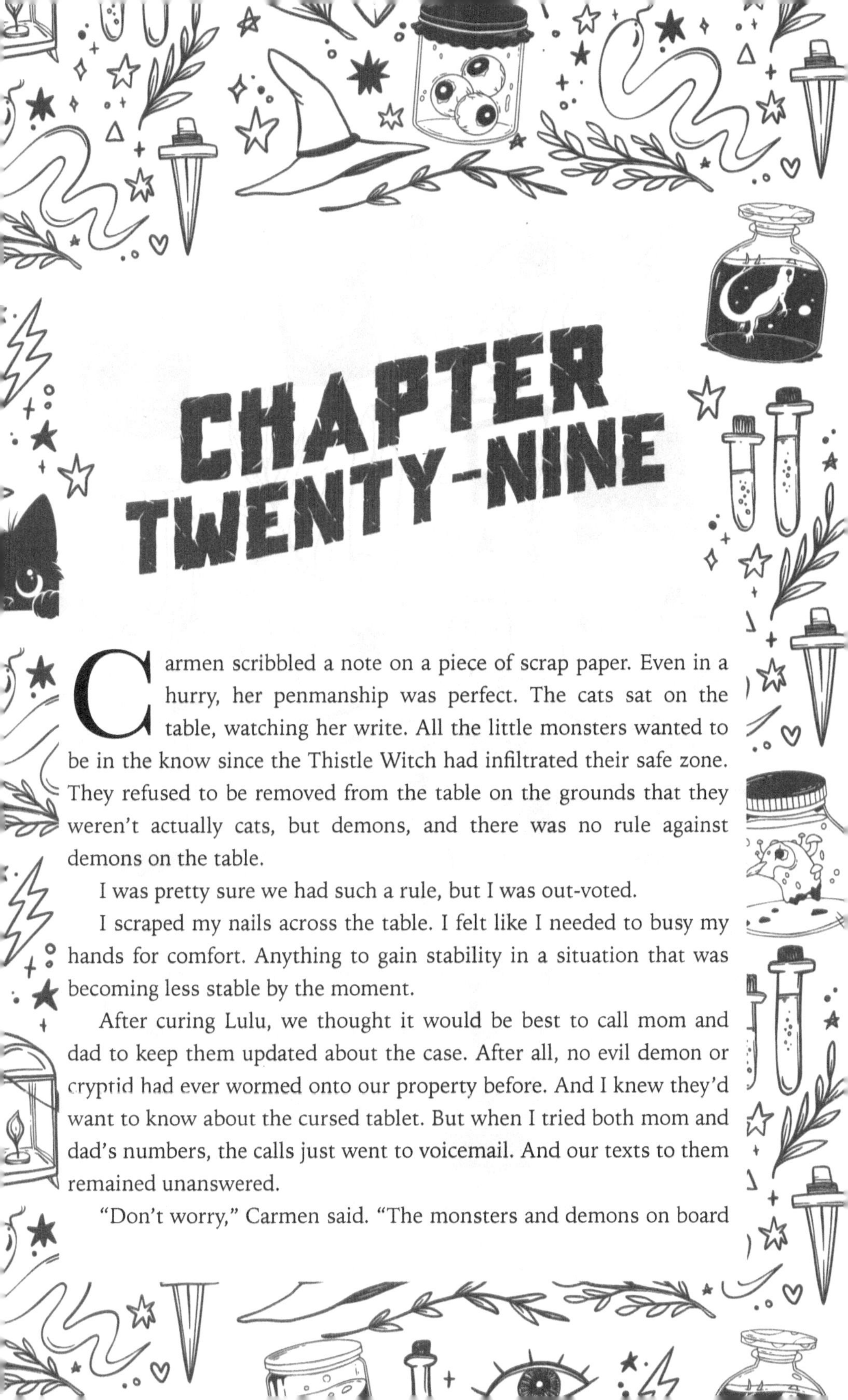

CHAPTER TWENTY-NINE

Carmen scribbled a note on a piece of scrap paper. Even in a hurry, her penmanship was perfect. The cats sat on the table, watching her write. All the little monsters wanted to be in the know since the Thistle Witch had infiltrated their safe zone. They refused to be removed from the table on the grounds that they weren't actually cats, but demons, and there was no rule against demons on the table.

I was pretty sure we had such a rule, but I was out-voted.

I scraped my nails across the table. I felt like I needed to busy my hands for comfort. Anything to gain stability in a situation that was becoming less stable by the moment.

After curing Lulu, we thought it would be best to call mom and dad to keep them updated about the case. After all, no evil demon or cryptid had ever wormed onto our property before. And I knew they'd want to know about the cursed tablet. But when I tried both mom and dad's numbers, the calls just went to voicemail. And our texts to them remained unanswered.

"Don't worry," Carmen said. "The monsters and demons on board wouldn't hurt them. Remember how they were cutting a rug together last time we talked?"

"They probably just took your parents' phones away, so they can't contact the outside world," said Lulu. "After all, if they're that afraid of the Thistle Witch, they wouldn't want her to find out that they're all on a cruise ship hiding out from her."

I knew that was more than likely true, but it didn't stop me from digging my nails into antique furniture. We really were adrift, with only our own magic to help us. And magic and me weren't close friends. But there was nothing to do but forge on.

"Thanks so much, Keith," said Carmen, talking on her phone. "You too. Goodbye."

"What's your cop friend know?" asked Lulu. She was trying to eat a taco while Ludwig tried to steal it.

"Can you believe it?" asked Carmen, leaning in. "Missy Borne and her husband are getting a divorce. You remember her, Immy? We were in band together. She was so nice."

I leaned back in my chair. "She was a bitch," I said.

Lulu smiled and threw a piece of taco to Ludwig. He thought anything less than a whole taco was a great insult. He threw it back at her.

"She was not," said Carmen, offended.

"She was," I said. "She liked everyone except me. And you two had your red hair twin thing going on. She made such a point of liking you, but not me. She turned her back whenever I walked up and acted like she didn't hear me when I talked. Bitch."

Carmen rolled her eyes. Lulu patted my shoulder.

"You can let that go, you know," said Lulu. "It was, what, fourteen years ago?"

"What's not to like about me?" I asked, furrowing my brow. "I'm pleasant all the time."

"Anything going on besides hot gossip?" asked Lulu.

"More bad news," said Carmen. "The Thistle Witch *has* killed again. A family from Brier. They must have been the ones we saw in that vision in the trees. Isn't that just dreadful? And get this, Immy. They were the Sullivan family. Remember them?"

I sighed. I had the terrible feeling that by the time this was over, the Thistle Witch was going to slaughter anyone who was even remotely acquainted with us.

"They had a poltergeist in their attic," I said, picturing the family. They were all light-haired, so light-haired that even their eyelashes were blonde. "The ghost was some guy who lived there in the 1950s. Really violent, angry spirit. Took two days to cleanse him out of there. They were pretty grateful because their kids had been so young then. They sent us a Christmas card for a couple of years."

Carmen looked at me like a proud parent.

"I knew you loved this work, Immy. You wouldn't remember things like that if you didn't."

I rolled my eyes and grabbed another taco. I was starting to feel better, but just to be sure, I was going to eat five more of those suckers.

"Way to bury the lead," said Lulu, staring.

"What?" asked Carmen.

"You could have mentioned the horrible family massacre before the divorce," said Lulu.

"I guess that's true, isn't it?" said Carmen.

We were momentarily distracted by noise from the parlor. For the tenth time that day, some of the demons were having creative differences about how to decorate the Christmas tree. The holiday was coming fast, and we hadn't had time to get a tree. So, the cats and demons had taken it upon themselves to go out back to the woods and cut one. They weren't going to be cheated out of their gifts and treats. That was for damn sure. The fact that most of them belonged to pre-Christian religions didn't seem to matter when candy canes were involved. They loved that peppermint. They stuck the tree where it went every year in front of the large bay window. By the way it shook every now and then, I had the sneaking suspicion it still contained an outdoor resident.

"I think we should go over the whole thing one more time," I said, taking my eyes off the moving tree.

Lulu grumbled and knocked her forehead against the table.

"Humor me," I said. "You're sure you don't remember *anything* from your time under the spell of the cursed tablet?"

Lulu lifted her head. Crumbs were smashed into the skin between her eyebrows. She wiped them away.

"Like I told you," she said. "I remember taking a shower. Then I sat down in bed and read my romance novel for a while, which was pretty silly considering our situation. And just imagine what it'll be like trying to keep all of this from the next person I hook up with on Tinder. Anyway, that's it. I woke up on the basement floor in pain."

"Can you remember a feeling?" asked Carmen, prodding in her delicate way. "Even if it seems like a dream? Anything at all? Even the silliest thing might be helpful."

"A feeling?" asked Lulu. She screwed her face up, trying to think. "I guess, if I had to say something, maybe I dreamt that I was cold. Like my feet, I mean."

"Maybe you were outside," I said.

"It was windy last night," said Carmen. "Her footprints would be gone or covered up by the tracks all the pocket demons left while looking for me."

"And I kind of remember…" said Lulu, staring off. She looked like someone trying to grab at a fading mist. "Yellow. I remember dreaming about the color yellow."

I crossed my arms. "Well, shit," I said.

"What does it mean?" asked Lulu.

"Even though yellow is the color of sunshine and tulips," said Carmen, smiling. "And people usually think of it as cheerful…actually throughout history and folklore, it's generally considered a bad luck color. Like a yellow rose, for instance. A yellow rose is a symbol of a love that doesn't stand a chance."

"I've been given yellow roses," said Lulu, grumbling. "That's some bullshit."

"So, whatever she did or *had* you do," I said. "It probably wasn't good."

We were still trying to process what this meant when my iPhone rang. I didn't recognize the number and prepared myself to be accosted by a computer claiming to be the IRS.

"This is Imogen," I said.

"Immy!" said Carmen, frowning.

"I mean…um… Otherworldly Investigations," I said. "The Exorcism professionals since 1932."

Carmen beamed. "I should put that on the business cards."

"Uh," said the voice on the other end.

Yep, I thought. *I freaked out the guy selling wreaths or the neighbor with the loose cat.*

"Imogen," said the voice. "This is Shannon."

"Shannon," I said. I stood up, not knowing why. Carmen and Lulu followed suit. "How are you?"

"I got let out of the hospital," she said. She sounded nervous. "That is you guys, then. I got your card in the mail."

I threw a tortilla chip at Carmen. She shrugged.

"Carmen sends those out sometimes," I said.

"A month ago, I would have thought you guys were nuts," said Shannon.

My feet felt stuck right into the floor.

"And now?" I asked.

"That dog was outside the house this morning," said Shannon. There was a weird note in her voice. A kind of finality. I must have looked alarmed. Lulu and Carmen got right in my face.

"What is it?" asked Carmen. "Should I get the 038?"

I waved Carmen and Lulu away with my hand.

"Are you at home now?" I asked.

"No," she said. "I just passed Deadwood. Is six and a half hours away far enough?"

I saw myself frowning in the reflection of the china cabinet. I looked fatigued.

"I don't know," I said, walking up to my reflection. "I was tempted to find out, but I don't think we have that option."

"It's something magical, isn't it?" asked Shannon. Her voice wobbled. "Bad magic."

I traced the outline of my face in the glass.

"How did you figure it out?" I asked.

"It turned into that woman," said Shannon. Her voice had a harsher note to it. "Then it disappeared. I grabbed what I could in five minutes and got into my car. What is it?"

"A witch," I said. I stared at the dainty little flowers on grumpy Euphemia's old plates. They were ones we only used for holidays. I wondered if we'd get another chance to take them out. "A very powerful witch."

"So, witches are evil," said Shannon.

"I don't know," I said, glancing back at Carmen. She sat at the table again, petting Norma Shearer in the rapid way she only did when she was nervous. "Some are, I guess. Me and my sister aren't so bad."

Shannon's voice lightened. "Then you can kill her," said Shannon. "You can kill her for me."

I turned back to the hutch, staring at the cups, but not really looking at them.

"That's up in the air right now," I said. "Witchcraft nowadays isn't much to write home about. This woman is a throwback. Nobody has seen power like this in a long time. But we're trying."

"Good," said Shannon. She said it like we had agreed to some kind of promise. But I guess we kind of had, and a long time ago, too. "Will it follow me?"

"I'm not sure," I said, resting my head on the glass. "She's distracted by us at the moment, I think. But maybe."

"Am I going far enough?" she asked.

"Just keep driving," I said. "Drive until you can't drive anymore. And then get on a plane and fly. Do you have a passport?"

"Yes," she said. She sounded like she was rummaging through her purse. "Where should I go?"

"Anywhere," I said, quick and quiet. "Just don't tell me. I don't want to know."

"Why not?" she asked.

The old teapot had a substantial amount of dust on it. I opened the cabinet and made a line with my finger across it.

"Because if she tortures me," I said in a low voice, "then all I can say is that you're in Deadwood. Because that's all I'll know. I should call Eliza and tell her to go, too."

"I just talked to her last night," said Shannon. "She's not around. She took Carter and went to her aunt's in…"

"Don't tell me," I said, with too much force. Carmen bounced up from her chair again. "But is it far from here?"

"Yes," said Shannon, in a whisper.

"Good," I said, whispering back. I felt like someone was listening in, right around my shoulder. It always felt like *she* was right there, watching, smirking at her upper hand.

"Will you call me when it's all over?" Shannon asked.

"Yes," I said, closing the cabinet again.

"What if you never call?" asked Shannon, nervous.

"Then keep moving around," I said. "Don't stay in the same place very long. Move from town to town, and then to another country. Make up stories. Lie to people about where you've been and where you're going. Lie to people about who you are. But never stop moving."

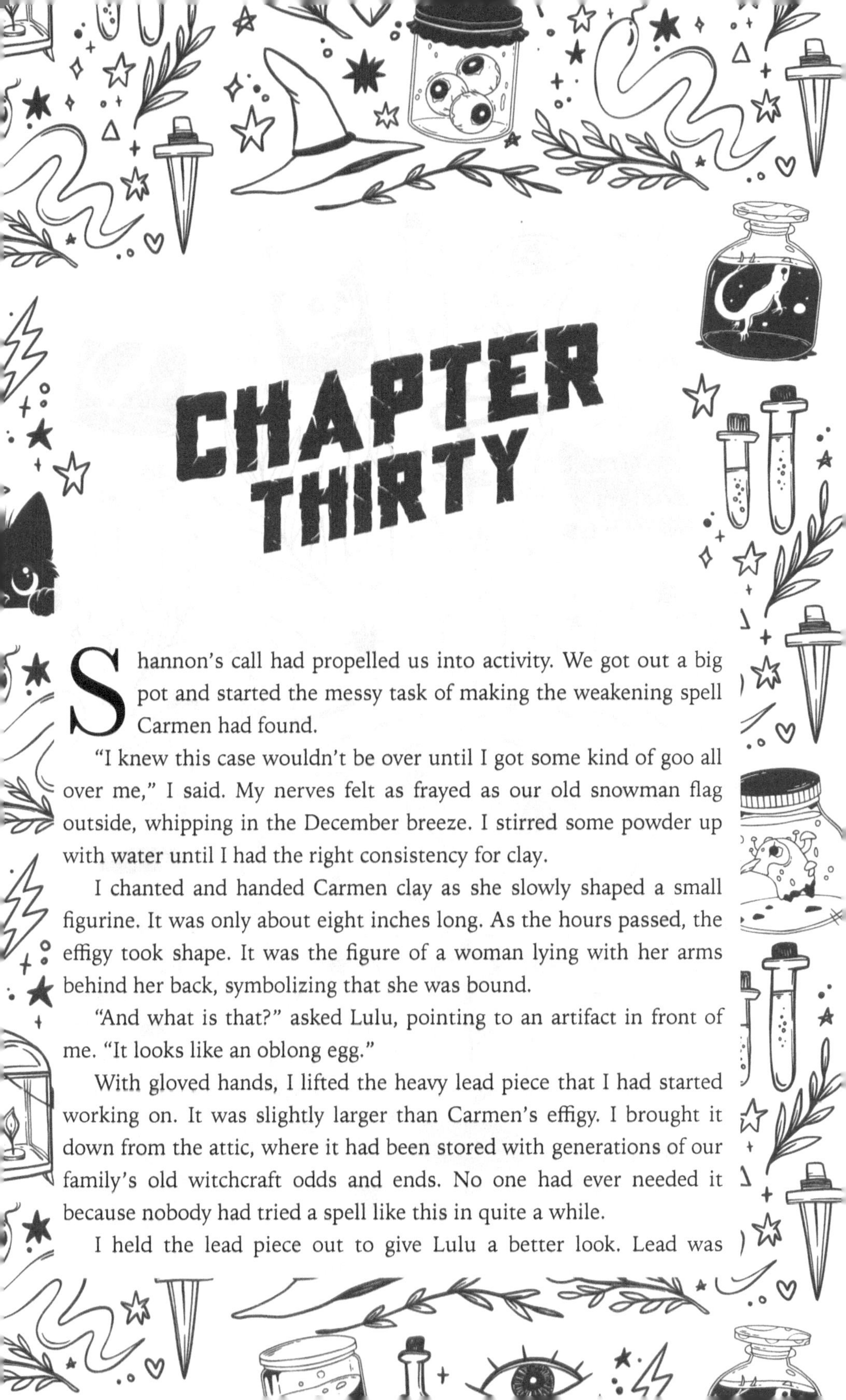

CHAPTER THIRTY

Shannon's call had propelled us into activity. We got out a big pot and started the messy task of making the weakening spell Carmen had found.

"I knew this case wouldn't be over until I got some kind of goo all over me," I said. My nerves felt as frayed as our old snowman flag outside, whipping in the December breeze. I stirred some powder up with water until I had the right consistency for clay.

I chanted and handed Carmen clay as she slowly shaped a small figurine. It was only about eight inches long. As the hours passed, the effigy took shape. It was the figure of a woman lying with her arms behind her back, symbolizing that she was bound.

"And what is that?" asked Lulu, pointing to an artifact in front of me. "It looks like an oblong egg."

With gloved hands, I lifted the heavy lead piece that I had started working on. It was slightly larger than Carmen's effigy. I brought it down from the attic, where it had been stored with generations of our family's old witchcraft odds and ends. No one had ever needed it because nobody had tried a spell like this in quite a while.

I held the lead piece out to give Lulu a better look. Lead was another thing that witches didn't look forward to handling. Last time, I'd ended up with adult acne all over my face and shoulders.

"It's supposed to symbolize a coffin," I said. "But I guess whoever made it back in the day couldn't do pointed corners."

"Huh," said Lulu, examining it.

"It's hollow inside," I said. "See?"

I lifted the top to reveal a hollow center. Lulu peered inside like a paleontologist on a fossil hunt.

"What exactly do you do?" asked Lulu. "I just got a vague idea from the spell we found in that book. But Carmen had to read it to me —it was in Greek."

It still felt weird to be with a regular human interested in magic and witchcraft. She hadn't even tried to run screaming in the opposite direction. I wasn't sure if that made me feel better or worse, but I had no choice but to go with it.

"When Carmen gets done making the effigy of the Thistle Witch, we put it inside here."

"And you carved words all over the top of it," said Lulu. "What do they say?"

She pointed at the symbols I'd just finished.

"I etched a curse onto the coffin lid," I said, feeling slightly icky about the idea. "It's Greek. Basically, it's a curse to weaken her powers. She'll be just like us. Once the effigy is inside this coffin, we have to bury it in a place of magical significance."

"And where's that?" asked Lulu, raising an eyebrow.

"The woods out back should work fine," I said, setting the coffin back down. It clanked onto the table and sent a shiver through me. "Forests are always places where magic abides. And it doesn't hurt that we used to have a troll living back there."

I took a deep breath and leaned back in my chair. I felt winded just explaining what we were doing. This was some serious magic, and I was feeling it. It was obvious that Carmen felt it, too. Her normally bright and chipper attitude had been replaced by solemn sculpting. Usually, doing crafts and creating things were surefire ways to boost

Carmen's disposition. But she just sat there, working and wiping her brow.

This was different from the usual case. Sure, we'd faced some apocalypses, but we'd never faced anything like a witch trying to kill us. Witches were family. Witches were the people who made me extra Oreo fluff at the reunion because they knew I liked it. Hurting another witch made me uncomfortable, even if she was a murderous, evil one.

"But this isn't enough, Immy," said Carmen, sighing. Minerva landed next to her with a dainty cup of hot cocoa. She pushed it toward Carmen, who thanked her with extra scratches on the pocket demon's neck.

"I don't see my cocoa anywhere," I said.

"If you gave them bubble baths, they'd bring you cup after cup," said Carmen, sipping the cocoa.

"I'll get my own cocoa and save myself from scratches. I know how Barnaby gets in the tub."

"What do you mean?" asked Lulu. "What won't be enough?"

"I always get distracted by devils," said Carmen, putting down her drink. "I meant that to complete the spell, we need something that belongs to the Thistle Witch, preferably a hair or a piece of cloth. We'll tie that around the hands of the effigy to symbolically bind her to the curse. Then we bury it."

"How the hell are we going to get cloth or hair from her?" asked Lulu. "We can barely get near her."

"It'll be loads of fun, I'm sure," I said, taking a sip of Carmen's cocoa. "And after all that, we'll still be damned lucky if the spell even works."

"Why?" asked Lulu.

I stared off, trying to think of an example.

"Have you ever baked anything that didn't turn out?" I asked.

"Croissants," she said. The very word made her nose wrinkle in disgust. "They can go straight to hell."

"And why is that?" I asked.

Lulu tried to find the words. "They're just so persnickety. They're layers and layers. And you can think everything is fine, then stick them in the oven, and they come out looking like a massacre."

Carmen brightened. "That's magic," she said.

"Witchcraft is some serious shit," I said. "Especially an old-timey spell like this. This spell is a croissant. We might think we have everything right, but we won't know until the timer goes off."

"Wonderful," said Lulu, sarcastically.

"That's why it would be nice if we could amp up our witchcraft, so we could be equally matched with the Thistle Witch," said Carmen.

"But your magic is already better than it was before," said Lulu. "Isn't it?"

"But that took me my whole life," said Carmen. "We don't have that kind of time. We need something to jumpstart our witchcraft now. But who knows if that's even possible?"

Carmen and I looked at each other. She was so proud of the way she had increased her magical prowess. I had always pictured Carmen as a witch walking down the street trailing a cloud of ethereal mist or flying off into the moonlight. Those images suited her. But all they did was give me a case of the flop sweats. But I knew the moment of truth was fast approaching, and when it did, we couldn't be standing around ready to face the most powerful witch in recent history with what amounted to a couple of measly card tricks.

I guess I fell asleep. Overuse of magic will do that. I woke up in a wingback chair in the parlor with a bunch of gunk in my eyes. I heard Carmen clanking pans and stirring something on the stove. Her soft, melodic voice drifted into the parlor, and even though I couldn't make out what she said, I knew she was offering something sweet to one of the pocket demons. They only made that kind of happy, high-pitched call when something sugary was involved.

I was surprised when I lifted my head and noticed Lulu sitting by the Christmas tree with a quilt over her. She stared out at the silent, purple morning. From the stillness and the ice on the windows, it looked like the kind of cold that made the snow squeak when you walked through it.

"What day is it?" I asked.

Lulu jumped a little, startled by the way I had broken the calm stillness of the room.

"It's tomorrow," she said, quietly.

"I don't even know what yesterday was," I said, willing myself to wake up.

Lulu's eyes drifted toward the Christmas tree. I knew she had a large family. I saw her on the phone sometimes and wondered what excuse she gave them for her absence. What did they think she was doing? Did they think she left them high and dry? Did they think she was in trouble? No, probably not. Lulu was good at spinning yarns. And whatever story she had given them was probably something very logical. A total doozy compared to the reality she faced.

As her eyes passed over the popsicle and construction paper ornaments that Carmen and I had made as kids, I saw a look on her face. *That look.* And I knew exactly what *that* look was because I had seen it before many times in the mirror. It was the look of a person who wanted nothing more than to get up, bid us all a very fond farewell, and step back into her normal, sane life. But somehow, she couldn't. Because now she was in the world of magic. And she knew that the Thistle Witch was a possible threat to everyone she loved, simply because I had worked with her at a bakery. I hoped that when this was all over, she'd be able to step back into her old life and not be haunted by the things she had seen.

But to have that future, we first needed an end.

"OK," I said, breaking the silence.

Lulu glanced over at me, confused.

"What?" she asked.

"I know what you want," I said. "We'll get you back there."

I didn't wait for her reaction. Instead, I got up and walked out of the room. I must have had a purposeful gait because Carmen and the pocket demons poked their heads out of the kitchen. Carmen had a serving tray full of waffles—the perfect carb solution to one too many spells. Her mood had improved because she lifted the tray and smiled at me, saying something. But I didn't catch it. I was on my way.

I charged up to the second floor and into the bright room that we used as a library. Huge windows let in the winter morning. That's what made it the logical room for books and reading. I passed rows of bookshelves, aiming for the back wall. My eyes were fixed on a small painting that hung there.

I didn't realize everyone was behind me until I stopped in front of the picture. But when I saw them all there, it didn't surprise me. Carmen nodded. She understood what I was up to.

I guess if we had been good, old-fashioned witches, the picture I stood in front of would have been some magical scene. Some fairies, maybe, or a woman leading a unicorn around a lake. But that would have been too obvious for a secret hiding spot. So instead, in true Midwestern fashion, the painting was of a pheasant taking flight over a cornfield. I lifted the picture off the wall and a thin layer of dust floated to the floor.

"A wall safe," said Lulu. "I'll be damned."

I brushed some dust off the safe. I couldn't remember the last time we had opened it. Then I sighed and turned the dial to the numbers we had been taught to memorize as children, right along with important phone numbers. Then I pulled the lever, and the safe opened with a squeaking crack.

There were quite a few trinkets inside. Some were old coins that had helped us out in a pinch, and some were artifacts that had caused a bit of trouble back in the day. And some were mementos of our childhood. But I moved them all aside. I was looking for something else.

It was under everything. After all, it was only a tiny piece of paper. There were a lot of stories in that safe. We could have taken each item out and told their tales for a week. But I shook my head and forced the shudder inside me to pass. Then I slammed the safe door and covered it with the picture again.

"What is that?" asked Lulu.

I held an old piece of paper. It was stationary that had probably come in the mail once as a gimmick to try to get my parents to buy something. There were only five names and five phone numbers written on it.

"The emergency numbers," I said. I held on to the list with sweaty fingers. "Witchcraft might scare me, but I'm sick of being scared. Increasing our power is the surest way to beat the Thistle Witch. Maybe someone on this list knows how to do it."

"Fabulous idea, Immy!" said Carmen. A line of pocket demons sat on her shoulder, peering down to look at the names.

"And if they don't?" asked Lulu.

I frowned, considering that very real possibility.

"If that's the case," I said. "Then maybe we can offer to buy them a pizza if they donate their time to the cause."

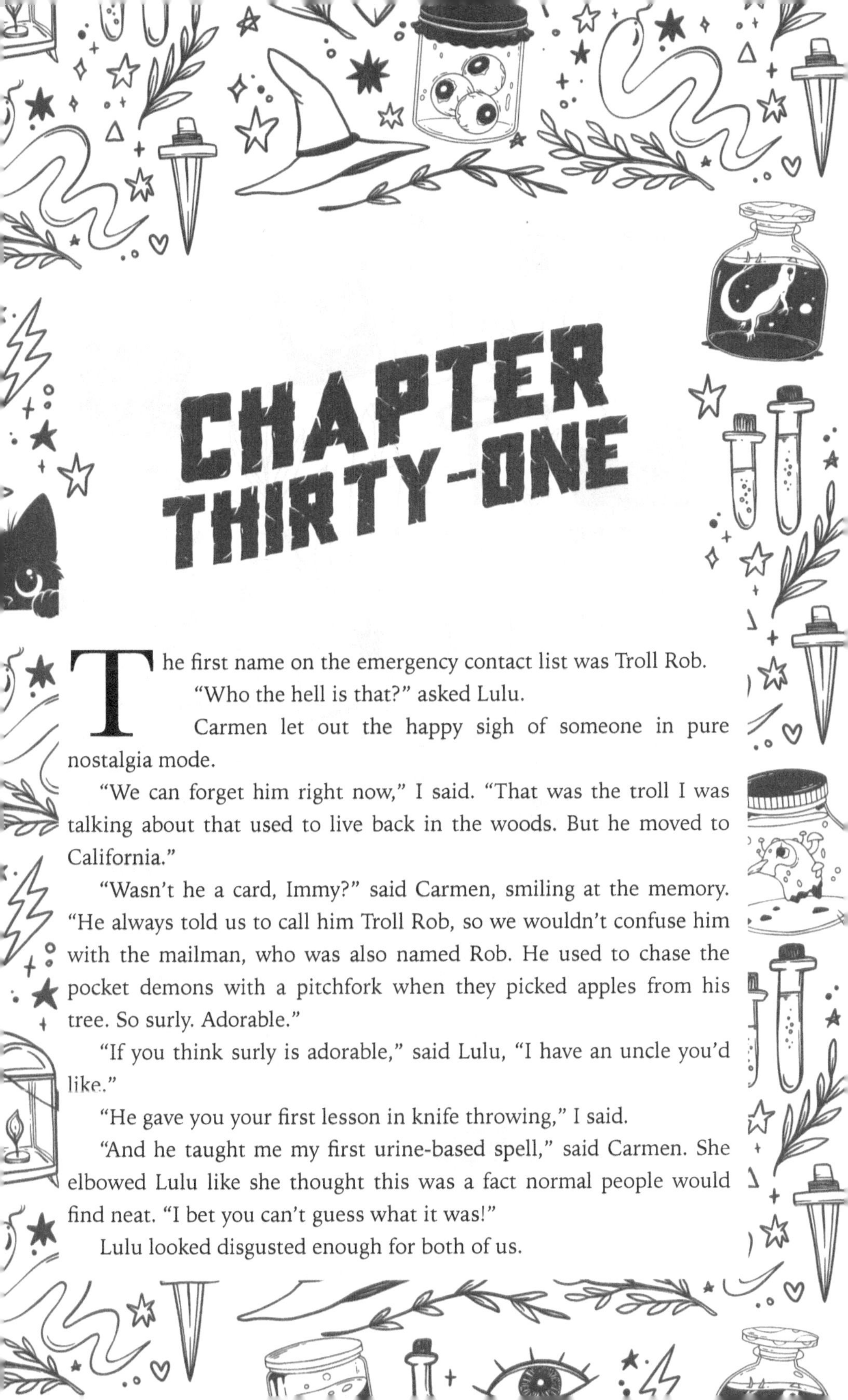

CHAPTER THIRTY-ONE

The first name on the emergency contact list was Troll Rob.

"Who the hell is that?" asked Lulu.

Carmen let out the happy sigh of someone in pure nostalgia mode.

"We can forget him right now," I said. "That was the troll I was talking about that used to live back in the woods. But he moved to California."

"Wasn't he a card, Immy?" said Carmen, smiling at the memory. "He always told us to call him Troll Rob, so we wouldn't confuse him with the mailman, who was also named Rob. He used to chase the pocket demons with a pitchfork when they picked apples from his tree. So surly. Adorable."

"If you think surly is adorable," said Lulu, "I have an uncle you'd like."

"He gave you your first lesson in knife throwing," I said.

"And he taught me my first urine-based spell," said Carmen. She elbowed Lulu like she thought this was a fact normal people would find neat. "I bet you can't guess what it was!"

Lulu looked disgusted enough for both of us.

"Nope," she said. "And I think I'm OK with it being a life-long secret."

"You never swore so much before you met him, Immy," said Carmen.

"I know," I said, thinking back. "He was one of my favorite role models."

We were both lost in thought for a moment. I wondered if the old troll still liked cigars.

"He's too far away to help us," I said. "Heck, he could be on that cruise with mom and dad."

"I wish I could text them and ask," said Carmen. "They'd love to get a picture with him."

"That would be one hell of a sight," I said. "Troll Rob spitting and swearing the whole time. He hated flashing lights."

The second name on the emergency contact list was our aunt, Joyce. Her phone must have rung twenty times before she picked up.

"It worked, Stephen," she said, when she answered. She yelled at her husband in her typical loud, brassy style. "I can't freaking believe it."

"Hi, Joyce," I said. "It's Imogen."

"My God, Stephen," said Joyce. Even though she spoke to her husband with the phone right next to her mouth, Joyce still acted like I couldn't hear her. "Stop staring out the window and come over here. It's Immy. It must be the apocalypse or something. She'd never call me otherwise. How are you, sugar?"

I didn't answer for a minute.

"Uh, are you talking to me?" I asked.

"Who else would I be talking to?" asked Joyce. She sounded fed up with me already. "*You* called *me*!"

I counted to ten several times and took a deep breath.

"I hope you're doing good and everything," I said. "And I'm sorry we don't have time to catch up, but me and Carmen have a little situation here."

"Is it the apocalypse?" asked Joyce.

"It might be, kind of," I said. I stared off, considering the all-encompassing nature of the word. "The witch apocalypse, anyway. Or maybe just our family's apocalypse."

"I knew it," said Joyce, shouting out into whatever room she was in. "Stephen, I was right. Come over here. Those birds can wait until later. God, that man. Anyway, honey, what is it this time? It's not werewolves, is it? I can't stand them. Did your parents ever tell you how I helped them with that werewolf outbreak back in 1977? I almost got turned by one when it pulled off my platform heel. Your uncle Stephen would have had his hands full if I had gone over to the dog side."

"It's the Thistle Witch," said Carmen, leaning over to the phone. "Hello, Aunt Joyce!"

"Hey, sweetie," said Joyce. "The Thistle Witch? She's real, huh? What do you know? I always thought she was just a demented bedtime story like the tooth fairy."

"She's incredibly powerful," said Carmen. Carmen's enthusiasm for powerful witchcraft made me want to lock her somewhere and lose the key. "It looks like the only way we can defeat her is to boost our witchcraft. You wouldn't have any hints, would you?"

"Are you gals serious?" asked Joyce. "Well, I'm not at home right now, so I don't have my spell books in front of me. We're in Venice! Stephen didn't think my cell phone would work, but the people at the place said it was all good to go. I told you, Stephen!"

"Venice sounds lovely!" said Carmen.

"You should see the water," said Joyce. "My God, it's everywhere. It's amazing. After years of thankless palm readings and eating bologna sandwiches, we finally decided to win a little something at the casino. Stephen wanted to do an ancestry trip thing. Next, we're going to Scotland, where one of our ancestors got caught up in the witch trials there."

I felt a pounding deep on the right side of my head. The conversation with Shannon kept running through my mind.

"Time really is of the essence here," I said. "Do you have any advice for boosting our witchcraft?"

"Beats the hell out of me," said Joyce. "Most witches say that's a lost cause and are happy to win at poker all the time. But taking this trip kind of reminds me of something you used to always read in the old folklore."

"What's that?" I asked.

"All those witches in the past were good chums with fairies," said Joyce. "That's where our powers originally came from, right? A fairy would endow a person with powers, you know? And they'd become a witch. Maybe you need to find a fairy."

"We talked about that before," said Carmen. "But everyone knows that fairies are dwindling."

"Stephen, give me that camera," said Joyce. "If you get water on that, I'll be pissed. Anyway, sweeties, that's all I've got. I'm not the Otherworldly Investigations type. I don't know much about fighting evil. I avoided helping when I was a kid, and only did two summers with your parents when I got out of college. That was enough for me. Give me tarot cards any day. But you'd sure as hell think you'd be able to find a fairy some damn place."

"You'd think," I said, not really paying attention. I was looking at my parents' list. "Just thought I'd ask since you're on the emergency contact list in case of apocalypse."

"That's pretty damn stupid," said Joyce.

I wanted to agree with her, but thought better of it.

"Right under you is another name," I said. "It looks familiar. Must be a relative, but I don't know her. The name is Henrietta MacCalzean."

Joyce made a thick, throaty noise.

"Petey needs to update his list," said Joyce. "That's some second cousin of ours. She was in a nursing home in Montana. She's been dead for ages."

"If this was baseball," said Lulu, running her hand through her frizzy hair, "I wouldn't like our batting average."

The fourth name on the list was Daphne Findlay. When I dialed the number, a familiar buzzing rang through my ear. Then the operator message began:

The number you are trying to reach has been disconnected or is no longer in service. Please hang up and try again.

"Shit," I said, tossing my phone onto the end table. "What the hell kind of list did they leave us?"

"Good thing you never needed it when you were kids," said Lulu, crossing her arms. "One of you would have been eaten by now."

"Try the last number, Immy," said Carmen. But I had lost my momentum and felt overwhelmed again by the sheer magnitude of what we had to do. Maybe we did need a fairy, like Joyce said. But how the hell would we find one?

"You call it," I said. "I temporarily hate life."

Carmen's smile was still optimistic and determined. She took my phone and called it. The first four names and numbers on the emergency list had been written in a black pen, in the tight, messy hand of my father. The last name and number must have been added later. It was written in blue pen with the big bubble letters my mom loved so much.

The name my mother had written was simply: Lubberkin.

"Who is that?" asked Lulu.

"I have no idea," I said. Lulu looked at me like she wasn't surprised.

"It's ringing!" said Carmen. Just getting through was cause for celebration. Somehow, the phone ended up back in my hand again.

"Polar Bear Ice Cream," said a high-pitched voice. It was a young girl, probably no more than seventeen. "Our special today is a bacon cheeseburger with hand-cut fries or a hot ham and cheese with your choice of soup. And our snowstorm of the month is crème de menthe with crushed Oreos."

I didn't say anything for a long time. I'm pretty sure that Lulu and Carmen asked me what was going on, but words failed me.

"Is this the ice cream parlor in Kirkwood?" I asked, perplexed.

"Yep!" said the voice. She was eager to talk, which wasn't a surprise. Running an ice cream shop in Minnesota in December had to be a nap-worthy experience. "But we have a bunch of food, too. After the new owner took over, he added daily meal specials. Business is way up."

"That's my favorite place to get ice cream," Carmen said to Lulu. "They make their own hot fudge. I usually get a puppy cone for the demons."

"I like the snowstorms," said Lulu. "But I don't get why they don't just call them Blizzards."

The girl at Polar Bear Ice Cream must have been able to hear Lulu's loud voice.

"We can't do that because of Dairy Queen," said the girl. "We don't wanna get sued."

I unfolded my parents' list, which I had nearly crushed from fiddling with it.

"This might sound like a weird question," I said. "But does the name Lubberkin mean anything to you?"

"Sure!" said the girl. "He's the new owner I was talking about. Mr. Lubberkin. He's super nice and very chill. Like, he put a ping pong table in the basement for when we're on break. His sister is a bitch, but what can you do? She's hardly ever here."

"Is that so?" I asked. Something felt like it might possibly make sense. My parents had met in Kirkwood. It was the largest town around, if a town of nine-thousand people can be called large. They had both hung out in downtown Kirkwood in the 1970s, which was apparently just what you did then. And Polar Bear Ice Cream had been a fixture in downtown Kirkwood since the 1920s. It was the oldest business still in operation in the area. "When did he take over again?"

"I guess about six months ago," said the girl. "But he's been around for longer. Probably about a year and a half. That's when he moved to town."

"Could I talk to him?" I asked. "He's a friend of my parents, and there's kind of a family emergency he should know about."

"Oh," said the girl. I felt like I had killed her good mood. "That's awful. But he left about an hour ago on a cheese run. He has a special place where he gets cheese. He's very serious about cheese."

I felt like I should comment, but decided not to.

"But he doesn't leave very often," said the ice cream girl. "He's a real homebody. He lives in the apartment right above the shop. If you call or stop by tomorrow, he should be around. He loves talking to people and giving free samples."

"All right," I said. I wasn't sure what else to say. My parents thought that an ice cream parlor owner could help us. To an outsider, that might have seemed a little strange. But over the years my parents had courted weirder ideas. "I guess we'll probably stop by tomorrow, then. Thanks so much for everything."

"No problem!" said the girl. "And I hope everything turns out all right."

"Thanks," I said. I put my phone on the table and looked at Carmen and Lulu.

"Are we going to get some ice cream?" asked Lulu.

"I think so," I said.

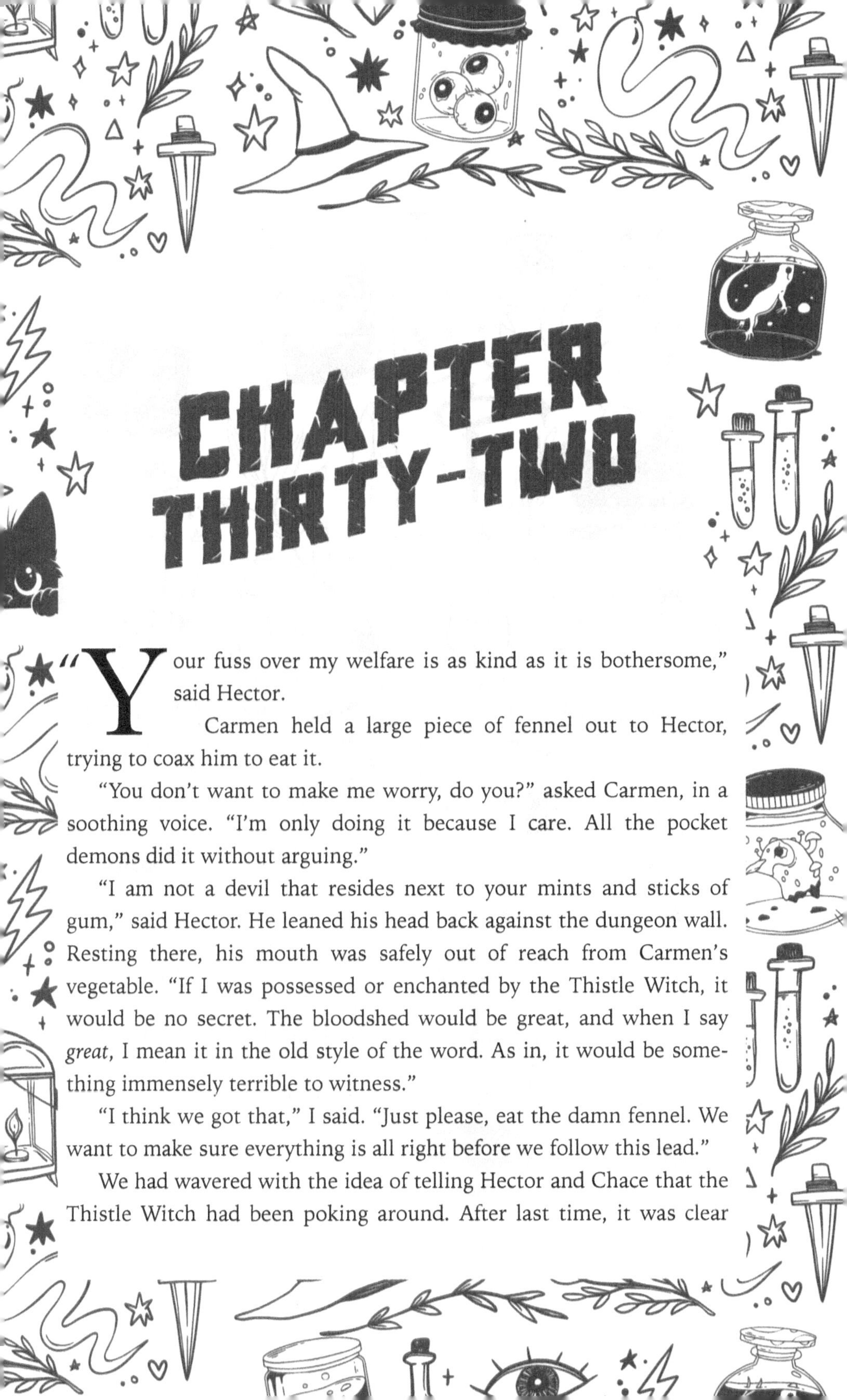

CHAPTER THIRTY-TWO

"Your fuss over my welfare is as kind as it is bothersome," said Hector.

Carmen held a large piece of fennel out to Hector, trying to coax him to eat it.

"You don't want to make me worry, do you?" asked Carmen, in a soothing voice. "I'm only doing it because I care. All the pocket demons did it without arguing."

"I am not a devil that resides next to your mints and sticks of gum," said Hector. He leaned his head back against the dungeon wall. Resting there, his mouth was safely out of reach from Carmen's vegetable. "If I was possessed or enchanted by the Thistle Witch, it would be no secret. The bloodshed would be great, and when I say *great*, I mean it in the old style of the word. As in, it would be something immensely terrible to witness."

"I think we got that," I said. "Just please, eat the damn fennel. We want to make sure everything is all right before we follow this lead."

We had wavered with the idea of telling Hector and Chace that the Thistle Witch had been poking around. After last time, it was clear that Chace was already nervous, and I didn't want his unease to spread to a ten-foot-tall minotaur. But we didn't know what the Thistle Witch had Lulu do, so we didn't have a choice but to go down and tell them.

"It's not so bad," said Lulu, taking a bite. "I put it in soup all the time."

I walked over to Chace in his cell. His skin still looked terrible, but no more terrible than last time. Somehow or another, though, he had managed to look even more tired.

I handed him a piece of fennel, and he chomped down on it without hesitation. Then he raised it to Hector.

"Cheers," said Chace. He took another bite.

"Bah," said Hector. He swiped the fennel from Carmen's hand and took a little bite out of it. He reminded me of a small child trying new fruits and vegetables for the first time. "This is truly awful."

"But neither of you look like you're breaking out," I said. "No shrieks of agony. So, I don't think you're under any kind of spell."

"Thank gods for that," said Hector, throwing down the fennel. "I cannot believe that the Thistle Witch was so near, and yet I did not smell the putrid vapor of her hate or experience the sickening recoil in my stomach due to her proximity."

"Hopefully, if you didn't sense her, that means she didn't sense you," said Carmen.

"You didn't hear anything that night at all?" I asked. "No possessed Lulu poking around or anything?"

"I hope not," said Lulu, looking sick at the thought.

"Nay," said Hector. "Since taking up residence within these dungeon walls, I have slept the calming sleep of an infant that belongs to a pack of mighty warrior monsters. Safe in the knowledge that it can rest without fear because it is at the top of the food chain."

"I wish I could sleep like that," said Lulu.

"How about you?" I asked, turning to Chace. "You didn't see anything? And please don't lie."

"I wouldn't lie," said Chace. He scrunched up the face that wasn't his, annoyed. "I don't have any interest in protecting the Thistle Witch. I'm the one that wanted to run from her, remember? I didn't see anything. I didn't sleep like a baby because this one snores like an old coal train pulling out of the station. But I didn't wake up, no."

My whole body wanted to relax, but didn't know how. Maybe the Thistle Witch didn't know that Chace and Hector were down here. Was that too much to hope for? Then what was she doing with Lulu? Did she just use Lulu to poke around our property? It seemed like a lucky break that the witch hadn't discovered our dungeon guests. We hadn't been lucky so far, and I was afraid to get too excited about it.

"That makes me feel a little bit better, Immy," said Carmen. "Maybe she doesn't know they're down here."

"Didn't you say you dreamt about yellow?" Chace asked Lulu. He stared at her with a pointed, groggy gaze. Lulu stared right back. She didn't hide her dislike for Chace.

"Yeah," she said, simply. "I did."

"That's probably not the best thing in the world," said Chace, looking away. "I wouldn't start celebrating just yet."

"Jade used to wear yellow when she went into battle," said Hector. He had a dreamy look in his eyes. "To frighten her enemies a little bit before she slaughtered them."

My mouth formed a shape that could have been a smile, but wasn't.

"That's nice," I said.

"She was a marvelous woman," said Hector, sighing. "And you, non-magical one. You do not feel any pain after the spell of the cursed tablet?"

"I'm all right," said Lulu. "I just feel like my nieces and nephews made me go on all the rides at Valleyfair."

"That's the spirit," said Hector. He patted Lulu on the back. "Now remember, when you face the Thistle Witch, you must smite her once for me. For me and Jade."

"That's the kind of confidence I like," said Lulu.

"Hopefully, this guy we're going to talk to can help us more than Joyce," I said.

"Joyce reminded us about the fairies," said Carmen. She held out Minerva, so Hector could pet her with his little finger.

"Good luck," said Chace. He rubbed his eyes. "Finding a fairy is no small feat. I've been alive for…well… I can't remember how long just now. But I guess that means a while. And I've only seen a fairy five times. And the last time was before your grandparents were born."

"Yeah, well, these gals are witches," said Lulu. "And if I've learned anything about witches, it's that they are good at gambling. So, I like those odds."

"Thanks so much," said Carmen.

"Soldier on, brave witches and non-magical brave human," said Hector. "Find this mystery man, so you can defeat that sinister witch. Worry not for us."

"He's right," I said. "We better go. There's a snowstorm coming, and I want to be back before it sets in."

Chace moved away from the bars and sat back down in his cell chair. The way he moved was like a caged animal confined for so long that it's no longer interested in putting up a fight. I had every reason in the world to dislike Chace. Still, though, the way he existed made me sad. I didn't like it, and I hadn't liked it since the first day we put him there. A bundle of guilt, sadness, and loss swirled around me, and I found myself walking up to him.

I must have been quiet because he didn't notice me at first. He already had a book open—but my shadow must have disturbed his light. He looked up with a startled expression.

"What?" he asked, closing the book again. "What's wrong?"

He almost dropped his book when he stood up.

"If you don't watch out," I said. "You're going to look like a person who cares about others, and not just like a demon who's wearing someone else for pretend."

I could feel the others behind me, watching.

"What do you want?" he asked. He tried to look disinterested again, but he wasn't fooling anyone. "I said I didn't see anything."

He was sick of all this, but I was sick of it, too. I didn't want to hold on to my old life anymore. It had all just been a lie, anyway. I needed to let go of it. And I couldn't let go if part of that old life still haunted the dungeon.

"I just wanted to tell you," I said, whispering. "That when all of this is over with the Thistle Witch, I'm going to let you out."

I thought he was going to laugh. Then he gained his composure and looked me right in the eyes. He leaned in toward the bars. It was closer than we had been in a long time. I didn't move. I just stared right back.

"And how do you propose that I get past all the eyes on the stairs?" he asked. I could almost feel his breath on my face, but I wasn't going to be the one to back away.

"I guess I'll just have to chip them off the steps," I said, matter-of-fact. "Then shove you out the door. And then after you're gone, we'll have to re-paint them."

He still stared at me, but his expression changed, like he was considering the possibility of a life beyond those walls. Thinking about a life that, until a few minutes ago, had seemed impossible.

"You're serious," he said. He didn't say it as a question. He said it like he couldn't process it.

"Yes," I said. I glanced around at the books and odds and ends in his cell. "So, start packing."

I turned to leave, but he made a strange noise, so I looked back at him.

There was a weird smile on the face that wasn't his. Like the smile a kid has when he's promised ice cream after dinner, but doesn't want to look too excited, in case he jinxes it.

"Aren't you afraid that when I get out, I'll come back and try to kill you again?" he asked.

I looked him over one more time, just to remember. He had messy, sandy hair, a short beard and mustache, dark eyes, and was barely taller than me. But none of that was really him. I'd never know what he actually looked like, not really. The only clue was the tiny, eraser-sized holes in his cheeks, where the purple scales poked through. It was so hard to believe that he was the man I had loved, but even harder to believe that I'd hated him. Now I looked at him and felt nothing but the need to never look again.

I stared him straight in the eyes and said, "You're the last thing in the world that scares me."

Then I turned and left.

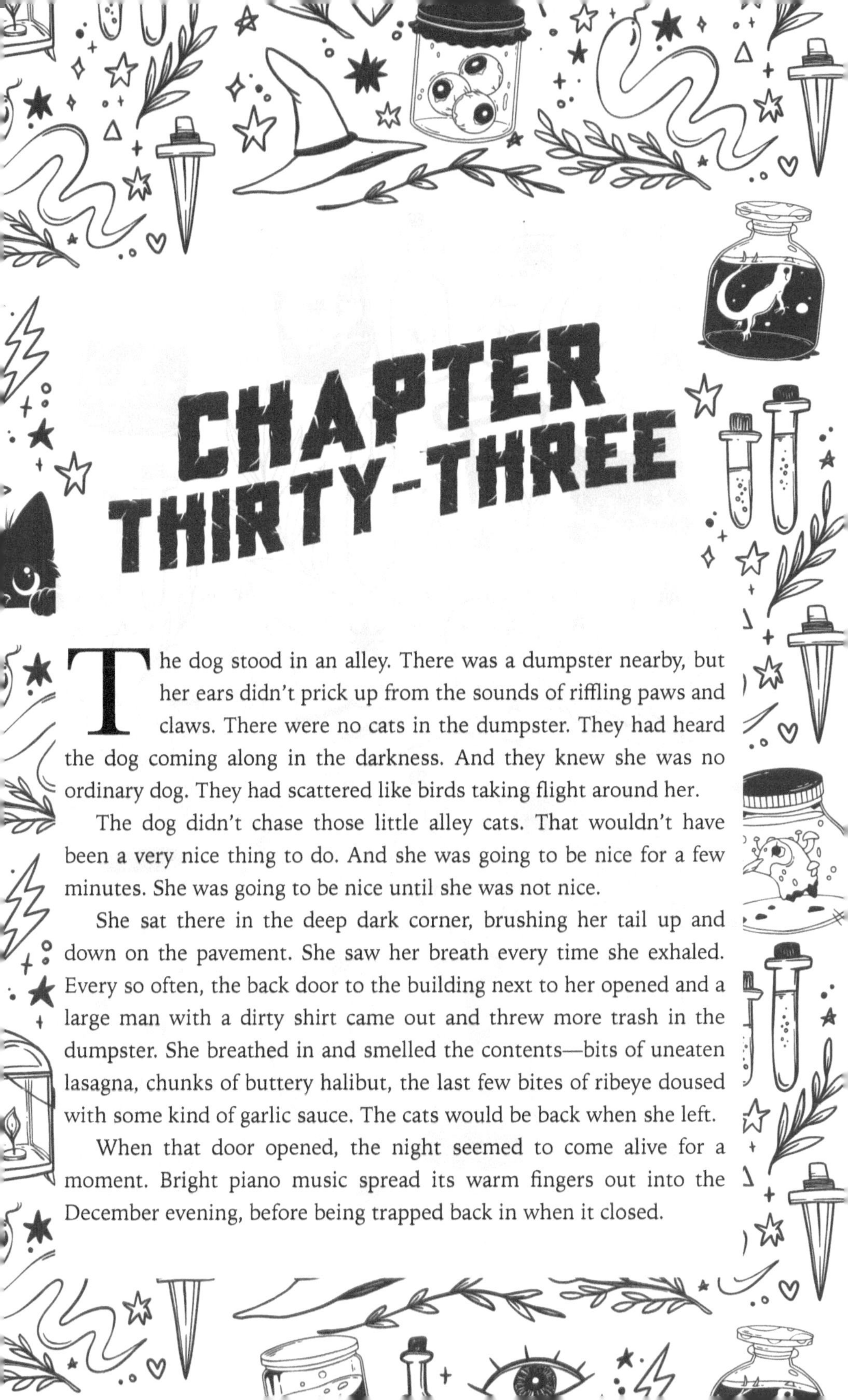

CHAPTER THIRTY-THREE

The dog stood in an alley. There was a dumpster nearby, but her ears didn't prick up from the sounds of riffling paws and claws. There were no cats in the dumpster. They had heard the dog coming along in the darkness. And they knew she was no ordinary dog. They had scattered like birds taking flight around her.

The dog didn't chase those little alley cats. That wouldn't have been a very nice thing to do. And she was going to be nice for a few minutes. She was going to be nice until she was not nice.

She sat there in the deep dark corner, brushing her tail up and down on the pavement. She saw her breath every time she exhaled. Every so often, the back door to the building next to her opened and a large man with a dirty shirt came out and threw more trash in the dumpster. She breathed in and smelled the contents—bits of uneaten lasagna, chunks of buttery halibut, the last few bites of ribeye doused with some kind of garlic sauce. The cats would be back when she left.

When that door opened, the night seemed to come alive for a moment. Bright piano music spread its warm fingers out into the December evening, before being trapped back in when it closed.

Once, when the door opened, she heard the cool sounds of a man with a deep voice.

"Make sure you have your martini for this one," he said. There was easy laughter and the tinkling of glasses. "This song has been covered by a lot of singers, but my favorite is still the Fred Astaire version…"

Somehow the dog thought the man sounded tall and sturdy, and she decided he must be brave to sing in front of all of those people while they ate.

He will do nicely, thought the dog. *Good and strong.*

When the door opened again, the dog heard that the singer had gotten everyone in the club to join with him.

"Make it one for my baby," they sang. "And one more for the road."

There are so many of them in there tonight. They will fill it out nicely.

The dog scratched her claws into the cold, icy pavement, thinking of the people eating their breadsticks and ordering their drinks, not knowing that she was out in the alley, waiting for a certain hour. Waiting until she knew the restaurant would be its busiest. She knew what time that was because she had been there every night for a week. She had watched people come and go. Soon it would be time.

The dog would have smiled if she had been in her other form. This would hurt the red-haired sister. And she very much wanted to hurt the red-haired sister. She didn't deserve to be a dog. No. What a dirty, filthy witch. And there was nothing in the world worse than a witch. Perhaps the red-haired sister knew the names of the people inside, from the man at the bar, to the singer by the piano, to the waiters bringing appetizers. Surely, she was friends with them all. The dog knew where the red-haired sister came and went. She had been watching her for a long while. The dog would put tears in that woman's big eyes. And then those big eyes would shut for good. And then the eyes of every other witch would shut too, to make a point.

Off in the distance, through the foggy winter air, a church bell chimed that it was midnight. The dog shuddered, but only for a moment. She had never liked bells. But there was no time to be angry about that now. She had been such a good dog not to hurt those cats. But now, it was time to be good at something else.

The next time the large man opened the door, the dog slipped past him, into the restaurant's kitchen. She was so fast that he spun around. He felt her tail touch his arm, but then he was alone there, in the alley, staring at the dark. He shrugged and threw the garbage in the dumpster, thinking it was only his imagination.

The door slammed and the dog was sucked into the sounds of trumpets and clarinets. The man at the piano sang for a full minute after the dog entered the building. That's when the screaming began.

CHAPTER THIRTY-FOUR

We were halfway to Kirkwood when the snow started. At first, it was just a flake or two, but then it seemed to come down all at once like balloons and confetti falling on a game show contestant who's won a big prize. Even with the defrost on, the windshield kept fogging up.

"Maybe we should wait and see this Lubberkin guy tomorrow," said Lulu. She frowned at the heavy flakes falling around us.

"No—" Carmen and I said it in unison, then glanced at each other with nervous eyes. We both had the same feeling of dread. I had felt it back before my parents had called to inform me that Carmen was a dog, and then again every time I thought about that witch. It was the curse of being a witch—knowing that something magical and most likely bad was about to happen, but having no idea what it was or when it would occur.

"I don't think that's a good idea," said Carmen. Her voice was constrained and quiet. "I have a queasy feeling like the Thistle Witch is charging up behind us. I feel like if I turn around, she'll be there."

Carmen flipped up the collar on her coat dress as if to keep an invisible breath from blowing on her neck.

"I feel it too," I said. "I'm pretty sure something's coming, and fast. We might not have until tomorrow to talk to this guy."

Lulu wiped the condensation off her window. She watched the snow pile up in the ditch from the plow ahead of us. She sat in the backseat like someone who had been asked to mimic the look of a relaxed person, but was doing a terrible job at it.

"I hope we don't go in the ditch on the way there or back," said Lulu. "It would be an unpleasant walk back to Holy Oak."

Chace turned a yellow page in his copy of *The Monk*. He blinked a few times against the harsh light of the dungeon. The wind was so loud that even underground he heard it, whistling and groaning through the shed above. But he kept his eyes on his novel.

Hector's attention was fixed on the dungeon ceiling.

"It is a veritable tempest out there. A tempest, I say!"

"Just try to ignore it," said Chace, in a bland tone.

"But the witches and their chunk of metal on wheels will be thrown off the road in this blizzard. The snow must be terrible to behold. I fear for their safety on this quest."

Chace didn't look up, but he wasn't reading anymore either. He only stared at the page.

"As long as they remember their protection spells, car accidents don't hurt witches," said Chace. The back of his neck felt hot. "Believe me, I know."

"Bah," said Hector. "You stopped being good company when we ran out of flesh-eating tales."

"They'll be fine," said Chace. "They'll find answers from whoever they're meeting…and then they'll beat evil as usual. Just relax."

"*Whomever*," said Hector.

Chace's face reddened. "Just work on that damn puzzle Carmen gave you."

Hector sat on the dungeon floor with a puzzle in front of him.

Only a small section had been shoved together. He lifted the little pieces in his immense hand.

"I cannot make heads nor tails of this cardboard amusement," said Hector. "The pieces are far too puny for me to manipulate with my grand digits. And there are more pieces of the same color than reason dictates. For the life of me, I cannot see how all of these small shards can join together to form this image on the box of three fluffy kittens in a wooden barrel."

Chace rolled his eyes. "Here, do you want my help? Put the pieces in the box and slide the thing in here. *I'll* make the damn puzzle."

"Brilliant!" said Hector, slamming the dungeon floor with his hand. With a flick of his fingers, he had all the puzzle pieces back in the box. He carried it over to Chace's cell and crammed the box through the bars.

"You shall assemble the puzzle," said Hector. "And I will observe your progress and provide helpful suggestions."

"Sounds great," said Chace, monotone.

"But once the kittens have been assembled, we must keep the puzzle in good condition, so we can glue and preserve the image, like Carmen mentioned. For posterity," said Hector.

"Yeah, yeah," said Chace, spreading the puzzle out on his cell floor. "We'll be lucky to get these pieces together with the way you bent them all."

When Hector didn't come back with a defensive retort, Chace glanced up. The minotaur was not looking at him. Instead, he was focused on an old iron skeleton key that stuck out of the keyhole in Chace's cell. A yellow ribbon hung from its circular end.

"What is that?" asked Hector, pointing at it.

Chace stood up slowly, feeling the real skin under his fake skin shift. There was sweat all over his brow.

"Look," said Chace. For some reason, he didn't dare point at the key. "A yellow ribbon."

Hector flared his large nostrils.

"Yellow," said Hector. "Just as the non-magical one dreamt about. You know what this means?"

"Lulu was down here when she was under the cursed tablet," said Chace. They both continued to watch the key as if it might move again or try to trick them.

"Or perhaps she had only to give it a mighty toss down the stairs," said Hector.

Chace scowled at Hector, and Hector scowled right back.

"You know of what I speak," said Hector. "That key is hexed."

Chace made shushing noises and put a finger to his lips.

"Saying it aloud will not bring perdition upon us any faster than if we refused to speak of it," said Hector. His eyes seemed to grow a size larger. "It is clear that the key is hexed. How else did it end up in that lock? Carmen and Imogen did not see it because it was not there when they were down here. And neither you nor I put it there. It has been waiting for its moment, and for some reason, its moment is now."

"Shut up," said Chace, quietly. "Just be quiet and give me a minute to think."

He paced back and forth, running his hands through hair that wasn't his. He stopped and felt it. It was starting to come out, strand by strand. He had almost started to think of it as his. But that was foolish. He didn't even have hair. He barely even had horns. Just a couple of nubs, really.

"Perhaps this is no ordinary storm," said Hector. "Listen to that wind. I have heard gales like that out on the open sea before, when a god would open the heavens and rain down vengeance upon a perfidious human."

"She wants to keep Imogen and Carmen away," said Chace, swallowing. "She wants to buy herself a little more time."

"And what exactly would she need that time for?" asked Hector. He stepped closer to the bars. "Why does the Thistle Witch seem so intent on setting you free? What do you know of this?"

"I don't know anything," said Chace, his voice rising. "I didn't want anything to do with her, remember? I wanted to get the hell out of here."

"A likely story," said Hector. "You were just biding your time until your master returned."

"You brainwashed cow!" said Chace. "She's not my freaking master!"

Their shouting match came to an abrupt end when the key clicked into place. Hector and Chace stood motionless as the cell door squeaked open an inch. It felt almost like a whisper, the way the door moved ever so slightly and then came to a stop. A whisper to someone above, perhaps, saying that everything was in place at last.

Chace backed away from the cell door with slow, cautious steps like it was something that couldn't be trusted. His face transformed into a look of desperation.

"Look at me," said Chace, frantic. "Look in my eyes. You know I'm not in cahoots with the Thistle Witch. You know she is no friend of mine. I didn't even believe she was real. And when I found out she was, I was terrified. I don't know what she wants from me, but I don't want anything from her."

Hector stared into Chace's eyes and then slowly nodded.

"I believe you, terrified short devil," said Hector. "What do you propose we do?"

Chace almost felt like laughing.

"Do?" he asked. "I have no idea. What the hell *can* we do? We're stuck down here. I'm not sure if that's a good thing or a bad thing."

He looked at his hands. He had to clench them to make the shaking stop.

"I think we might die down here," said Chace. "Somehow, she's going to kill us. She hates both of us because of our association with the Abernathys. And because you defiled her grave. And now she's going to kill us."

"Do not despair, shaking devil," said Hector. "This is still a protected place."

"I hope you're right," said Chace. "I don't know what all happened with that cursed tablet, but I'm not feeling particularly safe right now, are you?"

Drops of sweat ran down the side of Chace's bumpy face. It had never felt so hot in that dungeon.

Hector reached up as if to close the cell door, but thought better of it.

"Are you one of the demons that inhabits Hell?" asked Hector, in a quiet voice. "Or are you one that usually walks upon the Earth?"

"The Earth," said Chace, whispering. "So, I guess if she kills me, it'll be a change of scenery."

Hector made a somber noise but said nothing. The only sound was the hum of the lights and the howling wind above. Chace plastered himself to the dungeon wall at the back of his cell, waiting for something to happen. Hector once again stared up at the ceiling.

"I feel as if we shouldn't have spoken of the key," said Hector, sadly. "Just as you entreated. We should have ignored it and continued assembling the puzzle. I feel as if we have brought doom upon us now, just by speaking its name."

The wind surged above them. There was a crunching noise from an icy branch breaking and falling to the ground. Hector wandered to the far side of the dungeon, still looking up at the ceiling. It almost seemed like he could see the storm outside with the way his eyes were fixed upward like that. Then he disappeared to the left and down the hallway. Chace raised an eyebrow. He sighed and took a few deep breaths, waiting for Hector to appear again. When the minotaur didn't return, Chace's heart began to beat hard again. Had Hector abandoned him, disappearing out of the shed and into the storm? After all, Hector's soul wasn't dark the way his own soul was, if he even had one. Hector could leave anytime he wanted, no matter how ill-advised it might be.

Chace took a few small steps toward the open cell door.

"Hey," he whispered. "Hector?"

When Hector shot out around the corner, Chace put a hand on his chest, feeling a sudden wave of relief.

"What the hell are you doing?" Chace asked. "You scared the shit out of me. I thought you left."

"Salvation is upon us, my demon friend!" said Hector. He threw up his arms in victory. "It is a miracle among miracles."

"What the hell are you talking about?" asked Chace.

Hector swung open Chace's cell door. His large hand sizzled for the few seconds he touched the iron, but he seemed oblivious to the pain.

"It's her," said Hector. "Can you not hear her, even now? Her call is plain as day."

"Who?" asked Chace, frowning.

"Jade!" said Hector. "My mate. She has returned to me. She has come to save us from the Thistle Witch."

Chace ducked away from Hector, lodging himself back in the corner of his cell.

"That is not Jade, you idiot!" yelled Chace.

"Listen and you will hear her," said Hector. His eyes were glazed over like he had cataracts. "She is out there on the road beyond the Abernathy property. Come, she will take us to Imogen and Carmen. We can help defeat the Thistle Witch."

Chace kicked at Hector, but nothing he did was a match for the hulking minotaur. Hector didn't get mad when Chace resisted, but instead grabbed at Chace with a bright smile, like a parent trying to force his child to the dentist.

"Come," said Hector. "Do not be afraid. It is only Jade. She has come back to me! You must see her. She is a beauty even among beautiful monsters."

"No, you asshole!" said Chace. Hector gave Chace a sharp tug to pull him out of his prison, and Chace lost two fingernails in the cell wall. He clawed at the dungeon floor with such vigor that his real scaly finger poked out of Chace Mackenzie's skin. "It's the Thistle Witch! She has you spellbound. Snap out of it, you big, stupid shit!"

Hector pulled Chace through the dungeon kicking and screaming. Chace yelled in deep, guttural howls, begging to be let go.

"Coming, Jade," said Hector. They were halfway down the hall. "You will feel foolish, my small friend, when you realize you have put up this fuss for nothing. Jade will not harm you. I will insist that she give up consuming human and demon flesh, just as I did long ago."

"Listen to me!" said Chace. His throat was almost raw from screaming. "It's not Jade. Jade is dead. Her bones were scattered to the winds generations ago. It's the Thistle Witch, damn it. Don't you remember the key? You're bringing us to our deaths!"

But Hector only smiled. He paused at the bottom of the stairs and nodded.

"Only a moment more, Jade!" he called out.

"No!" Chace screamed. "It'll kill me!"

But Hector lifted Chace up and flung him across his right shoulder like a sack of flour. Then he ascended the steps.

He held Chace with a tight grip as the demon screamed out in pain. Then the screams were muffled by the blood streaming out of Chace's mouth. It ran down his chin and onto the eyes emblazoned on the steps. When Hector exploded through the door in the floor, a long bloody mass of flesh oozed down Chace's chin, and he didn't speak again.

"Jade!" said Hector, plunging himself into the snow. Chace's limp body bounced up and down, leaving a red trail in the snow.

The storm seemed to knock at Hector from every direction, distorting his view. He only knew where to go by Jade's strong voice, calling him through the wind. Inside the Abernathy house, the bravest of the little devils poked their heads out from behind the curtains and peeked outside. They barely made out Hector in the tempest. Then one by one, they ducked out of sight again and wrung their hands.

What should we do? Benedict asked.

There is nothing to do, Norma Shearer replied. *She is too powerful. We must wait for Carmen and Imogen to return.*

The pocket demons slid into the shadows and corners and deep, dark rafters, melting themselves into the wood to remain unseen. The grandfather clock ticked, the wind shook, and the devils in the dark corners waited for their mothers to return.

"Jade!" said Hector. He shouted above the wind. "I am here! Wait for me!"

The blood had nearly frozen to Chace's face when Hector finally made out the figure of a woman standing on the road beyond the stones. It was hard to see her with the snow and wind hammering against him. Then he heard Jade's voice once more and ran straight out to her. Hector was only four feet from the figure when his mate's voice faded from his ears. He stood on the road as the wind whipped between them. Hector was face to face with a woman he knew well. But that woman was not Jade.

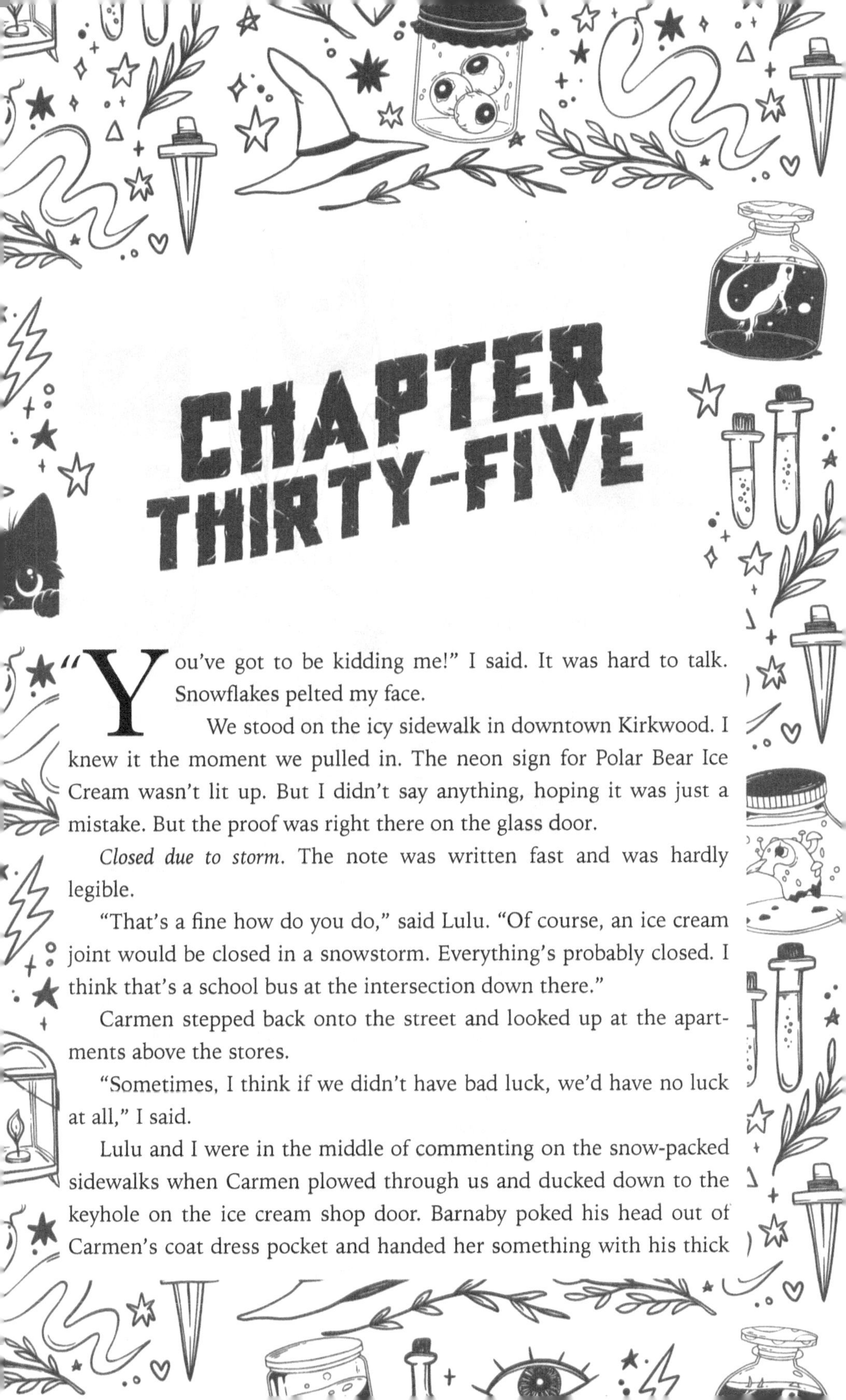

CHAPTER THIRTY-FIVE

"Y ou've got to be kidding me!" I said. It was hard to talk. Snowflakes pelted my face.

We stood on the icy sidewalk in downtown Kirkwood. I knew it the moment we pulled in. The neon sign for Polar Bear Ice Cream wasn't lit up. But I didn't say anything, hoping it was just a mistake. But the proof was right there on the glass door.

Closed due to storm. The note was written fast and was hardly legible.

"That's a fine how do you do," said Lulu. "Of course, an ice cream joint would be closed in a snowstorm. Everything's probably closed. I think that's a school bus at the intersection down there."

Carmen stepped back onto the street and looked up at the apartments above the stores.

"Sometimes, I think if we didn't have bad luck, we'd have no luck at all," I said.

Lulu and I were in the middle of commenting on the snow-packed sidewalks when Carmen plowed through us and ducked down to the keyhole on the ice cream shop door. Barnaby poked his head out of Carmen's coat dress pocket and handed her something with his thick paws. Carmen took it and said some words under her breath. Then she shoved the lock pick in the keyhole.

"As a small business owner, I'm not sure if I'm down with this," said Lulu.

"What if someone sees us?" I asked.

"Nobody's going to see us, Immy," said Carmen. She sounded like my apprehension about breaking into a business was the silliest fear I could ever have. "Everyone's worried about picking up their kids and finding babysitters for the afternoon. Nobody's watching three women in the most deserted part of town."

The way she finagled the lock pick around gave me the impression that this wasn't her first rodeo.

"I could see a light on above the shop," said Carmen. "I think Mr. Lubberkin is upstairs."

"That gal on the phone said he's usually around," said Lulu.

There was a clicking noise, and then Barnaby squealed with satisfaction. We were in.

As we entered the dark ice cream parlor, Carmen slid the lock pick back to the pocket demon.

"You might need to teach me how to do that," I said.

"Really?" asked Carmen, delighted.

"I can't believe I'm saying this," I said. "But it does look like it could come in handy."

"I'm going to watch out for you two on beignet day," said Lulu.

Polar Bear Ice Cream still had its original 1920s counter with creamy green, white, and yellow tiles laid out in an art deco style of rounded trumpet triangles. The stools seemed low to the ground, a sign of how short people had been back when the place had first opened. Behind the counter was a bevy of glass cups and bowls waiting to be filled with ice cream and cherry phosphates. There were photos of the store and its owners through the years, and paintings of the ever-changing façade of downtown Kirkwood.

Opposite the soda fountain wall were two lines of creamy green vinyl booths. The solid wood tables were old and dinged up from generations of use.

"What exactly is the plan?" whispered Lulu. "We're going to go up to his apartment and say, 'Hey, we just broke in to ask you a couple of things,' or what?"

"Probably not," I whispered back. That's when I realized that I, too, was out of the loop when it came to a plan. "Carmen. What's the plan? Are we doing reconnaissance, or going to talk to the guy?"

Carmen was admiring the sparkling glasses and sundae bowls behind the counter.

"Oh, dear," said Carmen, snapping out of her trance. "I hadn't thought beyond getting in here."

Lulu let out an annoyed huff.

"Look at this, Immy," said Carmen. She walked over with a sundae bowl in hand. "I should get a set of these for my homemade ice cream nights. They're so pretty. And nice and heavy. I could really bludgeon someone to death with one."

"Jesus," I mumbled.

"Witches sure aren't what I thought they'd be like," said Lulu, muttering. "We could get arrested for breaking and entering, and you two are acting like Laurel and Hardy."

"Pretty sure Laurel never joked about bludgeoning someone," I whispered, agitated.

"You never know, Immy," said Carmen. "They made over a hundred films together."

"You should be stealthy like cats," said Lulu. "Figure a way out of this. Should we go talk to him or get the hell out of here?"

Just then, a fluorescent light turned on in a back room. Large, bare feet came down the rickety old stairs.

We were all so befuddled about what to do that we did absolutely nothing. That was the day I learned that we'd make terrible cat burglars. Lulu threw her arms up in silent annoyance, sure we were all headed to the pokey. I shrugged, hoping it was one of those times we could use that old adage of begging for forgiveness instead of asking for permission.

The man reached the bottom step and sauntered into the ice cream parlor. The only place I had ever seen a guy quite like him was in a

Billy Jack film. He wore a plush avocado robe. I never found out if there were clothes underneath that robe. He had a hemp bracelet and messy, curly brown hair. There was definitely a Bob Ross look about him.

He rubbed the sand out of his eyes as he walked with drowsy steps toward the counter. Although he walked right by us, I felt that he hadn't seen us somehow. But then he lifted a hand and gave us a genial little wave. He took a few more steps, then stopped. He turned back to us.

"Snow's out of sight today, isn't it?" he asked. The way he talked was slow and easy, like caramel poured from a jar. "We're actually closed, but it's no sweat, man. You want some ice cream?"

He walked over to the bowls and cups. We motioned to each other, wondering what the hell to do. But the man seemed unconcerned with our break-in.

"I have, like, so much ice cream," he said. "We make it right here. The vanilla has bits of vanilla bean in it. It's some righteous stuff."

He opened the sliding door of a large metal freezer and bent over with an ice cream scoop. Then a shadow passed over his face, and he looked at us.

"You're not here to kill me, are you?" he asked.

"No!" We all said it so fast that it was one big blur.

"Of course not," I added, just to sell it.

The man's face melted into a relaxed smile again. "Right on," he said, bending back into the freezer. "Come on over, Red. I've got some butter brickle with your name on it."

"Oh, goody!" said Carmen, hurrying over to him. Lulu and I were left to stand in complete bewilderment.

"What the hell is this guy's deal?" said Lulu, under her breath. "This is your parents' big answer to the apocalypse?"

"You don't know my parents," I whispered back. "They've been suckered into every timeshare ever peddled to them."

"You came ready with your own bowl," said the man. "Righteous. Here you are."

Carmen took the ice cream and dug right in. There was nothing she liked as much as bonding with people over food.

"Thanks so much," said Carmen. "Would you happen to be Mr. Lubberkin?"

The man let out a goofy laugh. "Just Lubberkin," he said. "No *Mister*. It gives me the willies, you know?"

Carmen nodded the way you do when you think it's best to just agree with someone and let a topic die. Lubberkin disappeared into his freezer again, and then came back out with some rocky road for me and mint chocolate chip for Lulu.

"And who are you ladies?" asked Lubberkin.

"I'm Carmen Abernathy. And the one in the gray is my sister, Imogen."

"Loving the gray," said Lubberkin.

"And the one with the hair is our friend and bakery owner Lulu Marin," said Carmen.

"The one with the hair?" asked Lulu. She sounded like she didn't know if she should be offended or flattered.

"It's righteous hair," said Lubberkin, nodding.

"I think so too," said Carmen, taking another bite of ice cream.

"Do you have donuts at your bakery?" asked Lubberkin, scooping a bowl of chocolate ice cream.

"Of course," said Lulu.

"Cool," said Lubberkin. "I'm not down with bakeries that don't sell donuts. I don't get the point."

We ate our ice cream for a second. Lubberkin stared off like he was thinking.

"Did you say your name was Abernathy?" asked Lubberkin.

"Yep," I said.

"You must be Madge and Petey's girls."

"That's right," said Carmen, smiling.

"That explains the door," said Lubberkin. "You must be some far-out witches. That door might not look like much, but it's got a magic seal on the lock. Gotta protect my dairy."

The world stood still. Had the hippie wannabe uttered the words *witches* and *magic*? He didn't seem like the kind of person who would know about magic. He seemed more like the kind that would sit in the back of a van and smoke pot while staring at a wizard poster.

"Wait a minute," I said. "Are you a warlock?"

Lubberkin snorted when he laughed. "Imagine me, a warlock," he said. "That's far out. I could see that. Throwing some bones around, stirring a cauldron."

"But you're not?" asked Lulu.

"Nah," said Lubberkin. He pushed the chocolate ice cream toward Carmen.

"Who's this for?" asked Carmen.

Lubberkin looked Carmen up and down. "That's for all the pocket demons on you. There are, what, five of them in your coat?"

Carmen's face brightened. "One's either ripping up the back of my dress or giving me a massage. You can never tell."

Barnaby poked his head out of Carmen's breast pocket again.

"Hey there, little man," said Lubberkin. "It's been a long time since I saw one of you. Very cool."

The storm swirled around outside. Everything might have been cool and easy inside Polar Bear Ice Cream, but outside in the snow and wind, the Thistle Witch was still a very real threat. It felt like every moment we wasted was another moment she could use against us. We had to get answers from this guy. And then we had to hurry back.

"We don't have a hell of a lot of time," I said.

"Bummer," said Lubberkin.

"We have a serious otherworldly enemy we need to defeat," said Carmen.

"Otherworldly Investigations," said Lubberkin. "Your parents told me about it. I got a card somewhere."

"They're not around right now," I said. "But a very powerful witch wants to kill our whole family and anyone associated with us. And she seems to have a beef with cryptids in general. If you could help out at all, we'd really appreciate it."

"That sounds heavy," said Lubberkin. He stroked his stubble.

"Why don't you come up to my apartment? It's warmer up there. And then we'll see if we can sort things out in your favor. I've never been a big fan of the man trying to bring you down. And especially not the man trying to slaughter you. That's just not cool."

"If you're not a warlock, how do you know so much about magic and witches?" asked Lulu.

"Are you a demon?" asked Carmen. "Some demons are great. And I love my babies. But we had a bad experience." Carmen tried to point at me discreetly. I rolled my eyes.

"You must be a cryptid," I said. "Some kind of troll that's mastered how to look human?"

Lubberkin laughed, walking out from behind the counter. He made his way to the back of the store, and we followed.

"No way, man," said Lubberkin. "I'm no troll."

"Then how the hell do you know so much about magic?" I asked.

Lubberkin smiled a little. "Because I'm a fairy," he said.

We all stopped dead. We were as still as if we had been stuffed and mounted on a wall. A slow smile spread across Carmen's face.

"Should we go up and discuss fairy business?" asked Lubberkin. "It might help you."

"Absolutely!" said Carmen, running after him. "I've always wanted to meet a fairy. Ever since I was a little girl!"

Lulu and I stood back, still surprised. After a moment, Lulu shook her head.

"That is not how I pictured a fairy," she said.

"What were you thinking?" I asked.

Lulu shrugged. "Not someone with a five o'clock shadow," she said. "Or someone who looks like they know how to make a batch of special brownies."

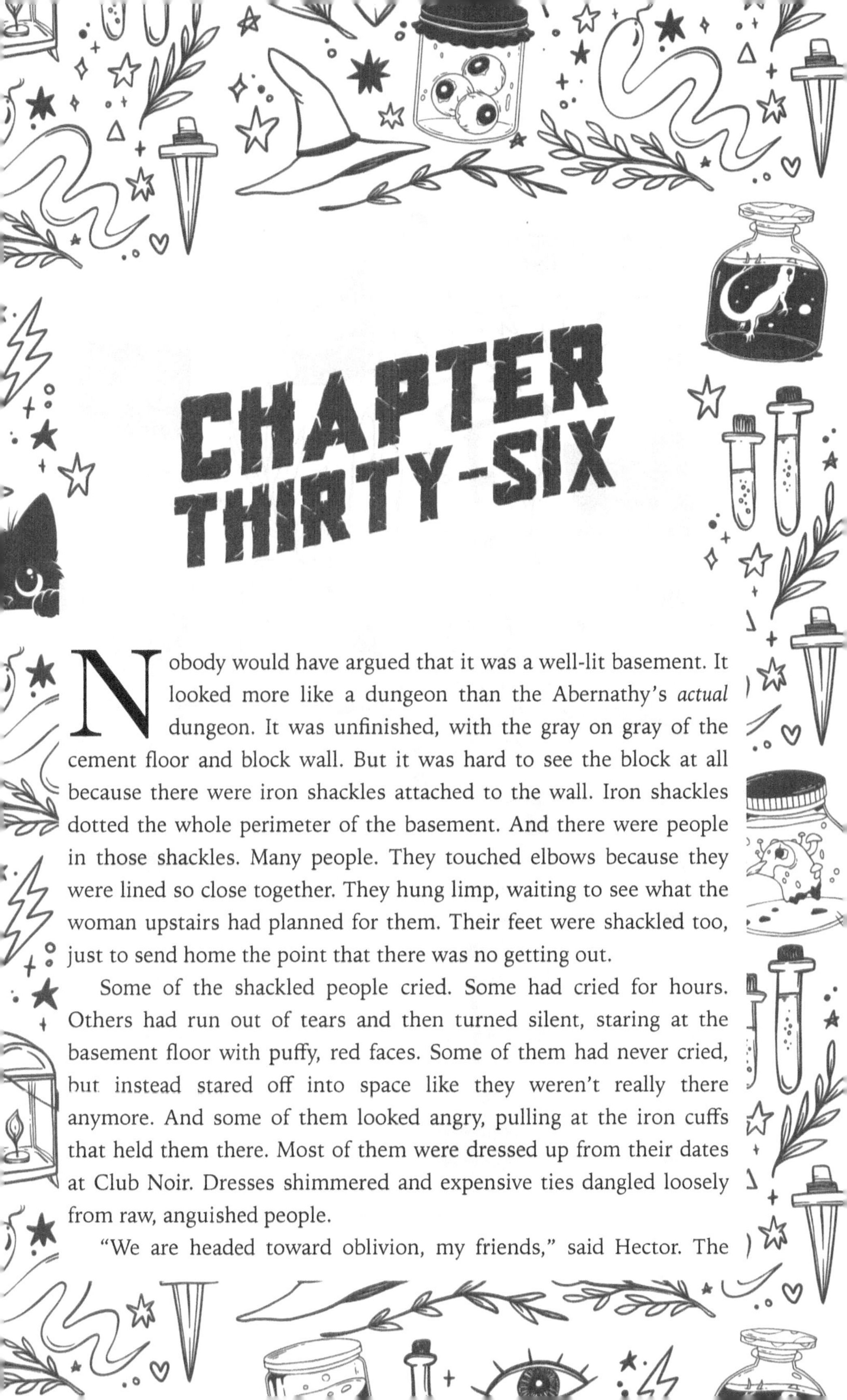

CHAPTER THIRTY-SIX

Nobody would have argued that it was a well-lit basement. It looked more like a dungeon than the Abernathy's *actual* dungeon. It was unfinished, with the gray on gray of the cement floor and block wall. But it was hard to see the block at all because there were iron shackles attached to the wall. Iron shackles dotted the whole perimeter of the basement. And there were people in those shackles. Many people. They touched elbows because they were lined so close together. They hung limp, waiting to see what the woman upstairs had planned for them. Their feet were shackled too, just to send home the point that there was no getting out.

Some of the shackled people cried. Some had cried for hours. Others had run out of tears and then turned silent, staring at the basement floor with puffy, red faces. Some of them had never cried, but instead stared off into space like they weren't really there anymore. And some of them looked angry, pulling at the iron cuffs that held them there. Most of them were dressed up from their dates at Club Noir. Dresses shimmered and expensive ties dangled loosely from raw, anguished people.

"We are headed toward oblivion, my friends," said Hector. The basement had a low ceiling, so Hector was not only shackled but hunched over. There was a perpetual sizzling sound from the iron cuffs touching his wrists. Chace's wrists also sizzled, so much that his human skin had worn through right down to his true, scaly flesh. It gave him the appearance of wearing human gloves. "Make peace and ready yourselves because she will show no mercy. I know firsthand the glee she derives from causing pain. She will mutilate us all."

"This isn't happening," muttered the man next to him. "This isn't real."

"It *is* real, my singing friend," said Hector. "The Thistle Witch will carve us up and reassemble us into her mindless murder machine. That I will be the vessel for her wanton destruction brings me much sorrow."

The singer shook his head again. He was not ready to accept the otherworldly.

"My only comfort is that when this is all over, surely the witch sisters will find all the parts of my body and give me a proper burial. And they will require the grandest of coffins to fit my colossal form. It will be awesome to behold!" said Hector.

"You aren't real," said the singer. He didn't look at the minotaur next to him. "Monsters aren't real. Magic isn't real."

"Shut up," said a young woman across from him. She had long since cried off her mascara. "You can see him right next to you. He's a minotaur. I read about them in my mythology class in college."

"Nope," said the singer, wide-eyed. "That's not possible."

"I don't know why you're scared of *him*, Lou," said another guy in a black tux. "He's a sweetheart compared to that thing upstairs."

Lou, the singer, muttered and gasped for breath. Sweat covered his brow.

"Magic is real, and it sucks," said the guy in the tux. "Make peace with it. You saw that witch come down and heal that sorry son of a bitch right there. Snap out of it, Lou."

The sorry son of a bitch he motioned to was Chace, dangling against burning chains. He didn't react to much of anything. He was too tired. The people next to him gagged at the smell of his cooking wrists.

"Why'd she fix him?" asked the man in the tux. "If she's just going to kill us?"

Chace blinked a couple of times as if he had returned to the land of the living.

"That's the whole point," said Chace, in a quiet voice. "She healed me so she could kill me."

"But why?" asked the guy.

Chace smiled. "Because that's her idea of fun."

"Before we are annihilated and forced to kill against our wills," said Hector. "I must tell you, my demon friend, that I am truly sorry for dragging you out of that dungeon. I cannot believe that I, Hector the minotaur, was spellbound. Such a thing has never happened in all my mighty years. The voice that drew me up out of the dungeon sounded so much like Jade. I know her voice like I know my own. She will always be my mate. After all these years, I am still sick with love for her. What a fool I am."

"Don't worry about it," said Chace. His voice was still strained from bleeding all over the stairs. He seemed reconciled to his fate. "You may have killed us both, but you're probably the best friend I've ever had."

"Many thanks," said Hector. "The feeling is mutual. I only wish we had time to finish our rendering of the fluffy kittens. Although, after being held by these burning shackles, manipulating the cardboard disks would be difficult."

Chace's wrists sizzled as he adjusted himself. "I know," said Chace. "It hurts so much that it almost doesn't hurt anymore."

"The first two hours were the worst," said Hector. He took a deep breath to smell his burning flesh. "Now it only feels like the annoying buzzing of a fly."

"A lot better than the pain I experienced earlier," said Chace. "Or the pain we'll experience later."

"Indeed," said Hector. "Gods help us."

"You're a demon?" asked the young woman. She stared at Chace. He nodded.

"But you look human," she said.

Chace opened his mouth, but something caught in his throat. He coughed and hacked for a moment.

"A few years ago, I killed a guy," said Chace. He said it nonchalantly. There was no point in pretending. The end was near, anyway. "He was by no means the first person I've ever killed. I dug him out and put him on."

Chace nodded toward the man in the tux. "Like your suit," said Chace.

"If that's true," said the man in the tux. "If you killed people, and you're a demon…that means you're no better than that witch, doesn't it?"

Chace's face remained blank. "I don't know anymore. I guess I'm evil. That's what everyone keeps telling me. I'm certainly not good, I don't think. But I'd rather be a demon than be human. Demons are supposed to be bad, so I fit right in. But humans…humans are supposed to be good, and boy do most of you fall short. You people eat each other for breakfast. Most of the time, you only care about other people when they look like you, or pray like you, or have sex like you. And if someone strays off the path, you feed them to the wolves."

The basement was quiet for a long time, except for the soft crying of people who didn't want to face what was coming.

"Perhaps we should go out with a song, like my ancestors of old. A great warrior's song, perhaps. You are a singer, are you not, crying man? Why don't you lead us?" asked Hector.

"This isn't happening," said Lou.

The crying and talking ceased like a light turning off when they heard a squeak on the basement step. Old leather shoes ambled down the stairs. Hector swung to look at Chace.

"Goodbye, my friend," said Hector.

Chace swallowed and nodded. "Goodbye."

"Maybe we shall see one another on the other side," said Hector.

Chace tried to smile. "I'll look for you. You'll be the one standing next to the love of your life, right?"

Hector's eyes lit up. A smile spread across his large face. "Yes," said Hector. "I will be, indeed."

The Thistle Witch slid into the basement the way a shadow slides across a floor. She stood at the door a long time, until they could have mistaken her for a statue. It felt like this was some kind of test, and the goal was to not react to her presence. Everyone remained silent, staring at the misshapen mask that revealed so little about the woman underneath. The only sound was Hector and Chace's sizzling flesh. Then finally, after what seemed like forever, the singer next to Hector lowered his head and began sobbing.

The Thistle Witch didn't make a sound, but seemed to float over to Hector and Lou. She lifted the man's chin, forcing him to look her right in the mask.

"Too loud," said the Thistle Witch. "Too much crying. Too much singing. Too much from you."

"Please, God, no," said Lou.

The Thistle Witch looked up at the ceiling and the blinking fluorescent light. She watched it like she was waiting for something, then looked down at Lou again.

"God remains silent," said the Thistle Witch. "You must puzzle out for yourself what this means."

"Please don't hurt me," said Lou. "I'll do anything. I won't tell anyone you're here. I swear."

The Thistle Witch leaned in and lifted Lou's face up a little more.

"You are good and strong," said the Thistle Witch. "You have kept yourself well. But too loud. Much too loud. Luckily, for my creation, you do not require a tongue."

In a flash, she had Lou's tongue in her crooked fingers. Screams shot up from around the basement as the Thistle Witch pulled a long, thin knife out of her dress pocket and sliced through his tongue. When she held it in her hand, she nodded and then threw it at the chained people on the other side of the room.

The basement dissolved into a state of total chaos from people crying, screaming, and pulling at their shackles. The only ones who remained silent were Hector and Chace, who merely looked on.

The Thistle Witch raised her arms. "Silence," she said.

It was like magic. Instantly, the room fell silent. The only sound came from Lou, who moaned and flailed around. Blood ran down his face as he choked and wheezed.

"Do not lose yourselves to despair," said the Thistle Witch. "I have done you a service. He brought an ill humor to this place, and put you all out of temper. I have silenced him, so you can feel merry again."

The Thistle Witch walked around the room like a fox circling a group of chickens, waiting to strike. She stopped at each person, inspecting them all. Nobody made the mistake of speaking or crying. Instead, they all looked away when it was their turn to be given the once-over. When she got back around to Hector, she raised a finger and pointed at them all. Some tried to duck, thinking that a spell might shoot out of her finger.

"Upstairs, I could hear you all," said the Thistle Witch. Her voice was only a whisper. "Not your words, but your thoughts. I could hear you begging for your lives. How was that possible? It is witchcraft! Witchcraft allows me to do such things. Is it not monstrous?"

She spun around, looking at each prisoner as she talked.

"You may ask yourselves if I will kill you," said the witch. "And the answer is yes, of course, I shall. I will kill each and every one of you, and I will enjoy it, too. But I offer you all something I have never offered anyone I've ever killed. I offer you the peace of mind of knowing that your bodies will be used for a glorious, noble purpose. You will be used in my effort to abolish witchcraft."

"But aren't *you* a witch?" asked the man in the tux.

The Thistle Witch turned to him and whispered some words under her breath. Then she raised her hand. As she did so, the man levitated toward her until there was no slack in the chains that held him against the wall. The man screamed as the Thistle Witch continued to motion him to her with the waving of her hand. The shackles tore into his skin as the witch pulled him closer and closer to her with magic. Then, with one quick entreating motion for him to come to her, the man was violently pulled forward. He collapsed on the floor as the room dissolved into screaming once more. The man's hands and feet were still in the shackles, while the rest of him cowered in a bloody heap on the cement.

The Thistle Witch raised her hand and the room turned silent again, except for the two men who moaned as they bled out.

"Any more foolish questions?" asked the Thistle Witch.

"Friends," said Hector. "I know she brings you great pain, but remember what I said. She enjoys your suffering. So, when she aims her destruction at you, do not give her the satisfaction of showing your agony."

The Thistle Witch slid up to Hector. Her dark eyes poked out at him through her leathery mask. She smelled like must and ashes. Hector stared back, showing no emotion.

"I have waited many years for this day," whispered the Thistle Witch. "I will have my revenge upon you."

"And I resolve to make it as anti-climactic for you as I can," said Hector. His nostrils flared as hot air shot out of his nose. "You say you hate witches, but you *are* one. You say you hate witches, yet you made a pact with Ignatius Abernathy, a known warlock. I don't know what agreement you made with him that day so many moons ago. But I do know that you need to sit down and decide which side of the battle you want to lay your sword down on. Or do you plan to be a self-hating, witch-killing witch forever? As Imogen Abernathy might say— you're a mess, bitch."

The Thistle Witch snapped her fingers and a large cleaver appeared in her hands. With one swoop, she lunged forward and cut off Hector's right leg. The room remained silent, but the prisoners gaped at the minotaur. He swiveled a little, then regained balance on his left leg. He pressed his mouth shut and flared his nostrils again, but made no other reaction to his severed limb, which lay discarded on the floor in front of him. Blood oozed from the place where his leg had been cut off, but he didn't look at it. He kept his eyes on the Thistle Witch.

A strange noise broke the silence of the room. It started small, but grew louder and louder. It was Chace Mackenzie. He hung there, staring at the Thistle Witch, laughing deep down from within his chest. Laughing until it almost seemed to hurt. Hector looked at him like the demon had lost his mind.

The Thistle Witch turned toward Chace and lifted her bloody cleaver at him. That only made him laugh louder.

Finally, Chace composed himself. He had to clench his jaw to make the laughter stop.

"Sorry," said Chace, smiling. "I just realized *it* all of a sudden, and I couldn't help laughing. It's just... I was wrong. And I'm so glad."

"Wrong about what?" asked the Thistle Witch. She floated in front of him.

"Imogen and Carmen are going to win," said Chace. "They're going to beat the shit out of you. Don't you think, Hector?"

"Absolutely," said Hector, steadying himself. Blood continued to stream from his severed leg to the floor below.

"What's the point of this?" asked Chace. "Look at you, trying to mutilate us to hurt Imogen and Carmen. Do you think this will send them cowering into a corner? They'll be sad, of course. Devastated. But being haunted by our deaths won't stop them. It'll make them fight harder. You know how many people they've helped? They'll come after you and won't stop. They're going to wipe the floors with you."

The Thistle Witch leaned in toward Chace. He stayed perfectly still.

"What makes you so sure?" asked the witch.

"Because you might have the magic and the experience, but they have each other. And you'd be amazed at the kind of difference that makes. Having someone who believes in you. Who's always there for you. It makes up for a lot." Chace smiled at the Thistle Witch. "They're going to turn you inside out. I wish I could be there to see it."

"But you will be there," said the Thistle Witch, standing tall again.

Chace's eyes seemed to brighten at the realization. "I will be," he said. "Won't I? You can weave me into your murder machine and make me fight against them, but I get to be there when they defeat you. There's that, at least."

"Hear, hear," said Hector, smiling.

The Thistle Witch played with the cleaver before she looked up at Chace.

"Then I suppose we should get to it," she said. "And see if your praise of them is ill-placed."

She raised her cleaver toward Chace, who didn't react. As it came down at him, the room once again turned into a sea of panicked screaming.

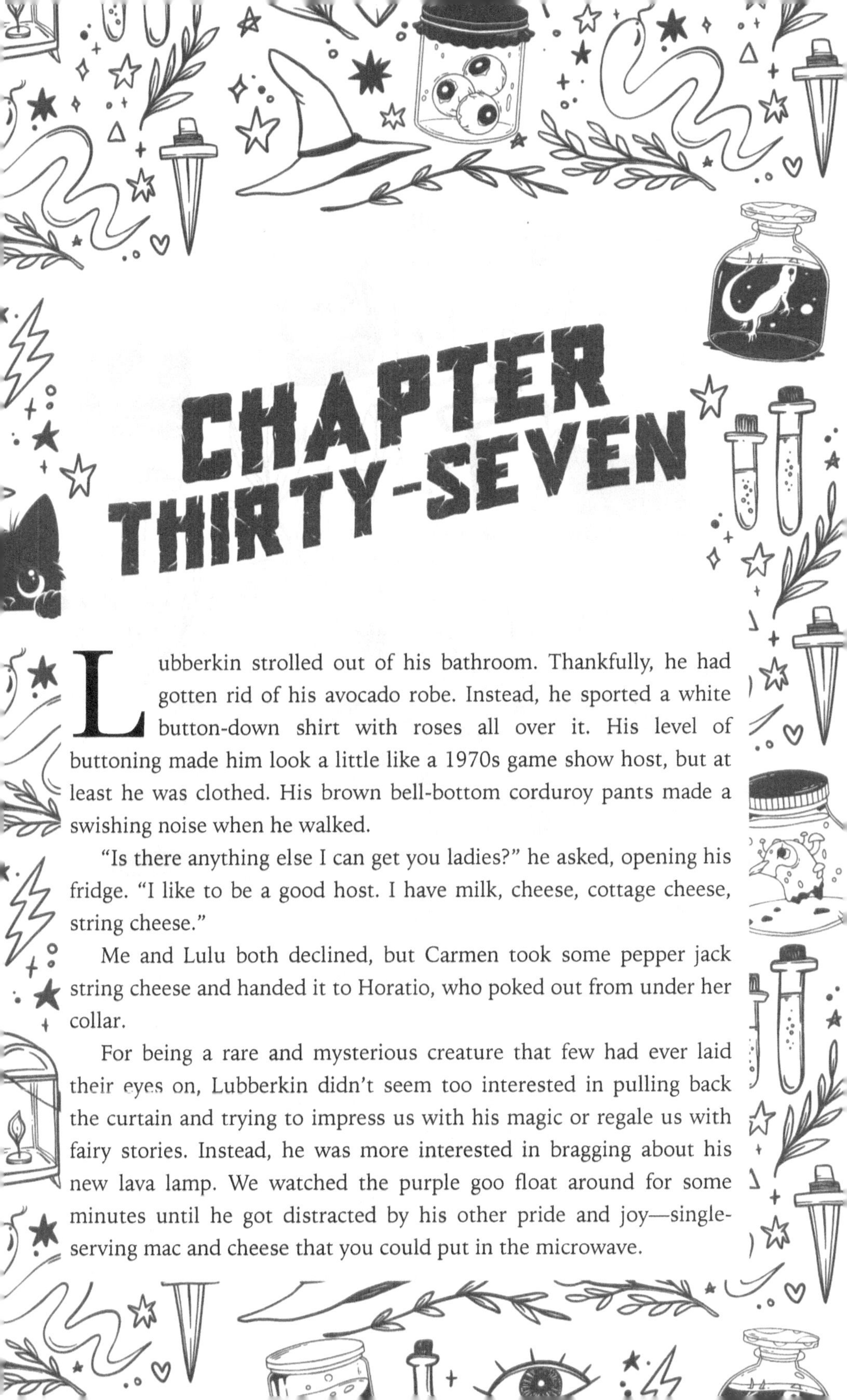

CHAPTER THIRTY-SEVEN

Lubberkin strolled out of his bathroom. Thankfully, he had gotten rid of his avocado robe. Instead, he sported a white button-down shirt with roses all over it. His level of buttoning made him look a little like a 1970s game show host, but at least he was clothed. His brown bell-bottom corduroy pants made a swishing noise when he walked.

"Is there anything else I can get you ladies?" he asked, opening his fridge. "I like to be a good host. I have milk, cheese, cottage cheese, string cheese."

Me and Lulu both declined, but Carmen took some pepper jack string cheese and handed it to Horatio, who poked out from under her collar.

For being a rare and mysterious creature that few had ever laid their eyes on, Lubberkin didn't seem too interested in pulling back the curtain and trying to impress us with his magic or regale us with fairy stories. Instead, he was more interested in bragging about his new lava lamp. We watched the purple goo float around for some minutes until he got distracted by his other pride and joy—single-serving mac and cheese that you could put in the microwave.

"Bless you, humans," said Lubberkin, staring at his reflection in the appliance.

Lulu and I exchanged dubious looks. This guy had the answer to our witch problem?

Carmen didn't seem to notice. She stared at Lubberkin like she had met her hero. She would have sat in that grungy little apartment and talked to our crumb-covered host for hours. And I'm pretty sure that if we hadn't veered the conversation back toward fairies, witches, and magic, Lubberkin wouldn't have mentioned it again.

"So, fairies, huh?" I asked, trying my best to steer our ship back toward reality. "You're a fairy. That seems neat."

Lulu looked at me like I wasn't exactly the master of subtlety. I shrugged.

"I can't get over it," said Carmen. Her wide-eyed look of satisfaction refused to diminish. "We're meeting a fairy. What are the chances?"

"We do kind of like to keep ourselves to ourselves," said Lubberkin. He pulled off some string cheese and ate it.

"Everybody said we had a snowball's chance in hell of finding a fairy," said Lulu. "I gotta say, I thought fairies would be…lithe, maybe. Fair-haired women with a temper."

Lubberkin took a thick brown pair of aviator glasses out of his shirt pocket and put them on.

"That's far out," he said. "But I guess that does describe a few friends of mine. Fairies are notoriously bad-tempered, you know?"

"I've heard that," said Carmen. "Sometimes, if they hear you playing the harp badly, they kill you right on the spot. Boom. You're dead."

Lubberkin laughed. "We're real assholes sometimes. I got mad once, too. I can't remember why, though. I think it involved sour cream."

"What kind of fairy are you?" asked Carmen.

"A Gray Neighbor," said Lubberkin. "We live north of here, mostly. We like the cold."

"Never heard of them," I said. I wondered if the rest of the Gray Neighbors spent so much time scratching themselves.

"They made sure of that," said Lubberkin. "They're secretive. Secretive to a fault. And if you step out of line, they can make it a real drag for you, man."

"Owning a popular ice cream shop and being secretive don't seem like things that go hand in hand," I said. "It sounds about as silly as witches having an investigation agency."

Lulu laughed, but Carmen shook her head.

"The pocket demons can hear you, Immy," she said, frowning.

"The Gray Neighbors don't exactly approve of me having this business, but there's not much they can say since I need to make a living. They banished me and a friend of mine. I call her my sister, but she's really just a like-minded fairy. But aren't we all brothers and sisters?"

"God, I hope not," I said, monotone.

"That's a lovely sentiment," said Carmen, ignoring me.

"What does a fairy do to get banished?" asked Lulu. She looked around as if the dirty clothes on the floor might provide a clue.

"Politics," said Lubberkin. He slid down on a bean bag next to me. "Nepotism, man. Friends helping friends. Everyone thought we were getting a little too interested in humans. But the only way we can make more fairies is by bringing humans in."

"Like the old legends of people being taken by fairies," said Carmen.

"Right on," said Lubberkin. "They were so uptight. When they brought in humans, it was fine, when me and my friend tried to, it was bad. There were lots of arguments. Lots of bad vibes. It was a hard time."

I was fascinated that we had finally met a fairy, even if this one didn't come in the expected packaging. But as Lubberkin talked, I felt my foot tapping the floor. We didn't have time for the inner workings of the fairy political structure. We needed answers.

"People suck," said Lulu. She patted Lubberkin's shoulder.

"It's all right," said Lubberkin. "Now I get to hang loose in the human world, talking to them every day. And I got to meet your parents. I knew they were witches right away. I was jazzed. Haven't seen a witch in a long time. We all used to be tight, you know?"

"We know," I said. "That's why we're here."

"Your parents stopped once to get ice cream on their anniversary," said Lubberkin. "They had their first date here. Very cool. Dairy brings people together."

"But you never get to go back home?" asked Carmen.

"We are banished for an undetermined amount of time," said Lubberkin.

I scanned Lubberkin's apartment. There were a lot of Joan Baez posters on the walls, and morose-colored tan and brown blankets were strewn on the floor. But there was no sign that he had a roommate.

"Where's the other fairy?" I asked. Lubberkin popped out of his reverie. He shrugged.

"She's kind of bitter about humans since all those bad vibes went down," said Lubberkin. "She visits from time to time, just to make sure the business hasn't burned down or anything."

"She sounds delightful," said Carmen. Carmen looked like she was determined to find everything about this fairy delightful, even though we sat in a room that smelled like spoiled milk and burnt hot dogs.

Lubberkin laughed. "You all would annoy the shit out of her," he said. "It'd be hilarious."

I decided that the only way to get out of that apartment in under ten hours was to be like Carmen and ignore my Midwestern roots. I had to plow right into the topic at hand.

"Do you think you'd be able to help us?" I asked. "This witch wants our heads on a spike."

Lubberkin leaned back and stroked his stubble. He stared out the window at the swirling snow and made a lot of humming noises. My face felt flushed. Wasn't he going to help us? Wasn't that what groovy, love-everyone dudes were supposed to do?

"You ladies know a lot about fairies?" asked Lubberkin.

"Of course!" said Carmen. Carmen had trained her whole life for this moment, like an Olympic athlete sliding onto the ice for the first time at age three. She had scores of old magical facts dedicated to memory. Some of them didn't seem particularly important. Like a fairy's favorite color—it's green.

"Then you know what fairies are like when it comes to helping humans," said Lubberkin.

Carmen's bright face faded into a concerned frown.

"Some fairies aren't very helpful at all," said Carmen. "No offense, Lubberkin. Some think it's funny to trick people in the dark, so they fall and break bones. And some agree to help humans, but then break their promise because they are prissy bitches."

Lubberkin nodded.

"But some are helpful," said Carmen, trying to stay positive. "Like Brownies, for instance. They'll come in at night and clean or finish making shoes. I guess it just depends on the fairy. I don't know what Gray Neighbors are like."

"Gray Neighbors belong to a subgroup of fairies that I'm sure someone well-read like you has heard of," said Lubberkin.

Carmen looked like an unsure trivia contestant.

"Look around," said Lubberkin. "Can you guess?"

Carmen scanned the room, furrowing her brow. Barnaby crawled up to her ear and whispered something. Carmen's eyes shot to Lulu's chocolate milk. Lulu put it down abruptly, like it was two weeks past expiration.

"What?" asked Lulu, alarmed.

Carmen's face brightened again.

"You *will* help us!" said Carmen. "Won't you?"

Lubberkin smiled and nodded. Lulu and I shot each other annoyed looks.

"Did I miss something?" I asked.

"Look at the dairy," said Carmen. "Gray Neighbors are in the subgroup of fairies known as household spirits. That means that they'll do the sweeping, tend to the baby, and clean out the fireplace in return for milk."

"Or any other dairy," said Lubberkin, wistfully. "I'm not fussy."

"Thank God, we have that settled," I said. "Now, about the Thistle Witch. It really is a time-sensitive problem."

"I'm perfectly willing to help you and all," said Lubberkin, standing up. It was the fastest I had seen him move. "But we've just established that fairies don't do nothing for nothing. So, there's just the matter of what you'll give me in exchange for my goods and services."

"I have a container of mixed berry yogurt in the car," I said.

"We all do," said Lulu. "Carmen packed them. So, you get not one, not two, but three."

Lubberkin rubbed his stubble again, but shook his head.

"I have a whole restaurant of dairy now," he said. "We have to expand our thinking."

He reached out his hand to help pull me out of my bean bag. As I took it, the touch of his weird, cold fingers nearly made my hand go numb. It felt like a little electric shock all over my body. In a moment, we all stood in a tight circle. I felt like we were members of the world's least sanitary secret society.

"Please don't let it be a blood brothers thing," said Lulu. "That's just icky. And no spit brothers either. And no giving you years of our lives in exchange for your help, either."

Lubberkin lifted his glasses. "Who do you think we are, sister?" he asked.

"I've seen a lot of TV," said Lulu.

"I think this ought to square us up just fine," said Lubberkin, taking a crumbled card out of his pocket. He handed it to me. "You witches have a reunion every summer, is that right?"

"How do you know?" I asked.

"It's the business of fairies to know about witches," said Lubberkin. He winked.

"It's every year in July," said Carmen. "We have a backup date if it's rained out."

"Groovy," said Lubberkin. "In exchange for my help, I sure hope that for the next witch reunion you consider Polar Bear Ice Cream for all of your catering needs."

Lulu exhaled. She was relieved that her blood and years would remain hers.

"Usually, the reunion is a potluck," said Carmen.

Lubberkin pushed his glasses back on his nose. "Not anymore," he said.

"The Thistle Witch wants to kill me and my family," I said. "And possibly all witches everywhere. And you'll only help us by blackmailing us into using you as our reunion caterer?"

"That's the long and short of it," said Lubberkin. "Like I said, I'm banished. I have to make a living."

I looked into the hippie's hazel eyes and shrugged.

"I get that," I said. "Makes sense to me. Where do I sign?"

"Let me get you a receipt," said Lubberkin. "Then I'll get some cheese and crackers, and we can bust open my fairy books."

CHAPTER THIRTY-EIGHT

Lubberkin pulled a bunch of old, musty books out of his closet. They were spread all over the floor. We, unfortunately, were also on that floor, along with a multitude of crumbs. Lulu thought she was smart when she snagged a throw pillow to sit on. But it had a ketchup stain.

Lubberkin fiddled with his glasses as he tried to read the small print in a crumbling brown book.

"I won't be able to help you directly," said Lubberkin. "Like, I mean, I can't go with you and fight the man. Firstly, the Gray Neighbors wouldn't be stoked about that. Secondly, as per my banishment, I've been stripped of my fairy powers, except for a few parlor tricks."

"So, you're like us," I said.

"Right on," said Lubberkin, holding the book closer to his face.

"Then how can you help us?" asked Lulu. She held a book tentatively, like she didn't want to touch it. I didn't blame her. It looked like it had mold on the cover.

"Don't sweat it, sister," said Lubberkin. "I have a few odds and ends in case times get hairy. You know, break glass in case of emergency stuff."

"I see," said Lulu.

"What was the name of the witch that's been flinging you the bad vibes?" asked Lubberkin. He turned the page and scanned it with his finger.

"The Thistle Witch," said Carmen. "She's a witch-hating witch. And I guess sort of a demon too, if the stories are true."

"I'm not the biggest fan of witchcraft," I said. "But she's taken her dislike of it a little far. She could have started with a strongly worded letter."

"Maybe she needs to meditate," said Lubberkin. He tapped his finger on the page. "Found her. The Thistle Witch."

"What is that book?" I asked. "We have about every spell and folklore book there is. I don't recognize that."

"That's because it's a fairy book," said Lubberkin. "It's like a who's who of witches. We have to keep tabs on our prodigies, you know? It's also kind of like a gossip rag. What do you want to know? Satan seems to think she's the cat's meow."

"A minotaur friend of ours met her a long time ago," I said. "He said she made some pact with our ancestor. And apparently, something happened with that pact because now she's out for blood."

Barnaby and Horatio paged through a book in front of Carmen.

"Let's see," said Lubberkin, looking. "She wasn't too lovey-dovey with her siblings, was she?"

Lubberkin hummed as he read through everything, looking for the right passage.

"Here it is," he said.

"It's in there?" I asked. I felt a surge of heat engulf my face.

"Sure is," said Lubberkin. He cringed. "Listen to this jive talk: 'To protect himself from injury against a being more powerful than himself, Ignatius Abernathy made a pact with one Thistle Witch. The pact stated that in exchange for sparing his own life, Ignatius would offer up the lives of his descendants. He acknowledged that the power of witches was fading, despite their best efforts. And would most likely continue to do so. The pact, therefore, stated that the Thistle Witch had to refrain from killing witches until an Abernathy descendant attempted, with serious ambition, to increase witch powers beyond their measly scope.'"

My whole body felt rigid. I let out a big breath. "What a pointless pact," I muttered. "Why would she decide *not* to kill an Abernathy, just to kill a few others at a later time? She could have just killed him, then strolled over to his house and killed his family. I don't get it."

"Here's the kicker, sister," said Lubberkin. "This is why she did it. Ignatius did some serious, dark magic with the Thistle Witch that night to make this pact. Real blood stuff."

"I told you," said Lulu. "Blood stuff is no good."

"This might have been one of the last big, dark spells to ever be performed," said Lubberkin. "It says that the pact they made meant that if the Thistle Witch waited to kill Abernathys until such time that a descendant attempted powerful magic, she would then be imbued with the power of every witch she killed. That's some powerful shit. He wanted to avoid a showdown with the Thistle Witch that night. How come?"

"He was on the trail of a mermaid he wanted to woo," I said, flatly.

Lubberkin's face remained firmly hidden behind the book. It muffled the sound of his voice.

"I can think of ways to woo mermaids without throwing your whole family under the bus," he said.

"We've already concluded that he was the family asshole," I said. "Apparently, he didn't think much of his wife or kids, or their kids into the future."

"What's a family without one asshole?" asked Lulu.

"It looks like after they made this pact," said Lubberkin. "The Thistle Witch took a little holiday down in the underworld, seeing as how she's an honorary demon and has a vacation rental down there. Apparently, she's been waiting around for an Abernathy to slip up."

We sat there, soundless. The pocket demons stared up at Carmen. She sweated profusely. Carmen never sweated. She hadn't even sweated when the Thistle Witch challenged us in that dream. I knew that look on her face. It was on my face whenever I thought about

Chace. It was a mixture of guilt and the feeling that you were about to throw up. She got out her knitted hankie.

Lubberkin set the book down and took off his glasses. He rubbed his eyes. "So, the question becomes, which of you sisters has been trying some Ph.D. level spells? Who's trying to be the professor?"

All eyes fell on Carmen. Horatio flew up and patted her sweaty forehead with the embroidered hankie. Carmen glanced at him with melancholy eyes.

"I was such a cute little dog," said Carmen. "But it probably wasn't worth killing us over, was it?"

I crossed my legs, not sure what to say. I kind of wanted to go back in time to punch my ancestor in the face. But I figured if most people knew what their ancestors were like, they'd probably feel the same way.

"Maybe I should have mistrusted magic like you, Immy," said Carmen. "Then we wouldn't be in this mess. Everything would be fine if I had fought the urge to be that dog."

We looked at each other and I raised an eyebrow.

"And if I had fought the urge to mess with the weather," said Carmen, slowly. "And if I had fought the urge to reanimate that bird… and reanimate that raccoon…and reanimate that deer… Oh, dear…"

For some reason, I had expected Carmen to react like me. I thought she'd be angry at our ancestor, the Thistle Witch, and the whole ridiculous pact. But as the pocket demons weaseled out of Carmen's clothing and began nuzzling against her, I knew that she had taken it to heart.

Carmen's eyes took on a wet and shiny glow. Tears ran down her face and hit the book below. Barnaby curled up in her arms and rested his head down on her sleeve. Lubberkin set down his book and mumbled something about making Carmen a nice mug of warm milk.

I sighed and scooted over to her. Sure, I had always been the wet blanket when it came to magic. I thought witchcraft was always waiting to bite you in the ass somehow. But it was just plain stupid for Carmen to feel like she was somehow in the wrong for not following guidelines set down by a couple of lowlifes.

"You couldn't have known," I said, running my hand through her hair.

"Don't feel bad," said Lulu. "It was a terrible thing for him to do. And she's an evil demon witch. Don't be mad that you broke their stupid rules. You just have a messed-up family. Who doesn't? Although, in retrospect, I think your genealogy book at home is really lacking."

"You're the most powerful witch I know," I said to Carmen. I rested my head against hers.

"I know, Immy," said Carmen, wiping tears away. "That's the whole problem."

"Don't you believe that crap," I said. "You never have to apologize for being strong. And you never have to apologize for wanting to be stronger, for having a voice, and for standing up for yourself. And don't you ever apologize for having goals. Don't feel bad because some misogynist dick ancestor of ours made some pact that we could never try to rise out of mediocrity. You've always wanted to be a better witch, and damn it, look at you. You're marvelous, you hear me? If I could be any damn person in this world, I'd be you. You're my hero, Carmen."

Carmen hugged me. She mumbled something, but it was hard to distinguish over her crying and all the random pocket demon cooing.

"Now I'm crying because of you, Immy," said Carmen. "That's the sweetest thing anyone's ever said. I love you."

"I love you too," I said.

"And you don't even like emotions," she said, hugging me again.

"I do not," I said, plainly. "But I like yours."

"You know I look up to you too, right?" asked Carmen. "I wish I could be more like you, Immy."

"What the hell for, you crazy bastard?" I asked, rolling my eyes.

"You never give up," said Carmen. "When things get bad, that's when you take charge."

"Imogen confidence, all right," I said. "It's really something."

"I'm serious, Immy," said Carmen.

"Yeah, yeah," I said.

There was a flash. We looked over to see Lulu taking a picture of us with her phone.

"That one's good," said Lulu. "I think I'll develop that one."

"Out of sight," said Lubberkin. "I love to see love. What kind of dog did you turn yourself into, by the way?"

"A corgi," said Carmen, wiping away tears.

"Sweet," said Lubberkin. "Dog of the fairies."

We sat for a moment, letting emotions settle, while Carmen drank her warm milk. Ignatius really was a scumbag. I knew that Carmen might understand that the pact was stupid, but she'd still blame herself for any people the Thistle Witch killed to craft her monster. I knew she'd feel responsible because, if the roles were reversed, *I'd* feel responsible. It made me more nervous about facing the Thistle Witch. Carmen would want to right a wrong, avenge those people. It made me want to lock her in Lubberkin's musty closet.

"Does that mean the Thistle Witch is going to eat you guys to get your power?" asked Lulu. "Like a zombie thing?"

"Some facsimile of that," said Lubberkin. "Not very chill."

"So, she's full of it," I said. "She says she hates witches, but she's going to kill us to consume our witchcraft."

"What will she do after that?" asked Carmen. "She'll be so power-ful. Think of all the cryptids on that cruise ship that are frightened of her. And then there's mom and dad. What'll happen to them if she has that kind of power? What'll happen to everyone?"

Lubberkin stood up. "We're not going to wait around to find out," said Lubberkin. "Come on. We're going to the basement."

CHAPTER THIRTY-NINE

Below Polar Bear Ice Cream was a storage basement illuminated by one naked bulb with a pull string. The place was filled with extra odds and ends for the restaurant, from boxes of spoons and forks to a backup mixer and milkshake maker. And in the middle of the room was the ping pong table that the employees were so excited about. But off in the corner was a separate space dedicated to Lubberkin's personal junk. A drab tan rug was rolled up against the wall, and a rocking chair with considerable dust sat next to it. But Lubberkin zoned right in on the big, chipped wooden wardrobe.

Lubberkin patted the wardrobe. Dust filled the air and floated back and forth before it finally settled down to the ground.

"Those old yarns about fairies and witches," said Lubberkin. "They don't tell the whole story. They act like a person would come into contact with a fairy and boom, she'd have witch powers for life. That'd be out of sight, but wasn't the case."

Lubberkin rammed his hand around his pocket and pulled out a rusty skeleton key. He inserted it into the old, worn keyhole in the wardrobe.

"How did it work?" asked Lulu. "How did a fairy make a witch?"

Lubberkin turned the key and smiled.

"The first witches were made by pigging out at the fairy café," said Lubberkin. The doors of the wardrobe creaked open, revealing cupboards lined with all sorts of food, from something wrapped in paper that looked suspiciously like fruitcake, to canned peaches and various condiments.

"It's fairy food," said Carmen. She gazed at it the way some people gaze at their true love.

"Wait just one minute," said Lulu, taking it in. "I might not know much about this stuff, but even I know that fairy food is supposed to be bad. In all those old stories, people would eat it and then waste away. Or be cursed somehow."

"Poor advertising," said Lubberkin. "That might have been the case with certain gnarly fairies. Some pixies are just jerks, you know? But most of those stories sprang from the idea that fairies are creatures of the underworld, so anything they peddle must be dark."

"And Lubberkin is a nice fairy," said Carmen.

"Thanks, sister," said Lubberkin. "Back in the day, when fairies were everywhere, sometimes they'd hang loose with a like-minded individual and give them food like this. The first witches had to have a steady diet of this stuff to keep their powers. But eventually, it was enough magic to pass on from generation to generation. For a while, anyway."

I took a parcel off the shelf and examined it. Then I went for it and took a big whiff.

"That's my own fruitcake recipe," said Lubberkin. "It tastes the best after six months. Lots of whiskey."

"That means this stuff isn't going to give us beefed-up powers forever, right?" I asked. I inspected the fruitcake with shaking hands. I wasn't comfortable enough with witchcraft to want sparkler fingers forever.

"Nope," said Lubberkin. "This is just a one-time deal. You'll chow down at the power buffet, and then hopefully you'll be ready to enter the ring with the Thistle Witch."

"How long will the powers last?" asked Carmen. She grabbed a mason jar of honey and turned it around in her hands.

"Twenty-four hours," said Lubberkin. "Maybe forty-eight if you're lucky. So only eat it right before your showdown with the Thistle Witch. And don't try to be a hero and eat too much, either. All that'll get you is the flu. Remember, a little dab will do you."

He handed a jar of peaches to Lulu.

"Me too?" asked Lulu, alarmed.

"If you want to, sister," said Lubberkin. "It'll work on you, same as them."

The peaches floated in their thick, golden syrup. "I don't know," mumbled Lulu. "I could get into a lot of trouble if I end up being able to do something like read minds for forty-eight hours."

"How much do you think we'll need?" I asked. I tried to hide the wobbly fear in my voice. The last thing I wanted to do was take a bite of that fruitcake. And that's not because it was fruitcake, either. Fruitcake is delicious when made properly, thank you very much. But the idea of suddenly being more powerful than I had ever been, or ever *wanted* to be, filled me with dread. "How much is too much?"

"Let's see," said Lubberkin. "You better bring some extra, just in case. Take the fruitcake, the honey. And here, take the maple syrup. I almost forgot about the maple syrup."

He reached high up into the wardrobe and grabbed a dusty bottle. He wiped it off and looked at it like it was his pride and joy.

"I made this myself," said Lubberkin. "I guess that's obvious, seeing that it's fairy food. This will do you good. Take the maple syrup first and keep the rest as backup. One nip should be plenty."

"You really think this will make us evenly matched with the Thistle Witch?" asked Carmen.

"She's powerful," said Lubberkin. "No doubt about that. She got her power in the womb from a spell. That's pure, concentrated dark magic. The witch that cast it was dealing some evil mojo. It's hard to make a witch that way. She must have been a prickly character. And no doubt she was puking her guts out for weeks afterward."

"Lovely," I said.

"And she's also a demon," said Lubberkin. "We can't forget that. But you ladies are getting your powers right from the cow, in a sense. That means you'll be incredibly powerful too, if only for a short period of time. So, watch your trigger finger."

"But you think that we stand a chance against her?" asked Lulu. I saw in her eyes that she wanted some sense of security. But nothing in the world of witchcraft was for sure.

"I think so," said Lubberkin. "But I *have* been wrong once or twice in the past. Like with bubblegum ice cream. I thought it would be a big hit. But it creeped most people out. Now I have fifty gallons of it."

I swallowed back bile and tried to steady my shaking legs. We had our answers. And we had a chance to defeat the Thistle Witch. That meant that there was only one thing left to do.

"All right," I said. "It's time."

The snow had stopped, but the wind was still going strong, pelting against us as we trudged out to the car. It wasn't late, but the sun was already starting to disappear behind the trees. The long nights of December.

We were putting the fairy food in the trunk with the delicate touch of someone packing away explosives when Lubberkin charged out of Polar Bear Ice Cream with his hands full.

"Chocolate malts for the road," he said, handing us each one. "And don't worry, I didn't rip you off. They *are* actually malts with malted milk powder. We need to start a campaign, so people understand that there's a difference between malts and milkshakes."

"I could get used to it here," said Lulu.

"Thanks so much," said Carmen. She struggled to suck the thick malt up the thin straw. "I love when people pay attention to detail."

"I've never thought about dairy so much in my life," I said, smiling.

"Your life will never be the same again," said Lubberkin.

"I think you're right," I said. I wasn't sure if that was good or bad.

"Are you sure you won't come help us fight the Thistle Witch?" asked Carmen.

"You could give her the smackdown with your good vibes," said Lulu.

"Nah," said Lubberkin. "I don't want to tick off the Gray Neighbors too bad. I might like living in the human world, but I got some good friends back home, and I'd like to see them again someday. Plus, I'm technically a pacifist. And as you can see, I've been untrue to my code today by giving you weaponry."

We smiled and thanked him. I knew we had to go, but my feet didn't want to leave that snowy curb, even with the moisture sinking into my shoes. I wanted to stay where there was warmth and laughter. I didn't want to go back to where darkness lived, even if we did have a glimmer of hope.

"No sense standing in the snow," said Lubberkin. "Better be off. Stay strong. Be brave. And peace and love to you."

As we got in the car, Lulu shouted to Lubberkin. He was halfway into the shop, but he strolled back out again.

"I just want to know one thing," said Lulu.

"What's that, sister?" asked Lubberkin.

"You said the Gray Neighbors bring in humans to make more fairies," said Lulu.

"Sure," he said.

"Does that mean you were a human once too?" she asked.

"I was," said Lubberkin, laughing. "I had a van and everything. And a different name. Maybe I'll tell you someday."

Carmen and I smiled.

"I was just wondering when exactly did you become a fairy?" asked Lulu.

"Let's see," said Lubberkin. "I think it was a week before Woodstock. Me and a buddy planned to go. But I never made it. I was bummed about that for a long time."

CHAPTER FORTY

Shadows spread across the gray basement. The shackles on the walls hung empty in the darkness. It was hard to believe that so much chatter had taken place in that room such a short time before. Chatter and crying.

The Thistle Witch stood down there in the darkness. There wasn't anything left to do or say. There was nothing left but the work. The work she was meant to do. But she was in no hurry. She always had quiet time before she set out for battle. This was her fourth creation, and she wanted to enjoy it. She ran her shoe around in the pool of blood that covered the floor.

"Sometimes I wish I could be a dog," whispered the Thistle Witch. She glanced over to a large figure that was hunched in the shadows. "Running free and happy through the woods. Not thinking of bad things. Not thinking of hurting anyone. Just a dog full of unbounded joy. Jumping into a river. Fetching a stick. I would be happy like that. It is my most secret wish. That someday I might turn into the dog and stay the dog. But not the dog with *me* inside. The *me* that only wrecks things. I want to be the dog and only the dog. Do you understand?"

The figure didn't move or make a sound.

"I suppose you couldn't," said the witch. "But understand that sometimes it's hard to be oneself when you know that there's something deep down in you, writhing and dark. And you can't get it out. And most of the time you don't want to. You like it there."

The Thistle Witch danced around in the blood, making figure eights in the blackness.

"I suppose it would have been better if I had not been born," said the witch. "Or if Mary Smith had let me remain a plain and simple human. But it was not meant to be."

The Thistle Witch spun in a slow circle and then stopped. She looked right at the creature in the dark.

"And then sometimes," said the witch, her voice rising. "I am very happy that I was born. I am very happy to hurt. I am very, very happy to hurt. I wonder why? I wonder why hurting people doesn't upset me. I wonder why killing people doesn't upset me. That seems very wrong, indeed."

The Thistle Witch looked at the blood on her shoe.

"This will take some time to clean," she said. "Perhaps when I injure those sisters in battle, I'll finally feel something. That would be different. Maybe I'll feel."

The Thistle Witch smiled under her mask.

"But I doubt it," she said.

She stepped toward the figure until she could just make out the eyes all over its torso. They blinked and watched her. Mouths began to sob.

"Come to me," she said.

The hulking figure crawled toward her. It couldn't stand upright, not in that small basement. Its huge, thin wings encapsulated it, making its body hard to distinguish in the dimness.

"We will have to destroy this house to get you out," she said. "You can't even stand up. You'd never get up the stairs. But that's no matter."

The creature bent its minotaur head down toward her. Its glazed eyes stared out, seeing nothing.

"I think you are my prettiest creation yet," she said. She leaned forward and kissed its head. The sound of her praise almost drowned out each head's cry of despair.

CHAPTER FORTY-ONE

I knew something was wrong the moment we pulled into the driveway. The snow and wind had ceased, and everything had a stillness about it that was neither serene nor relaxing. Instead, the whole world seemed afraid to make the slightest sound or the most careful movement.

The last violet rays of the day disappeared in the distance. It gave the illusion that the snow was blue instead of white. As I pulled to a stop in front of the garage, the pocket demons streamed from the house toward us. They looked like they kicked up turquoise sparkles with their paws and hooves.

"What's going on?" asked Lulu. The pocket demons screeched as they ran to us. It caught the attention of the demons in the car, and they hurriedly expelled themselves from Carmen's clothing.

"Something's wrong!" said Carmen. She almost threw herself out of the car in a panic. But I was still. I was always slow and careful when fear took hold of me. My eyes weren't fixed on the pocket demons. Instead, I was hypnotized by something in front of the car: a dark trail in the snow that was barely visible in the waning light.

My ears filled with a dull hum as I stepped out of the car. I knew there was commotion behind me, the sound of Carmen and Lulu trying to understand what the cats and demons were so upset about. But I didn't stay to listen. Instead, I walked to the side of the house. I bent down and grabbed a handful of snow. As I held it up, the dark substance came into better focus. The color reminded me of melted cranberries. Or jam. My chest tightened as I stood up and squinted in the dim light. The dark trail led back to the sheds.

The humming sound in my head was gone, replaced instead by my booming heart. The whole process of getting home, getting out of the car, and discovering the blood probably only took forty-five seconds, but it felt as if we had been back for an hour. Norma Shearer and Buster Keaton walked up to me. They pawed at the blood and meowed. But I already understood. The others gathered behind me. They understood too. It wasn't going to be next week or even tomorrow. It was going to be tonight.

Then it seemed as though everything snapped back into time. The world wasn't in slow motion anymore. Instead, everything seemed too fast. Everything seemed too real. And I'd have to face it.

"It's Hector and Chace," I said. That's when I looked down and realized I was running back to the shed. I didn't have to glance behind to see if the others were with me. We were like one entity with a united mission.

The door to the shed was off its hinges. Inside it, the door in the floor looked like it had been thrown open in a panic. The lawn ornaments and snow blower were heaped in the corner.

I stopped at the top of the stairs. The warm golden glow of the dungeon shined up at me. It was almost welcoming. If a dungeon can ever be welcoming. Juxtaposed against the state of the stairs, it made for an off-putting scene.

"Someone was murdered on the stairs," said Lulu, looking over my shoulder. Her breath was fast and frightened.

Blood covered the eyes on the stairs. It looked like more blood than a human body had. But then a cold shudder went through me. It was more blood than a human had because it wasn't human blood. Of course, it wasn't. I knew that. He was a demon. And demons were different. It was Chace's blood, of course. He must have been hauled up the steps.

Little tremors seized my body. Carmen reached around and grabbed my frozen fingers with her warm hand.

"It's all right, Immy," said Carmen. "We're with you."

I nodded.

Something came over me then because I quickly ran down the steps. I avoided the blood by staying on the outer edges. From the way it had dried to the steps, I figured it had happened only a short time after we left.

When I reached the dungeon floor, I raced down the hallway, then through the main room, and back toward Chace's cell. The wide-open cell door almost felt like a lie. I knew it had to be open or ripped down, but it still felt impossible. We had spent endless hours making sure it was safe. How had the Thistle Witch invaded it?

Everyone gathered around me as I stopped at the open cell door. The fact that all the pocket demons had come down with us was a testament to the fact that not all monsters are monsters. They inspected Hector's cat puzzle, which was scattered all over the floor. Chace's book was open on his chair like he might stroll back any moment, sit down, and start reading.

Something moved in my peripheral vision. I held my breath as I focused my eyes on an object sticking out of the cell's keyhole. It was something with a ribbon dangling on its end. Something that none of us had put there. I pointed at it. Carmen's eyes widened.

"Carmen," I said. I couldn't believe how calm my voice was. I sounded like someone ready to take charge. I sounded like someone ready to face trouble. How did I sound that way when inside I was filled with nothing but fear? "Go in and see if the skeleton key is in the salt jar! Go!"

I didn't have to beg Carmen to do anything. I barely got the words out when she turned and disappeared back up the steps and out into the snow.

The key pulled out of the lock with a grating scrape. It burned my palm. The frayed yellow ribbon hung limp on it. I stared at the key until it dissolved into ashes in my hand. Then I tilted my palm and let the ashes fall to the floor.

"Why did it do that?" asked Lulu.

But my only answer was anxious cursing.

Lulu and I were back up the steps and trudging through the snow when Carmen burst out of the house. She held the key in the moonlight.

"It was there, Immy," she said. She caught her breath as she handed it to me. "It was right in the jar where we left it. Are you thinking what I'm thinking?"

"Unfortunately, yes," I said. "The one in the keyhole turned to ashes."

Carmen and I frowned.

"What does it mean?" asked Lulu, frustrated.

I didn't want to tell her, but what choice did I have?

"I think we know what you were doing while under the cursed tablet," I said.

A pained look spread across Lulu's face.

"I did this?" she asked. Her voice turned slow and wistful. "This is my fault? Oh, no. No, no."

She ran her hands through her hair. She looked like a statue, standing half bent over, seized up with guilt, rage, and sorrow. Carmen rested a gentle hand on Lulu's back.

"Enough of this," I said. "We are done blaming ourselves for this crap. We are done blaming ourselves for senseless destruction. Carmen blamed herself for starting all this. Now you're blaming yourself for what that witch did to Chace and Hector. But we all know there's only one person to blame for all of this, and…"

"Two," said Carmen. The pocket demons and cats gathered around Lulu, doing their best to console her.

"What?" I asked, confused.

"It's just, there are technically two people to blame," said Carmen. "The Thistle Witch and Ignatius."

I stared at her. "I was on a roll," I said.

"I'm sorry," said Carmen. "Continue."

"We both know there are *two* people to blame," I said. "And one of them is long dead, so there's not much we can do about that…"

"Unless Carmen reanimates him so we can beat the piss out of him," said Lulu, wiping away a tear.

"But we can do something about the Thistle Witch," I said. "And we're going to do it tonight."

"We're ready, Immy," said Carmen. She rested her hand on my shoulder. "We can defeat her. I know we can."

"I sure as hell hope you're right," I said. "Because I don't like the alternative."

CHAPTER FORTY-TWO

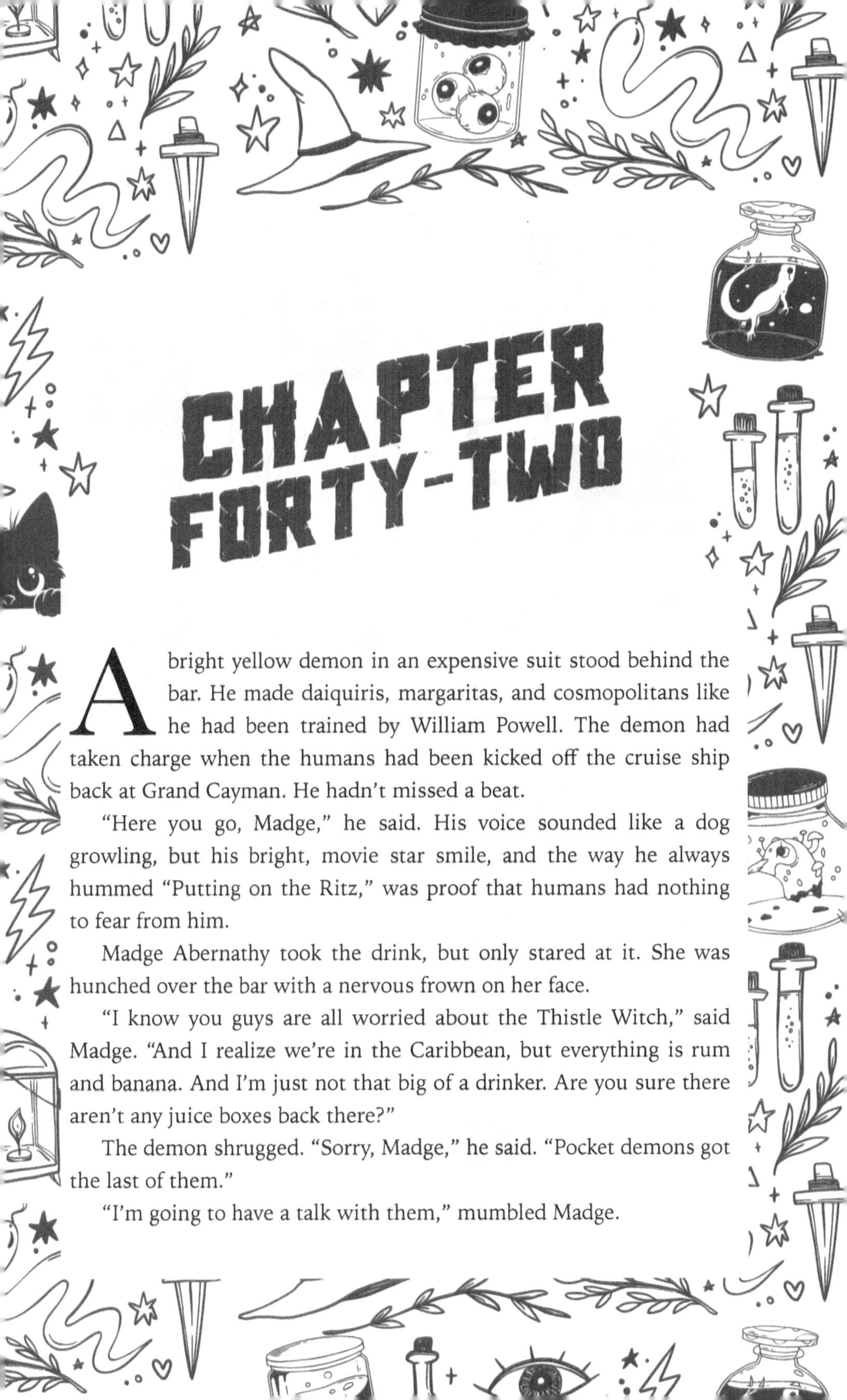

A bright yellow demon in an expensive suit stood behind the bar. He made daiquiris, margaritas, and cosmopolitans like he had been trained by William Powell. The demon had taken charge when the humans had been kicked off the cruise ship back at Grand Cayman. He hadn't missed a beat.

"Here you go, Madge," he said. His voice sounded like a dog growling, but his bright, movie star smile, and the way he always hummed "Putting on the Ritz," was proof that humans had nothing to fear from him.

Madge Abernathy took the drink, but only stared at it. She was hunched over the bar with a nervous frown on her face.

"I know you guys are all worried about the Thistle Witch," said Madge. "And I realize we're in the Caribbean, but everything is rum and banana. And I'm just not that big of a drinker. Are you sure there aren't any juice boxes back there?"

The demon shrugged. "Sorry, Madge," he said. "Pocket demons got the last of them."

"I'm going to have a talk with them," mumbled Madge.

Peter Abernathy ran into the bar. He was winded as he grabbed his wife's arm.

"What is it, Petey?" she asked, alarmed.

"You have to see this," said Peter. His face was cold and afraid.

Out on deck, the wind picked up. It was strangely cool after such a humid day. It made Madge shudder. The nervous bubble that had first formed back when they called their daughters, felt like it was about to pop.

"Look," said Peter. He pointed up into the murky night sky. All the demons on the ship gathered with them to look at the sight.

A huge, otherworldly mass of gray and blue light rotated slowly in the sky far to the west. It had a glow about it that lit up the night with a sheen of dismay.

"I haven't seen a symbol of evil magic usage like that," said Peter, "since…"

"Since those horrible evil snowmen," said Madge, frowning.

"That was Carmen's favorite Christmas," said Peter, holding his wife close.

Madge turned to the yeti beside her. "Can't I please have my phone back? Can't I call my daughters and warn them? Or tell them that I love them?"

"I'm sorry," said the yeti, bowing his head. "We can't risk the Thistle Witch finding out where we all are. She's out for blood, and we're all on her list."

Madge sighed. "Do you think they'll be all right?"

"They're our daughters," said Petey. "You know what that means."

Madge nodded. "That means a lot of swearing will happen before the night is over. And I blame you for that."

"It wasn't me," said Peter. "That was Troll Rob's fault."

Madge shook her head. "And it also means that if any two people have a chance of beating that witch, it's them."

CHAPTER FORTY-THREE

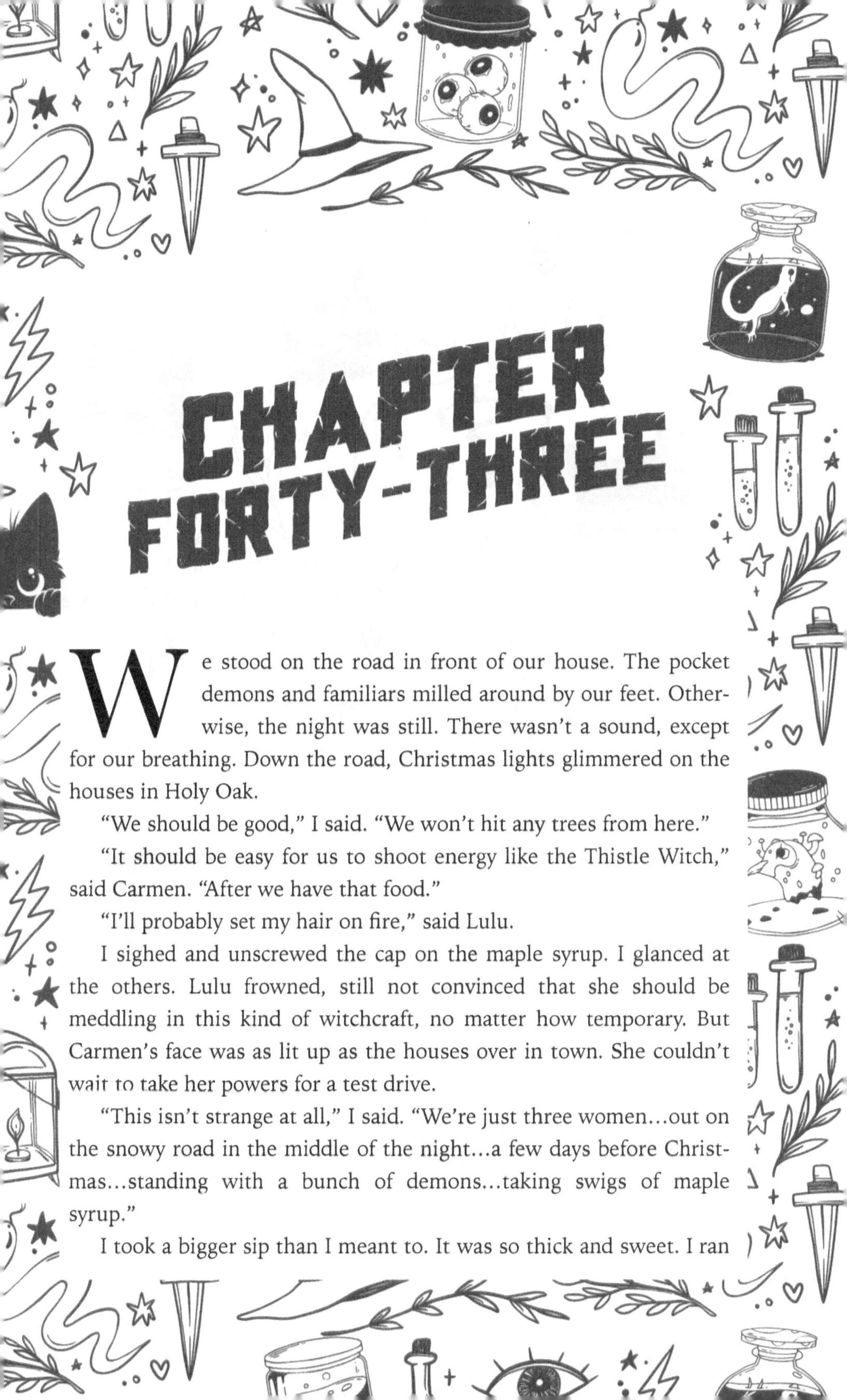

We stood on the road in front of our house. The pocket demons and familiars milled around by our feet. Otherwise, the night was still. There wasn't a sound, except for our breathing. Down the road, Christmas lights glimmered on the houses in Holy Oak.

"We should be good," I said. "We won't hit any trees from here."

"It should be easy for us to shoot energy like the Thistle Witch," said Carmen. "After we have that food."

"I'll probably set my hair on fire," said Lulu.

I sighed and unscrewed the cap on the maple syrup. I glanced at the others. Lulu frowned, still not convinced that she should be meddling in this kind of witchcraft, no matter how temporary. But Carmen's face was as lit up as the houses over in town. She couldn't wait to take her powers for a test drive.

"This isn't strange at all," I said. "We're just three women…out on the snowy road in the middle of the night…a few days before Christmas…standing with a bunch of demons…taking swigs of maple syrup."

I took a bigger sip than I meant to. It was so thick and sweet. I ran my tongue across my teeth and handed it to Carmen. She smiled as she took a drink, then passed it to Lulu.

"Looks like children's cough medicine," said Lulu. She took a drink and then shook her head. "Oh, man…"

"Can you feel the witchcraft coursing through you already?" asked Carmen.

"No," said Lulu. "It just seems weird without the pancakes."

I stood there, waiting to feel the magic take hold of me. But after a moment, nothing happened. I heard a noise and turned around. Carmen was hunched down, giving each pocket demon a sip of the syrup.

"That's not sanitary," said Lulu.

"Hey," I said. "What are you doing?"

"Come on, Immy," said Carmen. "They want to help. They're upset that the Thistle Witch was here twice, and they weren't able to do anything about it."

I shook my head. "If you guys get the runs, I'm not cleaning it up."

"Whoa," said Lulu.

"What?" Carmen asked.

"Look at your hand," said Lulu, pointing at my fingers.

It looked like a match flame was coming out of each of my fingertips. I turned my hands over and a shimmer went up my body. I looked at Carmen and saw her eyes sparkle an impossible deep green. Lulu's hair shimmered like fireworks until I almost thought that she *had* set fire to herself. But after a moment, the ethereal quality to all of us faded.

"All right," I said. "Let's get to work."

We each placed a hand on a protective stone that lined our property. Carmen and I said a Gregorian chant under our breath, and one by one the stones lit up. They shimmered for a minute and then faded back into their mossy sleep.

"That's witchcraft that hasn't been seen in generations, Immy," said Carmen. "Our whole property must be like a panic room now. All the demons on that cruise ship should be here. It must be the safest place on Earth."

"Are you trying to jinx us?" asked Lulu. "Don't. You'll get us killed."

"No cursed tablet magic should be able to get through again," I said. "That's for sure. I kind of hope it ticks her off. I'm in the mood to tick her off."

"Me too," said Lulu. "Let's crumble some Styrofoam when she gets here."

"Everybody knows the plan," I said. "The effigy and its coffin are sitting behind the white shed. We need to tear off a piece of the Thistle Witch's clothing, tie it around the hands of the effigy, put it in the coffin, then run back into the woods, say the enchantment written on the coffin, and bury it. One person has to go back and bury it while the other two distract the Thistle Witch…"

"And her monster," said Carmen, sadly. "If it's finished."

Lulu frowned. "Do you think Chace and Hector are dead?"

My heart beat against my chest. "If they're not dead already, they wish they were."

We stood silent for a moment, and then I nodded. "Remember the rest of the plan. She can't get on the property. But she can do a lot of damage if she thinks we might win. Everyone in Holy Oak could be in danger if she gets pissed. But once the coffin is buried, the Thistle Witch should be stripped of her powers. After we fire our warning shots, we probably only have a few minutes until she gets here, so be ready."

I opened my mouth, but wasn't sure what else to say. "I guess that's it."

Carmen patted our backs.

"All right, Immy," said Carmen. "Now remember, we're out on the road because we're trying not to hit the trees. If we do, there will be one very angry troll who will come back from California to give us a stern talking-to. He planted them and I promised we'd never harm them."

I raised my hands to the sky. Fire shot out of my fingers and wound around like a snake, shaping itself into a burning orb in my grasp. I could hardly breathe as my eyes filled with the fire I held above me. This was just what she had done in that dream. And now *I* was doing it.

"I'm not sure what to do," I whispered, sweating.

Carmen moved in toward me. "If you want to shoot it over to her house, trust yourself. Close your eyes and picture where you want the orb to go."

Carmen's voice was so calm. It made me want to fall asleep and pretend none of this was happening. But instead, when I closed my eyes, I pictured that snowy driveway, that chipped house, and the image of that poor family hanging in the trees.

As if the orb heard me, it shot out past my fingers and high up into the night sky, arching over the trees and disappearing into the west. Two more orbs shot out behind me, and I turned to see Lulu and Carmen with their arms raised.

"It feels so weird," said Lulu.

Carmen laughed. We shot off three more orbs and watched as their bright orange glow disappeared in the distance.

"Your move, bitch," I whispered to the sky.

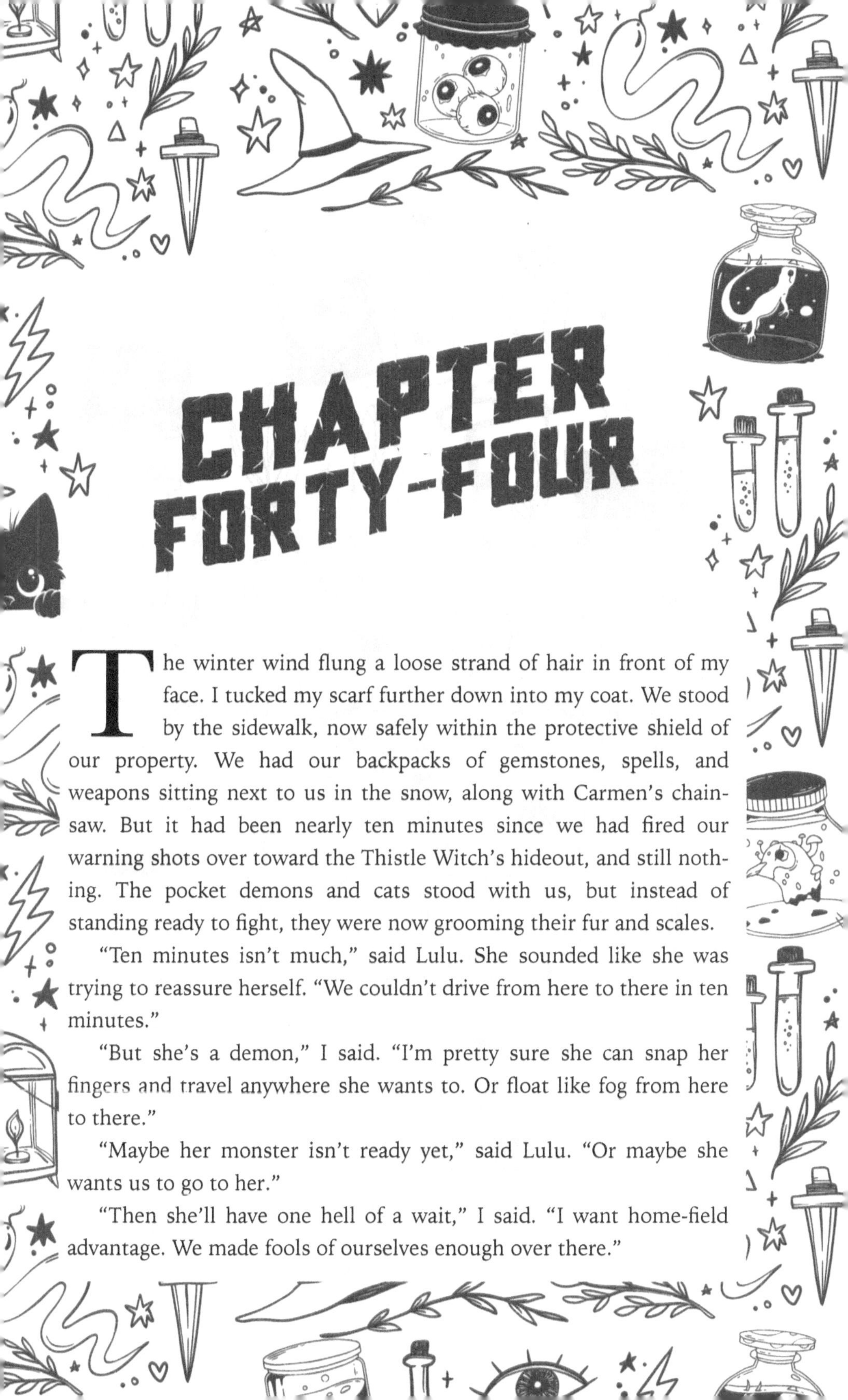

CHAPTER FORTY-FOUR

The winter wind flung a loose strand of hair in front of my face. I tucked my scarf further down into my coat. We stood by the sidewalk, now safely within the protective shield of our property. We had our backpacks of gemstones, spells, and weapons sitting next to us in the snow, along with Carmen's chainsaw. But it had been nearly ten minutes since we had fired our warning shots over toward the Thistle Witch's hideout, and still nothing. The pocket demons and cats stood with us, but instead of standing ready to fight, they were now grooming their fur and scales.

"Ten minutes isn't much," said Lulu. She sounded like she was trying to reassure herself. "We couldn't drive from here to there in ten minutes."

"But she's a demon," I said. "I'm pretty sure she can snap her fingers and travel anywhere she wants to. Or float like fog from here to there."

"Maybe her monster isn't ready yet," said Lulu. "Or maybe she wants us to go to her."

"Then she'll have one hell of a wait," I said. "I want home-field advantage. We made fools of ourselves enough over there."

"Maybe she's afraid of us," said Carmen. "She knows we shouldn't be able to shoot energy like that. Perhaps we've intimidated her with our new badass powers, and we'll never see her again."

Lulu stared at Carmen, horrified by the way she tempted fate. "You're jinxing us again!"

"I'm excited to see how our old charms and spells work with increased abilities," said Carmen. "They should be spicy."

Carmen hardly got the words out when a gust of wind knocked against us. The breeze sounded mournful as it circled around.

"Do you feel that, Immy?" asked Carmen.

"Even I felt that," said Lulu. "And I've only been a witch for ten minutes."

I swallowed hard.

"What was that?" asked Lulu, ducking and looking up at the sky. "Holy shit."

"What?" I asked, mimicking her stance. My eyes popped out when I saw the churning gray and blue light above us. A symbol for serious angry magic.

"I think you'll be able to test out your enhanced powers after all," I said.

"The sky is just like it was with those snowmen, remember?" asked Carmen.

"Don't get too excited," I said.

Carmen's face changed. "Did you hear that?"

"It's the wind," said Lulu, still staring at the sky.

"No," I said. I felt my face go red. "It's sobbing."

Carmen's eyes turned wet and glossy. "It's a lamentation of the dead."

"Does that mean what I think it does?" asked Lulu.

"She finished her monster," said Carmen. She sniffed to stop herself from crying. This was a monster made from people that were dead because they were connected to us. I would have cried too, but felt more compelled to smash something.

The wind blasted against us again, and down the road, something large fell to the Earth. The ground rumbled as it did so, nearly knocking us off our feet.

"There!" said Carmen, steadying herself. She pointed down the road. It was hard to make out in the blinking streetlight. It looked like a dark amorphous blob. Then it unfurled its wings and slowly walked up the street toward us.

"Son of a bitch," I said. "It can fly."

"It certainly doesn't look festive like I was hoping," said Carmen.

The figure took its time. Then, as though it had a mind to change, it stopped. It hunched a little, then soared upward, disappearing once again into the safety of the swirling night.

"I never thought I'd prefer a giant spider," said Lulu.

I only had a second's warning. Loud wailing filled my ears, so I knew the monster was close. I pulled Carmen and Lulu further back from the stones, just as the creature landed right in front of us on the road. The impact knocked us all down into the snow. The flightless pocket demons fell over with us, while the ones with wings tumbled end over end in the air before righting themselves again.

We shot up fast.

"Damn," said Lulu, shocked.

Chace had told us about the Thistle Witch's murder machines. The first had been a giant spider, then a huge snake, then a fifteen-foot werewolf, and now this—a hulking gargoyle. It stood nearly twenty feet tall. Its legs and arms were fashioned from the woven arms and legs of the Thistle Witch's victims. Its wings, which must have been fifty feet from tip to tip, were made from large strips of skin stitched together like a fleshy quilt with crude, brown thread. She saved everyone's heads for the gargoyle's abdomen. Eyes stared out at us while mouths opened and cried out in agony. In the golden street-light, my eyes were drawn to a head dead center on the gargoyle's chest. Chace's face stared out at me. He didn't cry like the others, but instead looked at me with an expression of utter despair. Our eyes stayed fixed on each other until everything else seemed to melt away. His dead fear drilled into me in such a way that I didn't know if I'd scream or tip over. All the blood drained from my face. But I didn't have time to grieve. That would have to wait. Instead, I steadied myself and tried to ignore all the bodies and misery in front of me. It wasn't easy.

The Thistle Witch had obviously seen Hector as a vital component of her monster. His body was woven throughout the gargoyle, from hands to feet, and everywhere in between. The whole creation was hard to look at, but if anything was worse than Chace's look of agony, it might have been the head of the gargoyle. It was Hector's head, staring out at us, with cataract eyes and an expression completely devoid of feeling. That was our friend, one who had begged us to keep him safe, trusted us to keep him safe. And we had failed him. *I* had failed him.

Lulu's mouth hung open in shock. Carmen stood stiff and was surprisingly expressionless, except for a single tear running down her face. I didn't want to know what I looked like because I probably resembled a wild, mad creature.

A cloud of ethereal fog drifted in front of the gargoyle and stayed there. Then it took shape, and the Thistle Witch suddenly stood in her human form, peering at us from behind her mask.

"What do you think of it?" asked the Thistle Witch. "It has a few familiar faces."

"I think you should have stuck with stamp collecting," I said. "Or model trains."

"How can you hate us enough to do this?" asked Carmen. She glanced up at Hector's face. "How can you hate *me* so much? You don't even know me."

"You are an abomination," said the witch. "Just like your ancestor before you. That is all I need to know."

"Then we're two of a kind," said Carmen, fixing her gaze on the witch.

"I have waited a long time to kill witches," said the Thistle Witch. "I will savor your deaths."

"I'm not sure about that," I said. "We're going to show you what abominations can do."

I didn't want to exchange pleasantries. I lifted my hands. Seeing what I was up to, Carmen and Lulu followed my lead. Red orbs appeared in our palms, and I threw mine straight at the Thistle Witch. I felt myself scream as I did so. Carmen and Lulu did the same, but when our orbs hit the protective barrier, they bounced back at us. We slammed ourselves into the snow as the orbs flew back above our heads, and went whirling up into the night sky.

"Shit," I said, my face plastered in snow.

"I think we made the border a little too strong, Immy," said Carmen, getting up.

"You think?" asked Lulu.

"You learned some new tricks since your interesting performance at my home," said the Thistle Witch. "But are you smart enough for them? Looks like you'll have to come out here to face me. Or are you frightened little witches?"

"Are you trash-talking us?" asked Carmen. Barnaby crawled up and jumped into her pocket. "Do you know who you're talking to? I throw knives for fun."

"You killed a lot of people," I said, staring at her. "And tonight, we're stopping you."

"We shall see," said the Thistle Witch, crossing her arms.

I handed Lulu and Carmen their backpacks and then picked up my own. One by one, we walked through the protective barrier onto the street. Then we turned and faced the Thistle Witch and her gargoyle.

I didn't wait around. The last thing I wanted to do was let her know how terrified I was. I wasn't sure if our powers gave us the upper hand or only made us equals. But I planned to at least feign some bravado. I had my hands outstretched with the orb in them before I even realized it. Lulu and Carmen did the same. We sent our orbs careening toward the Thistle Witch and gargoyle. The gargoyle acted quickly, stepping forward and knocking one orb out of the way, then another. He grabbed Carmen's orb out of the air and popped it in his hand like a tomato. The fire and energy melted down his arm like juice.

"It looks like we're evenly matched," said the Thistle Witch. "Your new powers are fascinating, if not disgusting. But didn't your mother teach you the golden rule of witchcraft? It's much easier on the body to create spells out of words and ingredients, bones and blood. It's much harder to create something out of nothing, like that."

She pointed at Carmen's hands.

"Oh, my goodness," said Carmen, staring at her palms.

That's when I realized that in all the adrenaline and nerves, I had ignored my own discomfort. But I couldn't ignore the truth etched across my skin. My hands were covered in big blisters. Lulu's were the same.

"It's not so bad," said Lulu. She looked at the Thistle Witch with more hatred than I had ever seen in her eyes. "I've been burnt worse."

"I hope you have old tried and true spells in your bags," said the Thistle Witch. "Or you may just be dead before you know it."

I found myself backing up. My mind scanned the books in my backpack, thinking of spells we could use against the gargoyle and witch. I knew Carmen was probably way ahead of me. I didn't want to face the gargoyle on the road. It might turn around and stomp over to the houses down the street, edging closer to Holy Oak. We needed to lead it away from where it could do damage, and where gawking townspeople might end up hurt.

The Thistle Witch rested her hand on the gargoyle. It looked down at her with vacant eyes. Then she pointed at us.

"Kill them!" she said, screaming. I'm not sure what filled me with more dread—the Thistle Witch morphing from an emotionless statue to something infused with hatred, or the gargoyle that suddenly sprang into action and ran toward us.

"Come on!" I said, grabbing at Carmen and Lulu. We sprinted down the street as fast as we could.

Lulu glanced back. "That big bastard can move!"

"Fried eggs right behind us!" Carmen screamed. "Fried eggs right behind us!"

"You don't have to use the code word," I shouted. "I know where the danger is. Run!"

"Where are we going?" yelled Lulu.

"The long grass covered in snow," I said, pointing. "On the other side of our property. It's just old Mr. Peterson's hunting land."

We slammed into the frozen grass, which was covered up with fluffy snow and a layer of harder slush underneath. It felt like a good place to fight. Maybe the gargoyle would get tangled up in the bramble. Plus, we were only about ten feet from our property line, so if the going got tough, we could make a run for the safety of the stones.

Carmen and the pocket demons took one of our old reliable spell books out of her backpack. She flipped through it as the gargoyle barreled into the long grass. Lulu grabbed her trusty iron rod. I snatched a few witch bottles out of my backpack and cringed at the way they irritated my already raw skin. I recited a few words, asking my aim to be true and painful, then I threw the bottles at the gargoyle. He howled as the glass broke against him. Nails, pins, and witch hairs burned his stolen skin.

Lulu lunged forward and slammed her iron rod against the gargoyle's leg, the same way she had when she first met Hector. But I didn't want to think about that. I didn't want to think about anything except destroying that monster and his maker.

The gargoyle howled deep and low, swinging at Lulu. But she ducked and sprinted away, hitting him again on the back. He shrieked and turned around, smacking his thick arm against Lulu. She fell flat down into the snow. I ran up and threw another bottle at him as he tried to grab Lulu. He knocked the bottle away.

Carmen flipped through her spell book in a frenzy, searching for the right incantation. The familiars and pocket demons waited around her. She nodded at them and began a deep, rhythmic Gregorian chant. The gargoyle clawed at the night sky and bellowed. Blood dripped out of his ears and down his face.

For all her bluster, the Thistle Witch didn't seem in a hurry to join the battle. She strolled up the street toward us all with slow, methodical steps. She was in no rush for this to be over. She wanted to enjoy it. And she wanted her gargoyle to do most of the dirty work.

The gargoyle broke free of the chant and lunged forward. Carmen sprang away just in time to avoid his massive, stamping foot. But the force of him pounding the ground still ricocheted through us. Carmen got up, dusting snow off herself. Then something seemed to take a hold of her. She opened her mouth and long, guttural words came out. It was a spell I'd never heard before, maybe one she had practiced with the pocket demons in her room late at night. All at once, Carmen turned a deep red, as if her whole body was on fire. My mouth gaped as she and the pocket demons hurled themselves at the gargoyle. He screamed in pain as Carmen latched on with her blazing touch. Lulu grabbed her rod and pounded the gargoyle again.

I walked up to the gargoyle, who was bent over. My mouth opened, and I recited a spell that I had only ever read about in the library, one that witches used long ago when they had more power. It was one that Carmen had tried once, too, with mixed results. As I spoke, a gust of wind picked up, and thick, fat snowflakes fell around us. As I continued chanting, the snow increased, the flakes became thicker, and the wind got faster. Soon we were all lost in the snow-storm of my spell.

"Good job, Immy!" said Carmen, racing up to me. At some point, she had detached herself from the gargoyle. The pocket demons remained, biting and ripping at their enemy. "Last time I tried that, it snowed in the house, but not outside. Remember?"

"I do," I said. "You look pretty good for someone who was on fire."

"The enhanced powers really cut down on the spell side effects," said Carmen. "I can only feel a rash forming on two-thirds of my body, instead of the whole thing. Isn't magic grand?"

"Just super," I said. We watched as the demons and Lulu beat at the gargoyle in the nearly blinding snowstorm. Sometimes the gargoyle sent the demons careening off into the snow. And sometimes he nearly knocked Lulu over with his wing. But they fought back with everything they had. The Thistle Witch stood calmly back on the road, only visible between gusts of wind.

Carmen disappeared into the snow, then reappeared with her chainsaw.

"I think this is a good time to take care of those wings," said

Carmen. "Immy, we can take the gargoyle. Can you get the piece of cloth from the Thistle Witch to complete the effigy spell?"

I felt like letting out a desperate laugh. Did she know what she was asking? Did she think I was brave the way she was? Of course, I didn't want to do it. But Carmen and Lulu's hands were full already. It looked like the gargoyle had honed in on them. It was as if the Thistle Witch was out on the road, daring me to face her.

"I can do it," I said, trying to sound sure of myself.

Carmen grabbed my hand. "I know you can," she said. "I love you, Immy."

"Don't say that," I said. Sweat dotted my forehead, even in the cold. "It makes me think something bad is going to happen."

"I love you, Immy," said Carmen, again. My eyes met hers and I saw the fear that dwelt deep down in her. The fear we both tried to hide. Sisters always know.

"I love you too, you crazy bastard," I said. "Now let's beat this asshole."

Carmen revved her chainsaw as I raced out to the Thistle Witch. It was so hard to see with the snow. All I wanted to do was turn and go a different way, but instead I aimed right for her. She didn't seem to realize I was there until the last minute. Then she looked right at me and said some words under her breath. The world became a blur, and my feet were above my head. I didn't know where I was, but I was falling, and I knew landing was going to hurt.

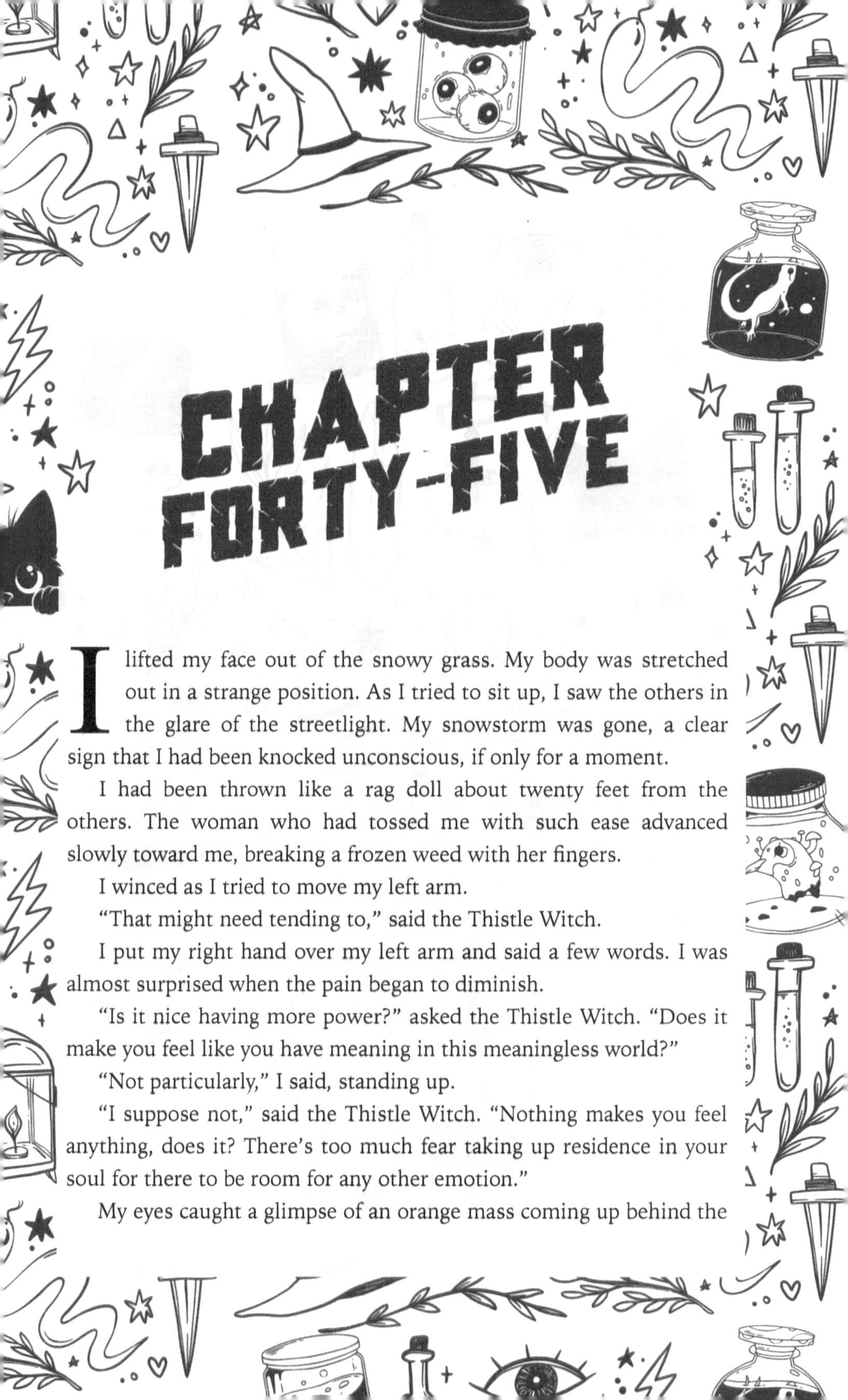

CHAPTER FORTY-FIVE

I lifted my face out of the snowy grass. My body was stretched out in a strange position. As I tried to sit up, I saw the others in the glare of the streetlight. My snowstorm was gone, a clear sign that I had been knocked unconscious, if only for a moment.

I had been thrown like a rag doll about twenty feet from the others. The woman who had tossed me with such ease advanced slowly toward me, breaking a frozen weed with her fingers.

I winced as I tried to move my left arm.

"That might need tending to," said the Thistle Witch.

I put my right hand over my left arm and said a few words. I was almost surprised when the pain began to diminish.

"Is it nice having more power?" asked the Thistle Witch. "Does it make you feel like you have meaning in this meaningless world?"

"Not particularly," I said, standing up.

"I suppose not," said the Thistle Witch. "Nothing makes you feel anything, does it? There's too much fear taking up residence in your soul for there to be room for any other emotion."

My eyes caught a glimpse of an orange mass coming up behind the

Thistle Witch. Buster Keaton and Norma Shearer stalked toward us. My eyes met Buster's for only a second, but we understood each other.

"You have mingled with demons," said the Thistle Witch. "And have tried like a child to hide from magic. I was looking forward to killing your sister for her hubris. But you will be fun to kill given your already miserable state. Like shooting someone who's already been poisoned."

I muttered, and icy weeds tangled around her. It was the same spell I had tried at her hideout and used on that jerk at the casino. But this time, my witchcraft was stronger, and the vines held her tight before she nodded and disappeared into fog.

I turned just as she reappeared behind me. I reached for her, but she turned to fog again, escaping through my fingers. It kept happening like that. Every time I thought I had her, she transformed into fog and disappeared into the safety of the dark, churning sky. How was I supposed to fight someone that could disappear and reappear?

I heard something behind me, and spun around in time to see the Thistle Witch reappear. I recited a Latin spell, but was cut short. With a wave of her hand, she smashed me against the snowy ground. Then she did it again and again. I completed the words to my spell, and the snow pelted hard against her, forcing her to return to fog.

The world was a blurry haze. Carmen and Lulu were suddenly there, with the gargoyle stomping after them. Carmen had blood all over her face. The reason was clear—the gargoyle was down by one wing.

Carmen leaned over to see if I was OK. Apparently, I wasn't. She said a few words while holding my arm. I must have wrecked it again.

"How many times have you hurt your arm, Immy?" she asked.

"A couple," I mumbled.

"Be more careful," said Carmen, with worry in her voice.

"The arm's the least of my worries," I said. "If you haven't noticed, she's kicking my ass."

My arm shimmered as Carmen healed me. My body creaked as I stood up again. Lulu held her arms out and shot an orb at the fog. It hit the Thistle Witch and smashed her hard against the snow. Lulu looked at her cherry-red hands and smiled.

"Worth it," she said.

I leaped onto the Thistle Witch and began muttering Carmen's fire spell. The gargoyle advanced toward me, but Carmen and Lulu lunged at him, tearing at his remaining wing with the chainsaw and a hatchet. I felt my whole body light up, just as the Thistle Witch disappeared from under me.

"Damn it," I said. Just then, the gargoyle broke free from Lulu and Carmen and lumbered toward me. I had to duck to avoid his punch. He tumbled to the ground as Carmen and Lulu cut into his other wing. The gargoyle sent a loud shriek into the night. It made me shake more than the cold.

Then I felt a strange tugging on my pants. Norma Shearer and Buster Keaton stood there, staring at me. Norma had something in her mouth. I kneeled down, and she spat it onto the snow. It was a brown, frayed piece of cloth.

"The Thistle Witch's dress," I whispered. "Did you get this while I was on top of her?"

Norma nodded.

"You were waiting for your moment, weren't you?" I asked.

The cats that weren't cats meowed at me, and I smiled.

"You did good," I said. "But I have something else for you to do."

I tried to pocket the cloth without drawing attention to myself. The Thistle Witch was out there in the wind somewhere. I didn't want to run the risk of her seeing what we had. This was our big chance, and I didn't want to blow it.

Carmen and the pocket demons nearly had the gargoyle's other wing completely off. Still, the Thistle Witch refused to reappear. It wasn't exactly a testament to her love.

Lulu ran up to me. "Do you have any more witch bottles in your bag?" asked Lulu. "I want to hurl them at the gargoyle while he's down. We might just be able to beat him."

I grabbed her arm and tried my best to look discreet.

"I need you to do something else," I whispered. "Carmen can handle the gargoyle now. You do this."

I flashed her the cloth for just a second and then shoved it in her pocket. Lulu's eyes turned glossy. She shook her head like she didn't even want me to ask.

"You take the cloth and tie it around the effigy," I said. "You remember where it's hidden?"

"Of course," said Lulu. "But…"

"Bury it in the woods like we planned," I whispered. "Then the Thistle Witch will be stripped of her power. Look at me, Lulu. You can end this."

"You or Carmen should do it," said Lulu, her face getting red. "You two know way more about magic than me."

"I'll send the cats with you," I whispered. "They can help. Listen, it has to be you. The Thistle Witch hates us a million times more than you. She'll notice if we're gone. She'll just think you're scared."

"I *am* scared," said Lulu.

I nodded and looked her in the eyes. "Me too. But we can't run the risk of her finding out what we're up to. She would haul ass out of here and kill everyone in town. We can't have that blood on our hands."

Lulu batted away tears. "You're covered in blood, Imogen," she said. "You're scaring me. If you have me do this, what are you going to do?"

"Just do it," I said. "You've been able to face magic in a way that I've never seen a normal human come close to. You can do this."

"All right," said Lulu, swallowing.

"Run away like you're terrified," I whispered. "To make it look less conspicuous. Like we don't have a plan. Like we're giving up."

Lulu nodded. "Just be careful, Imogen," she said. "Don't do anything stupid."

Lulu ran off panicked, just like I had instructed her to. She ran right onto our property with the Thistle Witch's dress hidden in her pocket. My heart lightened for a moment as she cleared the stones and got safely into our yard. Now all we had to do was distract the Thistle Witch until Lulu completed her mission. But Lulu's final words rang in my ears as she faded into the night.

"Stupid is the best way to distract her," I muttered.

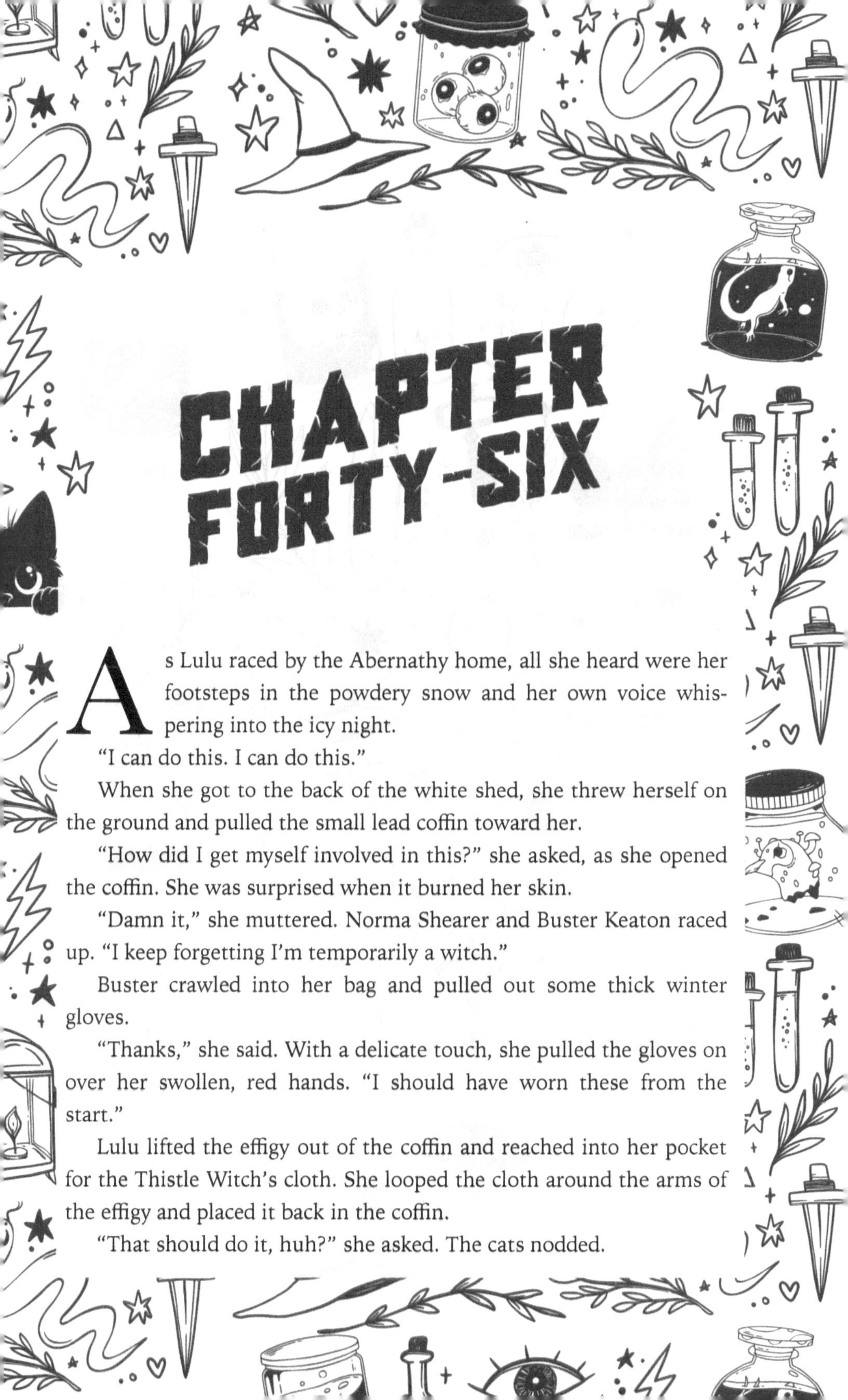

CHAPTER FORTY-SIX

As Lulu raced by the Abernathy home, all she heard were her footsteps in the powdery snow and her own voice whispering into the icy night.

"I can do this. I can do this."

When she got to the back of the white shed, she threw herself on the ground and pulled the small lead coffin toward her.

"How did I get myself involved in this?" she asked, as she opened the coffin. She was surprised when it burned her skin.

"Damn it," she muttered. Norma Shearer and Buster Keaton raced up. "I keep forgetting I'm temporarily a witch."

Buster crawled into her bag and pulled out some thick winter gloves.

"Thanks," she said. With a delicate touch, she pulled the gloves on over her swollen, red hands. "I should have worn these from the start."

Lulu lifted the effigy out of the coffin and reached into her pocket for the Thistle Witch's cloth. She looped the cloth around the arms of the effigy and placed it back in the coffin.

"That should do it, huh?" she asked. The cats nodded.

"Stay with me," she said, standing up. "I might need you yet."

I rummaged around in my bag as the gargoyle lunged at Carmen. She revved her chainsaw and ran at him. He spun away from her and growled.

I pulled on a pair of rubber gloves and stared at the item I had been looking for. It had been sitting at the bottom of my backpack the whole time. I hadn't told Carmen, afraid she'd only worry, or offer to do it herself. I had been anxious that it might come to this. That even though we had increased witchcraft, the Thistle Witch might still have an edge from her knowledge of how to wield powers that for us seemed so advanced. And she had that demonic ability to vanish and reappear. My heart felt like it would bang right out of my chest as I grabbed the item out of my backpack.

I held it tight as I closed my eyes. I knew the Thistle Witch was out there, somewhere on the wind. I blocked out the gargoyle's screaming. I blocked out Carmen's chainsaw and clever retorts. I listened for the fog.

And somehow, I heard it.

I carefully placed one end of the item on my safe, gloved wrist. Then I spun around and snapped the other end of the shackle on the fog. The Thistle Witch took form instantly and stared at me. Her eyes were huge within her mask.

"What have you done?" she asked, screaming.

Her wrist sizzled in the iron shackles that moored her to me.

"I bind you, bitch," I said.

The gargoyle tossed Carmen on the ground. She reeled as he loomed over her.

"I'm so sorry," said Carmen, looking into each of the faces that covered the gargoyle's abdomen. Then she looked up at Hector's head. "I didn't mean for any of this to happen."

The gargoyle bent over to stomp on Carmen. But Carmen grabbed her chainsaw, and with one fast motion, cut through the creature's left leg. It toppled to the ground. Carmen bent over and began sawing the gargoyle's other leg off. Its scream reverberated into the night.

The Thistle Witch tugged at me. Her wrist sizzled again.

"Your monster is looking a little worse for wear," I said.

"Carmen is an exceptional witch. But the same cannot be said of you. Where your sister hones her craft, you throw darts in the darkness, hoping something will stick."

"And you make a shitty dog, lady," I said.

"I thought you'd run away in the night like your scared human friend," said the Thistle Witch. "But I see you intend to torture yourself instead."

"If it means torturing you too, then sign me up."

The Thistle Witch flicked her hand and I went hurtling backward with her pulled right along with me. We both landed in the snow.

Carmen finished slicing off the gargoyle's other leg. Then she bent down and put her hand on his shoulder as he cried.

"I really am sorry," said Carmen, sadly.

The Thistle Witch lifted herself up. Her wrist sizzled again.

"That's a clever spell of yours," I said. "I think I caught the incantation just before you flicked your finger."

I closed my eyes and said the words, then flicked my hand at the Thistle Witch. We both soared through the air before landing in the snow again.

"I was right," I said, lying in the snow. My body felt too sore to move, but the Thistle Witch was already sitting up.

"You are doing a number on yourself today," whispered the Thistle Witch. "You must like pain as much as me."

"Not at all," I said. "I even hate waxing my eyebrows."

"Then you really won't like this," she said.

She reached her hand out to me and began chanting. But just as her hand took on a particular blue color and my whole body felt numb, Carmen ran up and reached out her arms. Horatio, Benedict, and Minerva leaped from Carmen with salt shakers in their grasp. They landed on the Thistle Witch and poured it on her. She screamed as the salt burned her skin. Barnaby tore into her arm as she writhed in pain. Her movements jostled me and a wave of fear soared through my body. Why had I done this? I had shackled myself to a wild animal and had no intention of breaking free.

"What did you do that for, Immy?" asked Carmen.

"She kept floating around," I said, spitting blood. "It was bugging me. I couldn't punch her. And I really wanted to punch that witch."

"But now she can *really* hurt you," said Carmen.

"No shit," I said. "I figured that one out."

"Let me help you," said Carmen.

"Be my guest," I said.

Carmen approached me, saying the same spell in Latin that she had earlier. She turned all red as she approached the Thistle Witch with outstretched arms. But the witch shook the pocket demons free and looked up at Carmen. The Thistle Witch said a few, deep, guttural words and Carmen screamed.

I reached out to my sister as she fell to her knees, clutching her stomach. The Thistle Witch said a few more words and Carmen was flat on the ground. The pocket demons ran to her aid as I smashed the Thistle Witch's face with my elbow. I threw myself on top of her and punched her again and again. But with a flick of her finger, she hurled us both into the air.

But something happened as we toppled end over end in the air. It was stupid, really. I just thought how much I didn't want to be thrown around in the air like a rag doll, and suddenly, I wasn't. Instead, the Thistle Witch and I floated there in the swirling night sky, hovering in the stars.

"You're flying," said the Thistle Witch, angry. "Even I can't fly."

It was so quiet up there. Tiny flakes cascaded around us.

"You want to take back that shitty witch comment now?" I asked.

"No," said the witch.

Carmen shouted from the ground. She wiped blood off her mouth and stood, gaping up at us.

"You make a pretty good witch, Immy," she shouted.

"The hell I do," I yelled back to her. "What do I do now?"

"I don't know," said Carmen. "I'd pass you the chainsaw so you could cut yourself free from her, but I can't get up there."

"That doesn't sound fun to me," said the Thistle Witch. "I suggest an alternate plan."

Then the world exploded in golden light, and I felt myself careening toward the Earth again.

CHAPTER FORTY-SEVEN

Lulu ran through the snow and into the woods. She didn't stop until she almost hit the river. Then she knelt down with the coffin and started digging. She threw the snow away and clawed down into the hard, frozen dirt. The cats dug with her until there was a place wide and deep enough to place the coffin.

"Shit," said Lulu, staring at it. "I'm supposed to recite the incantation on the lid. I can't speak Greek. What do I do?"

She looked deep into Norma Shearer's eyes, and as she did so, the cat didn't seem so much like a cat anymore. Neither of them did. Their bodies fell away, replaced instead by dark shadows and red eyes. Eyes that stared back into hers.

"Holy shit," said Lulu.

The shadow that had been Norma Shearer said a few words that Lulu didn't understand. When Lulu didn't respond, the shadow that had been Buster Keaton reached out and punched her in the shoulder.

"Ouch," said Lulu. "What? I don't get it. Am I supposed to repeat those words?"

The shadows nodded.

"Fine," said Lulu. "You don't have to punch me about it. Just go slow."

Norma said a few words, then waited as Lulu said them back to her. They continued on like that, saying a few words and repeating them, until the lid of the lead coffin lit up like a thousand sparkling blue stars. Gradually, the shadows faded and the cats were cats again. Lulu's eyes shined from the brightness of the lid. But Buster pawed at the hole, and Lulu snapped out of her reverie.

She placed the coffin in the hole just as the sparkles on the lid began to vanish. She covered it with dirt and then patted the snow down onto it.

"There," said Lulu. Her hands shook, and it felt like something was caught in her throat. "Is it done?"

It is done, the cats seemed to say. Lulu felt a shudder go through her. *It is good.*

I woke up as the Thistle Witch threw herself on top of me. Carmen came at her with fire hands again. She placed her palms down on the Thistle Witch, and the witch's back caught on fire. But she only laughed.

The witch curled her fingers around my throat and squeezed as Carmen kept burning her. Carmen shouted to me, but I couldn't understand her. I pawed up at the witch and got a hold of her mask. I ripped it off, and she let go of my throat. She flicked her finger and Carmen was propelled back into the snow. But my sister was up in a moment, racing back over to us.

The Thistle Witch's face was not what I thought it would be. Did I think she was an old crone? Or maybe some corpse with worms crawling on her? She was neither of those things. She had a round little face and bright brown eyes. Her hair was the color of dark straw. She was beautiful, almost. And so young, no more than twenty-two. I felt the shock plastered all over my face. She was anyone.

"You're barely more than a child," said Carmen, shocked.

"It's just another mask," said the Thistle Witch. Her voice rang out, loud and clear. "Would you like to pull this one off, too, and see what's underneath?"

The Thistle Witch rested her hands on my face. I felt heat radiating from her palms, so I reached up and did the same, reciting the words I had heard Carmen use.

It was all a blur. Where had Carmen gone? I felt my whole body turn red. My face was hot under the Thistle Witch's touch. So hot that I couldn't stand it. And then so hot that I didn't feel it anymore. Where was Carmen?

Your body has gone into shock, I thought. *Your face is on fire.*

I smelled burning flesh, but it wasn't just mine. I was burning the Thistle Witch too. I had singed her shoulders down to the bone.

"You fool," she screamed at me. "If you set me on fire, you'll burn up too. What was the point of all of this? To torture yourself?"

Then I saw something. It was faint at first, but then it came into focus with a bright glimmer. A thin wisp of light. It swirled around the Thistle Witch. But she was oblivious to it. Maybe it was the shock, but I swore the sky changed, too. The swirling gray and blue disappeared. It was like a light turning off.

Lulu, I thought. *You brilliant bastard.*

"The truth is," I said. "I only did this to distract you while Lulu buried your effigy. I didn't want you to find out our plan and go on one final killing spree around town."

"You lie," said the Thistle Witch, pressing her burning hands harder against my face. I didn't feel it. Not at all. Then she finally noticed the light swirling around her. She let go of me and screamed.

"No!" she yelled. That's when I saw Carmen racing up behind her. It seemed like she had been gone forever, but it was probably only thirty seconds. She had her chainsaw in hand.

I don't feel right, I thought, dreamily.

In one quick cut, Carmen severed the witch's shackled arm. Then she flicked her hand and the Thistle Witch was thrown away from me. The witch screamed at her bloody, severed arm. The swirling light stalked her, making fast circles around her. She cowered from it.

The light swam around the Thistle Witch until she couldn't be seen. My ears filled with buzzing as the light became brighter and brighter. It was so harsh that I had to avert my eyes. The Thistle Witch kept screaming from inside the intense glow. Then, as quickly as it had appeared, the light vanished. The night became still and dark. The only thing that remained of the witch was a crumpled mask, smoking in the snow.

Carmen leaned down and spoke. But I didn't understand. And I couldn't stop shaking. I shook so hard that my body hurt. I was afraid to know what state I was in. But somehow, I still had the nerve to feel my cheeks. But something wasn't right. Not at all. There was no skin. It was hollow.

How could there be no skin, but no pain? I couldn't feel anything! Fear wafted through me, and I reached up to Carmen.

If I didn't feel any pain, why did I scream? Why did I scream again and again?

I screamed up into the darkness before the night settled down on top of me. I closed my eyes and lost all sense of time.

CHAPTER FORTY-EIGHT

There was darkness for a long time. But time is funny that way. It's not what it appears to be, or lasts the way we think it will.

And then, somewhere in the darkness, there was a voice. It was a voice I knew, although I didn't understand what she said. Her voice had always been there in the darkness, guiding me out. I felt my eyes open and close, and in my milky gaze, the only thing I made out was her red hair. Her finger ran across my skin, making funny little squiggles on my face and neck. Then the movement stopped.

My eyes closed. I felt like sleeping to the tune of her voice.

"It'll be all right, Immy."

Her voice turned harsh and deep just as the bucket of water crashed into my face.

I sat up with a quick jerking motion. I gasped as the cold water ran down me. I reached out, not knowing what I was grabbing for. But

Carmen was down with me in a second, inspecting me like a doctor. That's when I noticed Lulu and the pocket demons standing behind her, looking at me with fear and wonder in their eyes. Lulu's hands were over her mouth. She looked like she'd been crying.

I yelled and grasped around at the night.

"I'm hurt!" I finally said, grabbing at Carmen. "I'm hurt!"

"You're all right now, Immy." Carmen grabbed my arms to stop them from flailing. "Relax or you'll start hyperventilating again."

I took long, deep breaths, and Carmen nodded.

"That's good," she said. "I'm sorry about the water, Immy. You must be cold. But I thought I'd better do the same spell we used to heal Lulu. I didn't want to take any chances."

I breathed in a couple more times and nodded. Then my shaking fingers reached up to my face. The tremors subsided a little when I felt cold skin on my cheeks.

"Was it bad?" I asked, my heart thumping. Carmen opened her mouth, then closed it again. Her eyes said everything.

"Was it bad?" I asked, looking up at Lulu. Lulu took her hands away from her mouth.

"It wasn't good," said Lulu. The words caught in her throat.

I kept my hands on my face.

"Did I look like a zombie?" I asked. I tried to smile, but I wasn't ready for that yet.

Lulu tried to smile back. "Yeah," she said. "One from the 1970s."

I rested my head on Carmen's shoulder. She put an arm around me.

"You've always hated zombies," said Carmen.

"I really do," I said.

"I don't get it," I said.

We walked through the snowy grass of Mr. Peterson's property. The snow was so soft and still. Like little feathers floating down to

Earth. There was no sense of the battle that had just taken place, except for the hulking dark mass that was stretched out by the road.

I held the Thistle Witch's leathery mask, rubbing the rough fabric between my fingers.

"The spell was supposed to weaken her," I said. "Not kill her."

"Maybe we were lucky," said Lulu. "There's a first time for everything."

I stopped in front of the gargoyle. He was on his back, panting softly as he bled out into the snow.

"Too bad the luck didn't carry over to them," I said, staring at the bodies that comprised the Thistle Witch's monster.

"Witches!" said Hector. We hurried up toward his head and knelt down. His voice was rough and slow. "The spell. I believe it is broken."

Hector's eyes were no longer glossy, and he looked out at us with a desperate, searching need. Carmen took out her embroidered hankie and dabbed the sweat off his brow.

"It's broken," said Carmen. "We defeated her."

"Thank the gods," said Hector. "You should have seen the way she chopped me up. No precision. No skill. None would argue that she is an artist. When I flayed enemies back in the day, they looked like poems when I was through with them."

"Is there anything we can do for you?" I asked.

Hector grimaced. "I do not even want to look down and see how she has cut me up, warped me, and sewn me back together with those other poor souls. Is it terrible? Tell me honestly, since I am a dying monster."

"It's pretty bad," I said.

"But you put up a great fight," said Lulu.

"That's true," said Carmen. "I have chains that really need sharpening now."

"Then I die with honor," said Hector. He struggled to breathe. "When I am gone, please separate me from the others as best you can. I know it will be grisly work."

"Don't worry," I said. "We'll do it."

"And if your pocket demons have some leisure time," said Hector, glancing at Carmen. "Perhaps you could have them finish our epic kitten puzzle."

"Consider it done," said Carmen, smiling just a little.

"But warn them," said Hector. "It's probably the most difficult cardboard amusement ever fashioned. It will take skill, luck, and a good deal of patience."

Tears dripped from Carmen's eyes down to the snow.

"They'll do you proud," she said.

"Imogen," said a voice. It was weak and scratchy, but I recognized it right away. I moved down to the gargoyle's chest and stared into Chace's eyes.

"We beat her," I said. "We did it."

He nodded. "I told her I'd get to see it," he said. His voice was thin. "I told her you'd win. She didn't like that very much."

I'd tried to smile. Chace stared into the night sky and took in a few raspy breaths. Then he looked back at me with tears in his eyes.

"Kill me," he said, weakly. "Please."

I had to take a few breaths to steady myself before answering. Everything was caught up in my chest.

"You're already dead," I said. The words froze in the air. "Just give it a couple of minutes."

He never broke his gaze from me.

"Good," he said.

We stayed with them, listening and nodding our heads to whatever few words they spoke. We sat there until the last head took its last breath.

The snow was still falling when we stood up from Hector, Chace, and the others. But it was nothing like the snowstorm I had made. These were meandering flakes. Ones that took their time twirling around in the streetlight. It made me hopeful, somehow, despite my still shaking hands.

"Immy," said Carmen. "Look."

There was something in the blackness right outside our porch. It was hard to make out, but it sat there, waiting. As we got closer, its tail started to wag.

"No way," said Lulu. She came to a dead stop.

The Thistle Witch sat there, in her dog form, looking at us. Her tongue hung out of her mouth. I should have been terrified, like I had been the whole case. She had killed a lot of people, after all. And she had burnt me to a crisp. I didn't have to wonder whether that would haunt me. But instead of being afraid, I was only angry.

"I knew it was too good to be true," I said. "I knew we weren't done with you."

I charged toward the witch, but Carmen held me back.

"Let me do it, Immy," she said. She walked slowly up to the witch, then knelt down next to her. Carmen leaned in toward the dog.

"Are you crazy?" asked Lulu. "She'll kill you."

Carmen whispered something to the dog, but it only cocked its head at her.

"Shake," said Carmen. The dog lifted its paw and rested it in her hand.

"What the hell?" asked Lulu.

"Just what I thought," said Carmen, smiling. "I knew it couldn't be the Thistle Witch anymore because the property is protected more than ever. Evil magic definitely can't enter."

"So, who is that?" asked Lulu.

"Our spell must have worked better than we meant it to," said Carmen. "It weakened her magic so much that she got stuck in her dog form. Now she's just an average pup."

"That would be nice if it wasn't so creepy," I said.

"What is that around her neck?" asked Lulu. "A collar?"

Carmen pulled a white, frayed ribbon off the dog's neck. There was a little gemstone attached to it. All the while, the dog just sat there, wagging its tail.

Carmen inspected the stone. Then her face lit up.

"What is it?" I asked.

Carmen smiled at me. "It's the maze," she said.

She stood up and stamped down on the gemstone. It shattered in white, sparkling light. When it faded, and we were in the dark again, nine little kids stood there in the snow with us. Nancy smiled at me and waved. I waved back.

"That's where the maze was hidden?" asked Lulu. "In a ribbon around her neck? I don't want to think about that."

We stood there, looking at the kids. They were mesmerized by the world around them. It had been so long since they had seen it.

"What are we going to do with them all?" asked Lulu.

"We'll figure out something," said Carmen, petting the dog.

"And what about that dog?" asked Lulu. Her question sounded like an accusation. Carmen just smiled.

"Oh, no," I said. "We are not keeping that dog. Don't you even think about it."

Carmen grinned.

"I'm traumatized already," I said. "We're not keeping that dog."

"It would be so morbid if you kept that dog," said Lulu, shaking her head.

"We can call her Thistles," said Carmen, beaming.

"No," I said.

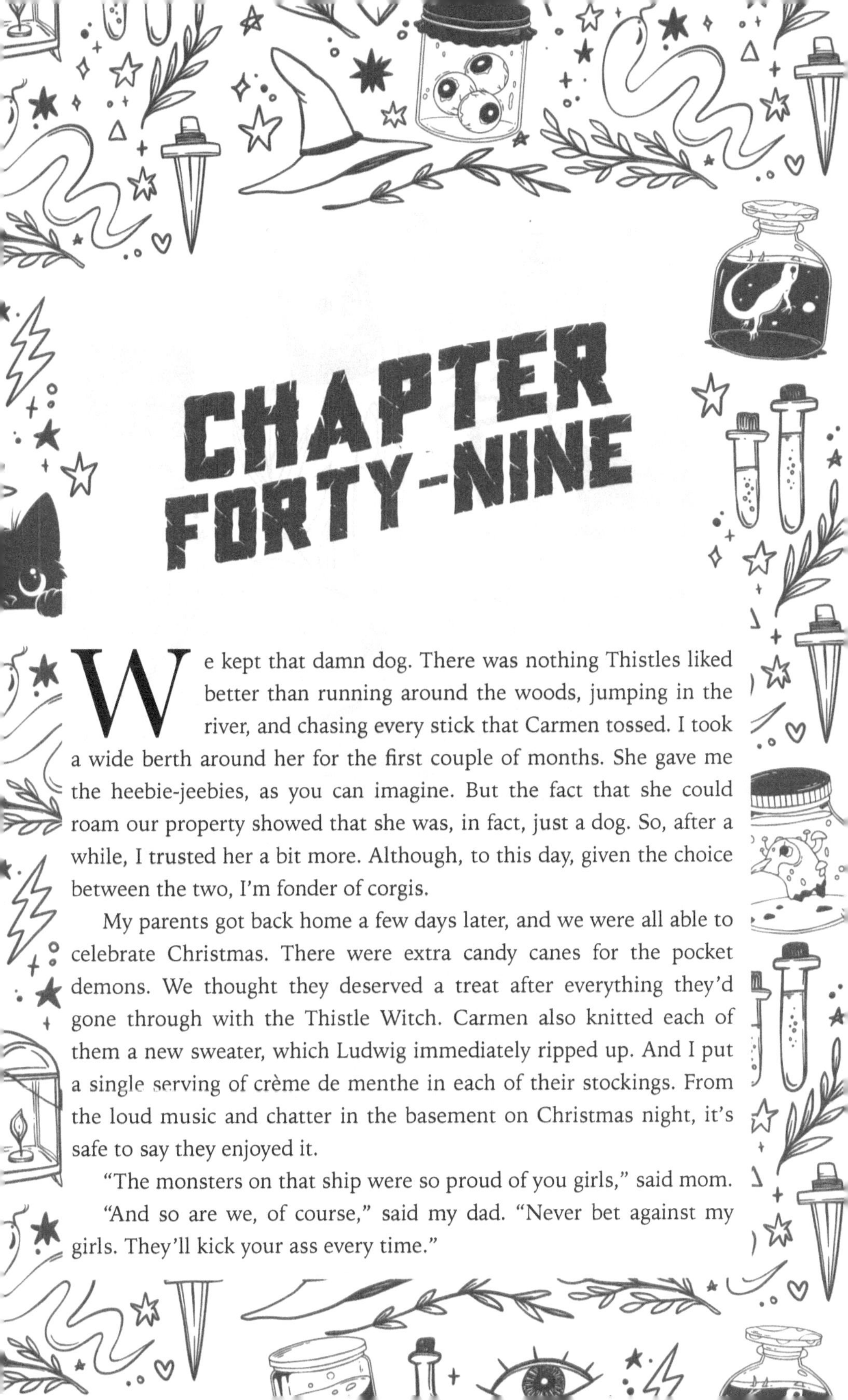

CHAPTER FORTY-NINE

We kept that damn dog. There was nothing Thistles liked better than running around the woods, jumping in the river, and chasing every stick that Carmen tossed. I took a wide berth around her for the first couple of months. She gave me the heebie-jeebies, as you can imagine. But the fact that she could roam our property showed that she was, in fact, just a dog. So, after a while, I trusted her a bit more. Although, to this day, given the choice between the two, I'm fonder of corgis.

My parents got back home a few days later, and we were all able to celebrate Christmas. There were extra candy canes for the pocket demons. We thought they deserved a treat after everything they'd gone through with the Thistle Witch. Carmen also knitted each of them a new sweater, which Ludwig immediately ripped up. And I put a single serving of crème de menthe in each of their stockings. From the loud music and chatter in the basement on Christmas night, it's safe to say they enjoyed it.

"The monsters on that ship were so proud of you girls," said mom.

"And so are we, of course," said my dad. "Never bet against my girls. They'll kick your ass every time."

"They wanted us to give you these," said my mom, putting two slips in my hand.

"Tickets for a cruise!" said Carmen. "How lovely! I don't want to sound full of myself, but I'm pretty good at karaoke. I've mastered 'Angel is a Centerfold,' with my own corresponding dance moves."

"How exactly did the cruise line explain a bunch of monsters and demons taking a ship?" I asked.

My parents glanced at each other. "Electrical issues," they said.

I stared at them. "That's the dumbest thing I've ever heard," I said. "That makes zero sense. It doesn't account for scaly and fuzzy monsters taking over a ship, and kicking everyone off. Who's going to buy that?"

"The way she kidnapped and hurt all those people from Club Noir was swept under the rug too," said Carmen, frowning. "The paper says they're just missing. But they're not missing. Their families will never see them again or know what happened. And how could we ever tell them? How would they ever believe it?"

"Normal people believe anything," said my mom. "To them, it's better than admitting that the otherworldly exists. You know that."

"Electrical issues like you've never seen," said my dad.

I called Eliza to let her know that it was safe for her and Carter to go back home. She was relieved and thankful, but didn't want to know much more than that. Like my mom had said, some people just didn't want to admit that things that shouldn't exist, did.

When I finally got a hold of Shannon, she had journeyed all the way to Scotland.

"I always wanted to come here," she said on the phone.

"It's safe to come back now," I said. "It's over."

I heard a sigh on the other end. "That's a relief. But... I think I might stay here for a while. Too many memories, you know?"

"I know," I said.

"Thanks for everything," she said.

"I didn't do much," I said.

"I doubt that," she said. There was a long pause. "It's nice to know that people like you are out there."

"People like me?"

"People who know that weird things are walking around," she said. "People who know how to deal with them. People who keep everyone else safe."

The Thistle Witch's siblings stayed with us for about a month. It felt weird to walk into the house and hear kids stamping up and down the steps or sliding down the banister.

"Stop that right now," my dad said, racing up the stairs to snatch one boy just as he was sliding down. "Are you crazy?"

"Sorry, sir," said the boy.

"That's fine," said my dad. "But that's no way to slide down a banister. If you're going to do it, do it like this—backward. Makes the adrenaline really pump. That's the way we always did it as kids."

I smiled and rolled my eyes.

For all of her arguing that she could never live outside the maze because the world had changed too much, Nancy and the others seemed to acclimate themselves pretty well. One of their favorite hobbies was to sit down in the basement with the pocket demons, eat their secret stash of cheddar popcorn, and play original Nintendo for hours on end.

When it was finally time for them to leave, my aunt Joyce brought them home to England to stay with a coven of witches she knew. They planned to teach the kids how to live in the modern world. And apparently, they did a good job because to this day, those kids send me emojis that I don't understand.

Lulu went back to work at the bakery, which made a substantial amount of tension leave my body.

"Monster fighting is all well and good," said Lulu. "But when I can make éclairs this delicious, I almost have to, you know?"

"I know," I said, smiling.

"But remember, I'm coming right back over next time you need help," she said.

I wandered into the bakery one snowy morning, just to see how she was getting along. When our eyes met, she scurried out from behind the counter and nearly slammed into me.

"My brother's here," she whispered.

"So?" I asked. "Your brother's always here."

"It's just," said Lulu, struggling to find the right words. "I had to account for all that missing time. So, I lied."

I shrugged. "I told you to blame me," I whispered.

"I did," she said.

My mind spun, wondering what she could have said to Louis and the others.

"Well?" I asked. I saw Louis in the back. He smiled at me and wiped his hands. I could tell he was about to come out to talk to us.

"You know what Lyme disease is?" asked Lulu.

"One of our cousin's friends had that," I said. "He was in bed for months. That's about all I know."

Louis walked toward us and Lulu whispered in my ear.

"Learn faster," she said. "Because you had it."

On a quiet, snowy day in mid-January, I walked into my parents' home and heard a weird scraping noise from a spare room. We only used it for storage, so I ducked my head in to see what was up.

Carmen and the pocket demons shoved a large desk around, then inspected its placement.

"That's perfect," said Carmen.

"What are you doing?" I asked.

"Immy," said Carmen. She pulled me into the room with a bright smile. "I'm turning this room into the new Otherworldly Investigations office."

"What a shame," I said, sitting down in a wooden, wheeled desk chair. "Where will we put that treadmill we never use, or store our third-best George Foreman grill?"

"I want to give it a 1940s, Sam Spade kind of feel," said Carmen. I wasn't surprised since she was outfitted in a 1940s two-piece caramel victory dress, black heels, and a black fedora swept over one eye like Veronica Lake. "I imagine a client coming in and telling me that he wants me to find his business partner. I sit here with the pocket demons, listening intently, but I have to tell him that his kind of case isn't the sort I usually take on. But then he leans forward out of the shadows and reveals that his business partner is a yeti. What do you think?"

"I hate it," I said, crossing my arms.

"Why?" asked Carmen, sitting down.

"You didn't mention me in that hypothetical at all," I said, staring at her. Carmen's frown transformed into a coy smile.

"You?" she asked, fiddling with some papers on the desk. "Does that mean… Are you coming back to the family business?"

I shrugged. "I figure I'm already warped by everything I've seen over the years and by the Thistle Witch. No point in warping some other poor bastard."

Carmen tried not to look too excited, but I could tell that she was bubbling over on the inside.

"I've noticed you've been haunting this place lately," said Carmen. "But I didn't want to push anything on you." Her face turned serious. "You know you don't have to, Immy. I don't want you to do anything that makes you unhappy."

I stared out at the snow. "It doesn't make me unhappy," I said.

"Not really. It just makes me angry sometimes. People getting hurt, you know? And some aspects of the job are a little absurd. Like that baby Loch Ness Monster in the bathtub upstairs. When were you going to tell me about him?"

"I was getting to that," said Carmen, biting her lip.

"But it's nice to help people," I said, thinking of Shannon. "We know the otherworldly exists. A lot of people don't. So, we're all that there is if people need help. It's just us."

Carmen nodded. We stared out the window. Tiny flakes drifted down from the sky, but it seemed like it might get sunny later. I wanted to tell Carmen that I hadn't been sleeping. I wanted to tell her that whenever I closed my eyes, I saw my own hollowed-out face, and the Thistle Witch hunched over me, her body also burning. But as we sat there, and Carmen glanced at me, I didn't think I needed to say anything after all. Somehow, I thought she already knew. Witch intuition, maybe.

"I hope we get a case soon," she said, petting Barnaby.

"We never have to wait long," I said, watching the sun stream out from behind a cloud. "Plus, I have a case we can investigate right now."

"Really?" asked Carmen, brightening.

"The case of the missing fairy food," I said, glaring at her. "You wouldn't happen to know where it is, would you?"

But Carmen was already up and out of the room. I didn't move, but instead shouted after her.

"Because those leftovers should really be put in the safe in case we need them someday," I said, raising my voice. "It's not something the pocket demons should eat to amuse themselves when their VCR breaks."

Carmen came back into the room, pulling a big filing cabinet along with her.

"Do you know where the fairy food spirited away to?" I asked.

"Oh, Immy," she said. "Don't you worry. It'll turn up. Now help me with this cabinet."

I got up, shaking my head. "That's what I thought."

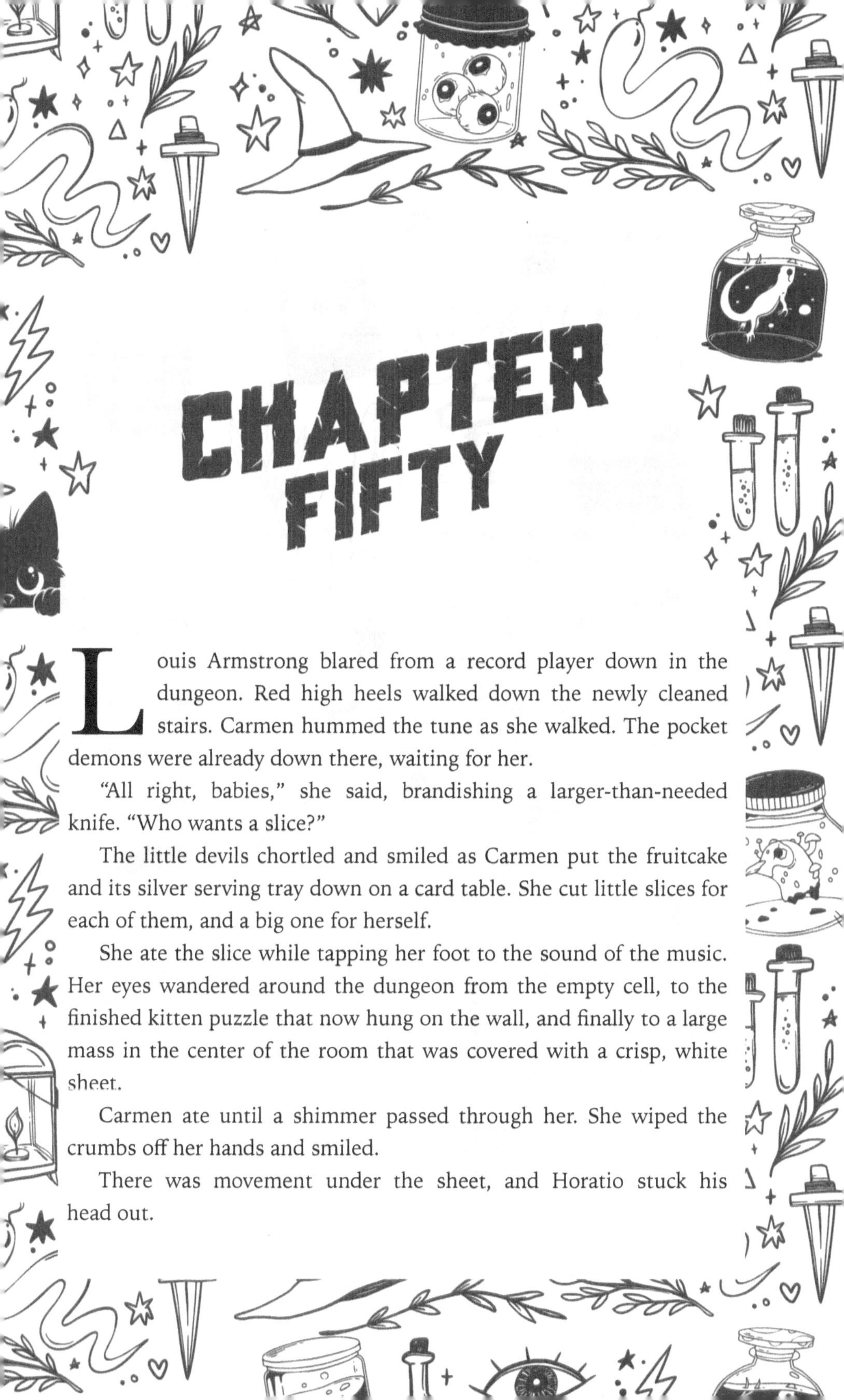

CHAPTER FIFTY

Louis Armstrong blared from a record player down in the dungeon. Red high heels walked down the newly cleaned stairs. Carmen hummed the tune as she walked. The pocket demons were already down there, waiting for her.

"All right, babies," she said, brandishing a larger-than-needed knife. "Who wants a slice?"

The little devils chortled and smiled as Carmen put the fruitcake and its silver serving tray down on a card table. She cut little slices for each of them, and a big one for herself.

She ate the slice while tapping her foot to the sound of the music. Her eyes wandered around the dungeon from the empty cell, to the finished kitten puzzle that now hung on the wall, and finally to a large mass in the center of the room that was covered with a crisp, white sheet.

Carmen ate until a shimmer passed through her. She wiped the crumbs off her hands and smiled.

There was movement under the sheet, and Horatio stuck his head out.

"Now, now," said Carmen, getting up. "That's no place to play. He isn't better yet. Not by a long shot."

The cats that weren't cats wound their way through Carmen's legs, and then looked up at her with glowing eyes. Carmen smiled.

"I think we're ready," she said. She bent down and peered under the sheet. The body was hard and rigid, and the horns had taken on a dull, chalky look. But every part was there.

The pocket demons gathered around her to see what she was doing.

"When I reanimated that bird," she said, petting Norma, "my body broke out in hives. When I reanimated that raccoon, I needed my tonsils removed. And when I reanimated that deer, I was in bed with pneumonia. What do you think will happen this time?"

The cats that weren't cats meowed at her, and Carmen smiled back with shimmering eyes.

"You're right," she said, winking. "There's only one way to find out."

ACKNOWLEDGMENTS

I wrote my first novel when I was sixteen, and if we all cross our fingers and hope really hard, that book will never see the light of day. I'm pretty sure it's still on my parents' old Dell in their basement. It might even be printed and shoved into a folder. Poor folder.

I was deep into my Jane Austen phase. Spoiler: I was *not* Jane Austen.

But I have always loved writing, and every new novel since then has felt like a step toward where I am supposed to be. And apparently where I am supposed to be is in some banter-filled, *Gilmore Girls*-esque (did I just invent a word?) world where fresh donuts are always readily available and magic is fun but also kind of creepy. Insert cackle of joy here. I hope you enjoyed reading this book as much as I enjoyed writing it.

Thanks to everyone who read this novel in all of its various stages. And thanks to my family for their endless support of it. A special shout out to my cousin Gabby, who talked this book up when it was still a baby and even made costumes and videos about it. You're the best. And thanks to my cousin Joel, who gave me my first radio interview. I wasn't even terrified! Insert nervous laughter here.

Thanks to my editor, Jen, for her lovely advice. You kept this novel on a path instead of letting it wander off into the trees.

A big, *big*, BIG thanks to everyone at the Nerd Fam. You breathed new life into this novel, and I am so grateful. The beautiful new cover! The advice! The help! You are so awesome that I might just emote about it!

Thanks to my parents for a lot of things over the years, including but not limited to the weird old cartoons, the weird old movies, that

Beanie Babies phase, pretending to be as invested as I was in *The Lord of the Rings,* for making me a cat lady, and for taping a special copy of *The Wizard of Oz* when I was little that completely omitted the scene with the flying monkeys.

And thanks to my husband Billy for encouraging me to write this novel, and for not looking at me like I was weird for talking to him at length about people that don't exist.

And thanks to you, the reader. Because without *you,* there wouldn't be *this.* I appreciate it so much. Lots of love from my computer screen in the past to your copy of this book in the future. Insert tears.

As a child, Amanda Braun Boe could often be found playing too much Nintendo, watching old movies, reading in a hammock swing, and daydreaming about fictional worlds. She obtained her M.A. in English and decided to start putting those worlds down on paper. When not writing, she enjoys baking, reading, searching for the best donuts in whatever town she's in, filling her phone with cat pictures, and testing the limits of how much coffee a person can consume in one day. She lives in rural Minnesota with her husband and their sofa-stealing furry friends. For more, follow her on Instagram and TikTok.

9 798218 500672